RELEASED FROM CIRCULATION

AUG 20 2024

**CENTRAL
GROSSE POINTE PUBLIC LIBRARY
GROSSE POINTE, MI 48236**

TOM CLANCY
SHADOW STATE

ALSO BY TOM CLANCY

The Hunt for Red October
Red Storm Rising
Patriot Games
The Cardinal of the Kremlin
Clear and Present Danger
The Sum of All Fears
Without Remorse
Debt of Honor
Executive Orders
Rainbow Six
The Bear and the Dragon
Red Rabbit
The Teeth of the Tiger
Dead or Alive (with Grant Blackwood)
Against All Enemies (with Peter Telep)
Locked On (with Mark Greaney)
Threat Vector (with Mark Greaney)
Command Authority (with Mark Greaney)
Tom Clancy Support and Defend (by Mark Greaney)
Tom Clancy Full Force and Effect (by Mark Greaney)
Tom Clancy Under Fire (by Grant Blackwood)
Tom Clancy Commander in Chief (by Mark Greaney)
Tom Clancy Duty and Honor (by Grant Blackwood)
Tom Clancy True Faith and Allegiance (by Mark Greaney)
Tom Clancy Point of Contact (by Mike Maden)
Tom Clancy Power and Empire (by Marc Cameron)
Tom Clancy Line of Sight (by Mike Maden)
Tom Clancy Oath of Office (by Marc Cameron)
Tom Clancy Enemy Contact (by Mike Maden)
Tom Clancy Code of Honor (by Marc Cameron)
Tom Clancy Firing Point (by Mike Maden)
Tom Clancy Shadow of the Dragon (by Marc Cameron)
Tom Clancy Target Acquired (by Don Bentley)
Tom Clancy Chain of Command (by Marc Cameron)
Tom Clancy Zero Hour (by Don Bentley)
Tom Clancy Red Winter (by Marc Cameron)
Tom Clancy Weapons Grade (by Don Bentley)
Tom Clancy Command and Control (by Marc Cameron)
Tom Clancy Act of Defiance (by Andrews & Wilson)

TOM CLANCY
SHADOW STATE

M. P. WOODWARD

G. P. Putnam's Sons
New York

PUTNAM
— EST. 1838 —

G. P. PUTNAM'S SONS
Publishers Since 1838
An imprint of Penguin Random House LLC
penguinrandomhouse.com

Copyright © 2024 by The Estate of Thomas L. Clancy, Jr.; Rubicon, Inc.;
Jack Ryan Enterprises, Ltd.; and Jack Ryan Limited Partnership
Penguin Random House supports copyright. Copyright fuels creativity, encourages diverse voices, promotes free speech, and creates a vibrant culture. Thank you for buying an authorized edition of this book and for complying with copyright laws by not reproducing, scanning, or distributing any part of it in any form without permission. You are supporting writers and allowing Penguin Random House to continue to publish books for every reader.

LIBRARY OF CONGRESS CATALOGING-IN-PUBLICATION DATA

Names: Woodward, M. P., author.
Title: Tom Clancy shadow state / M. P. Woodward.
Other titles: Shadow state
Identifiers: LCCN 2023055261 (print) | LCCN 2023055262 (ebook) |
ISBN 9780593717943 (hardcover) | ISBN 9780593717950 (e-pub)
Subjects: LCSH: Ryan, Jack, Jr. (Fictitious character)—Fiction. |
LCGFT: Spy fiction. | Thrillers (Fiction) | Novels.
Classification: LCC PS3623.O6857 T66 2024 (print) |
LCC PS3623.O6857 (ebook) |
DDC 813/.6—dc23/eng/20231213
LC record available at https://lccn.loc.gov/2023055261
LC ebook record available at https://lccn.loc.gov/2023055262

Printed in the United States of America
1st Printing

Title page photograph by BelezaPoy/Shutterstock.com

This is a work of fiction. Names, characters, places, and incidents either are the product of the author's imagination or are used fictitiously, and any resemblance to actual persons, living or dead, businesses, companies, events, or locales is entirely coincidental.

PRINCIPAL CHARACTERS

U.S. GOVERNMENT OFFICIALS AND CAMPUS OPERATIVES

JACK RYAN, SR.: President of the United States, founder of The Campus

MARY PAT FOLEY: Director of national intelligence, advisor to The Campus

ARNIE VAN DAMM: White House chief of staff

JACK RYAN, JR.: The President's son, a Campus team leader

JOHN CLARK: Operations director of The Campus

LISANNE ROBERTSON: Campus intelligence and logistics coordinator

CARY MARKS: Campus operator, active-duty Green Beret master sergeant

JAD MUSTAFA: Campus operator, active-duty Green Beret sergeant first class

KENDRICK MOORE: Navy SEAL master chief (retired), provisional campus operator

GAVIN BIERY: Campus director of information technology

HENDLEY ASSOCIATES AND GEOTECH CORPORATION

GERRY HENDLEY: President and CEO of Hendley Associates, a private equity firm

HOWARD BRENNAN: Chief investment officer, Hendley Associates

BRUCE STEPHENSON: CEO of GeoTech, a rare earth magnet mining and refining company

DAVID HIGHSMITH: GeoTech's president of Vietnamese operations

VIETNAMESE AND LAOTIAN CHARACTERS

COLONEL CAI QI: Nonofficial cover agent of China's Ministry of State Security (MSS) in Laos

LING AND TWEI: Cai's top two deputies, members of the Laotian Snakehead gang

MADAME MARIE ANH CLARÉ: Sister-in-law of David Highsmith in Hué, Vietnam

HENRI CLARÉ: Madame Anh's husband

ALANG NIK TRONG: Former Montagnard soldier allied with the US Military Assistance Command (MACV)

TOM CLANCY
SHADOW STATE

Mine honor is my life; both grow in one.
Take honor from me, and my life is done.
—William Shakespeare, *Julius Caesar*

PROLOGUE

ANDERSEN AIR FORCE BASE, GUAM
MONDAY, SEPTEMBER 30

LIEUTENANT COLONEL "MAGIC" MIKE HOLBROOK GRIPPED THE THROTTLES OF HIS specially modified F-15 Strike Eagle.

"*Raider One, doors open,*" crackled a voice through his headset.

"Roger doors," he replied into his oxygen mask.

Other than a red-lensed flashlight here and there, the cavernous hangar at Guam's Andersen Air Force Base was dark. So dark, in fact, that Magic couldn't see the hulking doors to either side. But as a test pilot, he'd learned to trust in the highly trained ground crew who'd flown out here with him from California. If they said the hangar doors were open, then, by God, they were.

The pilot lifted his boot soles from the rudder brakes. He felt the familiar dip in the hydraulic nosewheel strut as the plane moved. Bulked up with extra fuel and experimental electronics, the powerful old fighter surged forward.

Behind an enhanced-reality visor, Magic's eyes swept the dim instrument panel. "Exhaust gas temp good. Visual systems green," he reported. He pushed the button that activated the nosewheel steering and twisted the stick into a rolling turn. "Proceeding to three alpha."

Piece of cake, he thought as the jet thundered along the taxiway. Though this was no ordinary Eagle, maneuvering it around the airfield was as familiar to Magic as driving his F-150 around his neighborhood—even without headlights.

Before serving as an Edwards test pilot, Magic had commanded an Eagle squadron up in Kadena AFB, Okinawa, Japan. Later, installed at the storied test-pilot proving grounds on the high Mojave, he'd flown the exotic birds designed for the Air Force by Quantum Atomics, the Defense Department's largest, most sophisticated weapons supplier.

The F-15 he maneuvered tonight across Guam's airfield was a modified Quantum Atomics variant—one that few, outside of a handful of engineers and Magic himself, knew a damn thing about. Though Magic had strapped himself into dozens of experimental aircraft, he found it grimly amusing that his most dangerous mission to date should be in this familiar, old F-15 Strike Eagle.

"Raider One, this is Shotgun. Follow-me truck's to your right. Got it?"

Magic cranked his head around. Though the Humvee had its lights extinguished, the enhanced reality visor on his flight helmet made it visible. "Tally truck. Got him on infrared."

He twisted the stick into a sharp, following turn and bumped along at about thirty miles per hour to the end of the runway.

"Raider, Shotgun. *Viper Flight's at your nine. See 'em?*"

Magic twisted his head hard to the left.

Though the enhanced reality goggles were an amazing piece of DARPA tech, the Defense Advanced Research Projects Agency still required the pilot to turn his head into unnatural positions to aim the sensors.

"Roger, Shotgun. Tally Viper Flight."

Viper Flight consisted of two F-22 Raptors. They were running parallel to Magic's F-15 on a second taxiway, their anti-collision lights blinking as normal. Beyond them, Magic could make out a dozen B-52 and B-1 bomber tails rising in the dark like shark fins.

He waited for the planes of Viper to move ahead, then goosed his throttles to fall in behind them. "Shotgun, Raider One. In trail with Viper, headed to runway one-six. Will do run-ups and system checks at the hold-short."

"*Good copy, Raider.*"

Shotgun's head engineer was monitoring Magic's every move back at the top secret Quantum airfield in Palmdale, California, better known as "Skunk Works."

Magic checked his watch. It was one o'clock on Thursday morning in Guam. Back at Skunk Works, it was a lazy eight a.m. on Wednesday. He stifled a yawn and quietly envied the engineers' full night's sleep. No matter how fancy the plane or exotic the mission, jet lag was always a bitch.

"*Raider One, looking good. On standby until the hold-short.*"

Magic's F-15 gained the edge of the runway behind the two regular Air Force fighters. He moved the throttles to idle and pumped the brakes, jerking to a stop. "Shotgun, I'm at the hold-short."

"*Roger that, Raider. Initiate sequence alpha.*"

Magic double-keyed his mic in acknowledgment. With the fine movements of a pianist, he toggled each of the customized switches on the right side of his instrument panel. Normally, the

F-15 Strike Eagle would have a weapons systems officer in the back seat doing this kind of thing. But Magic's back seat was a solid mass of electronics.

"Shotgun, we're good here," he radioed, noting the various green lights on the panel and the digital metrics spewing down the right side of his visor. "Am I a go to power up the special mission pod?"

That, Magic knew, was the big question—the one that would require permission from the geniuses on the Potomac.

The special mission pod, code-named UMBRA, was a long tube of electronics in the Eagle's weapons bay. *Everything* in this F-15 had been modified to optimize UMBRA's performance. The Skunk Works engineers had coated the Eagle in black, radar-absorbent paint. They'd machined small changes in the wing strakes and control surfaces. They'd dusted the canopy with a transparent, reflective epoxy. And, of course, they'd replaced Magic's copilot with a stack of UMBRA system electronics.

Receiving no response, Magic wondered if Washington had gotten cold feet for this flight. He keyed the sat link again. "Shotgun, am I good to cycle the special mission pod to standby?"

He could picture the civilians in short-sleeve button-downs in California and the anxious Air Force generals leaning over their shoulders. He'd heard this mission had interest all the way up to the White House. He'd dismissed that as the typical military rumor—but part of him thought it plausible.

Now he was getting annoyed. "Shotgun, Raider. Looking for an update out here. We still a go?"

"Yeah, Shotgun, we hear you. Wait one. We're working the problem."

Problem.

Magic sighed and looked directly up at the night sky, through the clear canopy. Though he could see the white pinpricks of stars in his otherworldly digital goggles, he had the urge to pull the damned things off and look at the stars the old-fashioned way, like he used to do on his parents' cattle ranch in eastern Oregon.

Just like on those nights, Magic was looking at a pleasant, clear sky out here in the middle of the Pacific. He listened to his breath through the oxygen mask, and, still staring straight up, thought about his wife, then his boys.

The twin twelve-year-olds had just started peewee football at the Edwards middle school. A second-string tight end for the Air Force Academy a million years ago, Magic had stepped up to be the assistant coach of the boys' team, grateful to show them a few things. Their first game was this weekend. With any luck at all, he'd make it back in time.

"*Still waiting for final clearance back here,*" said Shotgun. "*Apologies for the delay, Magic.*"

He sighed into his mask and double-keyed his mic.

Classic hurry up and—

The speakers in his helmet startled him. "*Just got an update, Raider. Good news. We have clearance up and down the chain . . . Like way up. Mission's a go—so long as we get through the full flight-test telemetry package.*"

"Roger that. On to flight telemetry," responded Magic, dropping back into complete mission focus.

Like a sprinter limbering up before a race, Magic waggled his stick around and shoved his rudder pedals in and out. Back at Palmdale, the Quantum engineers followed along, narrating his every move. "*Raider, we see full aft stick now . . . Full forward stick now . . . Left rudder . . . Right rudder. Flight control checks look good. Put special mission payload on standby.*"

Magic lowered his thumb to power up the secret pod in the weapons bay, UMBRA. He scanned the cascade of numbers that was now running down the edge of his visor. "Shotgun . . . special mission payload is on standby. Lights are green, metrics in range. Decibels neg-fifteen."

"Roger that, Raider. We copy all. You are cleared for takeoff. Follow Viper Flight to Marshal Point Alpha."

Magic heard Andersen Tower give Viper Flight the go-ahead call. For secrecy, the tower had been ordered not to even acknowledge his F-15. The Viper fighters raced down the runway, then shot skyward, anti-collision lights blinking. Magic waited for the jet wash to dissipate, then told the Palmdale engineers he was ready to go.

"Shotgun, leaving hot mic on via telemetry. Contact me on button seven if needed. Otherwise, I'll get back on the net after departure."

He shoved the levers to the stops—*balls to the wall*, as the old saying went. Forty-three seconds later, he was aloft, racing through the clear dark sky at six hundred fifty knots, hurrying to catch up with Viper, following the digital positional data in his visor glass.

At ten thousand feet, he leveled and slowed. He fell into formation behind the two F-22s, shadowing them in secret, his lights off. They knew he was there, of course, but the mission's operational security protocol dictated they say nothing to him. Magic's eyes swept his gauges, preparing for the command from Shotgun he knew would be coming his way.

And then it came.

"Okay, Magic, we want you to activate special mission payload. Take it out of standby."

"Activating." Magic toggled the switch. The multiple lights of UMBRA glowed green in his visor.

"How we looking?" he asked Palmdale.

"Couldn't be better, Raider One. You just fell off the AWACS scopes," came the answer.

Magic chuckled into his mask. Even the Pacific Air Forces's own airborne warning aircraft, AWACS, had lost him.

This is one special F-15, he thought. Just for the hell of it, he did a snap roll in the dark.

Two hours later, somewhere between Guam and the Philippines, the three aircraft rendezvoused with a KC-10 tanker at twenty thousand feet. As instructed in the highly classified air tasking order, none of the fuel-boom operators in the back of the tanker acknowledged the existence of the black Strike Eagle that sucked down thousands of pounds of aviation gas.

Twenty minutes after the air-to-air refueling chore, while flying five hundred feet below and a quarter mile behind the F-22s, Magic's UMBRA lights went yellow, then red. For good measure, his seat vibrated, making sure he was paying attention.

Per procedure, he killed the alarms and focused on the UMBRA readings in his visor. "Shotgun," he broadcast over the link. "Be advised I've got targeting radars lighting me up. Special mission pod activated and functioning."

"Roger, Raider. We see that. Stay steady on course and speed. Put another mile between yourself and Viper."

Magic acknowledged the order and dropped back. The UMBRA sensors were blinking, the telemetry data spewing. Shotgun contacted him again. *"Raider, can you give us a detailed read on those radars painting you?"*

"Roger, Shotgun. Special payload identifies the radar as USS

Benfold, Block IV standard surface-to-air missile bearing three-zero-zero, sixty-one nautical miles."

"*Strong copy, Raider. Stand by.*" Magic knew they would check in with the Pentagon again. It took them forty-five seconds. "*Raider, you are still Charlie Mike.*"

Continue mission, thought Magic. *UMBRA lives.*

The special payload had successfully detected *Benfold*'s fire-control radar and created cloaking return waves as an echo. Coupled with the radar-absorbent coating on the Strike Eagle, UMBRA had nullified *Benfold*'s radar energy the same way noise-canceling headphones negate sound waves. Evidently, well enough that the brass was confident in moving forward to the next phase.

Magic turned northwest, straight over the friendly, ship-borne SAMs that were targeting him. He could hear Viper responding to *Benfold*'s fire-control radars now, communicating with the naval officers down in the ship's combat information center. While the Air Force and Navy officers chattered through the "blue-on-blue" exercise, Magic's F-15 flew on, undetected, cloaked by UMBRA, completely unacknowledged by *Benfold*.

Now for the hard part.

"We still a go for the neutral?" Magic asked Shotgun.

It took them about a minute to respond. "*Roger. Stay with Viper. Mission is cleared to Point Bravo, test neutral.*"

Point Bravo, thought Magic, settling in behind the stick, his bladder pinching him. From Alpha to Bravo would be the longest leg of the flight. After refueling from the KC-10, his Eagle certainly had the gas for it—his body was another matter. He put the Strike Eagle on autopilot, loosened his straps, rotated onto a butt cheek, and unzipped the crotch of his flight suit.

How many times, he asked himself, *have I pissed into one of these little plastic relief tubes?*

That unpleasant business done, he sat back, scanned gauges, and waited. During the remaining transit, he thought of several ways to improve his boys' receiver routes. Though it was just peewee football, Magic still hated to lose.

A tone in his helmet warbled. He'd made it to Point Bravo—over the Leyte Gulf, the notch of water between the big Philippine islands of Luzon and Mindanao. The UMBRA lights were flashing, his seat vibrating.

"Hey, Shotgun, I've got the PAF lighting me up with an early-warning radar. We still good?"

"Roger that, Raider, still good. Philippine Air Force is seeing the F-22s, communicating on Guard freq. They're not seeing you. Commence separation exercise."

Magic pulled the stick back and ascended, putting more distance between himself and the F-22s. He went to thirty-five thousand feet, becoming a big, fat, juicy target for the PAF's air defense operators up and down the archipelago. This would be the very first test of a truly foreign air defense system, the real thing—but at least it was a neutral country.

He put his radios in scan mode and listened for the reaction from the Filipinos.

There wasn't one.

"Raider, we are still Charlie Mike." The pocket protectors were clearly jubilant. Magic could hear some celebrating in the background of the transmission. *"Proceed to Point Charlie, Raider, hostile test approved. You've made us propeller-heads very happy back here."*

Magic acknowledged the call, tilted his stick to steady up on course two-seven-zero, and left Viper Flight behind.

He was alone now, headed over Palawan, a long candy bar–shaped Philippine island. It lay just east of Mischief Reef, a heavily fortified man-made outpost built by the Chinese to illegally take control of the South China Sea.

Magic's F-15 would soon fly right over it.

That's when he would know whether UMBRA *really* worked.

HIS HAIR BUZZED SHORT, HIS SKIN TAWNY, HIS FATIGUES UNMARKED BY INSIGNIA, Colonel Cai Qi stood next to a missile defense sergeant in a buried bunker on China's Mischief Reef.

Braced by the muscled shoulders and sinewy arms of the Muay Thai fighter he was, Cai leaned on the metal tabletop and studied the flow of real-time information coming in from the air defense radars. Heterochromia, a quirk in the genetic roll of the dice, had given him one brown and one blue eye, both of which squinted at the small digital symbols that represented aircraft over the South China Sea.

"What's that, there?" he asked the radar operator, pointing at a yellow contact on one of the flat-screen monitors.

"That's a Filipino cargo plane, sir. Took off from Cebu, destination Manila."

"Was it scheduled?"

"Yes, sir. And its IFF system checks as normal."

As a Laos-based non-official-cover officer in China's Ministry of State Security, MSS, Cai was certainly no expert on air defense systems. But it wasn't hard to follow what was happening on the screens.

Looking at another monitor, he could see an Air India 787 making its way to Mumbai, a Philippine Airlines triple-7 departing Manila, and an EVA 747 on its way to Taipei from San Francisco. He could also see the blips that represented the two J-20 fighter jets of the cumbersomely titled People's Liberation Army

Air Force, PLAAF, as they flew in a tight racetrack position ten thousand meters over the reef, just in case the missiles failed.

This man-made island, Mischief Reef, was shaped like a boomerang. Down one peninsula was the airfield and the underground surface-to-air missile control battery, in which Cai stood now. Down the other peninsula were the surface-to-surface missiles designed to sink ships, should they approach within fifty miles of the reef.

Standing upright and rotating his head on his stiff neck, Cai checked his watch. Zero-one-thirty—they were entering the mission window. He inhaled deeply and closed his eyes. The bunker's piped-in air smelled faintly of vinegar.

The man standing next to him was an MSS science and technology engineer in civilian clothes. Cai's handler—who he knew only as "Control"—had sent the engineer to accompany him on this rare, direct-action mission. The engineer touched Cai's thick shoulder.

"Zero-one-thirty," whispered the S&T man. He was gray at the temples, a little pudgy.

Thinking of Control's orders and their associated risks, Cai grunted. "Check the software again."

The S&T man squeezed between the operators at the monitors and typed several lines of code into an administrative console. When done, he turned to the sergeant in charge. "Run another systems check."

The noncommissioned officer standing watch at this battery on this night, didn't know these men. But they'd shown him the proper security credentials and a set of classified orders from the command base up at Hainan Island. Out here at Mischief Reef, where the PLAAF often tested experimental air defense systems, the sergeant wasn't all that surprised to have these visitors.

After punching some buttons, the sergeant wheeled away from his monitor so the S&T man could inspect his work.

"Good," the S&T man said. Out of view of the sergeant, the engineer shot Cai a self-assured glance.

Cai waited for the sergeant to replace his headset and resume his station. "You're sure?" he asked the Beijing-based engineer in a low voice.

"I'm sure. The code is operating perfectly."

"And the bunker comms are disabled? You guarantee that?"

You guarantee that?

Among the officers of the MSS, that question was a code. Should the subordinate violate the guarantee, retribution would be swift.

After staring at his shoes for a moment, the S&T man looked up. "I guarantee it, Colonel."

"Then leave."

The engineer turned his thick body sideways to make his way to the heavy bunker door.

For another three minutes, Cai watched the sergeants processing benign air contacts. Then, at 0136, Cai opened the bunker door and climbed the metal stairs to the grated roof. By the time he got there, the S&T man was gone, walking back to the airfield. Ling and Twei, Cai's men from Laos, were by themselves, leaning against a railing on their elbows, looking out to sea. Cai could hear the crash of surf on the reef. The water was invisible.

He looked at his men. In the same bland khakis Cai wore, their shoulder-length hair tied into ponytails made them look more like prison convicts than the radar technicians that the lanyards around their necks claimed them to be. Not that it would matter all that much.

"Hey," Cai called to them. He pointed at the heavy fuel cans near their feet. Control had arranged for those cans. They'd been waiting for them at the landing pad where Cai's helicopter had touched down a few hundred meters away.

"Now," said Cai. He made his way to the bunker stairs. Ling and Twei followed, carrying the cans. They left them outside the door before entering with Cai.

"Any new contacts worth noting?" Cai asked the sergeant.

"Negative, sir. There were some American F-22s over the Philippines, but they turned north. Looks like they're headed to their base in Okinawa. They came from Guam."

Cai registered the comment with a head bob, then moved to the right, making room for Ling and Twei. The three Laotian visitors got in position behind the three air defense sergeants, as planned. They waited.

A full minute passed before the commanding sergeant spat, "Hostile contact profile! American F-15, incoming!"

He then barked a dozen target indicators into his lip mic, believing he was passing the information up the chain to his leadership on Hainan Island. He ticked off the F-15's speed, bearing, altitude, electronic signature, and radar gain. His hands flew over the controls of the missile system, pulling up the hinged plastic guards that prevented an accidental launch.

"Master arm!" he shouted. The other two sergeants performed similar functions.

"Target acquired!" announced the man at the center scope.

A shrill electronic warning sounded. The lead sergeant put his hand near the SAM launch controllers. Over and over, he tried to make contact with headquarters. He couldn't raise them.

"Ready missiles one and four!" the sergeant barked.

The protocol when there was no response from Hainan was to fire on any foreign military aircraft that pierced the self-declared air defense zone around Mischief Reef. They would launch them in salvos of two, wait, then launch again.

"Sir—I'm going to have to fire on it. Are you aware of any other orders?"

Cai moved closer to the commanding sergeant on the left, his eyes fixed on the scope. "Show me the contact."

"Right there, sir. Ten thousand meters, bearing zero-eight-seven. Radar has positively identified it as an F-15 Eagle, Mach point seven, closing fast. No IFF. Mission profile hostile." He tried once more to raise Hainan. No response. To the operator, none of this made any sense. He turned to Cai with wide eyes. "Could it be the software you installed?"

"Keep tracking the target, Sergeant, but don't fire," answered Cai. "I'll go up top and get the engineer."

That was the signal.

Ling and Twei were looking at him, waiting for it.

Cai withdrew the knife tucked on the inside of his belt. It was a folding karambit, with a curved blade and a finger loop that acted like a brass knuckle.

"*Bai-ee,*" he said in his native Laotian, raising his voice to be heard over the sergeants.

The MSS colonel stepped briskly forward, seized the chin of the man at the leftmost scope, and sliced the karambit across the base of his neck. After the cut, he locked his forearms around the operator's head and twisted violently, cracking a bone. He could hear Ling and Twei following the same procedure to his right.

Then he heard something else.

Ling's man, the early-warning-radar sergeant at the center console, had fallen out of his swivel chair, making an ungodly mess as he collapsed on the floor. In the dim light of the bunker, the blood puddle was black, spreading quickly.

Twei was on the other side of Ling, making light of the mess, grinning. In a Laotian dialect, he noted that Ling had pulled way too hard on the man's chin—a rookie move if ever there was one.

Cai wiped his blade on the clean shoulder of the dead man in front of him, refolded the karambit, and stowed it in his waistband. He punched in the security code at the bunker door that Control had given him while alarms blinked and buzzed at the now vacant radar consoles.

The diesel cans were on the grated door stoop, right where Ling and Twei had left them. Cai stepped past them and hurried up the metal steps, his feet echoing in the quiet night. His two men would take care of the burnout.

Over the normal hiss of the surf at the bunker roof, Cai could hear the helicopter spinning up on the pad a hundred meters away.

Ling and Twei had made quick work of the burn. Cai could smell the fumes from the exhaust ports before they floated off on the sea breeze. He saw a sooty, black curl of smoke reaching up from below.

Accidents happened often out here on Mischief Reef. The island's fire marshal would conclude that the bunker's emergency generator had gone haywire. Cai didn't need to worry about the cover story. Control had said he'd take care of everything.

Ling and Twei joined him on the roof. Together, they descended the short stairs to the sand and sprinted to the idling helicopter. The three Laotians strapped in next to the S&T man, who'd been waiting for them. Cai noticed how the engineer never once made eye contact with him. With his unmatching eyes, Cai had found long ago that he could have that effect on people.

He took one last look at the bunker's square concrete roof,

barely visible in the spare light of predawn as the helo gained altitude. As a committed Taoist, he didn't mourn the spirits of the sergeants who'd given their lives in sacrifice. He believed they'd served their inevitable role, as ordained by the Tao.

And, in thinking of that Quantum Atomics F-15 flying on somewhere overhead, Cai thought he'd performed his inevitable role, too.

1

**KOWLOON, HONG KONG
TUESDAY, OCTOBER 1**

JACK RYAN, JR., STOOD A FOOT TALLER THAN MOST OF THE PASSENGERS EXITING Hong Kong's Star Ferry. With his tropical-weight suit jacket slung over a shoulder, his shirt sleeves rolled, and his tie askew, the American shortened his stride so he wouldn't bump into the people in front of him.

From behind his Wayfarer sunglasses, he scanned the commuters knotted at the ferry's prow, waiting to get off. He was in a hurry—desperate to get one more glimpse of the woman before she disappeared into this city of seven and a half million.

He dropped his eyes low, scanning briefcases, purses, and computer bags. She'd been carrying a string-handled white shopping bag, he remembered.

He felt elbows, shoulders, and knees pressing against him as the crowd packed together, ahead of the ferry's docking. The singsong Cantonese around him rose in pitch, the voices as indecipherable to Jack as squawking birds.

He kept searching, hoping to pick the woman out from the

crowd. He etched what she'd looked like into his memory—shopping bag, surgical mask, sunglasses, long black hair, a fashionable charcoal skirt suit.

Jesus, he thought, scanning intently. More than half the women on this ferry looked like that. Provided the shopping bag *hadn't* been a figment of his imagination, it would be the only feature that distinguished her.

The ferry door opened. The first of the riders surged through it. Jack was swept onto the gangway with the crowd, over the pier, through the turnstile, and past the last security checkpoint.

He wondered if the woman might be behind him. He forced his way to the edge of the throng and stood still. Commuters flowed around him like rapids around a rock. He cleared enough space to put his computer bag at his feet and throw his jacket on. He reached into the jacket's lower right pocket. His fingers touched the note the woman had passed him.

Knowing he was under surveillance, Jack only touched the note. It wouldn't be safe to read it until he spotted his MSS minders again.

It took six minutes for the crowd to leave him behind. Before the onrushing set of passengers mobbed the ferry, Jack strode down the open quay. Dying autumn sunlight warmed his shoulders. A stew of cigarettes, fish, diesel exhaust, and salt air burned his nose. He heard the buzz that opened the gate for the new set of passengers headed from this side, Kowloon, to the island, Hong Kong.

Jack turned and walked along the ferry's hull, staying away from the rush that surged over the gangplank. He watched dockworkers loosen thick halyards from massive cleats bolted to the pier. He heard the engine rev.

Facing the harbor, he watched the ferry depart. Beyond it, at the far shore, he noted the tall buildings of Hong Kong's central business district. He turned around and looked up and down the quay. With his MSS surveillants at least a few hundred yards away, he chanced a last look at the note the woman had slipped him, making sure he had it right: *Temple Street Night Market. Heirloom Watches, 2200.*

He balled the paper in his fist and tossed it in the harbor.

He knew his MSS minders would be somewhere up the quay, waiting for him. Delaying the inevitable, Jack stood at the water's edge. It was a pleasure to see the ferry thread between freighters and junks and admire the glassy skyscrapers on the distant island shore, shining gold in the sunset.

Jack was happy to be across the harbor from those buildings. He'd spent the day trapped in one of them on the thirtieth floor, going blind as he worked over spreadsheets. He could see that very building now, the HSBC tower, right in the center.

Jack thought of Howard Brennan, the Hendley man who'd traveled with him to Hong Kong. Howard was Hendley's chief investment officer, the man who directed the firm's capital strategy.

He and Jack had come to Hong Kong to line up the financing for an acquisition. Gerry Hendley was making a bid for GeoTech, an acknowledged leader in the refinement of rare earth magnets, an incipient power player in the green energy revolution. Hendley was old friends with the company's CEO. The deal, they all thought, was a good one.

To pull it off, however, would require three hundred million dollars in borrowed capital. It was Howard's job to negotiate the terms for the loan with HSBC.

Jack could picture Howard up near the top of that tall building now, schmoozing the bankers, skillfully arguing to shave a point of interest here, add a few months of bond maturity there. Jack felt his phone buzz in his pants pocket. It was a text from Howard, right on cue, as though the banker had been reading his mind.

> We're working through dinner to get the financing terms closed. You coming back?

Jack typed his response. No. Going to run the risk profile numbers in my room tonight. Will catch you in the morning and—

He stood still, thinking through his response. He knew MSS would be monitoring his communications. Before hitting send, he evaluated how they might read this note to Howard. After a moment's reflection, he decided it would fit with his plan. He sent it.

A fishy gust came in off the harbor. The sea air was gaining a raw edge in this first week of October. Glad for the suit jacket now, Jack closed one button. He hurried up the quay with his sunglasses still on, even though it was getting dark.

There.

He caught sight of his first MSS minder. It was the same man Jack had spotted that morning, the one in the blue suit jacket and gray trousers. Jack had mentally named him Blue.

Blue was standing by a bench on the wide promenade that abutted the harbor. He was trying to look natural, one foot up on the bench, a cell phone pressed to his ear. He was deliberately looking away from Jack.

Well, thought Jack, *if Blue is looking away, then Brown must be around here somewhere.*

There.

Jack spotted him at the far end of the quay, near the street.

He wore a leather jacket and blue jeans. He had unkempt hair. He was younger and more athletic than Blue. Jack figured that Blue was the leader and Brown was the muscle.

Jack strode over the promenade and ascended the steps to the Peninsula Hotel, knowing they would follow.

Along the way, he wondered about his duty to report the contact with the woman on the ferry to John Clark. Though on a purely "white-side" assignment for Hendley, Jack could at least let Clark know he'd been approached by an unknown contact with a request for a meet. That seemed to be something he *should* do.

If he'd been on a "black-side" op, the decision would be easy. Hendley's black-side was The Campus, an embedded national security team that took direction from the President in operations that prized speed, discretion, and deniability above all else. Hendley's white-side private equity business was legitimate. It also happened to serve as both a funding source and cover for The Campus.

As Jack rode the hotel elevator up, he visualized how the conversation with Clark might go. Mr. C had pointedly sent Jack on this all-business white-side assignment to Hong Kong. He'd emphasized the importance of GeoTech, telling Jack the acquisition was more strategic than the Campus op going down right now in the Philippines, where Cary, Jad, and Lisanne were tracking a known terrorist. He'd also given Jack's fiancée, Lisanne, her dream role, promoting her from logistics coordinator to a full-blown field intelligence operative.

As Jack saw it, the repercussions of Clark's decisions were twofold. One, he was missing out on the real action, stuck here on a city pier wearing a suit that felt like a straitjacket. Two, with his betrothed hopscotching the eastern hemisphere on a black-side op, there was no one left at home to look after Emily, Lisanne's niece, who was now living with them.

Lisanne had found a solution, naturally, arranging for the fifteen-year-old to stay with her grandfather for the week—but not before Jack had made a fool of himself, telling Lisanne she'd be putting herself in harm's way without him there to protect her. That crack had opened an old wound—and earned him a cold cheek when he'd gone to kiss her goodbye.

He'd taken his concerns to Clark, who'd been respectful but unyielding. Mr. C. was adamant that Jack accompany Howard Brennan to Hong Kong to close this deal. The old SEAL had said it would be good for Jack to take part in a more strategic initiative for the firm—while also learning to let the team operate without him.

And—as if that weren't enough—Clark had said that since Jack would be working in Hong Kong, a special administrative region of the People's Republic of China, he was absolutely forbidden to stay in touch with the team in the Philippines. Operational security was the name of the game, Clark had said.

Jack swiped his key and stood just inside the room, inspecting it carefully. After a quarter-minute, he put his phone up to his eyes to unlock it and opened the room-scanning app Gavin Biery, Hendley's infotech specialist, had created for The Campus. Per the app's instructions, Jack took a picture, then let the AI program compare it with the room photo from that morning.

The app returned three red dots on the new photo—three depressions in the carpet, likely from a man's oxford shoe, size nine Sendas, a Chinese brand. Jack had put a do-not-disturb sign on the door that morning, and since the room was still a mess, he could only assume Brown and Blue's helpers had searched it.

So be it. On this Hendley white-side assignment, he had nothing to hide.

He dropped his bag on the desk, kicked off his shoes, and sat at the edge of his bed. He opened another Gavin-Campus app on his phone, the secure communications portal, hoping to see a message from Campus ops that might redirect him to the real action in the Philippines.

If he was honest with himself, he'd admit that he also hoped to see a message from Lisanne, given the way they'd left things with each other.

A disappointed sigh escaped his pursed lips. His shoulders slumped.

The inbox was empty.

BY EIGHT-THIRTY THAT EVENING, JACK HAD EATEN A MEDIOCRE ROOM-SERVICE club sandwich and traded a dozen messages with Howard, who was still across the harbor, hammering away on the terms with the British bankers at HSBC. Jack sat at his hotel room desk, running the terms through the risk analysis tool he'd built for Hendley Associates.

He took the work seriously. Gerry Hendley, a former senator with deep ties in the energy industry, believed that within a year or two they could flip GeoTech for nearly three billion—the firm's biggest strike to date. But if Jack's analysis got any of the underlying numbers wrong, then the company could just as easily go bankrupt trying to repay the HSBC loan.

After analyzing GeoTech's disclosed financial statements and inputting the relevant figures, Jack updated his model with Howard's new terms. However Howard had managed to drive his latest bargain with the bankers across the harbor, he'd done a fine job. Jack's model showed the deal working well, the risk profile within acceptable limits. In his final email of the evening, he congratulated Howard on a job well done.

There, he thought. He'd done his white-side work, the equivalent of eating his vegetables. Now on to more flavorful fare.

The digital clock in the upper corner of his laptop showed 8:45. There was still time to make it up to the Temple Street Night Market and meet the woman who'd passed him the note.

And why shouldn't he? he asked himself. That woman might well be a disaffected citizen chafing under PRC rule, highly placed, a future asset. A year earlier, Jack and Lisanne had recruited just such a woman in Seoul, a defecting North Korean scientist who'd since paid big dividends to the American intelligence establishment.

So why shouldn't he? he asked himself again.

For starters, his mind answered, Mr. C. had warned him that MSS would be all over him in Hong Kong—Brown and Blue were certainly proof of that. Moreover, Clark had counseled him that MSS could play dirty, that they might even do something to entrap Jack. Especially since he was the son of the sitting President of the United States.

Then again, thought Jack, Mr. C. had also counseled him to trust his gut, to never forsake his duty, to look for every opportunity to gain the upper hand over his adversaries. As Mr. C. had said time and again, *Debate can be fatal. You must think, decide, act.*

Ensuring he was connected to the internet via Gavin's node-hopping, encrypted virtual private network, Jack alt-tabbed from his risk analysis spreadsheet over to Google. He looked up the Temple Street Night Market.

Condé Nast described the wet market as *not to be missed*. The travel writer harkened it to Hong Kong's roots as an exotic trading port, full of the sights, sounds, and smells of Asia. A deeper dive into Google located Heirloom Watches, smack in the middle of the market.

Jack finished the remains of his room-service ice water and rattled the old Rolex on his wrist. The watch had been a gift from his parents fifteen-ish years ago, back when he'd graduated Georgetown with a major in finance for his own passions and a minor in history for his father's. Heirloom Watches, indeed.

What the hell, he thought finally, checking his phone once more to see that Lisanne hadn't messaged. It was a nice night to do some sightseeing, wasn't it? And besides, he had ways to prepare for a contact meeting. Though Mr. C. had told him not to deviate from his white-side assignment, he'd given Jack the business card of a friendly local resource to be used *in case of emergency*, as the old SEAL had put it.

There was still an hour before the woman would be there, waiting for him. Time enough. Jack riffled through his bag and dug out the business card. Clark had said the man on the card was a hell of a tailor—and that MSS knew nothing of his black-market weapons business. According to Google, the tailor shop was on the way to the Temple Street Night Market.

He looked at his old watch again. His father, Jack Ryan, Sr., would never have ignored a contact bump like the woman on the ferry, right under MSS's nose.

And besides, Jack asked himself, who was he to disregard Condé Nast?

2

AFTER TAKING THE STAIRS TO THE GROUND FLOOR, JACK BURIED HIMSELF IN THE crowd at the lobby's English pub–style bar. Edging onto a stool, he ordered a Guinness and Bass black and tan, scooted his seat for a clear view through the whiskey bottles by the bar mirror, and studied the crowd behind him. He was looking for Brown and Blue.

His two MSS minders *had* to be down here somewhere, he reasoned, provided they hadn't been relieved by a separate detail. As a decoy, Jack had left his phone in his room. He'd also kept his network connection to Hendley's Virginia office live, sending encrypted data over the hotel wires. The fake electronic footprint, he assumed, would have kept Brown and Blue posted nearby.

Surveying the crowd with the bar mirror behind the whiskey bottles, Jack couldn't find them. To be expected, he supposed, since the two men were professionals. That wasn't going to stop him. He was committed now.

A good-looking ethnic Chinese woman took the seat next to him. She was about his age, shapely, fit. Brooding over his beer, Jack listened to her ask the bartender for a French 75 in a charming English accent. She briefly flashed her dark eyes and big teeth at Jack in the mirror.

Her interest made him feel a little better about the tiff with Lisanne—until the woman was lost in a big, touchy greeting when a tall Australian in a good suit arrived at her elbow.

After three more gulps of the black and tan, Jack dropped thirty Hong Kong dollars on the mahogany bar. He hadn't spotted Brown or Blue, so he guessed they were in the front lobby.

He walked down the narrow hall with the restrooms toward an adjoining restaurant. He breezed past the host station, threaded linen-topped tables with candlelit diners, and slipped through the swinging door that led to the busy kitchen.

Amid flames and steam, white-clad sous-chefs were heads down, hard at it, paying him no mind. Jack marched right past them, the walk-in freezer, the scullery, the baking station, the bloody meat counter, and a rack of metal cookware. He finally found the rear exit door.

Once through it, he was in the alley behind the hotel, standing on a loading bay, a dumpster just below him. Google's satellite view had nailed it.

Jack stepped on top of the green monster, balancing his feet on the open bin's slimy edges. There was a one-meter gap between the dumpster and the chain-link fence behind it. Jack coiled into a crouch with his hands below his quads. His high school basketball coach had once told him he wasn't genetically equipped to have a good vertical leap.

He'd been right.

Jack nearly fell backward as one foot lost its toehold on the fence. Were it not for the death clutch of his fingers, he'd have plunged into the dumpster, ruining his best tropical suit. But his strong hands held. He dug his dress shoes into the narrow gaps and clambered up. At the top, he threw a leg over and hopped to the hill into which the fence had been built.

He muscled through brambles, brushed off his pants, and stood on a narrow curving street. Just past a lamppost, he found the concrete steps that zigzagged between the buildings, carving a steep path that ended at the avenue. By the time he'd finished climbing Signal Hill, he was irritatingly winded.

This white-side work is making me soft, he chided himself.

He dug through his suit's breast pocket and pulled out the business card Mr. C. had given him. The numbers on the tightly packed apartment buildings told him he had about five blocks to go. He got moving, none the worse for wear.

"If the shit hits the fan out there, this guy can get you anything you need," Mr. C. had said when pressing the tailor's card into Jack's hand a few hours before the flight. "Emergency only. Don't say anything to Howard."

Well, thought Jack. Though Mr. C. might be furious with him for blurring the hallowed line separating Hendley's black-side operations from its white, could he really fault Jack for being careful?

He'd find out soon enough. After covering the five blocks, Jack double-checked the address and rang the doorbell.

"We're closed. Golden Week," said the old woman at the chained security door with rusted metal bars. She'd opened it just far enough to see Jack, studying him with a wary, wrinkled squint. Adjoining the door was the storefront of Fleet Street Tailors, Peter Chou, proprietor. Jack had found it locked. Having noticed the same name on this door, he'd given it a try, assuming it was Peter's residence.

He looked past the woman. He saw a light in a distant room, a narrow hallway, a few hanging houseplants.

Golden Week. He'd heard plenty about the holiday since he'd landed in Hong Kong. It was the Chinese Communist Party's commemoration of the founding of the People's Republic of China in October 1949. With the CCP's burgeoning presence in formerly British Hong Kong, locals were toeing the line, putting on a loyal show.

"An old friend asked me to get in touch," Jack told the crone, who looked at him through the crack in the door.

Unimpressed, she moved to shut it. "No friends. Not anymore. Not here."

Jack shoved his foot into the breach, scuffing his shoe. He shot her a crooked grin. "I think Peter does have a friend. His name is Clark. John Clark."

She exhaled a phlegmy sigh, slumped with resignation, and turned. Jack waited on the curb. It was 21:19, a little over a half-hour before the meet.

Careful to appear at ease, hands in pockets, he swiveled his eyes up and down the street, watching for Brown or Blue. There was an uninterrupted stream of vehicle traffic, much of it chirping scooters. To either side, he saw several shops like this one, most of them closed. Having climbed a fence, stumbled through bushes, and skulked through narrow alleyways, Jack told himself his surveillance detection route, SDR, had worked. Brown and Blue were probably still back at the hotel, oblivious to his departure.

Lights in the tailor shop blinked on. A bell rang as the door opened.

Peter Chou wore suspenders, round tortoiseshell glasses, and an expression of creased disdain. His gray hair was thick, his shoulders stooped. Jack judged him to be about seventy. Without a word, Chou led him deep into the recesses of the shop, finally stopping before a cutting table bordered by tightly packed bolts of fabric.

The older man cleared his throat and blinked behind his Coke-bottle lenses. "Who are you?"

"Ryan. Jack Ryan . . . Junior."

More blinks.

"John Clark sent me."

"You know Clark."

"Yes. I work for him."

Peter Chou took down a bolt of gray flannel from a shelf and threw it on the center of the table with a padded thump, unwrapping a yard. "What size are you?"

"Forty-four long."

The tailor darted Jack a wary, magnified glance and spooled out three folds of fabric.

Jack folded his hands behind his back. "Clark told me you're old friends . . . That you have history."

Chou ran his scissors through the wool, cutting rapidly. Jack repeated himself, growing worried that Clark's old contact had retired, that he was no longer the Campus friend he'd once been.

"You already have a suit," Chou said.

"Well. I didn't come here for a suit. I came here for something else."

The tailor held the scissors open, mid-cut. Through his thick lenses, he raised his head and squinted at his visitor. "And what, exactly, did you come here for, Ryan, Jack Ryan, Junior?"

"A gun."

3

TEMPLE STREET NIGHT MARKET
KOWLOON, HONG KONG
TUESDAY, OCTOBER 1

THE LAST TIME JACK HAD USED A SMITH & WESSON M&P 9-MILLIMETER WAS AT THE back of Mr. C.'s twenty-two-acre horse property, just south of Richmond.

Gerry Hendley had put up half the money for the gentleman's farm as a bonus for Clark on the SEAL's third anniversary with The Campus. The gift had come with a handshake agreement that the farm could be used as a Campus gun range and occasional safe house, should the need arise.

Jack had subsequently spent several days at Clark's horse farm, undergoing a weapons training regimen hosted by Mr. C. and his son-in-law, Domingo "Ding" Chavez. Training up new Campus agents had become a family business.

The old frogman had told Jack he had one rule and one rule only when it came to pistol selection in the field. And that was that the pistol needed to have a threaded barrel, a magazine that held at least ten rounds, and a raised sight so it could be used with a silencer, out of the box. Ding had agreed enthusiastically.

That had winnowed the pistol selection, according to Clark and Ding, to Beretta, CZ, FN, and the one clipped to the back of Jack's belt that he'd acquired from the tailor, an eighteen-round Smith & Wesson M&P.

In a back room behind a rack of suits, the old man had spread his wares. After selecting the Smith & Wesson, Jack had asked about knives. The three pink scars on his forearm—courtesy of his last encounter with the MSS in Tel Aviv—had spurred him to study knife fighting under Ding's watchful eye back at the horse farm.

With that in mind, Jack had picked a small, carbon-black folding knife that now hung around his neck as he walked through the crowded market. Though the tailor had insisted Jack buy a custom suit, he thought both expenses well worth it and charged them to his Hendley white-side account.

"*Chushou! Chushou!*" cried a leathery old woman in a blood-spattered apron. She raised a cleaver, buried it forcefully into a pig leg, and met Jack's eye. A mistake, he realized.

"Twenty a pound. Twenty!" she cried, staring at him. Blood dripped from her sagging chin. Jack looked away and quickened his pace, throwing himself into the mass of other shoppers.

The farther he got into the wet market's plywood stalls, the thicker the crowd. Suspended paper lanterns glowed and swayed in the night breeze over his head. Next to many of them fluttered broad red banners with the yellow stars of the People's Republic of China.

Ah yes, he reminded himself. *Golden Week, the Chinese Fourth of July.*

Oblivious to its political origins, children in school uniforms lit white-hot phosphorous sparklers and popping firecrackers. Jack kept walking, tightly packed against this bustling mob of shoppers. There were few other Western tourists, he noticed, making him an easy surveillance target, which he didn't much like. While scanning faces, he hoped his ruse against Brown and Blue was holding.

A horrible smell wafted under his nose. A gap-toothed old man was stirring a pot the size of a wine barrel with a wooden spoon as big as a shovel. He looked up at Jack with a gummy smirk, churning the steaming yellow sludge. "Stinky tofu," he said, exposing his remaining incisor. "Three dollar."

Jack's eyes watered. He put his hand over his nose and turned away, headed down another alley crowded with buyers and sellers.

Dripping, decapitated white chickens hung to his left. Purple pork sausages snaked to his right. He nearly tripped over a live duck at his feet, then bumped into the two five-year-old girls chasing the fowl, laughing uproariously. Fireworks crackled, red banners swayed.

After passing a station stuffed with slimy squid and hollering fishmongers, he realized—hoped, even—that he was coming to the end of Temple Street's infamous wet market and entering the garment district, where Heirloom Watches was supposed to be.

Closer to his objective, he again wondered about the woman on the ferry. Whoever she was, she was smart enough to guess that Jack had probably been under MSS surveillance. She'd also skillfully chosen this bustling market for their covert meeting, knowing it would be a difficult place for MSS to maintain surveillance.

These details indicated to Jack that she really might be worth the risk, that she might turn out to be a star recruit. White-side assignment or not, Jack couldn't let the opportunity pass.

A short, squatty matron tugged at his suit jacket, dangerously close to the pistol clipped to his belt. Out of reflex, Jack batted her wrist away.

"You like! You like!" she hissed, rubbing her hand, pointing at a rack of garish silk bathrobes. "Golden Week special! Only for you! America! America!"

He turned away, merging into the center of the busy aisle.

Up ahead, he finally saw the sign—*Heirloom Watches*. He angled from the center of the crowd, scanning faces. A loud crack made him reach inside his jacket, near his pistol.

Fireworks burst and blossomed in the night sky, cracking, whistling, and booming. Bathed in fiery light, the crowd around him was suddenly looking up, oohing and aahing. Jack used the distraction to spot any potential surveillants. With a quick scan of the crowd, he fixed on one face that wasn't looking up.

A military-age male. He had a broad nose, long hair in a ponytail, and a neck tattoo. He wore a tight black T-shirt. He was shouldering through the crowd toward Jack, while the people around him were looking up, watching the fireworks. His eyes were fixed forward.

Jack turned to follow the man's line of sight. He was threading through the crowd, apparently intent on the stall next to Heirloom Watches, Pantek Leather Goods. In that stall, browsing a rack with fake Dior handbags, Jack saw a woman in a face mask, wearing a charcoal suit, carrying a white, rope-handled shopping bag.

Her.

Ferry Woman was ignoring the fireworks, occasionally surveying the crowd through the pieces of hair that dangled over her forehead as she picked up one bag after another. Taller than everyone around him, Jack was easy to spot. Their eyes met. He bobbed his head once in recognition.

Breaking contact, she shook her head briskly, turned, and pressed into the stall between more racks of handbags. It seemed to Jack that she'd seen something and was calling off the meet.

To understand why, Jack looked over his shoulder. He saw the military-age male in the black shirt. He was twenty feet from Jack and closing, still on his way to the handbag stall.

As fireworks crackled overhead, Jack scanned the shop to find the woman.

She was gone.

4

JACK MOVED TO STAY IN FRONT OF THE MAN WHO WAS MAKING HIS WAY TO THE stall where Ferry Woman had been a moment before. He was still between the man and the stall.

His mind kicked into operational mode. Ferry Woman, he thought, had contacted him at tremendous risk to herself. Reciprocating that risk, Jack sensed he had a duty to protect her so they could meet again, later. And the likelihood that she was a Chinese dangle seemed remote. Black T-shirt was proof of that. She'd detected the surveillant and run for it. Had she been a dangle, MSS would have wanted Jack to meet with her to entrap him, he thought.

Nevertheless, Jack knew he couldn't put himself in the middle of a Chinese surveillance op. He also couldn't stand idly by. He came up with a third option.

If he could *accidentally* thwart the woman's pursuer, she might find another opportunity to approach him during the remainder of his Hong Kong stay. All he really needed to do was aid her in her getaway.

Knowing that Black T-shirt was behind him, Jack walked to the handbag shop, slowing his pace. Deliberately making himself wide, he spread his legs, put his hands on his hips, and surveyed the leather shop's racks.

He looked for Ferry Woman. She wasn't there. He saw a curtain behind the cash register. She must have gone through it, he concluded.

The six-foot-three American raised his arms as though sampling goods to either side, deliberately blocking the stall's entrance.

He knew Black T-shirt had arrived when he felt a hand on his shoulder, pulling him roughly aside.

"Hey!" barked Jack, facing the man with the ponytail and neck tattoo, swatting his arm away. "Watch it, man!"

Black T-shirt tried to shove past Jack. Jack backed with him, tangling their feet, blocking the route to the curtain behind the cash register.

"*Cay—ee!*" seethed the man, elbowing Jack roughly. Up close, Jack could make out the tattoo on his neck—it was a hooded cobra head.

Jack stumbled backward, blocking the way to the curtain.

"Get off me!" he shouted.

Black T-shirt had had enough. Sneering, he shoved Jack hard. In doing so, his hand glanced against the pistol lump in Jack's waistband. The man's look of anger switched to one of shock. His hand raced under Jack's jacket, going for the gun.

Jack turned sideways and moved his arm to block him.

They tussled and stumbled through the curtain into the narrow alley behind the stalls. Jerking the man's hand free, Jack touched the top of the pistol's grip. His fingers closed around it. He pulled it up.

The man wrenched Jack's wrist and tripped him. Jack landed face-first on the pavement with Black T-shirt on top of him. He felt a stabbing pain in his wrist and elbow—so sharp that it forced his hand open, letting go of the gun. Black T-shirt pulled it free.

The Smith & Wesson's barrel poked at the base of Jack's neck. *Oh shit.*

The alley was dark. The pavement cold and damp against his cheek.

"*Bu!*" snapped the voice behind him. *Bu* was among the few Mandarin words Jack understood. It meant *no*. Odd, he thought, that T-shirt should speak the language of mainland China rather than the Cantonese of Hong Kong.

This is bad, thought Jack, gasping. *Real bad.*

Either he'd fallen victim to a common street thug—or he'd just been burned by an undercover MSS officer. Maybe Mr. C. had been right. Maybe Ferry Woman *had* been a dangle.

Jack felt the pressure on his wrist loosening. He jerked his arm free, rolled, and got to his feet. Black T-shirt was already up, pointing the pistol at Jack's head.

The American's eyes darted left and right, up and down. The alley was about ten feet wide. To Jack's right was a mass of parked scooters on kickstands, packed tightly. The wall behind him was the brick bottom of a building.

The fireworks boomed in the night sky, lighting the alley red. With the gun still on him, Jack glanced up and saw laundry swaying on clotheslines. Hanging low, the lines were tacked to the top of the plywood stalls.

"*Bu!*" barked the man again, gesturing at Jack to get back on the ground.

Facing the barrel of his own weapon, Jack ignored the command. He nearly tripped over a scooter behind him. He backed until his shoulder blades met the bricks of the building.

Evidently unfamiliar with the short-barreled Smith & Wesson

9-millimeter, the man glanced at it. He gripped the slide and pulled it with his left hand, while still aiming at Jack with his right. Staring down the barrel, he examined Jack with his head cocked.

He's not sure what to do, thought Jack.

Fireworks strobed the alley in white when another skyrocket boomed overhead. Still aiming, the man lowered his left hand and withdrew a phone from the pocket of his baggy cotton trousers. It was a wafer-thin large-screen Android, no case.

The man took his eyes off Jack for a fractional second and slid his fingers around, unlocking the device. Jack could see that its big screen made it hard for his assailant to manipulate the smartphone with one hand.

Mr. C. had taught Jack that in every armed encounter, there comes a time when each combatant must decide what to do next. Clark had called it the OODA loop—observe, orient, decide, act. By now Jack had completed his observation, orientation, and decision.

Time to act.

Jack lunged, going for the pistol barrel. He swatted it down hard, breaking the man's grip, while throwing an uppercut to his chin. In the brief gap between fireworks, Jack heard the pistol bang off the pavement.

He hit Black T-shirt in the face with a quick right jab that backed the Asian into the plywood stall. With the man reeling, Jack glanced down, hoping to spot the gun so he could roll toward it.

Big mistake.

The thug slammed the heel of his palm into Jack's Adam's apple. Coughing and dazed, Jack tried another jab. His knuckles smashed into plywood.

The Asian had ducked. Now he came up like an uncoiling spring. He drilled a pointed fist into Jack's chin. The American was thrown backward, into the center of the alley. Before he could steady himself, the assailant landed a fast roundhouse kick to the side of Jack's head.

Unsteadily, Jack crouched low, going for a leg sweep, the standard counter to a roundhouse. The Asian anticipated the move. He hopped over Jack's sweeping leg. Jack jumped up, thinking about the knife on the chain around his neck.

He didn't see the next kick coming. The sole of the attacker's shoe connected with Jack's right eye, slamming his head into the bricks behind him.

Stunned and angry, Jack reached for the little folding knife under his open-necked collar. The necklace knife was attached to the chain with a small carabiner. Jack hurriedly flexed his thumb to free the knife. Before he could, a side kick slammed his rib cage with the force of a baseball bat.

Since his hands were already at his neck, Jack was able to lower them quickly to catch the assaulter's foot. He shoved the Asian's ankle straight up, sending the man to his back. In that moment of relative safety, Jack scanned the pavement for the 9-millimeter. He couldn't find it. He went back for the necklace knife.

From his position on the ground, the Asian delivered a vicious kick to Jack's knee, doubling him over. Jack cried out, but finally got the knife off the carabiner. Breathing hard, smarting from the pain in his knee, he unfolded the blade and raised it, ready to strike.

The Asian was back on his feet. He sneered through a grin at Jack.

SHADOW STATE

Black T-shirt pulled his own folded knife from the rear pocket of his cotton pants. With a wrist flick, he swung the blade free, then spun the weapon around his finger like a six-shooter in an old cowboy movie. He was twirling it, Jack saw, around a metal loop on his index finger that doubled as a brass knuckle. The unfolded blade was curved to a point, like a cat's claw.

From his training with Ding, Jack recognized this style of knife. It was as a karambit, a weapon favored by Southeast Asian street gangs, according to Chavez. Its curving blade followed the natural flow of a punch, rather than the awkward forward thrust of a jab.

No wonder the thug was grinning. Jack's little knife looked like a joke.

The man feinted a left jab, then swung the karambit at Jack's neck with his right hand.

Jack squatted low. He thrust his own knife, going for the Asian's exposed ribs. Jack's attacker batted the thrust away and hurled a backhand swing of the karambit at Jack's heart. The American leaped to the side, nearly tripping over the parked scooters.

The knife-wielding assailant closed in. With his left hand guarding his face, he kept the karambit in his right hand in constant motion. He wheeled the blade at Jack's midsection.

Jumping back, Jack collided with the scooters. On two sides, the bikes were closed in by the plywood stalls of the night market. On the third, they were bunched against the brick building.

The Asian kept coming.

Out of room, Jack had no choice but to climb up onto the scooters. They'd been pushed together tightly, one touching the next, as though crashed in a massive highway pileup. He stood with his left foot on one scooter seat, his right on another. He glimpsed down to keep from falling—every angled handlebar represented a different trip hazard.

Reaching over the first row of scooters, the attacker swung the karambit at Jack's ankles.

Jack raised his right foot to avoid the knife. When he brought it back down, the cuff of his trousers caught on a handlebar mirror.

He lost his balance and windmilled his arms by instinct.

He feared that if he fell between the bikes, he'd be trapped, an easy target. As his hands flew over his head, they touched fabric hanging from the clothesline. Desperate not to fall, Jack clutched at it, losing his grip on his puny knife. As though trying to climb a rope, he pulled hard.

He fell anyway.

On his way down, his head banged off a scooter's front fender. He jerked to get to his feet, but found his legs hemmed in by the bikes. Tangled in the fabric he'd pulled from the clothesline over his head, he flailed desperately, trying to get up before the Asian could make his move.

He tore at the sheet, trying to see. His fingers found a thin cord. It was the broken clothesline he'd yanked as he'd fallen. He ripped the sheet from his eyes.

The attacker was standing over Jack, the karambit swinging for his throat.

Jack raised his arm to block the thrust. Again he tried to get up, turning to his side. Without a better move, he flung the sheet at his attacker's face.

It landed on Black T-shirt's head.

Jack sprung to his feet with the broken clothesline in his hand. He tackled the assailant, smothering him on the pavement, the sheet still tangled around his shoulders. He whipped the clothesline around the Asian's neck, coiling it. He pulled the two sides of the cord as hard as he'd ever pulled anything in his life.

Between the scooters and the wall, the knife-wielding assaulter thrust his blade wildly, slamming it against wheels, bricks, and pavement.

From his position behind the attacker, Jack ignored the karambit. He focused only on pulling his improvised garrote. For more leverage, he shoved his knee into the Asian's back and grunted.

The karambit thrusts grew weaker and weaker.

Until they stopped altogether.

5

**VIRGINIA BEACH, VIRGINIA
TUESDAY, OCTOBER 1**

"HELLO, MASTER CHIEF," SAID JOHN CLARK.

He'd spotted the shining bullet head and hulking shoulders of Master Chief Kendrick Moore from a distance. Clark had arrived at the beachside coffee shop right on time, ten-thirty a.m. Apparently, Moore had gotten there early.

The master chief was sitting awkwardly at a sidewalk table, wearing Levi's and an untucked short-sleeve shirt. His tarp-sized windbreaker was draped over a nearby chair. Rising with an extended hand to greet Clark, the big SEAL nearly knocked the dainty metal table over.

"Thanks for coming, sir."

Clark rarely met men whose hands were bigger than his. He returned the firm grip. "It's John, Master Chief."

Kendrick Moore inclined his shining bald head with deference. "John it is. Aye, sir."

They sat. The master chief's thick thighs poured over the seat bottom. Clark worried the small café chair might collapse.

Having never met before, each knew the other only by reputation. They started in on small talk. Clark began with questions about Moore's family situation.

Kids? Negative. Wife? Not anymore. Girlfriend? A sad shake of the head. Clark sipped his coffee quietly and looked over the street at the gleaming Atlantic.

"How's Ding?" Moore asked when the interval grew awkward. "I understand he married your daughter."

Clark put the cup down. "Yeah. He did. Made her a mother, too."

The corners of Moore's lips curved up. "The famous John Clark's a grandfather now. Why am I the one who feels old?"

"You have no idea, Master Chief."

Moore followed Clark's wistful gaze over the ocean. "Not sure if Ding told you, John, but I worked with him in an op out of Majorca. Maritime interdiction. Iranian freighter headed for Syria."

"Yeah," returned Clark. "He told me." The sea breeze whipped into a gust. "Ding said you're a hell of a leader. That you run a tight team."

Moore curved his hands around his paper cup and leaned over it. His knee bounced under the table. "Ding's, uh, in your . . . outfit now, right?"

Clark studied the man across from him, logging the freshly shaved jaw, the flinty eyes. He also noted Moore's faintly embarrassed expression, the mouth that moved before speaking, as though not sure what would come out of it. Master Chief Kendrick Moore wasn't at all what John Clark had expected.

Moore's forearms were resting on a manila folder, holding it in place so the wind wouldn't catch it. The big man nervously twirled the empty cup in his fingers.

"Hey, Master Chief," offered Clark, noting the bouncing knee, "you need a refuel?"

"Negative. Had three of these already."

"Got here early, did you?"

"Yeah." The master chief raised his wide face, squinting against the breeze. "I, uh, kind of didn't want to screw this up—if you know what I mean."

Clark locked eyes with the SEAL. Like so many of the operators he'd known, they were prematurely wrinkled for a man of only thirty-eight.

"Come on," said Clark, rising. "Let's walk the beach. Not many sunny days like this left."

It was the first of October, a weekday. The air was cool, the summer beach crowds a memory. Moore stood, donned his jacket, and placed the sheet of paper into a manila folder, which he pressed to his side under his elbow. They tossed their cups in the garbage.

With Moore at his side, Clark took the steps down to the sand. They walked thirty yards over the dunes to the hardpack. Waves crashed and hissed. Sandpipers ran back and forth, avoiding the surf.

Clark breathed deeply and looked out at the blue-green horizon. "I never miss that smell," he said. The sun was forty-five degrees above the Atlantic, shining brightly.

"Same here."

"There's just something that draws us back to the sea, isn't there?"

"Said like a true frogman, Mr. Clark."

"I told you. It's John, Master Chief." Clark glanced at the folder at Moore's side. "Hey, what is that you've got there, anyway?"

Kendrick Moore carefully extracted a white paper from the

manila folder. The strong breeze made it flop over in his hand. "Ding said to bring a résumé. I worked on it all night."

Clark didn't reach for it. "Why? I know your rep."

"You don't want to read it?"

"Put it away, Master Chief."

Moore put his résumé back in the folder. He and Clark walked in silence for a dozen yards, the waves crashing rhythmically next to them. "Not sure how this is supposed to work," Moore finally said. "Ding told me to have a résumé. If you've got some other approach, I'm fine with it."

Clark looked south, his eyes sweeping the sky. They both heard a low, approaching buzz and caught sight of a small dot over the sea. It was a Black Hawk helicopter, nose down, level to the horizon, engines screaming, blades whopping.

As it sped past them, Clark noted its long refueling probe. He guessed it was a special ops bird, likely from the base at Dam Neck, just to the south. That's where Development Group, formerly known as SEAL Team Six, trained. They were the Navy's finest, tier-one operators all, the elite of the elite, specially selected from the other SEAL teams.

Moore's last assignment had been with DEVGRU.

The Black Hawk turned east, headed out over the waves. It grew smaller and smaller. The two men watched it intently. "You miss it?" asked Clark.

The helo arced into a low southern turn, likely returning to Dam Neck. Moore's eyes never left it. "Yeah. I do indeed."

"It will get easier."

Moore released a pent-up sigh, grumbling, "The only easy day . . ."

". . . was yesterday," finished Clark, completing the old SEAL motto with a side-eyed grin. They resumed walking as the helo beats faded. "So," continued Clark. "Are you . . . officially a civilian now? Or are you riding out the weeks until retirement?"

"As of last Friday, I'm a civilian. Whatever the hell that means. I got my DD-214, my white ID card, all of that."

"Weird feeling, right?"

"Yeah. Very."

Three seagulls hung in the wind over their heads and screeched before diving away.

"Look," said Clark after the birds had quieted. "I don't need to see your résumé. I don't need to ask what three adjectives you'd use to describe yourself or to give two examples of your last work contribution. At the end of the day, I really only have one question."

"Shoot, sir."

Clark looked the SEAL in the eye. "Is your head right, Master Chief?"

Moore blinked against the wind, his eyes slitted. He looked away from Clark and shoved his big hands into his pockets. "Yeah. I'm all right."

Clark marched on through the sand. "No shame in saying you need to take some time. You've been through a lot—the legal proceedings, the media . . . your trident-pulling."

"I have. But I've also learned to accept responsibility for what happened. I accept all of it."

"You've learned to accept the responsibility for your team, you mean."

"My team was my responsibility. It was on me. Sure, I accept that."

Clark turned to face him. He jabbed a finger into Moore's enormous chest. "You got a raw deal, Master Chief."

Three months earlier, an ISIS defector had told a *New York Times* reporter that a band of SEALs had viciously killed a suspected terrorist under interrogation. The story fingered the DEVGRU team's leader, Kendrick Moore, as a ruthless maniac. Lawmakers anxious to curb defense spending had made Moore infamous, calling him a war criminal. Everything had gone south from there.

They strode along in the companionable silence of brother operators for a while. It took a hundred steps before Moore felt an obligation to say something. "Look, John. I'm not going to lie. Pulling my trident hurt. I'd have almost preferred a bad-conduct discharge to that."

They stepped over a dead horseshoe crab swaddled in seaweed. Swarming with flies, the mess was the size of an ottoman. "Nothing to be ashamed of now, Master Chief. Charges were dropped."

"Yeah. Thanks to President Ryan."

At Clark's urging, Ryan had asked his chief of staff, Arnie van Damm, to step in and hammer out a deal to keep the sanctimonious senators at bay. From the President's perspective, the SEALs hadn't done anything wrong. The ISIS scumbag they'd hit had been on the Air Force's drone kill list. The problem was optics. And media.

"The President wishes he could have done more," Clark added. "But at least you left with an honorable discharge. You also got to keep your E-9 retirement pay."

"Yes, sir."

"So why are you looking for work already?"

"Because, John, it's . . . not enough for me."

"You mean the money?"

"That's part of it. The divorce takes half. Then there are the legal bills for the trouble that came with the Senate inquiry. And, well, there's the boredom, the uselessness . . . the . . ." He clenched his mouth shut, his jaw muscles flexing.

"Lot of demand out there for an operator with your skills, Master Chief."

Moore angled to study the waves. "I can't even get an interview."

"You've applied to the mercenary groups? Blackwater? Northbridge?"

"Yeah. Losing my trident has marked me. I'm bad news, John."

Clark stared down at the sand, noting their stunted shadows. It was more than the stain of a pulled SEAL trident, he knew. He'd learned that potential employers like Blackwater had passed on Moore because of his disorderly conduct arrest after smashing up a Virginia Beach bar. A divorce, a DUI, and a DEVGRU operator who'd lost his trident added up to a man with some serious problems.

They started walking again, a little faster. "Ding said you guys operate a tight ship. But that's about all he'd tell me."

"Right," said Clark.

"Ding wouldn't say exactly what you guys do. He just said you might have room for an experienced operator. Do you?"

A particularly big wave forced them to walk up the beach. Clark had to raise his voice to be heard over the hiss of the retreating water. "Yeah. I might. I run an outfit that does things for the government."

"An outfit. As in . . . Other Government Agency? Special Activities?"

"Not the OGA you're thinking of." Among operators, OGA was the generally accepted term for the Central Intelligence Agency.

Moore looked sideways at Clark. "So if not OGA . . . then a commercial group? Private security?"

"I'd call it a hybrid. We do a bit of both. Very small. Keeps us agile."

"What's the chain of command?"

"I run a flat org. You'd work for me, plain and simple."

Moore's fingers twitched on the folder he carried. "Listen, John, if I haven't been clear . . . I'd like to be a part of it. Is there a fit for me?"

Clark took a breath. "It's a small group. A few former SOCOM. We also have a few ex-Marines, SWAT, and FBI trigger pullers. Ding probably told you some of this, though he shouldn't have."

"He told me a little when he said you might have an opening. But he didn't say what you were looking for—only that we should talk."

"Well, I'm looking to deepen the bench. I need someone with experience. The team's skills are solid—but they're young. It's their judgment I worry about, their maturity. I want someone who's willing to challenge their thinking—tactically and strategically."

"I can do that, John."

Clark slowed and turned to face Moore. "You sure about that? Your last mission went a little sideways. Someone might question my judgment if I were to hire you for this job."

The master chief's hands finally stopped twitching. "I'll prove you right—and them wrong."

Clark looked out at the sea, thinking for a while. The wind rustled the folder in Moore's hand, making it crackle. "It'd be pretty understandable, Master Chief, if you harbored a few grudges."

Moore's face flushed, his thick shoulders sagging. "I'll admit it. I did. I was . . . angry, for a while. Now I'm just sorry."

"Sorry doesn't mean better."

"I'm better, too."

"Yeah? What's changed?"

"Ding called. This meeting got on the calendar. It gave me . . . hope, I guess. A goal. With my pin pulled, I'd lost the goals that gave me purpose. That defined who I am. That's what messed me up."

Clark scanned the horizon. He listened to the waves and the rising buzz of another helicopter coming up from the south. He'd known men like Kendrick Moore his whole life. Not once had he met one who'd had his trident pulled—the meanest punishment Clark could imagine.

The helicopter roared by. Moore didn't watch it this time, Clark noticed. The master chief was staring down at his sandy shoes, his head and shoulders forming an isosceles triangle.

Clark made his decision.

"Okay, Kendrick. If I said I had an op for you—but that you had to get on a plane tonight—you think you could handle that? We're helping a Filipino SEAL team bag a high-value target."

Moore's head sprung up. His shoulders squared. "Of course. Who's the HVT?"

"Suffice it to say . . . a jihadi who seems to have gotten cozy with the Chinese. This op has to be one step removed. Full denial. You know the drill."

"I know the drill, yeah. And I know Lieutenant Commander Santos out in Manila. I worked with one of his teams in an op in the Spratlys."

"It's Captain Santos, now. And he has the whole Filipino SEAL command under him. He remembers that Spratly op, too.

He speaks highly of you. *He's* one of the reasons I'm here this morning. My team needs someone like you. So does Santos. But you'd have to leave immediately."

Moore rolled the manila folder into a tight scroll. "John, I live in a month-to-month Airbnb garage attic. I don't even have a houseplant. I'll drive straight to the airport now if you tell me to. I'll eat a goddamned snake for breakfast if that's what you want."

"What I want is for this op to stay quiet. It's why my team's there instead of SOCOM. Like I said, I have a couple of good people there—two Green Berets, a woman who runs intel and logistics. She's a former Marine and cop. But they're all a little junior. You'd need to figure out how to lead them on the hit. Think you can do that?"

"I know I can."

"The whole thing might go down in the next forty-eight."

"I'm ready."

Clark looked out at the ocean, his lips puckered, eyes narrowed against the breeze. After about ten seconds, he said, "Okay. Let's get you jocked up. You're going in."

The master chief blinked. "I'm hired?"

"Consider it a provisional hire. This goes okay, then yeah, I'll support you coming onto the payroll full time."

Moore seized Clark's hand, shaking it vigorously. "As God is my witness, John. You won't regret this."

6

**THE WHITE HOUSE
WASHINGTON, D.C.
TUESDAY, OCTOBER 1**

TWO HUNDRED MILES TO THE NORTH, PRESIDENT JACK RYAN RESISTED THE URGE to put his feet up on the Oval Office's hulking Resolute desk. He was leaning back, fingers interlaced behind his head, just itching to throw his wing tips up on the desk's solid oak planks.

He wondered whether that would be sacrilegious, a show of disrespect toward the office. The hallowed presidential desk had been built from remnants of the British arctic exploring ship HMS *Resolute*, a gift from Queen Victoria to Rutherford B. Hayes. Would old Queen Vic mind?

No, thought the President of the United States. If the *Resolute*'s timbers could handle arctic ice, they could certainly handle Jack's size twelves. Besides, he told himself, he'd earned a little relaxation in this office. Because, for once, Mary Pat Foley's intelligence update had been *good* news. The sweetest thing he'd heard in months.

UMBRA, the stealth pod they'd retrofitted to an old F-15 Strike Eagle in the Pacific, had worked.

Absorbing the report, canted back, the President placed his feet on the desk. He was almost reluctant to probe, to ask the hard questions. Couldn't good news go unmolested for once? But it was his job to keep the spooks honest.

"Nothing?" he asked Mary Pat, his director of national intelligence. "The Chinese PLAAF didn't do a damned thing? You're absolutely sure?"

"Nothing in this business is absolutely sure, Mr. President," she replied. "But our assessment is that the PLAAF never saw the F-15 when it crossed over Mischief Reef."

Though the news was good, Ryan thought Mary Pat looked severe this morning. She'd worn her gray pantsuit, black blouse, and hair pulled back in a bun. Her arms were crossed over the secret-stuffed leather portfolio that rarely left her side. She looked, thought Jack, a bit like Sister Judy O'Keefe, the nun who'd terrified him into memorizing his times tables as a kid at St. Joe's.

And, the President considered further, much the way Sister Judy would have disapproved of his supine posture in the Oval, he sensed that maybe it bothered Mary Pat, too. He planted his feet back on the thick blue carpet and straightened his chair.

"Well, then," he said. "Give me the detailed tactical assessment of the Chinese air defense reaction to UMBRA. If it's as good as you say, I'd like to savor it."

Mary Pat angled her head toward one of two yellow damask sofas that faced each other a few feet away. "Clarence—you want to give the President your analysis?"

Army lieutenant general Clarence Gill was the current

director of the National Security Agency. He was sitting at the right sofa's edge with his hands folded over a crossed knee.

He'd only been the DIRNSA for sixty days—it was his first time in the Oval Office. Gill's boss, Secretary of Defense Bob Burgess, sat next to him. On the facing sofa sat Arnie van Damm, Ryan's chief of staff. Arnie was hunched forward in the watchful pose of a gargoyle, as always.

General Gill cleared his throat. "Mr. President, as part of the UMBRA operational test, we had every national electronic collection system aimed at the Chinese air defense radars in the South China Sea. We also had two PARPRO flights tuned to their destroyer squadrons within the Taiwanese Air Defense Identification Zone."

Ryan took a point of pride in decoding the acronyms that formed the bulk of the DoD's vernacular. PARPRO, he knew, meant Peacetime Aerial Reconnaissance Program. They were usually Navy P-8 Poseidons that loitered in the airspace off the east coast of China.

"You said *two* PARPRO flights, General," noted Ryan. "The whole point of this UMBRA test was to look like business as usual. Was it a risk to put up two?"

General Gill looked between Bob Burgess and Mary Pat Foley. Since the NSA is run by the military as an intelligence-gathering organization, Gill reported to both Mary Pat and the secretary of defense.

Burgess spoke first. "Mr. President, the Navy Poseidons were flying the same racetrack patterns we've been running for three months. You're right that we don't usually have two birds up—but it's not unprecedented. The Chinese didn't react to it."

"We also had assets from NGA looking for SIGINT," added Mary Pat.

By that, Ryan knew, she meant the National Geospatial-Intelligence Agency, the arm of the DoD that operated spy satellites. SIGINT, signals intelligence, referenced the combination of electronic and communications emissions that the satellites sucked up for analysis.

"The Chinese must have seen something," said the President. "I thought we were going to bird-dog them with two F-22s before the F-15 broke away on its solo path."

"That's right, sir," said Burgess. "The Chinese had their early-warning radars up and the usual check-ins. One of the radars picked up the F-22s and reported it back to their ground control intercept headquarters on Hainan Island. But there wasn't a single report of the F-15—even though it flew right over Mischief Reef."

The news was just too good, thought Ryan.

It meant that the Pentagon could retrofit the entire Pacific fleet of F-15s in Okinawa with UMBRA pods. For a sum less than a single B-21 stealth bomber, the President had just acquired a vast fleet of stealth strike aircraft. He considered it the defense procurement judo move of the century.

He looked at his defense secretary. "Bob, what about our naval units? Could they see it?"

The SecDef tented his hands. "We had an Arleigh Burke, the *Benfold*, deliberately sailing in the F-15's path. The *Benfold* was operating under the assumption that they were doing an air defense exercise with the F-22s as the red team. They never saw the UMBRA-equipped Eagle. We also had an Air Force AWACS up. It didn't pick up our F-15, either. She was invisible."

Ryan laughed, smacking his hands together. "Our own Air Force missed it?"

"Not a blip," added Mary Pat. "We looked at post-exercise

mission statistics. UMBRA worked flawlessly. It defeated every system we have. Not a single echo, not even a faint one when we knew where to look."

"I'll be damned," said Jack. "Is there some way for me to fund steak dinners for the Quantum Atomics team out at Palmdale? Do they know they've built something that could change history?"

And at least give us a fighting chance to retake Taiwan if the balloon ever goes up, he thought.

Burgess leaned forward. "We'll figure something out for those propeller-heads out at Quantum."

"Please do. Hell, I'd like to pay Palmdale a visit personally."

"I'll set it up," chimed in Arnie. "We can make it about the new B-21 bomber they're finishing up out at Skunk Works. That will make a good cover story for UMBRA, right?"

"Yeah," Jack replied. "But please make sure I meet the actual UMBRA team. Quietly. They need to know how important this is."

Burgess rapped his knuckles on the coffee table, showing off his West Point ring. "Mr. President, this might be a good time to press Congress on the supplemental appropriation for a lot more UMBRA pods. They cost a hell of a lot less than new stealth bombers—but that doesn't mean they're free."

"We can't go back for more defense funding," objected van Damm. "You'll just have to take it out of some other program, Bob."

"Arnie, you know how strapped we are. We're supposed to be retiring all those F-15s. Keeping them alive with UMBRA will need a funding package. It's a major rework."

Ryan's mouth flattened. Both Arnie and Burgess were right.

The defense budget had been cut to the bone—and Congress would be unwilling to give him another dollar after the months-long negotiation gauntlet they'd all survived, barely.

"A new DoD-funding bill is going to be dead on arrival in the Senate," said van Damm. "We've got a lot on our plate right now."

"And we've got the Chinese saber-rattling over Taiwan again," shot the SecDef. "It's not like our military *asked* for that."

Van Damm raised an eyebrow at Jack.

"For what it's worth, I agree with Bob," offered Mary Pat, coming to the President's rescue. "I know I'm just the spook in the room here. But as a taxpayer, I see this as a lot of bang for the buck. If UMBRA lets F-15s evade Chinese detection, then it's a bargain. Maybe cancel one of the new Columbia subs, Bob—put the reallocation into UMBRA."

"Whoa, now. I wouldn't go that far, M.P." Burgess frowned. "The next war with China will be naval. We need every nickel going into those ships."

Van Damm piled on. "And the new Columbia-class boomers are made in swing districts. You want to upset Congress? Mess with those carefully negotiated allocations."

"I'm just saying," said Foley. "China's big advantage is in missiles—hypersonics and theater ballistics. If UMBRA gives us bombers that can fly right up to those sites and take them out, then we can negate the Chinese capability with the forces we have in theater now."

"True," said Arnie. "Which is why we should brief the Armed Services Committee on UMBRA."

Mary Pat looked doubtful. "That's a good way to lose our advantage."

"She's right," agreed Ryan. "UMBRA is huge, a game changer.

Norden bombsight, Enigma machine huge. I want a complete lockdown on this thing. *No one* can know about it. We sure as hell aren't going to risk a congressional leak."

"Of course, Mr. President," said Mary Pat. "This is all eyes-only, special access." She hugged her portfolio closely to her chest and dropped her eyes to the floor. Ryan didn't like the look on her face.

He got up from behind the *Resolute* desk and rounded it, touching the button that would summon the Navy steward.

He took one of the padded upright chairs in front of the fireplace and waved Mary Pat to the free spot on the sofa, next to van Damm. Ryan had installed the big portrait of Teddy Roosevelt over the mantel, framed on either side by smaller paintings of Washington, Jefferson, Lincoln, and Madison.

The hidden curved door that led to the private dining room opened. The steward appeared with a silver coffee service, set it up, and departed silently. None of them spoke until he'd gone.

The President added a little cream to his coffee and stirred. "Well . . . budget battles yet to come notwithstanding . . . I'd still like to call for champagne over UMBRA. But you know. That would start rumors in the kitchen as to what the hell we're talking about in here." He grinned over his cup.

"Have a cocktail in the residence tonight," said van Damm. "Until then, cheers, folks. Nice work. UMBRA lives. We'll figure some way to pay for it."

"Thanks, Arnie," said Burgess. "But it's more than a question of funding. We also have to make sure we can supply enough of these pods. Ninety percent of rare earth magnets come from China. Quantum only has one supplier for them so far."

Ryan munched a cookie. He'd read in one of his Commerce Department papers that there was a race on to secure rare earth mineral resources. The Chinese had cornered the market on refining them and that was a big no-no when it came to weapons procurement. He'd asked Commerce and State to follow up with some suggestions on how to encourage private industry to find friendlier, allied links for the supply chain—but he was still waiting on an answer.

"Let me check my understanding of how UMBRA works," the President said to Burgess.

The SecDef scratched his neck. "Please, sir. Go ahead."

The President lowered his voice. "UMBRA consists of rare earth magnets that take an incoming radio pulse—like a radar—and turn that into a mirrored, reciprocal electric field."

"Yes, sir."

"And our biggest defense supplier, Quantum Atomics, builds this wizardry into a long pod carried in a plane's weapons bay."

"Correct, sir. It takes quite a bit of engineering."

"Right. Because the pods are highly specialized. The electric fields come from very specific types of magnets made from rare earth minerals."

"Yes, sir. The magnets are made from samarium. Almost all samarium mining and refining is done in China. Avoiding Chinese mines, refiners, and magnet suppliers has been the hard part."

"We don't let U.S. defense suppliers source magnets from China. Where are these coming from?"

"The samarium magnets Quantum is using come from Vietnam," said Burgess.

"Vietnam. A traditional enemy of the Chinese, a country we're courting as an ally for precisely that reason. Right?"

"Correct, sir."

"Then what's the problem? The Vietnamese supply chain shouldn't be at risk."

"The problem, Mr. President, is that those samarium magnets are in high demand for electric cars. I'm not sure we're going to be able to get enough of them—especially if you're looking to outfit every fighter plane in the Pacific. All the magnets used in the UMBRA pods are coming from one company with operations in Vietnam. GeoTech."

"They're *all* from GeoTech?"

"For now, sir, yes. GeoTech's the only company that's tapped a substantial load of samarium. Samarium magnets are great for electric motor efficiency—even better for producing the right electromagnetic wave convergence for UMBRA."

Jack sighed. "Okay. I get it." He glanced up at van Damm. "Arnie, ask Alice and Tony to swing by this afternoon. Commerce and State need a sharper plan to get more American companies into the rare earth magnets game—or at least to import them from allies. And we have to figure out how to make sure Quantum has priority for the existing supply. Bob's right. UMBRA's too big a deal to leave to one company."

He sipped his coffee again. "Well, anyway. This is fantastic news, folks. Good work."

When in the Oval Office, if the President is happy, everyone is happy. They all smiled broadly. Except for Mary Pat.

The President's secretary, Alma Winters, stuck her head through the door. She was under standing orders to do so when Ryan's meetings went more than ten minutes over the tight schedule. He glanced at his watch. Sure enough, he'd taken longer than he'd intended.

"I know, Alma, I know," he said to her. "Who's up now?"

"Brotherhood of Locomotive Engineers, Mr. President. They're coming in with Secretary Cobb to discuss terms. Mr.

Cobb said it's urgent . . . That they're threatening to strike tomorrow."

"Jack," said Arnie. "You need to take this."

Elliott Cobb was Ryan's Secretary of Labor, who'd failed in keeping the rail management and union folks from the mutually assured destruction of a strike. The President glanced up at Teddy Roosevelt's pince-nez spectacles and soup-strainer mustache. T.R. had threatened to send troops to settle a coal strike more than a hundred years ago. *Teddy, give me strength.*

"Shall I show them in, sir?"

Ryan still didn't like the look on Mary Pat's face. "Give me another minute, folks. Mary Pat, stay put." Alma retreated, taking the rest of the staff with her.

After they'd all filed out, Ryan looked intently at his director of national intelligence. "Okay, let's have it."

"Have what?"

"Whatever's on your mind, Mary Pat."

"I've given you my two cents on UMBRA, Jack. It's all good news."

"Then why don't you look happy?"

"I am happy. But I'm worried. It's . . . kind of my job to worry."

"Right. Mine, too. I'm worried about how to prevent a rail strike. I can't figure out what you're worried about."

She rushed a sigh. "I agree with you that UMBRA is an important countermeasure, a strategic advantage."

"Right."

"But, Jack, technical countermeasures only work if they're asymmetric, where *we* have them and the bad guys don't. Otherwise, they'll just find a way to counter it."

"UMBRA *is* asymmetric."

"For now." She crossed her legs. "Dan Murray's got the FBI opening a new Chinese counterintelligence investigation roughly every hour of every day. There are *thousands* of them, most focused on industrial espionage."

"I know," said Ryan. Dan Murray was Ryan's attorney general. "I gave Dan that priority. Of course I want the FBI director to do that. Why does that worry you?"

"Because . . . I don't know what I don't know."

"Jesus, M.P. What the hell am I supposed to do with that?"

"Sorry, Jack. It's just that the MSS industrial intelligence collection effort is on a scale we've never seen before. Something like UMBRA would be at the top of their list."

Now the President frowned. "You really know how to rain on my parade, don't you?"

Her forehead creased. "Sorry, Jack. It's just that we're seeing MSS activities everywhere, beyond the pale. Real violence, not like the last cold war. This is more like a hot war, only it's taking place in the shadows, one step removed from the real fighters."

Ryan waggled his foot, staring at it. "You're going to tell me more about that theory of yours, aren't you?"

"Yes."

"You give it a code name yet?"

She opened up her folder and stared into it, frowning. "We're calling it TALON. I didn't want to report this to you with the others in here . . . so I left it out of your PDB." She was referring to the President's Daily Brief.

"Why? What have you got that makes TALON seem real?"

She handed the President a decoded intercept from an Abu Sayyaf terrorist in the Philippines. The translated, decoded phone call showed a Chinese intelligence officer asking the terrorist to hit the current Filipino president, a new American ally who'd pledged to allow U.S. troops to return to the islands as a bulwark against China.

After reading the paper, Ryan handed it back. "China's trying to assassinate the president of the Philippines because they don't like how things are shaking out in the South China Sea."

"Looks that way."

"And they're going to make it look like a hit driven by an Islamist sect on Mindanao."

"That's the essence of the MSS TALON ring. They're recruiting bad actors all over the world, creating a shadow force."

"Do you have someone working on this? CIA or . . . otherwise?"

"Otherwise," she said, holding his gaze.

The President held up his hand. "This is one of those ops you said I shouldn't know about."

"Correct. And between us, it's not the only one. We're seeing similar communication with MS-13 gang leaders down in Central America. More TALON."

"Glad you're working it."

"Me too. But you can imagine why I might worry. The MSS will do whatever it takes to root out something like UMBRA. Every system we have is vulnerable."

The President looked at Mary Pat. The joy he'd felt at the UMBRA report had passed into something that felt like anxiety. Why did it always have to end up that way? "Well," he said, clearing his mind. "As much as I hate to say this, Mary Pat, I have to get on with the rest of my day."

"Yes, Jack."

As she went out, Alma Winters came in. Only those who'd occupied the Oval Office knew it had a constantly swinging door, leaving the President few moments for reflection. Jack's mood was off—the apprehension over MSS interference climbing.

"Mr. Cobb says they're getting antsy, sir."

Behind the *Resolute* desk again, Ryan drummed his fingers on the oak, thinking about UMBRA. He stared at Alma's imperturbable face. Then he looked up at Teddy Roosevelt again.

Speak softly . . .

That part was easy, he thought. The hard part was figuring out how best to wield the big stick.

7

**HONG KONG ISLAND
WEDNESDAY, OCTOBER 2**

"JACK, YOU LISTENING TO THIS?"

Howard Brennan, Hendley Associates' chief investment officer, and architect of the GeoTech financing strategy, leaned into Jack Junior with a sharp elbow.

"Yes, Howard. I'm on it," Jack whispered back, lowering his eyes to his laptop screen.

A moment before, those eyes had been fixed on the towering skyscrapers of Kowloon on the other side of the green harbor. Twelve hours earlier, Jack had nearly been killed up the hill from those skyscrapers in one of the city's famed wet markets.

By whom or what, he still didn't know.

"You sure you're all right?" whispered Howard when the HSBC bankers huddled together for a private chat. Jack had a right-eye shiner. He'd told Howard he'd been mugged on a trip up the hill when he'd gone out to buy a new suit. On his return to the hotel, he'd ended up in a fight with a mugger to hang on to his old heirloom Rolex.

The bankers on the other side of the table finished conferring and addressed Howard. "Right. Now, here's how we see it," said their leader, a tall angular Londoner with a fringe of white hair. "We're willing to come down twenty-five basis points. Provided, mind you, that we get undeniable proof of GeoTech's operating income by the end of the week."

As an experienced negotiator, Howard Brennan forced himself to look disappointed. "Twenty-five basis points? That's it?"

"Yes, I'm afraid so, Howard. That's the best we can do. We find the offer very generous—and keep in mind, it will expire. There are many other GeoTech suitors afoot."

The Hendley executive drummed his pen against his legal pad. "Well." He frowned. "Can you give us a minute to run the new numbers?"

"Certainly." Following their leader, the bankers filed from the room.

When the door closed behind them, Howard spun his chair to face Jack.

"Come on," he urged. "Run the numbers, will you? You heard the man. We may have to act quickly here to keep this deal from ending up with the Germans."

"Yes. Okay . . ." answered Jack, still preoccupied with the prior evening's exploits.

"Hey, Jack. What's with you this morning?"

In the blink of his bruised eye, Jack pondered that question.

Yes, he'd killed men before. As a trained Campus operative, he'd logged several critical missions. In each, cloaked in the usual requirements of secrecy, deniability, and zero footprint, he'd led Campus fire teams against mercenaries, terrorists, and Special Forces units.

But what had happened to him at the wet market had been

altogether different. With his bare hands, he'd killed a man—strangled him—without sanction.

He'd gone on to cover up the crime, if that's what it was. He'd smashed the man's phone and tossed it in a trash bin. He'd dropped the Smith & Wesson acquired from the tailor into a murky canal. He'd even snuck back into the Peninsula Hotel the same way he'd exited it, climbing over a dumpster into the room-service kitchen.

"Earth to Jack," said Howard. "Come on, man. Run the numbers."

"Sorry to interrupt," said the HSBC lead banker. He'd pushed his snowy head through a crack in the door. "Do you need more time?"

"A bit," said Howard.

"What about you, Jack? Can we get you something for that eye? Aspirin? Ibuprofen?"

The HSBC team had been shocked by Jack's appearance that morning. They'd offered local police and medical help. Jack had waved the assistance away, telling them he was fine. The mention of police had sent a cold stab through his gut.

"I'm good," he told the banker, who left again.

"Come on," said Howard. "Crunch the numbers."

Jack shot Howard a harried glance and typed revised figures into the ten highlighted cells on his spreadsheet. He thumbed the return key and tilted his laptop toward Howard. "There you go. That's a twenty-five basis-point reduction on the three-hundred-million-dollar bond with a maturity of ten years and a lower balloon payment in year four."

Howard's mouth twisted in thought as he scanned Jack's model. He rubbed his chin, swiveled back and forth in his chair, and muttered to himself, as though doing math in his head. After a full minute, he slid the laptop back to Jack. "Make it a twenty-seven basis-point reduction," he said.

Jack complied and displayed the new numbers. Howard blew out a lung full of air. He stopped swiveling in his chair. He was no longer mumbling. "I'll go get them," he said, rising.

The HSBC bankers resumed their position across from the Hendley men. "Do we have a deal?" asked their leader.

"We do," said Howard. "If you make it a twenty-seven basis-point reduction."

The leader's eyes shifted among his team, then settled again on Howard. "And you can get us the due diligence on GeoTech's Vietnamese samarium mining operation by the end of this week?"

Howard nudged Jack. It was the junior man's job to cover the due diligence—an audit into GeoTech's books to ensure their revenues and expenses were exactly as depicted in their financial statements. The audited proof was critical to the HSBC bankers because their loan would be collateralized by the Hendley Associates firm—which, by extension, would soon include all the assets of the GeoTech Corporation.

In other words, should Hendley Associates default on the three-hundred-million-dollar loan, HSBC would end up owning both companies. The HSBC bankers wanted to make sure they weren't getting suckered.

"What do you think, Jack?" asked Howard. "Could we get an audit done in Vietnam by week's end?"

Jack unconsciously touched his black eye. He wouldn't normally mind performing this type of work. He was good at it. But he hadn't quite anticipated the curveball of finishing it by the end of the week. And he'd still harbored the dim hope that Mr. C.

would whisk him away to the Philippines on the black-side op in the archipelago.

Vietnam would be taking him in the wrong direction—physically *and* spiritually.

Muddling through mashed-up thoughts of Mr. C., Lisanne, the Philippines, a rushed audit, and the man with the deadly karambit he'd strangled the previous evening, Jack sighed heavily. "Yes. I can complete a GeoTech audit in Vietnam by the end of the week. No problem."

"Then," said the lead HSBC banker, rising with an extended hand, leaning over the table, "contingent on that audit, gentlemen, we have a deal."

Hands were shaken, backs slapped. Howard scribbled out a pen-and-ink term sheet. The three HSBC lenders and the two Hendley borrowers signed the paper with a dignified flourish, as though adorning a historic document.

When the impromptu ceremony was finished, Howard glanced at his watch and turned to Jack. "Let's get Gerry on the phone," he said. "Quick."

AMONG OTHER THINGS, GAVIN BIERY HAD BUILT A SECURE VIDEO COMMUNICA-tions service for Campus employees. Outwardly, it looked just like Zoom—should any nosy MSS agents get hold of their laptops. But the underlying code used blockchain-based non-fungible tokens to authenticate each user for a secure, virtual private network. Gavin had bragged that the Campus comms setup couldn't even be broken by the NSA.

As a side benefit, the app was also useful for communicating details of Hendley's white-side business.

Gerry Hendley was in the private study of his Chevy Chase home, dressed casually in a polo, a row of green books behind him. John Clark occupied the other video square. Clark was still in Hendley's Arlington, Virginia, office. It was nine p.m. there.

"What the hell happened to your face, Jack?" asked Hendley, squinting at his web camera.

"I got mugged in Kowloon. Bastard took a hundred bucks off me. I fought back when he asked for my watch." Jack raised his wrist to show that his old Rolex was still there.

The former senator's mouth dropped open. "Jack, you serious?"

Jack told Gerry the same story he'd given Howard, though in this version he didn't mention that he'd been shopping for a new suit. He only said he'd run into a knife-wielding gangbanger who'd relieved him of the money.

He'd reported the brush pass and blown meet to Clark the prior evening in a terse after-action-report email. He'd left the juicier details out of the AAR, preferring to discuss them with Clark after a good night's sleep, a reasonable breakfast, and a resting heart rate somewhere below ninety.

While Gerry uttered the appropriate sentiments of concern, Clark gave Jack a flinty stare.

They turned to business.

"So, Howard. You like their latest offer?" asked Gerry.

"Hell yeah," said Howard. The banker walked through the HSBC interest rate, the convertible warrants in the case of default, and the equity terms for HSBC if such a default were to occur. "We just have to provide the due diligence from GeoTech to guarantee the revenues and expenses. They want proof of operating income in Vietnam so they can securitize the bond. Once we deliver that, HSBC will be ready to fund. I think we need to move fast. They keep hinting that the Germans are sniffing around to buy GeoTech."

Jack was too distracted by Clark's brooding face in the upper left corner of the screen to listen properly—but he could tell that Gerry Hendley liked the contours of Howard's financing deal.

Howard tilted the laptop to show more of himself, stealing it from Jack. "Gerry, with those Germans out there, we need to make a decision here, pronto. I think we should get over to Vietnam to get that due diligence in motion. Like today."

"Yeah, I get it. Before we get into that," replied Gerry, "I'd like to hear what Jack thinks about the risk profile."

Jack briefed his bosses on the risk coefficients in the Bayesian decision model he'd created, which assigned probabilities to an array of outcomes. Jack had originally developed the model as an intelligence tool for The Campus. It was only later that he'd massaged it into an analytical decision framework for the white-side private equity business.

Jack aimed Howard's laptop camera back at himself and cleared his throat. "Based on my model I see fourteen probable outcomes. The top five all show this acquisition paying off. It would take a seismic event to dent GeoTech's growth prospects, given international regulations on reducing fossil fuels, subsidies, and the resultant growth in electric vehicles. There's also the contract they have with Quantum Atomics. Their samarium magnet technology is going to be the hottest thing on the planet. If GeoTech's financial statements are correct, then I agree with Howard. The deal's good. We should move fast."

"Did you include the geopolitical aspect in your analysis?" asked Clark.

"Yes, that's part of the risk model. Overall, it's in our favor.

With most of the world tilting away from Chinese rare earth refining and magnet production, GeoTech's looking at fervent demand. That's why Howard and I don't think HSBC is bluffing. We really do believe there could be another buyer in the wings. Probably the Germans."

"Yeah," agreed Howard, stealing the laptop back again. "I'd like it, Gerry, if you could set us up with Bruce Stephenson, GeoTech's CEO. I know he's usually in Singapore, but if you talk to him, maybe he'd fly over to meet us in Vietnam so we can run through those books in a hurry."

All of them knew that Gerry Hendley had a long friendship with Bruce Stephenson. Ages ago, the two men had served together at the tail end of the Vietnam War.

"I'll get Bruce on the horn immediately," he said. "We definitely want this deal to go through. Bruce will probably also want us to work with David Highsmith, his president of operations in Vietnam. He's based in Da Nang."

"Sounds good," said Howard. "Jack, here, will wrap the duedil up by Friday. That will get us both home by Saturday night your time."

Hendley addressed Clark. "I agree with Howard. John, can you work with Lisanne to get them a jet? I want these guys in Ho Chi Minh City in the next few hours. I'll tell Stephenson they're on the way."

"Yeah," said Clark. "I'll get in touch with her. We'll set it up."

With the business wrapped, Howard moved to close the call. He was in a hurry to get back across the harbor so they could pack.

"Just one more minute," said Clark. "I'd like a private word with Jack, if that's all right with everyone."

Ah, shit, thought Jack.

"I'M BEGINNING TO THINK YOUR AAR DIDN'T GIVE ME THE WHOLE STORY," SAID Clark, his blue eyes locked in an appraisal of Jack's face. "You didn't say you were injured. You just said the meet was broken up by a possible agent and that you bailed out."

"True enough."

"And the black eye?"

"Listen, John. I knew we'd be talking today. I thought it would be easier for both of us to discuss it live. The outcome in the AAR hasn't changed."

"Uh-huh. Walk me through exactly what happened."

Jack glanced at the closed door behind him. He pulled the laptop camera closer to his face. "That suspected agent took my gun, pulled a knife on me. I took him out in self-defense."

"Took him out?"

"Yes. He's a kilo. Sorry for not putting it in the report—but I didn't want to worry you until you had more context."

Kilo, killed. John Clark briefly shut his eyes and sighed. "This could be a serious problem. You're on white-side. You had specific instructions to stay clear of MSS."

"I know. I did. I eluded surveillance and performed a good SDR. I even set up a decoy. This morning my regular MSS minders haven't reacted to anything."

"What part of 'stay on the white side' didn't you understand?"

"The part when I was contacted on a ferry by a potential agent."

"A huge risk. To you . . . to Howard . . . to the deal."

"I was following my instincts," Jack replied, defending himself. "Like you and Ding always tell me to do. All I did was head up to a market after an SDR for a potential discussion."

"I see," said Clark. "Well. Peter Chou called me. He said you stopped by and bought a Smith and Wesson on the Hendley account. He wants his money."

Jack sighed. "All right."

"I'll reimburse him for the pistol. The suit you bought is on you."

"That's fair."

"I warned you that MSS plays dirty, Jack. This could have all been a setup."

"No," insisted Jack. "It wasn't. I've had two MSS minders on me since I set foot on this rock. They tailed me to the hotel yesterday and I gave them the slip. I was black when I went into that wet market. The guy I tangled with was someone following the woman. If they'd been trying to entrap me, they would have let me go on with the meet."

"You don't know that. I told you. These bastards play dirty."

"Sure. But, Mr. C., this morning, when I came across the harbor with Howard, the same two MSS minders were tracking me, like nothing had changed. If they wanted to zing me for killing one of their people, they'd have done it by now."

Clark looked away from the camera, considering Jack's defense.

Sensing a reprieve, Jack pressed on. "Listen, Mr. C., I know this GeoTech thing is important and all, but I think I should hang around Hong Kong for another day or two. That will give the woman from the ferry another chance to contact me. I'd hate to pass on someone who could be a critical asset for us against the Chinese."

"Negative," said Clark. "I'm getting you out of there as quick as I can. For all you know, local police could be hot on your trail."

"I don't see how. It was a blind alley and I got rid of the gun."

"You said he had a phone. Please tell me you didn't keep it, Jack."

"No. I smashed it up and threw it away."

Clark rubbed his eyes. "I'm going to have Gavin check the NSA China wires this morning—make sure we're not seeing any chatter out of MSS HQ."

"I can do that, John. You don't need to worry about it."

"Negative. Let me take care of that. I need you focused on this deal."

Jack knew he was out of runway. "Understood," he said.

"I don't need to remind you . . . you're Hendley's top risk analysis expert. As I understand it, if we get this deal wrong, we lose a whole lot of dough."

"I've got it, Mr. C. I promise."

Clark's eyes rested on Jack's for an uncomfortably long period. Finally, the old SEAL said, "I'll get Lisanne to charter a plane ASAP. I want you to get out of Hong Kong right now."

"Roger that."

"Check in with me when you get to Vietnam. We may have to take some extra steps to keep your six clear. Hopefully not, based on the way you took care of the scene. Sounds to me like you did what you could. Just be a helluva lot more careful from now on."

"I will, Mr. C.," said Jack. "And . . . if I finish the due diligence in Vietnam in the next day or two—would you consider sending me over to the Philippines to join Cary, Jad, and Lisanne?"

"You really don't know when to quit, do you?" mumbled Clark.

"What? Why?"

"Your value to The Campus right now is to do the best job you can on the GeoTech deal. It's strategic, Jack. Not only for Hendley's finances, but for American national security. Hell, you just explained all that in your risk analysis. Right now, you're not a trigger puller. You're a critical link in a geopolitical strategy. I need you to act like it."

Jack sighed. "I said I'd do GeoTech due diligence first. I understand its significance."

"Good. Keep it that way."

"I will. I promise. But tell me, Mr. C., who've you got leading the team in the Philippines? If it's not me, you must be shorthanded."

Clark harrumphed as he moved his finger to close the connection. "Like I said. You don't know when to quit, Jack. Let me worry about the Philippines. Now go pack up for that trip to Ho Chi Minh City."

A half second later, Jack was staring at a blank screen.

8

MINDANAO, PHILIPPINES
THURSDAY, OCTOBER 3

UNDER A SAGGING GREEN ARMY TENT, SODDEN FROM THE NONSTOP JUNGLE RAIN, Lisanne Robertson's Campus-issued Panasonic Toughbook was anything but blank. She'd set it up with a split view—and both sides of the screen were suddenly alive with activity.

On the left, in the encrypted Campus messaging app, she could see the urgent order from Clark, demanding that she set up a private jet for Jack Ryan, Jr., and Howard Brennan to travel from Hong Kong to Ho Chi Minh City ASAP.

On the right, she could see her Campus teammates, Cary and Jad, creeping through the jungle, appearing through the valley fog as two white blobs on infrared.

Rain shook the tent roof, drooping the fabric wherever it wasn't supported by a pole. Distracting her from her duties, a new drip had begun, splashing off the makeshift table she'd created by stacking two empty ammo crates. Before responding to Clark's message, she rummaged through the tent, found an old metal coffee cup, and arranged it so it would catch the drip.

She opened a new window on her laptop to find a charter service for Jack and Howard. She could see almost immediately that the job wouldn't be simple. She put her radio to her mouth.

"Cobra One and Two, be advised I'm going off-net for a minute."

Through the IR picture provided by the small drone she'd launched, she watched Cary and Jad respond. They stood still, their rifles pointing forward.

Over the link, Cary whispered, "*Negative, Cobra base. We're almost to the river ford. Before we cross it, we need an intel update, fresh G2.*"

"Copy, Cobra One. I get it. But I have an immediate tasking order from Charlie One actual," she said, referring to none other than John Clark. "It's going to take me a few minutes. I have no choice."

"*Come on, Cobra base,*" Jad chimed in over the radio. "*Give us one last update at the HVT camp before you sign off, over.*"

Lisanne scratched the healing mosquito bite on her knee. She could at least do that for them, she thought. "Roger, Cobra Two. Stand by."

She'd let her hair fall loose and removed her prosthetic arm. She'd lost the real one a few years earlier while on a mission for The Campus.

To avoid questions from the Philippine SEAL team with which they'd been deployed for the past two weeks, she'd kept the prosthetic discreetly out of sight under a long-sleeve shirt. Now, alone in the leaking tent, she had the luxury of baring all, wearing nothing more than a sports bra and running shorts in the cloying, damp heat.

She touched her laptop's trackpad to rotate the camera angle from the drone that flew seven miles away from her. She'd launched the small U.S. Army RQ-11 Raven with a fling of her wrist some thirty minutes before. Now she was maneuvering the aircraft on the far side of the river, gaining an angled side view under the tree canopy, switching to optical to see if the visibility had improved.

"Fog's still degrading optics," she told Cary and Jad.

One storm after another had battered the island, since it was still the "wet season" in the Philippines. She zoomed the drone cameras in and out, scanning the river for the Filipino SEAL "red team" posing as the enemy for this exercise. She switched back to IR and took another scan.

"I got nothing along the river," she announced. "You're clear, Cobra."

Master Sergeant Cary Marks, Cobra One, married father of three, decorated Green Beret, and leader of this small Campus detachment, answered her. *"Base, we heard an aircraft about five klicks south of our pos a little while ago. Propeller-driven, likely C-130 or recon bird. Can you get us any intel on that . . . You know, unofficially?"*

"Negative, One," she answered. She'd heard those propellers, too.

With the helicopters grounded by fog, she'd taken an electronic dip into the Filipino air traffic control system. She'd learned the prop plane was a Philippine Air Force C-130—but she couldn't tell Cary Marks that. The rules of this exercise forbade her from giving her team any further amplifying information.

"Come on, base. What team are you on here?" pleaded Cobra Two, Sergeant First Class Jad Mustafa, Marks's second-in-command. Jad's job in the exercise had been to develop a route that could lead to a hit on the mock Abu Sayyaf terrorist camp

the Filipinos had created a few miles downriver. Both Green Berets were eager to best the Filipino SEALs defending it.

"You really want me to cheat, Cobra Two? You guys seemed pretty sure of yourselves a couple of nights ago at chow, making those bets with Captain Santos and his guys."

That, she knew, would shut them up.

In a chest-thumping display of Green Beret pride, the two Campus operatives had told the red-team SEALs "defending" the notional Abu Sayyaf camp, that they were sure they'd be able to score a hit on the HVT, undetected.

So sure, in fact, that they'd bet a case of San Miguel beer. The Filipino SEALs were now *highly* motivated to upstage the cocky Green Berets, an intraservice Special Forces rivalry that had spilled into the allied realm.

"Give us a read on the HVT," tried Cary.

The real-world HVT was Adnan Al Sheikh, an Abu Sayyaf leader who'd executed three Duke students while on a dive trip to Palawan. Now Al Sheikh was upping the ante. According to Clark, he intended to assassinate the Philippine president, which would clear the path for a China-friendly opposition candidate to take charge.

Lisanne held the radio close to her lips. "Roger that. Be advised, I'll be blind on your pos for the next few minutes."

Marks double-clicked his acknowledgment.

She flew the drone south, over the fog-shrouded snaking river, to the mock Abu Sayyaf camp. Though the real thing was another ten miles on, the Filipino SEALs had created a replica that was accurate to the tiniest detail, painstakingly assembled according to satellite imagery supplied by The Campus.

She looked at the IR picture on the right side of her Toughbook screen.

In the real camp downstream, fifteen Abu Sayyaf fighters lived in a collection of huts along the river. A Campus CIA link enabled by Mary Pat Foley had told them Al Sheikh was still in hiding in Manila, but that he might show up at the camp at any minute. It was standard practice for the Abu Sayyaf terrorists to dash between their scattered island hideouts via the long, outrigged native craft known as bangka boats.

The moment he did, the Filipinos—assisted by The Campus— were to take him out in a deniable, zero-footprint op.

But that hit would happen at the real camp. In the exercise version, Adnan Al Sheik was represented by a broomstick and bucket.

Lisanne watched the red-team huts in her screen, noting the white blobs of Filipino SEALs arrayed around it as sentries on the river. She keyed her radio. "No change, Cobra. HVT is still in hooch three. Five tangos on patrol near the river. Going off net now. I've got to get to that Charlie One actual order. Good hunting, Cobra. Out."

The tin coffee cup had overflowed. Lisanne took it to the bucket in the corner and dumped it. She could hear a Humvee grinding past the camp sentry. Through an angled tent flap, she noted Captain Santos in the passenger seat and wondered what the wily Filipino SEAL commander had been up to. He, too, was determined to thwart the cocky American Green Berets on this exercise.

No time to worry about Santos. She couldn't keep Clark waiting. She hunched over her stacked crates and got to work on arranging the private flight from Hong Kong to Ho Chi Minh City for Jack and Howard.

She typed in the name *Ryan, John Patrick, Jr.* She saw his face in the digital passport image she'd uploaded and hammered out the details required for a Vietnamese electronic visa.

Throughout this exercise, she'd done her best not to think about Jack.

Now she had no choice.

APPROACHING THE RIVERBANK, MASTER SERGEANT CARY MARKS PULLED HIS FOOT from oozy, swampy sludge. The New Hampshire native's face was striped olive and black, topped by a thoroughly soaked, floppy jungle hat.

Marks pushed the hat slightly to the right, causing a stream of warm water to flow over his shoulder. He ignored it and kept a firm grip on the long-range Barrett sniper rifle he'd swaddled in green rags. He concentrated on freeing his boot from the sucking mud.

Two weeks earlier, when he'd gathered his kit and kissed his wife goodbye for this op, he'd been itching to get back in the field. At the time—though he relished his role as Arlington super dad to his three kids—he'd found himself bored. There were only so many soccer games he could stomach. Now, suffering in this jungle hell, he wondered why he'd been thinking that way.

You know why, he chided himself when his boot finally got free.

Cary Marks had leaped at the chance to lead Clark's proposed advisory op in the Philippines. It would be the kind of Campus deployment that would let the Green Beret flex his experience.

Best of all, he'd help the Filipinos bag a cold-blooded terrorist scumbag. How could he have turned all that down?

Nine miles of slow humping had made him sore and hungry. The constant search for leeches on his body had made him twitchy. He sure as hell hoped that Jad hadn't sent them on a route that the Filipino SEALs could follow.

He stopped and let his feet slide into a new bog of ooze. He shifted his arms to avoid the chafe at his shoulders from his heavy, armored plate carrier vest that also held his spare ammunition—blanks for this exercise.

Cary raised his Barrett rifle to his eyes to look back at the foggy trail through the thermal scope. He could see Jad slogging forward, sweeping his M4 carbine. A few seconds later, his second-in-command broke from the brush. Cary lowered the Barrett and held up a fist.

The lead Green Beret turned and pulled his boot free. He did it again and again for ten more minutes, fifty-seven sucking steps, until, finally, landing on solid dirt. Using a GPS-based land navigation app, he'd located the big toog tree, the last waypoint before the river crossing.

Marks slumped to a seat on the tree roots and pulled a shriveled hunk of beef jerky from his plate carrier pocket. He took a few sips of water and swallowed four ibuprofen. His back was killing him, fatigued by carrying the big Barrett.

Eleven years ago, when he'd first gotten through Robin Sage, the final gauntlet before earning his coveted Green Beret, he'd felt like an Olympic athlete. Now he felt like a retired NFL running back. Leaning against the tree, he steeled himself by mumbling a few lines from "The Ballad of the Green Berets."

That helped. A little, anyway.

Jad Mustafa emerged from the leaves, fifteen yards back. Like his team leader, the sergeant sat on an adjoining root, M4 at the ready.

"You got any of that jerky left?"

Cary swallowed. "Negative. Just finished it. Sorry."

"Not cool."

Faces painted, still as lizards, they moved only their eyes, watching the jungle for movement. Cary picked up a stick and traced the rest of their route in the dirt, reviewing the plan. It went across the river, up one hill, around another, and then to their planned sniper hide. "Terrain's going to get easier," he said to Jad. "Once we cross the river and climb the hill."

"It'd better. Getting pretty sick of this mud." Jad touched his watch. "We're supposed to be in place by sunset."

Cary swatted a mosquito hovering near his ear. "Mud slowed us down. We'll have to double-time the hill."

"Hope Santos's men aren't waiting on the other side of that bank. We can't lose this bet. We'll never hear the end of it."

"Yeah, well, I'm less worried about losing a case of San Miguel than having Captain Santos tell Clark we gave them a bad plan."

Jad checked the mechanism of his green M4, then wiped the barrel free of mud. He looked at his boss carefully. "Got any leeches?"

The two of them took a moment to inspect their bodies. Jad found one on his chest. With a grimace, he plucked it off and tossed the hated creature into the leaves.

"Okay. Let's hustle up that hill. We're late."

"We're not that late. Not like Ding could have done any better," offered Jad.

Marks grunted. They both knew that with Jack Junior sidelined, John Clark's next best choice had been for Domingo Chavez to lead this op. But Ding was down in Central America, chasing a gang leader with Chinese connections.

"Let's see if Lisanne's back, get some fresh G2," said the lead sergeant. He tilted his face closer to the mic near his shoulder and whispered, "Cobra base, this is Cobra One. You back online yet?"

Her voice crackled softly over the net. *"Roger, Cobra One, I have you at Point Bravo."*

"Copy. ISR showing any tangos on the other side of the river?"

"Negative," she answered. *"Just looked. River ford is clear."*

Cary shot Jad a triumphant grin. "Strong copy, base. Proceeding to cross the river."

Jad clapped Cary on his soaking-wet shoulder. "The SEALs don't see us coming, brother. I can already taste that San Miguel."

Twenty slow yards later, they were at the foggy bank. The river's snaking, estuarine current varied with the tides. For the moment, it was slack, bubbling under the rain. The fallen logs they'd identified on ISR as a crossing were just to the north, only a few yards away.

Before climbing on the top log and exposing himself as a target, Cary radioed Lisanne. "Cobra base, this is One. We still clear? You sure?"

"Roger, One. I'm watching. You're clear."

With his head low and the Barrett in his arms, Cary sprinted from the tree cover and stepped carefully onto the fallen logs. Moments later, he was slinking along the makeshift bridge.

He was halfway across, watching his muddy boots to make sure he didn't slip.

He could hardly believe it when two big hands surged from the brown water and grabbed his ankles, dragging him off the log.

9

MASTER CHIEF KENDRICK MOORE STUCK HIS THICK BALD HEAD THROUGH THE TENT flap. At his side, the former SEAL carried three cold, sweating bottles of San Miguel beer in his meaty hands. He shoved the rest of his body past the flap to get out of the rain.

"I brought a couple over for you guys. Don't tell our Filipino friends. Cap'n Santos would kill me."

Cary, stripped down to shorts, T-shirt, and Teva sandals, stood up to accept the cold beers. Forty pounds lighter without his gear, shorn of bravado, his voice was subdued. "Thanks, Master Chief. That's nice of you."

Moore rolled a woolen army blanket and found a mostly dry portion of the tent floor, next to a bucket that collected drips. He grunted as he sat down on his improvised seat and watched Jad take a long pull on the brown bottle.

The master chief was wearing a long-sleeve khaki combat shirt and a pair of gym shorts, which revealed a *VI* tattoo on the inside of his calf. The Green Berets had already figured out that it stood for SEAL Team Six, the unofficial name for the tier-one operators of DEVGRU.

Jad regarded the big, bald interloper who'd so easily

embarrassed them in the field that afternoon by toppling Cary into the river. After he'd washed off his camo paint and stripped down to shorts, Jad thought Moore looked like a giant Mr. Clean. "What's with you operating against us, Master Chief? You might be a SEAL, but we're still on the same side."

Moore chuckled. "Just sharpening the tip of the spear, is all. Feel free to thank me—and Captain Santos."

"You know him well?"

"Yeah. Real well . . . From back when he was a lowly lieutenant commander. And this isn't the first time he and I have run an op on Abu Sayyaf. They're some seriously bad hombres."

The master chief put a sweating bottle on the desk in front of Lisanne. "Hey, Lisanne, this one's for you."

"But how did you get *here*, Chief?" she asked, popping it open. "The helos have been grounded in this soup."

"Yeah, I know. That's why I jumped."

"Jumped?"

"Yeah. Santos cleared a PAF C-130 to bring in his new guys from Manila. I tagged along. I went out at ten thousand feet on a HALO, opened my chute at two thousand, then descended through the fog to an LZ on the beach. Great ride. Wet as hell, though."

"Well, then, it's officially not fair," said Jad. "It's not like we knew there was a new recruit from The Campus parachuting in here. Especially one who knows Captain Santos. Jesus."

"Love and war, fellas. Love and war."

Reclined on the bed, Jad nudged Lisanne with his foot. "Hey. Come on, Lis. Be straight with us. Did you know the chief was coming? Did you guide us into his ambush? When Captain America here landed in the middle of camp, is that why you went off-net?"

She laughed. "Sorry, boys, but no. Master Chief Moore got the drop on me, too. I never saw him on ISR. I still don't know how he didn't show up on thermals."

"But you arrange Campus transpo and logistics. You must have known the chief was coming in."

Lisanne waved a dismissive hand. "I had no idea the chief was coming. I knew Clark was looking to hire a new operator, given how thinly stretched we are right now. But I didn't know he'd done it."

Cary looked at the big SEAL curiously. "Clark made you a full-timer with Campus, just like that?"

"No, not yet. I guess you could say I'm on probation, waiting to see how things go. But yeah, he brought me in as a temp for this job."

"When?"

Moore glanced at his dive watch. "About . . . seventy hours ago, I guess. Clark told me to get my gear and buy a ticket to Manila. Santos's SEALs were waiting at the airport and got me jocked up on the jump bird. Guess they wanted me to be the X factor."

"Yeah. X factor. Thanks." Jad tilted his beer and swigged.

Lisanne stole a look at the new man. There was something about him that seemed familiar. She noted his big empty hands. "Not a beer man, Master Chief? You won it, fair and square."

"Negative. I don't drink."

Jad was looking at the bottom of his beer bottle, tilting it high. "How 'bout family, Chief? Married? Kids? What's your story?"

"Not married, no kids. Well—I *was* married, twice, around 9/11. She lasted five years. And then I got hitched again, but, well . . . that wrapped up last year." The chief was staring down at his muddy bare feet now.

"Hear that, Lis?" asked Jad with a nod to the intel specialist. "Still sure you're going to want to actually marry Jack?"

Lisanne's head snapped up, staring bullets at the Green Beret. Against her better judgment, she'd shared with them the brief spat she'd had with Jack before they'd deployed from Arlington.

The night before she'd departed, Jack had told her he didn't want her to go to the Philippines without him. He was being characteristically overprotective of her, a trait that tended to set her off. She was a former Virginia state trooper and a Marine, for God's sake. She could handle herself.

But she could have forgiven Jack for his baser instincts. What had really angered her was when he spread his overprotectiveness to Lisanne's niece, Emily. Jack had suggested that Lisanne should *turn down* the promotion to Campus intelligence analyst because it would be too hard on the fifteen-year-old.

Nonsense, Lisanne had thought. The fact was, Emily was doing great. She'd *wanted* to go stay with her grandparents. Two weeks with her direct family would be good for everyone—except Jack, apparently.

It bothered Lisanne to no end that Jack didn't recognize that she could operate perfectly well without him—a point she intended to prove here in the Philippines.

She sipped her beer and checked for any new messages from Clark on her Toughbook while the younger Campus members drank in silence.

"Well . . . How do you know John Clark?" Cary eventually asked.

Moore raised his head and glanced at the sagging tent roof before responding. "Well . . . I don't really know him—except by reputation. But I know Ding pretty well. I worked with him on an op in Majorca, another one in the Baltic—GOPLAT takedown."

Lisanne rejoined the conversation. "What's a GOPLAT?"

"Gas and oil platform. Standard SEAL maritime op. I assume you guys know Ding."

Nods.

Cary had been steeling himself to ask his big question, biding his time, looking for the right opening. "And . . . what's the chain of command here, Master Chief? Jack Junior's not around. Ding's on the other side of the world. Did Clark say we work for you . . . or . . . ?"

A flicker of concern crossed over the SEAL's face. "He just told me to get my ass over here to help work up an operational plan—in case this op against Adnan Al Sheikh goes hot. He thought I could help. Other than sending me the mission brief, that was about it. He's a man of few words, isn't he?"

"He is definitely that," sighed Lisanne.

"Well it would help me," said Jad, "if you told us how *exactly* you got the drop on us today. We never told Santos where we were going. That was the whole point of our two days of jungle misery."

The chief grunted. "Sure. I can do that. You guys still have your tactical planning map?"

Lisanne riffled through a case at the side of her desk. She found the laminated map and pushed Jad out of the way to spread it on the cot next to him. It was marked in grease pencil with the location of the mock camp and the path the Green Berets had carefully planned. The chief got up, leaned over the map, and traced a line with his finger. Cary moved to stand next to him. He was four inches shorter than the SEAL.

"Okay, here's how I looked at it," said Moore. "Clark told me the hit on the Abu Sayyaf camp is supposed to be ultra-low footprint, plausible deniability. So I knew you'd want to go with a sniper raid. I knew you'd completed the Green Beret sniper course and been trained up on that big-caliber Barrett. I figured you'd try to set up a long-range shot with enough cover to get in and out undetected."

Cary inched closer to the map, studying the area where Lisanne had marked Al Sheikh's camp. "Okay. You got that much right. But how'd you know we'd be at the river at that exact spot? Jad and I were out there for two days. Nobody knew where we were going."

"Simple. I studied the terrain. Pretty obvious you needed to get the right angle for a sniper hit. That made the hill your most likely hide."

"But it's a big hill. And there are a thousand places we could have crossed that river."

"Nah. There are really only four places. The fishing villages to the north and south limited your options. And I knew you wouldn't want to go for a swim with that Barrett around your neck. When Santos showed me his sat photos here on the ground, I spotted the same fallen trees you did and went for 'em."

Nearly done with nursing his beer, Cary shifted his legs. "Yeah . . . but how'd you get on-site? Lisanne had an IR-capable drone up all day. She had the rest of red team ID'd and tracked."

"You have the drone video, Lisanne?"

She tabbed to another window on her Toughbook.

"Back it up to about fourteen hundred, just north of the fallen logs." She scrolled through the recorded drone footage, which rotated between IR and visual feeds, depending on the fog cover. The chief stood behind her. Cary and Jad joined him, hands on hips.

Moore pointed at the screen in one of the optical shots, clear of fog. "There. See that cluster of twigs floating on the tide before it went slack?"

"Son of a bitch," Lisanne hissed. "I should have caught that. Explains how you beat the thermals." Proving herself an indispensable intel asset wasn't going exactly as planned.

Jad pushed back his thick black hair. "But how the hell'd you breathe? You weren't wearing a Dräger."

The chief pulled a clear plastic tube from his pocket. "This. Took it off my CamelBak."

Moore settled back down to his spot on the floor. He and the Green Berets fell into a detailed discussion about the vagaries of the target camp, the proper sniper angles for this hit, and the weather challenges. Cary told Moore that they weren't sure whether or when Adnan Al Sheikh would arrive at the camp. The intel had been sketchy. Clark had only told them to be ready.

"Isn't that right, Lisanne?"

The detachment's intelligence analyst had been quiet since the chief had shown them how he beat her drone. She broke out of her funk and set aside her worry that she wouldn't be good enough at her new job to keep her team safe.

"That's right," she said. "But we have a real-time feed through Campus headquarters."

"Yeah? What's the latest, then?" asked Moore.

She glanced at her laptop and reread the last chunks of message traffic. "Nothing new. Our man Adnan dropped off communications last night. CIA *thinks* he's headed here to the Sayyaf camp by bangka boat, based on some HUMINT asset they have. But we don't really know."

They spoke of other contingencies and wondered aloud if Clark might pull them out altogether if the terrorist stayed dark.

"How'd you guys go after Abu Sayyaf before, Chief?" This, from Cary Marks.

Moore told them about his previous experience in the Philippines. As he went on, Lisanne noted the way Cary and Jad were hanging on the SEAL's every word. The sense that she'd met him before returned to her. He had a familiar face. From behind her Toughbook, she googled *Kendrick Moore, Navy Master Chief, SEAL*.

Ah, she thought a moment later, reading the *New York Times* story about the rogue SEAL in Syria. The story went on to report the removal of his hallowed trident.

That's who Clark's added to The Campus?

Clark constantly preached judgment, patience, and prudence. This guy's rep certainly defied that.

What the hell?

TWICE DURING THE NIGHT, LISANNE EMPTIED THE POTS ON HER FLOOR, ONLY TO listen to them fill up again, drip by maddening drip. Still upset with herself for missing Moore's ambush, she lay awake, worrying.

If the fog dissipated the next morning, they'd rehearse a helicopter-borne assault and a fast-rope into the camp. That's the way the Filipino SEALs had originally wanted it done. Cary and Jad had mapped the other route to prove to them that there were lower-profile options.

Listening to the rain, she dozed off a little after nine with one of Jad's detective novels on her chest.

She nearly rolled to the floor when the long barrel of her satellite phone buzzed against her ribs a few hours later. Clark calling.

"Hi, Mr. C."

"You awake?"

Lisanne coughed into her fist. "Always, Mr. C."

From twelve thousand miles away, Clark chuckled. "Good. There's an update. I sent you a message. I hadn't heard back yet, so I thought I'd call."

"Oh? I've been checking the intel feed constantly. Something new came in?"

"Yeah. The op's on. Priority one. Needs to happen before dawn tomorrow."

She swiveled upright and put her feet down, her toes landing in a puddle. Rain drummed on the tent roof, hard as ever.

"What?"

"Yeah. Our high-level intel contact called and gave me a dump. I'm passing it to you. We need to act. Right now."

Our high-level intel contact. Lisanne suspected Clark was referring to Mary Pat Foley. Intel didn't get much hotter than that.

"I'm listening, Mr. C. What's up?"

"HVT's at the camp. Arrived by boat an hour ago—came over from a nearby island airstrip where the weather's better. He made the mistake of calling a CIA asset from there. We verified his location with other national systems, ELINT, IR satellite, phone fix, and so forth. Al Sheikh might not be there long. The op needs to happen—tonight."

"But the helos are down for fog and it's not supposed to clear for days. Filipino SEALs will have a tough time getting in there right now."

"The Filipinos are out. This is going to be Campus only."

"What? I thought we wanted to minimize American involvement."

"Yeah, we do, but it's no longer an option. Our high-level intel contact has learned there's a leak inside the Philippine government. For Captain Santos to move on this, he's going to need an order from Manila. Anything that comes out of Manila is going to leak. The boss wants us to get this done. Tonight."

Lisanne gripped the sat phone tightly, trying to shut out the constant thump of raindrops overhead.

Cary's failure to get to the sniper hide and her own miss of Kendrick Moore gnawed at her confidence. "Mr. C., I don't know. We've been having a hell of a time out here—only three guys, limited ISR, no air support. The new guy, Moore, just got here. We'd be a lot better off with Filipino SEAL help."

"Not an option. The boss wants Al Sheikh gone. He's ten miles south of you. This might be our only chance."

"Could we get a real drone from Japan? Put a Hellfire on him?"

"We can't bomb the Philippines, Lisanne. You know that."

"But Mr. C.—"

"Hey, Lisanne. I hear what you're saying—but this is what we do. I put you in the intel role on this op because your instincts and technical skills are as good as they get. And you're with three top-tier operators who know this terrain and are the best at what they do. Now jock up into your gear. I'm calling the master chief now."

The call dropped.

She stared at the sat phone's blank screen, wondering how in the hell they were going to pull this off. They had a brand-new master chief with an infamous reputation, her modest ISR setup, and two wily Green Berets who usually took orders from Jack.

Jack.

It was around midnight in Vietnam. She could use Jack's counsel about now, his take. If she was honest with herself, she'd admit that she could use one of the pep talks he often gave her.

With the phone still clutched in her hand, she dialed the first half of his number.

Then she deleted it.

Clark was right. This was The Campus—and she'd earned her spot as an intelligence analyst.

She rose from the cot, Velcroed her boots tight, and trotted to the command tent.

10

**HO CHI MINH CITY, VIETNAM
THURSDAY, OCTOBER 3**

EVEN IF LISANNE HAD FINISHED DIALING JACK'S NUMBER, HE WOULDN'T HAVE heard his phone ring because he'd ditched it in Hong Kong.

Before leaving the former British colony, Clark had ordered Jack to switch to a burner, just in case the wet market dustup surfaced as a problem with the local police—or worse, the MSS. Dutifully, Jack had run Gavin's wipe app and blanked out his old phone. As a farewell FU to Brown and Blue, he'd buried it in the dumpster behind the Peninsula Hotel's kitchen, hoping they'd have to dig for it.

Here in Ho Chi Minh City, formerly known as Saigon, his new Android was on vibrate, sunk in the pocket of his suit jacket. He was sitting in a leathery booth in a dimly lit nightclub.

Bruce Stephenson, GeoTech's CEO, and David Highsmith, the company's president of operations, were sitting across from Jack and Howard, slushy drinks before them. Dinner had concluded a few hours before.

They were in Highsmith's private club on the eighty-first floor of Vietnam's grandest, newest building. Here, businessmen rubbed elbows with government officials, greasing the country's commercial prospects.

Stephenson, who worked in GeoTech's corporate Singapore office, had come into town at Gerry Hendley's urging to help speed the due diligence effort, a process that Jack had begun the moment his chartered jet had touched down.

He'd spent a day and a half vetting GeoTech's financial statements. So far, the work was complicated by GeoTech's crude, paper-based information management system. He hadn't said as much to Howard yet, since the banker was anxious to tell HSBC they were all good to go—and Jack didn't want to worry him.

While Stephenson and Highsmith chatted up a waitress, Jack leaned over to Howard. He gestured with his drink at the young women who sat conspicuously alone at the bar in short skirts, high heels, and red lipstick. "What's with this place?" he asked, his mouth twisted in disgust.

Howard stirred his cocktail and answered in a low voice. "I know. I find it distasteful, too. Just part of the drill when entertaining international clients. Highsmith picked the place."

Jack listened to Nancy Sinatra's "These Boots Are Made for Walkin'" coming over the oversized speakers. "Let's just thank them for dinner and get out of here. I have a lot of work to do. So do you."

The older man tapped Jack's thigh under the table. "Play nice, okay? Just until this thing wraps. Gerry says we have to get this thing over the line."

Jack arched his eyebrows and looked away.

"What a great club," said Howard, now that Highsmith was done ordering and the music had settled back down.

"It suits, I suppose," said the Englishman.

"Oh, more than that. It's so nice of you to host us in this beautiful country on short notice."

"I agree with you there," the Englishman replied. "It *is* a beautiful country. Politically, of course, it's a mess. But the communists haven't figured out how to screw up the beauty of all this." Highsmith swept his arm as if to indicate the far reaches of the territory—as well as the women at the bar.

"They also can't screw up the profits underground," added Stephenson in his Texas twang. "As long as they let you dig."

Howard faked a laugh.

Jack thought about what Stephenson had said. "Has government permitting been a problem, Bruce?"

"Oh, here and there. But that's really Sir David's area. I'll let him comment."

Highsmith shrugged his narrow shoulders. "Government interference is a constant issue. But we have some good connections—including several critical men in *this* club."

"I understand you have a family connection to the country, Sir David?" Howard offered, keeping the conversation light.

"Ah. That. Yes. Back in the nineteenth century, my wife's French family amassed quite a bit of land here. Rubber plantations, mostly, in the northern interior. GeoTech leases those lands now, giving a nice return to the Democratic Republic of Vietnam. That keeps the commissar off our backs."

"Right," said Jack. "I saw some of the tax paperwork today. It does appear you pay a hefty load." In truth, Jack had seen piles on piles of carbon paper receipts that were hard to track, making it impossible to discern a reliable tax rate for due diligence purposes. Following Howard's advice, however, he said nothing.

Highsmith smirked at Jack. "You know, it's a shame you'll only be here for a day or so, Mr. Ryan. Otherwise, I'd have liked to have shown you around a bit, take you out to the provinces, maybe even up to our little family compound in Hué."

"Is your wife up in Hué, Sir David?" asked Howard.

Highsmith laughed. "*God* no. She's back in France. Hates the climate here."

"You must miss her," said Howard.

Highsmith laughed again. "Claudette's brother, Henri, and his wife, Marie, live up at Hué, permanently. Marie's Vietnamese. Her connections were helpful to our mining operations in the early days. They help me in my lobbying efforts in Hanoi."

"You live here, in Saigon? Or up in Hué?" asked Jack. He'd seen another murky set of carbon receipts that loosely tracked to Highsmith's travel expenses.

"I live in Da Nang to manage the regional headquarters," said the Englishman. "I rarely get back up to Hué these days."

"And you, Bruce?"

"Oh, you know, I have to run the whole GeoTech operation across Asia. I only come back here to Vietnam for fun these days. Sir David really runs things here."

Jack lifted an eyebrow. "The HSBC team has asked for reassurance that you're staying on for another two years, Bruce. You're comfortable with that provision, right?"

"Yeah," said Stephenson, grinning. "I'm not going anywhere. I love this business. And it will be a pleasure to continue on under Gerry Hendley. A good man—served with him in 'seventy-four when we started the evac out of this country."

Howard stirred the fresh tropical drink that had arrived at his elbow. "What about you, Sir David? Are you going to retire here? You seem to like it."

"Lord, no. After we finish the acquisition, I'll head back to

England—my family estate at Gloucestershire. Finally." The Englishman took a gulp of his cocktail.

"Sir David here is an earl," Stephenson drawled wryly. "Earl of Gloucestershire. Has a big horse property in that country. It hosted a king once."

"Which one?" asked Howard.

"Edward the Eighth," said the Englishman. "My grandfather hosted him with Wallis Simpson—a lawn tennis tournament."

"That's cool," said Jack. "So you're an earl. Not a knight?"

Stephenson had introduced Highsmith to Jack as *Sir* David. Jack's own father, Jack Ryan, Sr., had been knighted when he'd rescued the current English king from IRA hit men decades before. He'd assumed he was looking at a fellow peer of the realm.

"Not like your father, Jack, no," admitted Highsmith with a sheepish glance. "The *Sir* is Bruce's idea of irony, though it seems to have stuck. How naughty of me to let that fester."

"How often do you get back here to Saigon?" Howard asked Bruce.

"Since I lost Lori two years ago to cancer, God rest her soul, I basically stay in Asia year-round. Mostly Singapore."

"You have a place in the States?" asked Howard.

"Oh yeah, sure. San Diego. I try to get together with the kids once or twice a year there. But they're pretty busy these days with their own families. I was just out there last week, visiting our biggest customer, Quantum Atomics."

"*Very* big customer," said Howard knowingly. "Major revenue driver."

"Hell yeah. Anyway, I prefer Vietnam. Sir David, here, has been kind enough to rent me his house up at his wife's family plantation in Hué, since he lives in Da Nang. I head up there on weekends to unwind, enjoy the beach, deep-sea fishing, and fly my old helo."

Stephenson turned to Jack. "Your old man should come out, Jack. He's probably got a Vietnamese diplomatic trip planned somewhere on the horizon. If he does, by God, I'll fly him up to the Hué villa personally in my helo—assuming he'd be willing to get out of Marine One for a change."

Jack pushed the umbrella around in his fancy rum drink with the sprig of lemongrass. "My dad hates helicopters."

"Yeah, but Sir Jack Ryan hasn't seen *my* helicopter, now, has he?"

"Oh yeah? What's so special about this helicopter?" asked Howard.

Stephenson's eyes lit up. "Ten years ago, the team came across an old Huey submerged in a lake up in the mining highlands. It was shot down in 'sixty-nine or so, preserved in the mud like an old dinosaur. I bought her from the government and spent a king's ransom getting her restored—*sans* the door gun, of course. Now, when I do get to come back here to Vietnam, I like to fly her up and down the coast without dodging antiaircraft fire the whole time. I'd love to show it to you guys. Her name's *Austin Belle*. Check out the nose art."

The CEO plucked his phone from his pocket, flipped through photos, and finally showed the Hendley men a picture of the helicopter.

On the fuselage, just aft of the pilot's cockpit door, was a painting of a sexy redheaded cowgirl aiming a shotgun. Underneath was the stylized name *Austin Belle* in gaudy red.

"Alas, Bruce," said Highsmith as the phone was passed back. "Our new owners won't be here long enough."

"Maybe a future trip," Howard agreed. "I'd love to see that

Huey. But first thing's first. We need to stay focused on that due diligence audit. Jack's on it. We'll wrap it fast."

Jack responded with a noncommittal dip of the head. He wasn't so sure.

"Good," said Stephenson. "Now, how about another round? Mr. Ryan, you in? Another of these special club rummies might help heal that shiner you got there. At least dull the pain a bit. Best medicine in the tropics."

Jack pushed his drink away. "I'd better not," he said. "Head's still killing me. And while I'm sure your financials are clean, Bruce, getting at them has been rough. As you're probably aware, the records are all paper-based, almost nothing digitized. The going's slow."

"Well, there's a reason for that," Highsmith interjected, quick to defend his operation. "The Vietnamese government requires it. It's not like business in the States. At all. Believe me."

Jack rubbed his temples. "I understand. But it's still a slog. I'm afraid I only made it halfway through your supplier accounts today."

Stephenson reached for the bowl of nuts at the table's center, but found it empty. "That's a little concerning, I guess. Sir Dave, Jack might need records access up at your shop in Da Nang." The CEO turned to Jack. "No hanky-panky in my company, Jack. You have my word on it. And you can bet your ass that the Germans would make quick work of organizing those papers."

They all laughed. Jack took it as his cue to make a safe exit. He could leave the rest of the schmoozefest to Howard, who was better at this sort of thing.

He stood and offered his hand. "Thanks, Bruce. I *do* take your word for it. I look forward to getting through everything as quickly as I can. Happy to give the Germans a run for their money."

"Oh, Jack, don't go," said Highsmith. "The party's just getting started. What is it they say? All work and no play makes Jack a dull boy?"

Jack forced a grin. "I'll be up early. You guys enjoy yourselves."

Highsmith stood and offered his hand. "Let me at least have my driver take you back to the hotel."

"That's okay, Sir David. I could use the fresh air of a walk."

JACK WAS GLAD TO SEE THE RAIN HAD STOPPED WHEN HE EXITED THE BUILDING. Now approaching midnight, the streets were shining, splashing with traffic. The air was humid, tainted by the faint soot of vehicle exhaust.

Jack trudged along the empty sidewalk with his tie in his pocket and his shirt collar unbuttoned. Back in Hong Kong, he'd recovered his necklace knife, which bounced reassuringly against his chest. At this point in his travels, he thought of the little knife less as a weapon and more as a good luck charm, like a rabbit's foot.

He walked through Ho Chi Minh City's glitzy central business district. The lights were bright, the products in the blazing windows high-end. He passed one glassy storefront after another, offering up goods from Hermès, Bally, and Chanel. Most of them were advertised by the famous, perfect faces of Hollywood actors.

He passed an enormous roundabout stuffed with speeding scooters. It was so busy that he couldn't walk directly across it, so he walked its circumference. The circling scooters made him think of Hong Kong.

He followed his phone's directions down another street, still busy despite the late hour. He was out of the high-end luxury district and into the neighborhoods where normal people shopped. To either side were stores with American brands the world knew by heart—Coca-Cola, Marlboro, Levi's, Nike.

The juxtaposition of Hong Kong and Ho Chi Minh City struck him. It was as though the two cities intersected in time, on opposite paths from one another. Hong Kong was the ghost of a capitalist past. Ho Chi Minh City its spiritual future.

The wide boulevard he walked along was evidence of its French colonial origins. He was nearing the district of his hotel, the Caravelle, where American reporters stayed during the war. Jack had read that it had been the headquarters of MACV, the Military Assistance Command of Vietnam. They were the original advisors who'd come to the country to help fight off the insurgency of the Viet Minh and its violent sister organization, the Viet Cong.

His stomach growled. The dinner Highsmith had organized had been French, which to Jack's way of thinking meant the portions had been tiny. He ambled along a side street alive with the strobing lights of a bar. It thumped with bass and spewed its drinkers onto the sidewalk. Many of them were gathering around a food cart. Jack caught the aroma of meat as he got closer.

There were many young Western tourists, he saw—girls in tie-dyed shirts, short shorts, and flip-flops. He heard a polyglot stew of voices when a pop song ended. European languages, a sprinkling of English.

He stood behind a tall, tattooed kid in his early twenties. The Westerner was in shorts and a T-shirt, a girl in similar attire tucked under his arm. When they ordered their meat sticks, Jack thought they sounded like New Zealanders. They were laughing, hanging on each other—until they saw him, standing there in his wrinkled suit with a black eye. They went back into the club.

Jack ordered a stick of fried chicken and ate it on the sidewalk, feeling conspicuous.

After eating, he hurried along the path to his hotel as directed by his phone. He was soon on a darker street, where the beeping scooters were spaced farther apart, the sidewalks gone.

He stopped to consult the map. Zooming in, he could see that he was only a block away from a busier road. With a half mile yet to go, he decided he'd walked enough. Once he got to the avenue, he'd flag down a tuk-tuk, the ubiquitous three-wheeled mini-trucks that served as taxis in Ho Chi Minh City.

Still staring at his phone, Jack felt a trickle of unease. Involuntarily, his senses went on high alert. He wasn't sure why.

Then it came to him. A few seconds ago, he'd heard a scooter's exhaust on this barren street, somewhere behind him. It should have passed by now. But it hadn't. There'd been no fading exhaust as it went down a side street. The scooter had gone quiet.

He raised his phone as though studying the map. He opened Gavin's room-scanning app, which triggered the selfie camera. With the flash off, he took two photos of whatever might be behind him. Then he resumed walking to the busier boulevard and let the app do its magic. Studying the phone as he moved, he saw the marker immediately.

In the photo, a man was behind him standing next to a scooter, thirty yards back. He'd moved his arm in between shots, which had alerted the app. Though he was standing in the shadows beneath the awning of a storefront, the app's machine learning algorithms had completed the low-light picture.

Without breaking stride, Jack zoomed in to get a better look at the man in the photo. His hair was to his shoulders. Where his neck met his collar, Jack could see the outline of a dark tattoo. He'd been staring directly at Jack.

The last time he'd seen a long-haired man with a neck tattoo had been at the Temple Street Night Market.

A chill ran down his spine as he hurried toward the brighter lights of the avenue.

He threw his hand up to flag a ride.

A tuk-tuk stopped almost immediately, recognizing an easy mark, an American businessman. The goofy little vehicle was draped in Christmas lights. Its ancient, grinning driver eagerly accepted the American twenty-dollar bill Jack took out of his wallet—ten times the normal fare.

While it sputtered over the fifteen bumpy blocks to the Caravelle, Jack compared what he could see of the tattoo in the photo with his memory of the night market thug.

A quick Google search told him many Asian street toughs had neck tattoos. Jack had been wandering alone on a dark street after midnight, flashing his wallet. By the time he slid his key card into his hotel room door, he'd dismissed the man who'd watched him as a coincidence.

After brushing his teeth and telling himself he was paranoid, he got into bed. He checked the secure Campus apps on his burner.

Lisanne hadn't messaged him.

Thinking of her in the jungles of the Philippines, it took him an hour to drift off.

11

**MINDANAO, PHILIPPINES
FRIDAY, OCTOBER 4**

THE ROADS ALONG THE RIVER WERE A SOUPY MESS, THE SKY BLACK. THE FOG hadn't lifted since Lisanne had taken Clark's call. That meant the helicopters were out.

"Let us off here," said Master Chief Moore to the driver.

The Filipino SEAL had given Moore, Cary, Jad, and Lisanne a ride in a Humvee to the outskirts of the fishing village. As she got out, Lisanne could see a few homes on stilts. They unloaded their gear and piled it up. The vehicle drove away, leaving them alone in the rain.

"Kit up," said Moore. They pulled their plate carrier vests on, then smeared dark camo paint on their faces. They strapped up with radios, spare ammo mags, and weapons.

"Keep it quiet. Let's go." Moore took point. They hurried beneath the buildings, trotting for the landing where the villagers kept their boats.

Twice, dogs barked at them. They zigzagged through the shadows until they came to the clearing at the water. Moore led them back downriver a few hundred yards, stopping in a tall grass thicket.

"Jad," he said, "you're up."

Sergeant First Class Jad Mustafa flipped his four-tube night optical device, NOD, over his eyes. He darted for the mass of low hulls pulled to the bank.

A minute later, he returned in a drifting boat. Moore saw him coming. The master chief waded into the river and caught the boat as it drifted, pulling it to the shore.

Cary ran his hand over a splintered gunwale and whispered just loud enough to be heard over the rain. "Little small, isn't she, brother?"

Jad hopped out of the boat and held it so it wouldn't drift off. "Not like it was a showroom."

Moore riffled through the boat's contents, finding various grades of nets and fishing tackle. "We can use this," he said.

The master chief gathered one of the fishing nets along with three red floats used for crab traps. He cut the floats free with his Ka-Bar knife and wadded them up in the rolled net. "This will be our floatation device. Copy?"

After acknowledging the point, Cary and Jad began stowing the heavy Pelican case with the drone in the boat's stern while Lisanne stood sentinel. The chief threw the suitcase-sized net bundle between the front two thwarts. He then inspected the small outboard engine, checking its fuel level. Satisfied, he pulled the starter cord. The motor sputtered to life.

"Load up," he said.

The four Campus operatives climbed aboard. As planned, Lisanne took the aft thwart, acting as coxswain. Cary took the bow. The SEAL master chief and Jad were in the center.

Lisanne twisted the throttle and launched them into the

current. Her Velcro boots were resting on the hard plastic case. Once in the center of the river where the current was strong, Moore told her to kill the engine and use its propeller shaft like a rudder.

"Weapons check," said the chief.

Cary and Jad hoisted their long M4 barrels up and swept the black treetops. Their laser scopes put red dots against the shining leaves. Captain Santos had given the team free rein over the Filipino SEALs' weapons cache, letting the Americans take anything they wanted.

Moore carried two rifles—a silenced M4 and a SAW, an M249 Squad Automatic Weapon. He put both guns across his knees and tugged at the rows of grenades along the bottom of his breastplate. "Okay," he said. "All good?"

Cary, Jad, and Lisanne each gave him a thumbs-up.

The frogman directed his red-lensed flashlight at the muddy water. "Lisanne," he whispered hoarsely. "Mind your head. The river curves up there. Copy?"

She slid forward on the Pelican case so she could hear him better. "What's that, Chief?"

"Your heading. Keep us along the bank. We're too far into the middle."

"Roger that." She pushed the tiller to the right, steering for the mangroves that overhung the elevated banks, following the red beam of Moore's flashlight. They drifted in silence for ten minutes, hugging the bank.

"Coming off NODs." The chief flipped his tubes back up on his helmet. "Let your eyes adjust to the dark for now. Lisanne—give us a position fix."

She looked at the tablet she'd strapped to her knee. The device was bulked up with a ruggedized case and a bulbous satellite antenna. She also used it to control the drone. "We're nine air klicks north of the camp." With the river bends, the drifting distance would be nearly double—but the chief was aware of that.

"Good," he said. "Nose us into the bank. We'll hold while you ready the drone."

The wooden bow scraped against the mangroves. Jad clutched a dripping branch to steady the boat. Lisanne pulled the two-foot-long drone fuselage free of the Pelican case and slotted its wings into place. After testing its control surfaces with the tablet strapped to her thigh, she leaned forward. "Chief," she said, tapping him on the shoulder with the tail assembly, "you can probably hurl this thing farther than I can."

"Sure," said Moore. The former SEAL scooted back, violently rocking the boat. Standing precariously, he held the drone at arm's length while Lisanne manipulated the tablet. The aircraft's electric engine whined to life.

With its systems all showing green, Lisanne gave Moore a final nod. "Send it, Chief."

Moore reared back and threw the drone skyward. The aircraft buzzed away. It disappeared in the rain.

He sat down again. "We hold here until it's on station."

"ISR has contact," Lisanne announced six minutes later. She manipulated the tablet strapped to her thigh, steering the remote aircraft. "I've got hot spots on thermal. Tangos."

Moore's jaw tensed as he gave a thumbs-up. "Distribution?"

"Two at the river, standing. Looks like the same place where we saw them on imagery."

"Good. And in the camp interior?"

Lisanne spread thumb and forefinger to zoom in. "I count about nine bodies . . . in the center. They're all close together, not moving. Likely asleep."

"Any separates?"

"One. Northwest corner. He's alone."

"That'll be our HVT," Moore said under his breath.

"Concur." She looked up into the chief's painted face. "The Langley profile on Al Sheikh said he sleeps alone."

"Probably kicked out the other Sayyaf people to take the best spot," offered Jad from the bow.

"Listen up," said Moore. "We'll drift farther south, then hold at the initial point. Copy?"

Cary pushed them off the mangroves. As the boat entered the current, Lisanne put the drone into an autopilot surveillance orbit and steered the boat close to the banks.

In front of her, Moore stayed silent. Every so often, he flashed his red beam at the water to keep Lisanne on course.

After riding the current for twenty minutes, Lisanne announced that they were nearing their final rally point, just a half klick north of the camp. The chief told her to steer the boat into the mangroves again.

"Comms check," said Moore.

They went through the sequence of testing their waterproof UHF radios. The men had them strapped to their plate carriers connected via Bluetooth to a lip mic and earpiece. Lisanne's radio was at her side, resting on the thwart.

The chief leaned back to take a final look at the tablet on her knee. He noted the white blobs that represented the two tangos at the river's edge a half klick south of them.

"Everybody good to execute the plan?" he asked.

Thumbs-up all around.

The SEAL looped a leg over the boat and lowered himself into the waist-deep water. He held the craft steady while Jad and

Cary followed. Finally, Moore pulled the bundled flotation device free and let it bob next to the hull.

The chief leaned over the bulkhead, close to Lisanne. "Hey," he said. He pulled a Glock 19 from the holster on his plate carrier and held it in front of her. "Just in case."

The one-armed former Marine lodged the pistol in a slot on her own plate carrier vest. When she looked up again, she saw that Cary, Jad, and the chief were adrift, floating into the center of the river, clinging to the improvised device Moore had made from the fishing gear. Their heads were just above water.

She waved.

Cary acknowledged it with a dip of his helmet as they floated away.

"HOLD HERE," WHISPERED KENDRICK MOORE EIGHT MINUTES LATER, HIS FACE BURied among the float's netting. Cary dug his feet into the muddy bottom, stopping the drift and nudging Jad to do the same.

Moore walked the float toward the bank on the far side of the camp, staying submerged. They were still a hundred yards north of the target.

"Base," whispered Moore into his radio. "How's the camp looking?"

"*Still two tangos at the waterline,*" crackled Lisanne's voice over the net. "*On thermal, I'm seeing what looks like a small cookfire by the beach.*"

"Copy," said Moore. He turned to the two Green Berets. "We good?"

Still nearly submerged, clinging to the float, the commandos whispered their replies.

The chief tugged Cary's sleeve. "Hey."

"Yeah, Chief."

"This is still your op, Cary."

"Aye, Chief."

"I made sure Clark knew that. You've got command once you're on the X."

Cary replied with a grunt. The chief gave a final thumbs-up, then pushed the float into the current. With his two rifles slung over his back, he scrambled up the bank and disappeared.

The Green Berets floated down and across the river, reaching the bank just north of the camp's beach. With their NODs barely above the surface, they studied the two sentries at the waterline.

"Mine has an AK slung on his right," whispered Cary. "He's holding a cigarette with his left hand."

"Mine's got an AK by the stock, barrel down," answered Jad. "He's looking south."

Cary keyed his mic. "Cobra One, this is Two. We're in position."

"*Copy,*" answered Moore. "*Your overwatch is set. I've got eyes on you. Proceed at discretion.*"

Jad and Cary switched off their NODs and tilted them up over their heads.

"You good, brother?" whispered Cary.

"Always, Sergeant Marks."

The Green Berets shoved the improvised flotation device into the mangroves. Jad stretched out his breathing tube and backed farther into the water. He let the current take him. A moment later, Cary did the same.

After moving fifty feet underwater, Master Sergeant Cary Marks felt the muddy bottom thicken with rocks. He knew he'd reached the camp's gravelly beach. He spat out his air tube and let it drift away. He steadied himself against the current and raised his mouth just enough to breathe.

He could hear the chief whispering in his earpiece. *"You're both five feet from sentry positions. Ready?"*

Cary double-clicked. He heard Jad do the same.

"On my mark," whispered the master chief. *"Five, four, three..."*

Cary took a breath and went under, covering the last five feet. Above the rippling, rain-spattered surface, he could see the blurred silhouette of his assigned sentry, standing dumbly on the bank. He continued the chief's count. *Two, one...*

The sentry's head snapped back, then fell from view.

Moving as fast as he could without creating a splash, Cary slithered out of the water and crawled up the beach on his belly. The Green Beret dragged the dead sentry into the current. To his right, he glimpsed Jad doing the same.

Cary noted the neat hole in the terrorist's forehead courtesy of a 7.62 round delivered by the chief's silenced M4.

He took in the dead sentry's wispy beard, open eyes, and threadbare shirt. To deflate the corpse, the Green Beret shoved his Ka-Bar knife into the rib cage, holding the body in place so the perforated lungs would fill with water.

Lisanne's voice sounded in his ear. *"All call signs, this is Cobra base. The sentries are down and out of sight. Camp still quiet."*

The chief answered. *"Roger. No movement at all?"*

"Negative, One," said Lisanne. *"Thermal shows no moving bodies."*

Cary crawled up the gravel beach. Through the fog and rain, he could smell the remnants of the cookfire. With his night vision tubes in place, he saw Jad to his right, the M4 cradled over his forearms. They stopped to look at each other.

Cary rose slowly to his feet, his rifle barrel sweeping the camp. Jad remained to his right, looking for targets near the tree line. Cary dashed to the small hooch where the HVT slept. He raised his rifle at the hut, studying its entrance.

Through his NODs, he saw hanging vines over an opening. He stopped and waited, listening for movement. He used his M4 barrel to part the vines before creeping inside. His pulse pounded in his ears.

In the green glow of night vision he saw a sleeping man—grizzled beard, slack mouth partly open, chest rising and falling. Cary recognized the shape of the sleeper's nose, the closed, sunken eyes.

This man, he recalled, had sliced the heads off four Duke students, putting the spectacle on YouTube. Now he was planning to take out the president of the Philippines, simply because he'd gotten friendly with Americans.

Cary pulled the trigger twice.

Phht. Phht.

The Green Beret's two silenced M4 sounds struck Adnan Al Sheikh in the chest.

"Jackpot," he whispered into his mic. "I call winning number."

He pulled his phone free of his vest and flipped on the red light on his helmet. He snapped a picture of the dead terrorist's face. The eyes had popped open.

"*Copy Jackpot, winning number. Now get out,*" whispered Moore. "*We're RTB.*"

Returning to base.

Cary killed his light, stowed his phone, and carefully backed out. He felt the door vines sweep over his shoulder, then the rain drumming on his helmet again. He rotated into a sweep with the M4 aimed at the camp's center, checking for targets.

They were all asleep, he thought.

Wrongly.

"All call signs, I have movement on ISR," whispered Lisanne over the net. Her hushed voice sounded distant, slightly garbled. *"One tango coming out of the main hooch. He's headed your way, Two. He's at your three o'clock. He's almost on you."*

Cary lowered himself quietly to his knees, then his belly, pointing his rifle to his three.

Watching the main hooch in the otherworldly glow of the NODs, he saw a man emerge. Five yards away, the shirtless tango was stepping through the threshold. He was unarmed, eyes slits, half-asleep. Probably on his way to take a piss, thought Cary, hoping he'd walk to the tree line.

No such luck. The man headed right for him.

"I got him," whispered the chief in his earpiece.

A second later, the man fell sideways, his head pierced by an M4 round. The terrorist's shirtless body crashed through the flimsy hooch wall.

Cary heard voices. A light came on.

"Go!" seethed the chief from the far shore. *"Two, get to the river. Now!"*

"I have multiple tangos stirring in the hooch," updated Lisanne from sixteen hundred yards upriver. *"They're awake."*

Cary rose to a knee and pulled a flash-bang grenade from his vest. He yanked the pin and threw it into the center of the hooch.

Known as a "nine-banger" for the nine ear-shattering pops the grenade rattled, Cary knew the terrorists would mistake it for gunfire. He'd seen it a dozen times in Afghanistan. He threw a second flash-bang into the smaller hooch, where he'd dispatched Adnan Al Sheikh, to act as a decoy.

"*Counting close to twenty tangos,*" said Lisanne urgently. "*Must have been doubled up in bunks or—*"

Cary didn't hear the rest of her broadcast. While the nine-bangers went off, he saw two men dash from the tent, backlit by the flashes. The first fell, shot through the head by Moore. Cary glanced back into the camp. He saw Jad there, covering him.

The second man out of the tent tripped over his fallen comrade. Regaining his balance, he raised his AK and cooked off a ten-round burst.

At Jad.

Cary shot him in the left cheek.

He crawled frantically for the river. Jad and Chief Moore were calling out targets over the earpiece. With AK rounds whipping over his head, Cary trusted they had his back. He focused only on reaching the safety of the water.

The nine-bangers had stopped. He could hear voices again. The crawl was taking too long. Cary sprung up to run for it. He glanced to his left through his NODs to see where Jad was, hoping he'd be right there, when his vision whited out.

The terrorists had flipped on the camp's floodlights, blotting out the NOD sensors.

Cary tore at the tubes on his face. He stumbled over a rock. He fell. His outstretched arm burned. He coughed on ash. The cookfire embers, he realized.

He rolled to his back in time to see a man coming at him. He pulled the trigger, full auto, and shot the tango in the chest with four rounds. He saw two more men gunning for him. He popped a smoke grenade. "Frag out!" he said into the radio.

A shadow ran through the smoke. Cary saw the man stop, then fall backward. Master Chief again, thank God. He heard ricochets as unaimed rounds bounced off the firepit rocks. The smoke was helping.

"*I've lost ISR at your pos, Two,*" said Lisanne. Cary knew the smoke grenade and fire embers had ruined the thermal sensors on the drone. He'd also lost sight of Jad in the smoke.

"Lost you, Three," he said. "Where are you?"

"*Cut off from the bank,*" answered Jad. "*Evading north, on foot. Frag another smoke, Two. That's good cover.*"

Cary threw his second smoke grenade at the main hooch. He followed it with a full fragmentation grenade, then another, until he was out. He hoped the tightly packed iron pellets would kill the bulk of the terrorists.

For good measure, he unleashed three-round bursts at the huts until he ran out of ammo. "Two's Winchester," he called on the radio. "Reloading."

The smoke was bright in the floodlights. It hung over the center of the camp like a wall. Cary ran in a crouch for the river while fumbling over his chest pockets for a fresh mag.

His hands flew over the snaps on his vest. He felt the cold metal of the mag. He tugged it so hard that it flew free of his slippery hands and embedded itself in the mud a few feet away from him. *Oh goddamn you.*

Shadows crossed over it, moving quickly, just to the north. They were wispy and long, filtered by the brightly lit smoke.

They'd flanked him.

The terrorists had run down a trail on the south side of the camp. Cary heard them firing and dropped to the dirt. He reached for another mag in his vest, telling himself he could still reload, swing up with a tearing volley that would be just enough to—

His head snapped forward, blinded by pain at the base of his skull. He heard the low rattle of Tagalog, the native language of the Philippines, squelching Lisanne's voice in his ear. Then she was gone, too. They'd ripped his earpiece off.

They were screaming at him, incomprehensible, furious, an inch from his face. *They're going to take me alive*, he thought. His shoulder burned as they dragged him by an arm, his useless empty rifle trailing on its sling.

Cary caught a glimpse of a face over his head, long hair dangling down. He looked a lot like the sentry he'd bagged four minutes earlier.

The man's head suddenly came apart. He dropped Cary to the mud.

Cary heard a steady roll of machine-gun fire. He watched pink tracers whip by a few feet above him. The three terrorists who'd been standing over him a second ago lay shredded and bloody next to him.

He intended to roll over the dead men, but instead found himself moving. His boot heels laid tracks in the mud as he was dragged toward the river. Confused, he squinted into the smoke as ear-shattering gunfire exploded right next to his head.

It was Master Chief Moore, he realized.

After swimming across the river and mowing down the Sayyaf killers, Moore had seized the Green Beret's plate carrier with his left hand. The master chief was still firing the big Squad Automatic Weapon with his right, its mechanism next to Cary's ear. The firing didn't stop until the chief had pulled Cary over the beach and into the river.

"Swim!" he roared, the red-hot gun barrel sizzling in the water.

His ears ringing, Cary kicked hard. The current took them.

"We don't have long," Moore growled. "They're hot on Jad's ass. And in another few seconds they're going to—"

The chief pulled Cary down. In the underwater blur, the Green Beret heard bullets splashing over his head. Without a warning to take a breath, he was quickly running out of air. Now he could see flashlight beams strobing the surface, more bullets striking. He felt Moore's forceful hand keeping him under.

He heard a strange buzz amid the splash of bullets. The chief tugged him up. Cary's head broke free, grateful for the fetid air. The low fishing boat they'd stolen was headed their way. Its hull was slicing right for him.

Lit up by the sweep of an enemy flashlight, Cary saw the boat was dragging something at its side. It got closer, nearly clipping him as it shot past without slowing. The next thing he knew he was whipsawed onto his back with water streaming behind him. Moore still held him, anchoring them both to the trailing fishing net.

Lisanne had tossed the net over the side and secured it to a cleat. As she'd careened past, the master chief had wrapped his hand in it, without releasing his grip on Cary. Now Cary climbed up it, hand over hand, using it like boarding netting, until he was alongside the hull.

Moore resumed firing his weapon, holding the SAW just above the water with one arm while clinging to the net with the other. Lisanne swerved the boat into the river's center. Jad was there, swimming. He grabbed the section of net that trailed behind Cary.

The craft swerved around a bend. Moore stopped firing. He threw his hot M249 into the boat and clambered over the side. He reached down and helped the Green Berets come aboard.

With the sounds of gunfire receding, Lisanne put the motor into a sputtering idle and sat back.

"Let's get the hell out of here!" the chief barked at her. His face was smeared, chest heaving.

Lisanne didn't answer him.

She was slumped against the idling outboard.

She'd been hit.

12

DA NANG, VIETNAM
FRIDAY, OCTOBER 4

"WHERE DO YOU WANT THESE?" ASKED MALCOLM TRANG, GEOTECH'S DA NANG-based financial manager.

Jack looked up from the desk he'd improvised in the large conference room. Trang had already stacked boxes so high along the side table that Jack had lost his distant ocean view.

"Over there . . . on that table, I guess. With the others. If you can find room."

Frustrated by the gaping holes in the records in GeoTech's Ho Chi Minh City office, Jack had asked to move the audit north to Da Nang, the company's Vietnamese operational headquarters. Though Highsmith couldn't attend himself, he'd arranged the visit for Jack.

"What are these new boxes?" Jack asked, groaning inwardly at the sheer number Trang stacked on the table first, then the floor. Jack had expected two or three. He saw six or seven.

The accountant hefted another to the table. "Mr. Highsmith

said you wanted all the records from our leasing companies, right?"

"Right," said Jack. "You're saying these are *all* leasing agreements?"

Trang slid a box sideways to make room for another. "The first three are. We have quite a bit invested in mining equipment here."

Jack referenced one of the loose papers before him, though he'd practically memorized the numbers by now. "Thirty million dollars of capital equipment, according to your balance sheet."

"Sounds about right." The accountant slid a box onto the floor. "Trucks, hydraulic shovels, dozers, transport barges . . . Takes a lot to get metal out of the ground. And that's just extraction. It doesn't include refining minerals to magnet grade."

Jack stood and walked next to him. He popped the lid off a box and whistled at the mess of papers inside. "You *have* heard of computers in this country, right?"

The accountant, a Singaporean with an English accent, laughed and wheeled his hand truck backward. "Welcome to operating a capitalist business in a communist country, Mr. Ryan. Paper only." He leaned against the doorjamb, noting the wall clock. "Umm . . . do you think you'll need anything else? We usually wind down around this time on a Friday . . ."

"Just one more thing," said Jack. He searched frantically through a sheaf of papers he'd pulled from the first set of files. Finding the one he wanted, he lifted it with a flourish. "Here it is. This place. Are you familiar with an operation up at Lay Táo?"

Trang took the pink carbon paper from Jack's hand and studied it. "Yes. That's one of the larger samarium refineries up near the border with Laos. It does extraction as well, though I think the lode there is nearly spent."

"Right. Do you have accounting files specific to that site only?"

Trang gestured at the boxes with his chin. "They'd be somewhere in there. We have hundreds of individual mines up in that area and their output constantly shifts. We basically group all the mining ops together in a single set of financial records. Why?"

Jack picked up a flimsy yellow carbon paper, ink-stained with Vietnamese script. He'd been having conversations like this with lower-level GeoTech finance managers for the past two days. He'd been told that anyone who knew anything about mining operations was out in the field, at the mines.

He hoped Trang would be the exception.

"Can you help me understand this invoice? I'm having a hard time matching the gadolinium purchases to the samarium output. A lot of money goes into buying the gadolinium, but then the eventual samarium production is all over the place. It doesn't match up."

Samarium was the refined rare earth mineral that went into making GeoTech's magnets, their bestselling product. Gadolinium was a second rare earth mineral used in samarium refining.

The accountant looked at the paper and grimaced. "Refining is an inexact science, Mr. Ryan. It would probably be best to talk to the geologists up in LT."

Of course it would, Jack thought, sighing.

"Are you at least familiar with this gadolinium supplier?" Jack referenced his spiral-bound notebook, his best effort at piecing together a financially sound paper trail, since the company hadn't bothered. "The company's called Han Tach Limited."

Trang offered a slow head shake. "Can't say I'm familiar with them. But as you see, we have a vast supply chain." The accountant had one foot through the door, eyes looking out the window at the golden beaches of Da Nang.

"It's okay," said Jack, exhaling. "Hey, thanks for all this, Malcolm. I'll tell Mr. Highsmith you got me what I asked for. Go ahead. Take off."

The accountant left.

Jack riffled through his notebook, trying to organize the suppliers into categories. Occasionally he dug into a box, trying to find matching paperwork. He was well on his way to missing the deadline HSBC had set.

"Jesus, Jack," Howard groaned ten minutes later, leaning against the doorjamb, just as Malcolm had a moment before. He was in a short-sleeve blue shirt. His graying hair was oiled neatly in place. He wore gabardine slacks and Italian loafers. "*More* boxes? When are you going to be satisfied?"

Jack gestured at the multiple hues of colorful carbons he'd spread on the table. "I know."

"We're going to blow the deadline."

"I'm aware of that. We've got a problem, Howard."

Howard waved him away. "I just got off the phone with Gerry and Stephenson. Quantum Atomics signed a big deal this morning for a shit ton of refined magnets, revenues guaranteed for at least three years. That alone ought to be enough to satisfy HSBC. What are you so worried about?"

Jack put the lid on one box, then popped off another. He looked at Howard. "That Quantum supply deal is for rare earth magnets that are made of refined samarium, right?"

"Yes. Exactly."

"And that samarium comes out of GeoTech's ops up in the Vietnamese highlands to the northwest, specifically Lay Táo, right?"

"I don't know. Who the hell cares?"

"I care, Howard."

"Why? What's the problem?"

Jack put his hands on his hips. "The problem is that the expenses in that area are all over the place. Highsmith's reports say the operations out here are highly profitable. But if I do one double-click on operating expenses, I can see that isn't necessarily true. I see accounting entries involving government agencies that they classify as 'regulatory charges.' I see random payments for refining chemicals to companies that have no background."

"What's the worst that could happen?"

"Howard, the cash flow statements we've seen could be bullshit . . . They could be hiding an overrun in raw material costs that we don't even understand."

The older man dug his hands into his trouser pockets and said nothing. He looked wistfully out the window at the wide stripe of reflective afternoon sun on the flat ocean. Jack followed the older man's gaze. The shadows of palm trees lining the beach were stretching.

"You know I'm right, Howard," said Jack. "I can't certify to HSBC that this is all solid. We're taking on an enormous risk here. *You're* taking an enormous risk."

Howard murmured an acknowledgment, speaking almost to himself. He kept his eyes focused outside.

Jack went on. "And what's with the paper records? Highsmith keeps saying it's because the Vietnamese government demands it. That's all well and good, but these boxes are going to belong to *us* when this deal closes. I didn't get my license as a certified auditor just to rubber-stamp flimsy carbon papers written in a foreign language and call it satisfactory due diligence."

Howard approached a box and tilted the lid to look inside. He pulled his reading glasses from his shirt pocket and held a flimsy carbon paper up to the light, reading it top to bottom. "Is, uh, this typical of the kind of thing you're seeing?" he asked over the rim of his glasses.

"Yup. It's all like this. Until they type up their pretty financial statements. The ones we've been showing HSBC."

Howard thumbed through the files in the box, looking at the papers.

Exasperated, he sat down at the table and rubbed his eyes. "Jack, I want to do the right thing as much as you do."

"I know. We will. I'm just saying I need more time. Or better access."

"Yeah." The older man sighed huskily. "I'd hoped to get on that plane tonight. Minnie's birthday is on Sunday. And, well, I know it's kind of a stupid thing at our age . . . but I've never missed one."

Jack took the seat next to him. "Then go. Get back to Arlington. I'll stay here and run this to ground. You stall Hendley and HSBC. You're good at that, Howard."

The older man looked sideways at Jack. "No. I'm in this with you. All the way. Gerry may be the one pushing hard for this deal—but it's my job to close it. I'll stay."

Jack put his hand on Howard's arm. "You sure?"

"Yeah. Hundred percent."

"With the commission Gerry's paying you for this deal, you can bring Minnie one hell of a souvenir."

Howard smiled wanly. "Doesn't work."

"Sorry, Howard."

The older man jerked his head at the door. "Come on. Bruce Stephenson's up in his office. If we can't get answers out of these records, let's take it to the CEO."

SHADOW STATE

STEPHENSON'S OFFICE WAS ON THE TOP FLOOR OF THE GLOSSY DA NANG BUILDING. Though he normally worked in Singapore, the company founder maintained a presence at each of the GeoTech subsidiaries in Australia, Malaysia, and Vietnam.

Once Jack stepped through the glass door, he immediately guessed the Da Nang office was Stephenson's favorite.

The wall behind the desk was hung with Vietnam War memorabilia from the CEO's Air Cavalry medevac days. Jack saw a plaque commemorating five hundred rescue missions and a framed picture of a youthful Stephenson shaking hands with General Creighton Abrams, commander of American military forces in Vietnam. There was another photo of a Huey on the top of the American embassy. At dinner, Jack had learned that Stephenson had been one of the last American pilots in South Vietnam before Saigon finally fell.

Those glory days had wrapped nearly fifty years ago. Presently, the CEO was standing with the cord from his desk phone stretched to his ear. He held up a finger when he saw Jack and Howard at his desk. He motioned them to the two facing chairs.

"Yes, Minister," he was saying into the phone. "I'll take care of it . . . Yes, Minister . . . Right away . . . Of course, Minister . . . Thank you . . . *Tạm biệt.*"

The CEO hung up. "That was the Vietnamese minister of the interior. Quan Tach." He leaned forward on his knuckles. "Highsmith usually deals with him, thank God. The little SOB is the son of an old NVA infantry colonel. You can imagine how much I like kissing his ass."

"Is everything okay?" asked Howard, worried at the CEO's tone.

Stephenson's leathery face suddenly crinkled with a grin. "More than okay. You gentlemen will be pleased to know that the minister is going to carry on with our arrangements after you complete the acquisition. I know you asked me to certify that, Jack, to get it in writing. Now we'll have it. They're sending papers over tonight. Always papers, never email . . . Damned commies. Maybe this time that will be helpful."

"Great!" erupted Jack, genuinely happy to hear it. The government leasing certification was another niggling detail on his long list of audit requirements.

Stephenson sat down heavily behind his desk. "I never doubted we'd get it. Sir David's up in Hanoi schmoozing the various committee heads. That's his real talent, you know, the reason I let him run this division. I'd have never gotten this company off the ground without his help."

"Relationships like those are hard to put a price tag on," offered Howard.

"Yeah. Anyway." Stephenson glanced at his wall clock. "You finish up yet, Jack? Now that you've spent two days in the country, can we put a bow on this thing for HSBC and get you fellas to the airport?"

Howard put a hand on Jack's knee, answering for him. "You know, Bruce, I guess I'd start by saying that we're really pleased with how open your team has been, all the information we've been getting. But we're—"

"Here's the thing," interrupted Jack. "I don't like the look of your expense reporting for the mining and refining operations up in Lay Táo." He went on to explain the mismatch in gadolinium inputs and samarium outputs.

Stephenson twisted his mouth. After a few beats of consideration, he asked, "Have you talked to Sir David about all this, Jack? This is all Vietnam stuff."

"I have. He referred me to Malcolm Trang here, in Da Nang. Malcolm just told me that only the people up at the mines could answer my questions."

"Well, you shouldn't be too surprised at that answer. Refining's an inexact science."

"So everyone tells me. *Absolutely* everyone."

Stephenson offered a slight, crooked smile. "You know I'm a chemical engineer."

"Of course."

"Then let me tell you, Mr. Ryan, that getting to pure samarium is a little like alchemy. I'd like to say it's as simple as one plus one equals two, but sometimes the answer is point five . . . other times it's six. Either way, we're making enough of these magnets to satisfy that new contract we inked this morning with Quantum. That revenue's a *hell* of a lot more than these expenses you're chasing down. Am I right, Howard?"

"You're right about the revenue, Bruce," answered Howard. "It's just that—"

Jack waved a blue carbon paper, cutting Howard off again. "The revenues are only half the equation. If gadolinium ratios aren't consistent, then you have no idea of your profitability. Are you familiar with this company? Han Tech Limited? They're the gadolinium supplier for the Lay Táo refining operation."

Stephenson glanced briefly at the carbon, stained with Vietnamese script. "They're *one* of the gadolinium suppliers. Have you any idea just *how many* vendors we have, Jack?"

"Here in Vietnam, I'm up to three twenty-five and counting. All of it by massing up little carbon copies like this one."

"Then you'll have a lot more counting to do, if that's what you're after." Stephenson looked out at the shining sea. "Point is, Jack, I don't know the operational details of this side of the company. Mining is—"

"An inexact science."

Jack felt Howard's hand squeeze his knee. He gently brushed it away, keeping his eyes fixed on the CEO. "Bruce, look. We appreciate that you wouldn't know the details on a single supplier. But who would? It seems to us that no one here in the Da Nang office does. *Someone* in this company must. This isn't a small, one-off supplier. From what I've pieced together, they make up a big chunk of the op-ex in Lay Táo."

"The guys up at Lay Táo would know the supplier," said Stephenson. "They operate their own books up there. I prefer a decentralized, horizontal operation so they can make quick decisions. I'm sure you can understand that. There are no communications up there, no cell sites. They need to be able to do what they gotta do. All I really care about is them sending the samarium down the river barges."

"Got it," said Jack. "Makes sense. Would you have a problem with us visiting the team up at Lay Táo?"

Howard's right hand rose, palm outward. "Jack . . . we've got a timeline here. HSBC is waiting on us. Gerry hasn't authorized us to—"

"Be careful what you wish for," Stephenson cut in, getting up from his big, padded chair. "LT's mighty remote. And though it might not look like it today, we're still dealing with the rainy season. Especially up in those mountains."

Before Ryan could respond, the CEO walked to a wall map of Vietnam. It was stabbed generously with blue, red, and yellow pins.

SHADOW STATE

The CEO pointed to a blue marker on the western side of Vietnam, near the Laotian border. He circled it with his finger. "This area here is Lay Táo." The finger tapped. "It's one of the richest samarium ore lodes ever discovered. Our operation sits next to a river for easy transport of materials back here to Da Nang."

He looked at them, his finger still stuck to the map. "I took over the lease on that land from Highsmith's in-laws—on spec, mind you, the greatest gamble of my life. Now those hills are GeoTech's crown jewels. Soon to be *your* crown jewels, gentlemen."

"I'd like to see the operation," pressed Jack. "What good are crown jewels if you can't check them out now and then?"

Howard touched Jack's arm. "We should probably call Gerry."

Stephenson made the trip back to his desk chair. "Gerry's a doer, Howard. I think he'd agree with Jack."

"Sure," answered Howard.

"Look, fellas," continued the CEO. "If it gets us over the line . . . if it will satisfy your audit, Jack, then I don't mind you poking around up there. I haven't been up there in a dog's age, either. I'll take you myself."

"Thank you, Bruce. We all want this audit completed as quickly as possible. Could we get up there tonight?"

The CEO chuckled as he sat. "Easy, tiger. No, we can't go tonight. Tomorrow maybe. I'll need to talk to some of the geologists . . . make sure they're going to be around on a Saturday." He lowered his palm to his desk blotter with an audible slap. "But yeah, I'll make it happen. In the meantime, let me offer you gentlemen some hospitality. Come with me tonight up to the Hué plantation. We'll put you up in the guest villa. Highsmith's brother-in-law is supposed to cook for me tonight. Henri is a hell of a chef, trained at Cordon Bleu. You guys will be blown away."

Howard slowly rubbed his hands together. "Bruce, do you guys have broadband up at your plantation? Is it good enough that I could make a Zoom call? I'll need to check in with the wife . . . You know."

Stephenson grinned. "I get it. Sure, comms aren't the best up there, Howard, but we'll fix you up."

Standing up, Howard put his hands on his hips. "Okay. We'll need to get back to our hotel to get our bags. How long's the drive to the plantation at Hué?"

"A couple of hours," said Stephenson. Then, his face lighting up, he revealed a wide set of surprisingly white teeth, reminiscent of the youthful medevac pilot in the photos behind him. "But screw that. I have a much better way to get us there. You boys ready for a ride in *Austin Belle*?"

13

JACK LOOKED DOWN AT HIS DANGLING FEET AS STEPHENSON'S OLD HUEY BANKED right. He sat at the helicopter's open door, his butt on the deck plates, his feet hanging over the skids. A canvas "gunner's belt" clipped to a ringbolt kept him from falling as the helo twisted and turned.

Humid air whistled through his bulky, war-vintage flight helmet. Acrid smoke stung his nose. The steady beat of rotors thumped his chest. He was thrown sideways as the helo banked hard to follow a river. When level again, Jack looked down on the jungle with trees bunched like broccoli. The helicopter ascended a peak. From this height, the trees turned to dark, leafy folds. The helo suddenly banked left, flinging Jack's feet outward.

"That creek there," Stephenson narrated through the intercom speaker in his helmet, "is the headwaters of the Perfume River . . . We'll follow it right into Hué." Throughout the flight from Da Nang, the pilot had pointed out natural features and old battle sites.

They bumped through a turbulent turn. Jack looked back into *Austin Belle*'s cabin bay at the cockpit. The GeoTech CEO was flying in the left seat, Army style. Without a copilot, the stick on the right side moved in sync.

"Can you tell us again how you got this helicopter?" asked Jack into his lip mic. He watched as another fuzzy green hill approached, then receded beneath his feet.

"Oh, yeah. Our Army left her behind as a gift to the South Vietnamese army, the ARVN. Eventually, it crashed in a lake on our leased lands, just this side of Laos. Sir David wrestled with the government ministers to let us have it if we could get it out. I brought in some pros to restore her and modernize the avionics and engine." He laughed at the memory. "She's all mine now."

Howard's voice sounded far away over the intercom. "And . . . you fly her just for fun when you're back here on weekends and vacation?"

"Yeah, pretty much," answered the CEO. "And, oh yeah, Jack. I told our accounting department to take this bird off our balance sheet yesterday. She doesn't come along with the acquisition." The CEO cackled over the intercom.

"Okay," Jack said, chuckling. "We'll consider it a signing bonus. Isn't that right, Howard?"

Jack leaned back into the cabin to check on his colleague. Howard was clinging tightly to the rails of a canvas seat at the cabin's rear bulkhead. Jack gave him a thumbs-up. Howard dipped his head in reply, but kept his hands squeezing the seat. Jack thought he looked pale.

"What's our airspeed now?" asked Jack.

"Ninety-five knots."

"Feels faster when you're hanging out the door, a few feet over the ground."

"Oh, this ain't nothing, Mr. Ryan. Now, you just hang on . . ."

Jack felt the floor drop from beneath him as the Huey dove.

SHADOW STATE

The aircraft's nose tilted down. Jack slid forward, banging his thigh against the doorjamb until the *Austin Belle* leveled, flying thirty feet above a muddy river.

Looking through his knees at brown water, Jack saw a sampan with a thatched canopy as it crossed under the skids. It was visible for a flash before the river wound around a bend, the helicopter twisting with it.

"Now we're *really* flying!" Stephenson chortled over the intercom. "Get ready for the best part, fellas. When they redid the avionics, I had them put in a sound system, too."

The first twangy notes of the Rolling Stones' long intro to "Gimme Shelter" burst through Jack's helmet speakers. The engine pitch rose, the blades chopped the air with loud whops, and the CEO sounded at least forty years younger, hollering over the music. "Hundred and ten knots, twenty feet, gentlemen!"

The pilot jinked to the right and buzzed a long narrow boat. "Welcome to Vietnam!"

The brown water below Jack's feet splashed white as the rotor churned up the surface. The sampan rocked under the helicopter's blade wash, its owner raising a fist in protest. Stephenson roared with laughter. Mick Jagger sang over the sound system.

Grinning, Jack looked back at Howard to see how he was doing now. The older man had his eyes closed, chin raised, mouth mumbling, as though in prayer.

"Hey, Bruce," called Jack into his lip mic, shouting to be heard over the Rolling Stones. "My dad made me promise I'd never get in a military helicopter. You know, he broke his back in a crash."

"Don't be a party pooper, Jack. Your old man crashed in a Marine helo. You're with the Air Cav now, boy. Safe as in your mama's arms."

Jack looked at Howard again. The Hendley banker had a death

grip on the sides of his metal-framed seat, knuckles white. He'd stopped moving his mouth. His eyes were screwed tightly shut.

"Hey, I'm sorry, Bruce," said Jack. "But I'm feeling a little airsick. Do you mind slowing us down? I need some straight-and-level time. Can I come up to the cockpit?"

"Yeah, sure, Jack. I'll ease us out."

The music faded to the background. The helicopter climbed and slowed. The engine pitch got lower and steadier, like a big truck climbing a hill.

Jack pushed himself backward, sliding on the deck. When he was far enough inside the cabin, he released his tether. He crawled for the cockpit and climbed into the vacant right pilot seat, strapping in. Next to Bruce Stephenson, he watched the countryside scroll by in the glass chin bubble at his feet. He saw that the river was smaller. Shining rice paddies stretched to the sea, met by towering pink clouds.

Stephenson pointed ahead. "Tet Offensive got real nasty through here in 'sixty-eight, the Siege at Hué. Up there to the right, you can see the walled buildings where Marines fought house to house. Ugly."

The helicopter zoomed over Vietnam's ancient capital, the imperial seat of both Chinese and Vietnamese dynasties. Jack noted the multiple colors of buildings—some very old, dingy, and gray. Others new and white. Between them, he saw the Perfume River.

The city receded. They were nearing the coastline. The helicopter banked left.

"See that cluster of white buildings on the big green straightaway up there on the peninsula?" asked the pilot.

"Yeah," said Jack. "Looks like a country club."

"Uh-huh. That's Highsmith's plantation. His wife's family,

the Clarés, owned all this going way back. I rent Sir David's house to the left. The one in the middle is where Henri Claré and his wife, Marie, live."

"A lot of land," noted Jack.

"Two hundred acres running right up to the sea. Heart of the old rubber plantation. Pretty, isn't it? Hang on, men. We're coming into the LZ."

The helo slowed and hovered over the landing zone. Jack watched the green grass loom larger in the chin bubble, coming nearer.

"My crew's waiting for me," added Stephenson as the skids settled on the manicured lawn with a thump.

Tropical foliage at the edge of the clearing whipsawed green and silver in the rotor wash. Four grinning teenage boys stood in front of the jungle near a fuel tank towed behind a vintage Army jeep, their T-shirts flapping in the wind. A white tuk-tuk waited on a paved driveway. An old, wiry Vietnamese man grinned behind its wheel.

"Goddamnit that was fun," said Bruce through the intercom, throwing switches over his head as the engine wound down. The boys ran forward, ducking, opening his door. Stephenson pointed at the tuk-tuk. "Mr. Bac will take you over to the guest villa."

It was a white stucco cottage with a red roof that sat on the edge of a ravine, two hundred yards from the old plantation's larger houses. The guest villa had tall narrow windows and a mahogany front door. Mr. Bac showed Bruce and Jack around with elaborate hand gestures. The only English word he seemed to know was "here," which he repeated often.

Finishing the tour, he pressed his hands together and bowed. Not quite sure how to proceed, Jack gave him a twenty-dollar bill before the old man remounted the tuk-tuk.

Standing in the driveway, Jack inhaled the fresh tropical air. The lawn before him fell away to the ravine. He walked to its edge and looked into thick vegetation. He heard a rushing creek and singing birds. Beyond the ravine, he could see the helicopter as the sun set behind it.

Small wonder Bruce spent his weekends here, he thought.

When he went back into the villa, he found Howard on his hands and knees. "I'm not seeing an Ethernet cable," the banker reported, crawling. "No Wi-Fi."

"Maybe over at one of the bigger houses," Jack said. "Between Stephenson's and Henri Claré's homes, there's got to be internet."

After grabbing a beer out of the bar fridge, Jack settled into a thick rattan chair and popped the top off the Saigon Red. He swallowed three gulps before setting the beer down. He put his feet on the coffee table and closed his eyes, tired from a long day of accounting work.

"We need to talk to Bruce," shouted Howard from the far bedroom door. "My cell phone doesn't work here, either."

Jack pulled his burner phone from his pocket. No signal bars.

Howard emerged from the bedroom in a fresh blue shirt worn untucked over his gabardines. He still had on his Italian loafers with the metal clasps. "It would have been good to check in with Gerry. I shot him an email before we left the hotel—but I'm thinking he'd better keep the HSBC people warm. Damned Germans are probably lining up their own financing by now."

"Well," said Jack as Howard sat across from him. "We're here with the GeoTech CEO, Gerry's old friend. He's not going to turn us down."

Howard sighed and opened his own beer. "Highsmith's up in Hanoi . . . supposedly. He could be talking to the Germans right now, setting up some change of control protocol with the government. We don't know."

"Highsmith likes our deal. He's going to make, what, thirty million on his equity? Why jeopardize a sure thing?"

"Jack, let me tell you something. Though he's going to make a lot, he'd rather make more. I've seen it a hundred times when trying to acquire companies. In the end, people don't care who they sell to. They just want the most dollars."

Jack thought of Highsmith at his fancy club in Ho Chi Minh City, eyeing the pretty women at the bar. "I don't know. Highsmith seems to like it here. I mean, look at this property. You really think he'll leave Vietnam?"

"His real value to the company has been the government relationships. Now that Bruce has that new, extended lease from the Interior Ministry, there's really no point to Highsmith staying. And let's not forget. He's an earl back in England."

"He'll have to deal with his wife."

"Or—finally have enough money to make her go away," said Howard.

"You know," said Jack. "For a happily married man, you're a bit of a cynic."

Howard looked at Jack seriously. "I have *got* to make that birthday call, Jack."

THE DINING ROOM WAS AT THE CENTER OF THE HOUSE THAT BRUCE STEPHENSON rented from David Highsmith. Its long dark table was flanked by mahogany benches. The GeoTech CEO sat at its head, surrounded by flaming hurricane lanterns under glass.

Stephenson passed a wide white platter with dark red sauce

and a silver spoon. "Try this one, gentlemen. Henri, remind me. What do you call it?"

The man across from Jack, Henri Claré, wore a rumpled cotton jacket with lapels that refused to lie flat. His yellow shirt was opened down to three buttons at the neck, exposing a tuft of unruly gray chest hair.

"That one, Bruce, is *bún bò Huế*," he said with a thick French accent and a gesturing hand. "*Bún bò* dates to the Nguyen dynasty, a royal tradition. Though I think you'll agree, the egg yolk gives it more of a . . . Gallic flair. I hope you do not find it too spicy, Jacques."

"No problem. I like spice," answered Jack as he accepted the plate. "I'd love to try it."

Madame Marie Anh Claré, Henri's Vietnamese wife, demurely inclined her head. "Of all Henri's cooking . . . *Bún bò* is my favorite."

Jack ladled the stew into his bowl, then passed it to Howard. Though the chicken was spicy, he also found it sweet and smoky. Jack inclined his head at her. "I can see why it's a favorite of yours, Madame Anh."

"So can I," agreed Howard. "It is very generous of you to cook for us, Henri."

"My pleasure," purred the Frenchman. "You should take more sauce, 'Oward. Please. Do me the honor of more sauce."

"When are you heading home, Jack?" asked Madame Anh. "Have you already made arrangements?"

From the flickering light of the hurricane lamps, Jack took in her features. He judged her to be about fifty, though her flawless skin and careful makeup made it hard to tell.

"We hope to leave by Monday," said Jack. "Howard needs to get home."

"Oh, 'Oward," said Henri, the lines at his mouth deepening like fish gills. "Why the rush back?"

"Work," said Howard, dishing rice onto his plate. "Every acquisition is complicated, thanks to the lawyers."

"A pity," said Madame Anh. "But that means you both still have Sunday here. Maybe you'll let me show you around Hué? So many colonial buildings to see, so much history."

"That sounds very charming, Madame Anh," replied Howard, smiling at her. "Maybe internet service will be back up tomorrow."

"I'm sure sorry about that, Howard," Stephenson chimed in. "Happens every now and then during the rainy season out here. It'll be back. You'll be chattin' with your missus in no time."

A young female server in an ankle-length dress came through the swinging door. She placed another dish on the table while Madame Anh spoke to her in hushed Vietnamese. The girl responded with a demure bow before leaving.

"Jack, you're an adventurous eater," remarked Madame Anh. "You should try the one Danielle just brought. It's called *dê cay*. Another favorite."

She spun the turntable to present a dish with saucy, dark brown lumps.

Already impressed with Henri's cooking, Jack spooned it onto his plate, then passed it to Howard. He dug in. It tasted like sweet and sour chicken, he thought.

Madame Anh covered her teeth with her hand, watching the Americans. "Look at that. Jack and Howard both like *dê cay*."

"*C'est bon!*" approved Henri. "Very few Americans like *dê cay*. Bruce, here, won't touch it. Perhaps because he is a Texan. Well done, Jacques and 'Oward. Well done."

Howard looked over his fork. "Why don't you like it Bruce? Tastes good to me."

"I don't like it, Howard, because it's made of crickets."

Jack swallowed hard, then gulped a chaser of white wine. In his periphery, he could see Stephenson grinning at him.

"Here, Jack," offered the CEO. "If you want to kill the creepy-crawlies in your mouth, try putting some of this orange sauce on your rice quick. I call it napalm."

Jack dipped a spoon into the sauce bowl. His mouth was swiftly ablaze.

"The hot stuff's good here," continued the CEO. "I caught a bonito last time I was in town and fried it up into fish tacos. That napalm sauce is the clincher, like being back on the Gulf Coast."

"You fish, Bruce?" asked Howard. He'd downed his entire water glass, chasing away the crickets.

"Oh yeah, whenever I can. I keep a boat in the Da Nang marina. Named her *Longhorn* for my alma mater. She's an old Navy river patrol boat. I restored her like the *Austin Belle*."

Henri yawned. "Bruce likes to play with all the old war toys. He even has a U.S. Army jeep here on the property, out near the springhouse."

"Yeah," said Stephenson, chewing. "I call her the *Lone Star*. You saw her at the landing pad today. I know, my toys are expensive. I like to tell myself I'm preserving history."

"Very good of you," said Howard.

Two hours, three wine bottles, and a full belly later, the pretty young woman in traditional dress arrived with a coffeepot. Under the watchful eye of Madame Anh, she poured carefully.

Jack stirred cream into his coffee as the girl left. He turned to Bruce. "Howard and I are both anxious to get back to the States. How early can we take off tomorrow?"

"How's seven-ish? The Lay Táo sites are spread all over the place up there, about two hundred miles away. Long flight."

"You're going to Lay Táo?" the Frenchman quickly asked. "Why is that?"

"Part of the audit," answered Bruce. "Jack can't close out the deal until he sees for himself a few operational details at the refining sites."

Henri scratched his nose, then lifted his cup. "Audit? Really? Sir David told us the deal was already done. It isn't true?"

"Almost done," answered Howard. "Our financial underwriter is making us cross the t's and dot the i's, of course."

Henri's hands had frozen with his cup six inches in front of his face. "Do you think it will be a long visit? Have you told Sir David?"

"Hopefully not a long visit," said Stephenson. "Sir David's up in Hanoi. We intend to get this wrapped before he's back. Why, Henri?"

The Frenchman shrugged and sipped. "Oh. Well, there is an herb that grows near the rivers out there in Lay Táo. Pak kao tong—the heartleaf. If you have the chance, Bruce, perhaps you could get me some. There are a few markets near the refineries."

"I doubt there'll be time for that," said the Texan.

"Oh, please consider it. If you can, Bruce, I will pack you your favorite banh mi sandwiches. Mr. Bac will put a cooler in *Belle* tonight. What do you think? A fair trade?"

Stephenson nodded slowly, then tossed off the rest of his coffee. "The heartleaf, ah?"

"Yes. Very rare. Please, Bruce."

"Okay, Henri," the CEO said. "You got yourself a deal."

14

HANOI, VIETNAM
FRIDAY, OCTOBER 4

DAVID HIGHSMITH, EARL OF GLOUCESTERSHIRE, STOOD ON THE BALCONY OF HIS room at Hanoi's Apricot Hotel and stared at the bright lights reflecting on the lake.

One of his hands rested on the wrought-iron railing. The other held a glass of chilled Sancerre. Having removed his suit coat, he absorbed the cool of the evening and reached into his trouser pocket to check his phone. The girl, he was told, would arrive at eleven. She was already twenty minutes late.

Annoying. But, he thought with a sigh, likely worth the wait.

He sipped his wine, reminding himself that the girls up here in Hanoi were in high demand, often overscheduled. He'd paid extra for one of the northern beauties. Proximity to China gave them grace and symmetry. French heritage softened their edges.

Not *too* much French heritage, he thought, swallowing, shuddering at the image of his French wife, Countess Claudette Claré Highsmith. He banished her from his head, preferring to dwell on the ideal racial qualities of Northern Vietnamese women.

SHADOW STATE

Take Madame Marie Anh Claré, he conjectured. She traced her lineage to the Nguyen dynasty. In her younger days, Marie had been just the right mix of intelligence, grace, and beauty.

Lord, he reminisced. What a stunner she'd been when Henri had first brought her to live at the plantation twenty-five years ago. *My*, how Claudette had been jealous—and rightly so.

He grinned at the memory of young Marie Anh. He continued grinning until he recalled the many times she'd rebuffed him at Hué, long after Claudette had returned to Europe.

He stole another glance at his phone. The girl he'd ordered was now twenty-four minutes late.

Annoyed, he went inside, stood at the bathroom counter, and studied his face in the mirror. He tugged at the skin below his chin and smoothed back his hair. *Not all that bad*, he told himself. *For a man of sixty . . . ish*. These women could do a lot worse—how dare they keep him waiting.

He'd make her pay for this. He removed his pants and shirt. He hung them carefully on the towel rack.

Standing in only his boxer shorts, he dabbed cologne at his neck and rubbed the latest miracle cream under his eyes. He pulled the underwear away from his waist, looked down, and inspected his equipment. It still worked—usually.

As if that mattered.

Given the money he was paying, if he wanted to lie there and have them read Shakespeare aloud while he watched their lips . . . then that was *his* prerogative. One got what one paid for. Money was the only thing that ever *really* mattered.

He glanced at his phone again. Twenty-seven minutes late now. His thoughts turned back to money.

Enough people in his life had demanded it of him, hadn't they? The Lombard Street bankers who held the mortgage on his

Gloucestershire estate . . . Claudette, burning through tens of thousands a month on domestic staff and shopping in Paris . . . And what of their son, Cedric, who read ancient languages at Oxford, mistakenly believing that his aristocratic roots meant he'd never have to dirty himself with a word like "work"?

How wrong the boy was. He himself, earl of Gloucester, had been reduced to charging rent to his boss to reside at the Hué plantation.

Rent. Imagine.

He released his grip on his underwear, swirled some green mouthwash around, and spit forcefully into the sink. He saw that the girl was now twenty-eight minutes late.

Easy now, he said to himself. The equipment worked better when he was relaxed. And, for heaven's sake, why should it be so hard to relax? Deliverance was finally, *finally* at hand. The Geo-Tech deal was happening.

He was still clinging to this comfort when he heard the knock at the door. With a last dab of eau de toilette on his speckled neck, he went to answer it.

In the routine he'd followed for years, his preference was to unlock the door and rush into bed with the lights off before he or the girl could see each other. From long experience, he knew these young women were shy and—oddly—that they preferred to maintain a certain decorum.

All that was a major turn-on for Highsmith. He got into his bed and waited, fully aroused. Only, this time, when he saw the silhouette crossing the footboard, he knew something was wrong. The hair was long, but the shoulders were broad. Too broad.

Bloody hell. His blood running cold, he threw on a bedside lamp and sat up.

"What are you doing here?" he shot.

"Get dressed. He doesn't want to see you this way."

"My clothes are in the bathroom."

The man found the shirt and pants on the towel rack and hurled them at Highsmith.

The Englishman had seen this Laotian before—Ling. Cai's right-hand man wore his hair in a ponytail and had the cobra tattoo on his neck that Highsmith had come to abhor. The thug parted the curtains and went to the balcony—just as Highsmith had done twenty minutes ago.

Knowing what would happen next, Highsmith rolled out of bed and dressed in a hurry.

"Hello, *Sir* David," said Cai as he entered the suite. "How nice to see you."

The earl of Gloucestershire swallowed. Cai put the chain over the door, while Ling waited on the balcony.

"What's the meaning of this?" Highsmith demanded.

"*What's the meaning of this*," Cai mimicked, nailing the English accent. He went to the suite's sitting area, took a padded white chair, and lit a cigarette.

"We're done, you and I," blustered Highsmith, finishing off the top shirt button. "You have what you want. I updated you earlier tonight. What more can you want from me? Our arrangement is finished, Cai."

The end of Cai's cigarette glowed orange. "Our . . . *arrangement* . . . is not finished."

"How can you say that? The deal is happening. Quantum Atomics placed a huge order with GeoTech that ensures the HSBC financing will come through. I've kept you informed of all of it."

The Laotian blew a jet of smoke. "You said there were no obstacles to getting the deal closed."

"There aren't."

"Then why are Stephenson and the auditors flying to the mining sights tomorrow morning?"

"They're just doing the due diligence. That's a standard practice in acquisitions. It's normal. It's nothing to be worried about."

"How do you know?"

"Do you forget, Cai, that I was a banker at HSBC once?"

"That was a long time ago."

"Cai. This deal wouldn't have worked as quickly had I not introduced Hendley to the HSBC team in Hong Kong. And what? *Now* you think I'm keeping something from you?"

Cai studied Highsmith intently, holding his cigarette in place. Control had only said they were seeing delays in the deal due to a worrying audit, an unexpected wrinkle. Beijing had developed doubts about the true intentions of this asset of Cai's, David Highsmith.

Then again, Cai knew Beijing could be a little too careful at times. He didn't think someone as craven as the earl of Gloucestershire would have the balls to play him. He had to be sure, of course—which was why he'd already planned his next move.

After another drag on the cigarette, the Laotian said, "I have good news for you, *Sir* David. You're about to be promoted."

15

SUBIC BAY, PHILIPPINES
SATURDAY, OCTOBER 5

"HOW WOULD YOU ASSESS THEIR SKILLS?" ASKED CLARK.

Kendrick Moore had risen early, laced up, and run the five miles up the jungled hill to the hospital. With a final sprint, he'd hustled up the steps to the top of the building, all seven floors.

Now, chest slowing as he stood on the roof, he looked down the massive jungle hill, across the old American base and the deep blue bay.

"They're good," Moore responded. "ODA guys are always good." ODA—Operational Detachment Alpha—was the official Army designator for Green Beret teams.

Clark took a few seconds to respond. "You can be honest with me, Master Chief. It's why I hired you."

"I am being honest."

"Okay, then let's break it down. Would you trust them to lead another op?"

Moore dug his running shoe into the roof gravel. He had a routine after hairy ops, usually carried out belowdecks on a ship. He liked to exercise until his body couldn't take any more physical stress. That's why he'd run the hill and the stairs.

"Cary's a leader," he began. "Jad's got talent, a good athlete. They're both tight with Lisanne. I see them as a unit."

"What about judgment? Your AAR said Cary popped smoke, which ruined overwatch and ISR. His hit was good, but hardly quiet. Half the camp was killed. That's not zero footprint."

"Yes. But the whole team got out because of Cary's quick thinking. My after-action report also said we had limited intel and zero planning time. And our weapons were borrowed—they weren't what I would have chosen."

"Santos said he gave you everything you asked for," Clark reminded him.

"He did. But the Filipino M4s were all piston recoil. I prefer gas. The rifles had long barrels. I like short for this kind of op."

"This is The Campus, Master Chief. You're not in DEVGRU anymore. Cary and Jad have faced these issues before. I don't see that as a valid excuse."

Moore watched a Philippine Airlines 737 touching down in the distance on the long runway that bordered Subic Bay. Old-timers still thought of this former American naval air station as Cubi Point. In the mid-nineties, it had become a Philippine free port.

"Well," said the master chief. "My assessment stands. They're a unit. You, Ding, and Jack Junior have done a nice job shaping them."

While waiting for Clark to respond, Moore watched the jet on its landing rollout as it reversed its thrust and roared, slowing dramatically. The sun was cooking his head. He felt some sweat run down his nose and wiped it.

"Mr. Moore. There's something else," continued Clark.

Wary of Clark's tone, the master chief braced himself. "Blowback?"

"Yeah. Blowback."

"How bad?"

"A Muslim village kid on Mindanao was quick to get video of the dead. It's up on YouTube now. Comments are throwing the word 'massacre' around. Of course, Al Sheikh's body is long gone. They claim he was never there."

Goddamnit, Moore swore to himself. "Are they putting the hit on the U.S.?"

"Naturally. They allege our Special Forces or CIA. China's giving them a boost on TikTok and Telegram, of course."

Moore released the breath he'd been holding. "The op got messy. That's on me, John. It wasn't Cary's doing."

"This was supposed to be a deniable op. It's getting harder to maintain that."

The chief's gut tightened. His drab Virginia Beach attic apartment suddenly flickered across his mind's eye. He pictured the secondhand desk with the stacks of legal bills, the window that looked out on the driveway, where the homeowner's kid shot free throws all day.

He put his hand to his head, flicking off more sweat. "Like I said, John. It's on me. I own it."

Moore counted the seconds until Clark responded. The chill he'd already felt in his gut turned to ice, then crushed ice. If other mercenary units wouldn't take him before this, what the hell would they do if they learned he'd failed John Clark?

Clark still hadn't answered. Moore wondered if the call had dropped. He glanced at the phone screen, verifying it hadn't.

"Look," said Clark finally. "I'm going to have to address something tough here, Kendrick."

Moore tilted the phone away from his mouth so Clark wouldn't hear his uneven breath. What would he do now? If his soldiering skills weren't marketable, then maybe he could swing a hammer, work construction, or—

"Campus work is different," Clark went on. "Transitioning from active duty in an operational role is tough. I don't expect everyone to get it. When it comes to you, we both knew it was a risk, that we . . ."

Moore tuned out, not wanting to hear another conciliatory word. For the next few seconds, he thought of his cousin Frankie, a roughneck who worked the rigs on the Permian fields. The panhandle was hot as hell in the summers, but Frankie had said the pay was good. Moore had been dreading making that call.

"I appreciate the opportunity," he said when Clark finished.

"Yeah, I know you do. Anyway, while I process the next steps," said Clark, "I've asked a high-level contact to work out a cover for you and the team."

"Aye, sir."

"It may take a few days to get fully established."

"Copy, sir."

"For now, I want you to lay low. Stay within the fence line of Subic. If this Sayyaf video keeps escalating and the news crews get involved, I'm worried that if someone sees your . . ."

Face, Moore finished. *My big, dumb, doughy face.*

Months ago that face had been plastered all over the web, with him labeled a warrior turned sociopath who killed for the fun of it, who'd turned honor into horror, who'd embarrassed his nation, the vaunted Navy SEALs.

Foolish face. Worthless face.

He shoved his hand hard against his eyes. "No problem, sir. We can all lay low. Or . . . you know, I can get out of this country right now. I can even use my own money, take a roundabout way to get home."

"Easy, Chief. We're not there yet. I've got Gavin working up a cover story. While you wait, just huddle with the squad, out of sight. Then we'll figure out the travel. No need for extreme measures at this point."

"Aye, sir."

"Oh, and Master Chief, last thing. Ditch your phones and get burners, just in case China's got a lead on you. Make sure there are no communications with anyone. Not even other Campus resources, only me. Lisanne might want to call Jack. Don't let her. I think you know they're engaged."

"Aye, sir. I'll take care of it."

"We need Jack Junior to finish the white-side work he's doing now. He can't get distracted."

"Copy."

"How's Lisanne doing, anyway?"

Moore's eyes were closed, his hand still covering them, sweating against his brow. "I just saw her downstairs. She took a shot to her chest armor. It didn't penetrate."

"Is she an up-round, then?"

"The impact reopened scar tissue from an older wound. She lost some blood, but X-rays show she's okay. The docs are springing her this morning. She's anxious to get out of the hospital."

"How about Cary and Jad? How are they handling this?"

Moore dropped his hand and opened his eyes. "They won't leave the side of her bed."

Clark grunted. "Okay. Sit tight. I'll be back with instructions when I can. Talk soon, Chief." The connection closed.

Moore took a deep breath.

Still holding the phone to his mouth, he said. "Goodbye, Mr. C."

16

**HUÉ, VIETNAM
SATURDAY, OCTOBER 5**

STEPHENSON LET JACK STRAP IN AS COPILOT FOR THE FLIGHT UP TO LAY TÁO. HE SAT in the cockpit at the *Austin Belle*'s starboard controls with the GeoTech CEO to his left, flying the old Huey westward toward the mountains.

Howard was in a folding jump seat behind Stephenson, which gave him a good view through the front windscreen. Belted to the rear bulkhead of the *Austin Belle*'s cargo bay was a cooler with iced drinks and the carefully wrapped banh mi sandwiches Henri had promised.

The morning sun was bright, the sky clear, as the *Belle* beat her way to the northwest. The old Air Cavalry medevac pilot behind her controls navigated without ground-based aids, since, he said, there weren't any.

Finding his way by landmarks, they flew over a seemingly endless scroll of rice paddies, hills, rivers, and scattered villages. The GeoTech CEO kept the *Austin Belle* low, about three hundred feet. He loosely followed the Perfume River out of Hué to the wider Ca, while subjecting Jack and Howard to his music over the intercom. To preserve fuel, Jack noticed, the pilot flew at a manageable seventy knots and refrained from the wild jinking turns that had so terrified Howard the day before.

"Hey, Jack, hop back there and get us a couple of Cokes, will you?"

"Sure, Bruce."

"Kind of hot down here in the rice paddies," added the pilot over the intercom. "It'll cool down once we climb up into the highlands."

Jack turned the three-way metal buckle that kept his shoulders and legs strapped to the seat. He pulled his vintage Army helmet's intercom cord from the instrument panel, immediately losing Jimi Hendrix's "All Along the Watchtower."

Wearing his Levi's, a casual button-down short-sleeve shirt, and a pair of hiking boots he'd borrowed from Stephenson, Jack pushed himself backward, through the gap between the two pilot seats.

Along the way, he felt Howard's hands helping him. The Hendley banker's freshly shaved face was squashed in his helmet. Jack grinned encouragingly at him, thinking the banker looked noticeably better on this flight.

Howard was still a nervous flier, but seemed to enjoy the distraction of Stephenson's guided air tour of the Siege at Hué and the infamous Hamburger Hill. Howard had asked many attentive questions, much to Stephenson's delight.

With the exhaust-tainted, humid air swirling around him, Jack crawled over the deck of the *Austin Belle*'s cabin, staying low. Since the starboard cargo door was wide open, Jack crawled on hands and knees to the huge cooler at the rear bulkhead. He picked up three Coke cans.

Near the thermal bag Henri had packed next to the cooler,

Jack could still smell the leftovers of the almond croissants they'd devoured in the first twenty minutes of the flight.

The Frenchman was a hell of a chef. Now, at ten-thirty a.m., Jack could hardly wait for the banh mi sandwiches he saw resting in the cooler.

"Attaboy," said Stephenson once Jack had reversed course and strapped into his copilot seat. The CEO popped the top of his can and swigged.

Jack plugged the intercom cord back into the dash panel and watched the Vietnamese countryside scroll by while enjoying his soda. The *Austin Belle* threaded between thatched-roof villages, soared over lumps of wild jungle, and whisked just above the palm trees at the river's edge. He tapped his boots to the music.

"Say, Jack," said Stephenson when the song shifted to CCR's "Fortunate Son." "How's about a little flying lesson?"

"No thanks. My dad would kill me. He told me never to get in one of these—let alone fly one."

Stephenson laughed. "Your dad may be the President of the United States. But he isn't here. Come on. We're straight and level. We got a half hour before we're in the mountains, where the winds will pick up. Go ahead, put your right hand on the stick. It's called a cyclic."

Nervously, Jack did as Stephenson asked. He could feel pressure as the stick moved under the CEO's control.

"Okay, good. The cyclic controls the rotor blade angle, which guides the aircraft forward or backward. Now, here, take your left hand and put it on this lever. Yeah, there you go. That's the collective—it controls the power from the engines."

Jack dropped his left hand along his seat and gripped the collective. Again, he could feel Stephenson's small movements under his own hand.

"Now, take your feet there and put 'em on the rudder pedals. They control the tail rotor. Its job is to counteract the torque from the main rotors overhead, got it? You can tell if the aircraft is centered by that gauge in front of you. The goal is to keep the ball in the middle, within the white lines. That means she's facing straight. Ready to take over?"

"You sure this is such a good idea?" asked Howard from behind.

"Hell yeah, I do." Stephenson grinned, looking at Jack. "Take it, Fortunate Son. Go on."

The pressure on the cyclic, collective, and rudders eased as Jack took control. The *Austin Belle* leaped fifty feet, yawed ten degrees to the left, and banked awkwardly. Stephenson jumped in to straighten out their flight path, then relinquished the controls again.

Jack did better the second time.

"Look at that, boy. You're Air Cav now," said Stephenson. "You're whippin' an old UH-1 Iroquois up the Ca River in the 'Nam. The spirits of a lot of good men we lost down there are talking to you right now, Jack. You hear them?"

"I hear Creedence Clearwater Revival."

Stephenson laughed and resumed the controls. "Okay. First set of mountains is coming up. We're about two hundred klicks from Lay Táo. I'll take her back and get us over the hump, up to the highlands."

In the windscreen before him, Jack could see rising hills. Stephenson pulled the collective, climbing to get over them. The Ca River they'd been following disappeared in the narrow confines of a valley.

As they ascended, the air became noticeably cooler, the haze fainter, and the sky a deeper shade of blue. Jack could see the lumps of clouds building in front of them, gathering on the high mountain peaks.

"Hey, Howard, do you recognize that valley over there?" Stephenson pointed to the south.

Howard leaned forward, stretching to see through the window. "I just see mountains and plateaus."

"Yeah," said Stephenson. "But you see that one plateau with red gashes? See the dark valley just to the other side of it?"

"Yes. I'm with you. I see it."

"That's Dien Bien Phu—last stand for the French forces back in 'fifty-four. The one that kind of started it all for us here in the 'Nam." Stephenson glanced at the dash. "What the hell," he said. "We got plenty of fuel. Check out this other famous battle site."

As the terrain rose below them, alternating between mountains and plateaus, Stephenson steered the *Belle* westward. He pointed to a distant highway. "That's the old DMZ," he said. "That hill there south of the highway, the flat one, is the site of the Marine combat base at Khe Sanh."

Once they reached the old siege site, the *Austin Belle* tilted abruptly to the left. Stephenson killed the music and circled. He looked down silently at the scarred, red earth. Jack wondered what he was thinking.

"Anyway," said the old airman, "let's get you boys up to Lay Táo so we can finish off that audit—and all get rich, ha ha."

He leveled the *Austin Belle* and pointed her nose north, climbing into the mountains.

Along the way, Howard remarked, "Terrain's rugged here. How do you get the refined samarium out of Lay Táo?"

"Trucks take it down to the big Ca River," answered Stephenson. "Then we float barges back to Da Nang."

"I guess that explains a lot of the equipment leasing I've been tracking," said Jack. "You have a huge fleet of vehicles."

"Well, yeah," said Stephenson. "Getting ore out of these mountains is the first headache. Getting it back to civilization is the second."

"What's so hard about it?" asked Howard. "You've got the trucks and barges."

"Well, first there's the terrain, of course. I mean, just look at it. Then there's the weather. We're just finishing up the wet season. The heavy rains make the roads unusable. Jack, you probably saw in the cash-flow statements that most of our port activity in Ho Chi Minh goes November to April."

"Yeah, I did notice that."

"Rest of the year it's damned hard to get stuff out of these hills. There's also the security problem."

"What's the security concern?" asked Howard.

"Drugs. We're technically operating in the Golden Triangle. It's not really been a problem for us, though. The druggies don't seem to want to bother us. I think it's because they know we work with the government. They don't want any reprisals, and neither do we. We just steer clear of each other."

Jack recalled a DEA whitepaper he'd read on heroin smuggling in the Golden Triangle. He'd flagged it as a concern for Hendley's acquisition of GeoTech.

"Okay, gents. The hills are getting tall. It'll feel a little slow while we ascend, but we're making progress."

Now that Jack was more familiar with how to fly a helicopter, he recognized the movements in the controls. Stephenson pulled the collective to increase the power to the main rotor. The *Belle* climbed, passing through two thousand feet above sea level. Jack felt his ears pop.

"This altitude's no fun in a little Huey," said Bruce, still increasing power. "Controls get a lot looser as the air is less dense."

The helicopter gears ground and sang while Jack looked out at the impressive landscape. Getting hungrier, he was waiting on those sandwiches. That made him think of Henri—and by extension, his wife, Madame Marie Anh Claré.

Jack wondered at her offer to guide them around the city of Hué. She'd been curiously insistent. As they were leaving Stephenson's rented house after dinner, she'd pressed Jack's hand longer than natural before letting it go. The look in her eyes had given him a sense of déjà vu, though he wasn't sure why.

"We have to rise up to four thousand to make it over this ridge," said Stephenson over the straining engine. "Should be just a—"

A shattering bang cut the pilot off.

Jack felt his shoulders surge instantly against their restraints as the *Austin Belle* twisted. A wind that hadn't been present before swirled round his neck. The mountains in the window were sliding by in front of him, slowly at first, but accelerating. Warning buzzers and bells sounded in his ears.

As the helicopter rotated faster on its axis, Jack tried to turn his head to see what had happened. The increased gravity from the accelerating spin kept his helmet pinned to the window.

"Spin!" shouted Stephenson over the intercom. "Lost tail rotor. I don't know how it—" He stopped speaking with a groan. The fast spin had knocked him against the port cockpit door. Using his arms to prop himself, Jack managed a glance rearward.

Howard was there, his helmeted head leaning to the left, his jump seat straps locking his body firmly in place. Beyond him, Jack could see the source of the wind.

At the back of the cabin, through a tear in the riveted metal, hydraulic hoses flailed like snakes in the open air, spewing purple fluid. A hole had been torn in the rear fuselage. Based on Stephenson's comment about the tail rotor, Jack guessed a blade had flung free and ripped open the rear of the aircraft.

Pinned against the starboard door, he shifted his eyes as far left as he could. Jack could see that Bruce was similarly pasted to his door as the centrifugal force pushed them outward. Jack saw the yaw gauge on the instrument panel. Like a carpenter's level, it had a ball that rotated left or right of center line, depending on the power of the tail rotor. Jack saw that the ball was pegged to the right, that they were in an uncontrolled spin.

"Rudder not responding . . ." growled Stephenson, struggling to push himself upright. "Hydraulics are mushy . . . Just gone . . . Come on, *Belle* . . ."

Jack looked at the altimeter spinning counterclockwise.

"What can I do?" he barked into the intercom.

"I'm trying to . . . to . . ." Bruce was attempting to raise his arm toward the cockpit ceiling. His hand moved shakily, as though struggling under an eighty-pound dumbbell.

Through the forward window Jack saw alternating colors—green mountains, blue sky, and white clouds. *Belle* spun wildly, her nose rising and falling as she rotated like a carnival Tilt-a-Whirl.

"Trying . . . to . . . kill the engine," Stephenson groaned, his hand still trying to reach the ceiling controls. With a flash of understanding, Jack seized the pilot's elbow, giving him a boost.

"How will we fly without engines?" Jack shot.

"Auto . . . rotate . . ." said Stephenson, throwing a switch to cut the fuel.

Autorotate.

Jack knew what that meant. Without engines, the helicopter

blades would spin on their own, using gravity as the force to bite the air, the rotor-wing equivalent of a glide. Theoretically, autorotation would allow the *Austin Belle* to fall to the earth like an oak seedpod twirling off a branch.

Theoretically.

"We're descending through fifteen hundred feet," said Jack. He watched the altimeter continue its counterclockwise spiral. The kaleidoscope of blue-white-and-green through the windshield was turning into a blur.

"That's mean sea level," said Stephenson. "We're only a few hundred feet above the plateaus." Finished with the fuel switch, the pilot's hand was back on the cyclic. His helmet was still pinned to the port door.

Jack strained to move his hand back between the seats. He felt Howard's shoulder. The banker was also pinned sideways, his helmet jammed against the port bulkhead. Jack gave his shoulder a squeeze.

With fuel cut off, the grinding roar of the engines had stopped. Now Jack could hear the wind whistling in his helmet.

"We're going down. Brace!" called Stephenson.

As though on the inside of a tornado, Jack glimpsed a flashing strobe of treetops and sky. He heard branches breaking. His head slammed hard against the door window.

The intercom in his helmet stopped buzzing. The kaleidoscope outside shifted to varying shades of darkness. He heard metal tearing and screeching. His helmet whipsawed between the center console and the door, smashing the glass. Rotor blades thudded against dirt and brush, then beat against metal, as if the *Austin Belle* were eating herself alive.

She shuddered to a stop, lying on her side. Jack's straps held him suspended in place, hanging over the tilted cockpit, pinching his shoulders. Stephenson was below him, pinned to the port door.

Jack looked behind him. He saw that the *Austin Belle* had been ripped open like a torn aluminum can.

And that Howard Brennan was gone.

17

VIETNAMESE HIGHLANDS
SATURDAY, OCTOBER 5

JACK SMELLED FUEL. THE *AUSTIN BELLE* HAD COME TO REST ON HER PORT SIDE, shaded by the tall jungle canopy.

Desperate to find Howard, Jack twisted in his seat, seeing what used to be the ceiling and was now an open gash. The *Belle*'s top-mounted turbine engine had broken loose, taking her roof along with it. Jack looked out the shattered windscreen, hoping to see Howard outside.

Instead, he saw a dislodged rotor blade, snapped at an angle. It was embedded in a tree trunk like a knife blade.

Oily black smoke filled the cockpit. Jack coughed. "Howard!" he called.

Stephenson coughed next to him. The CEO was pulling his helmet off. Jack pulled the strap at his chin and did the same, casting it off.

"Bruce! Where's Howard?"

The pilot used his arms to push up from the door beneath

him. Like Jack had done, he looked behind him into the *Belle*'s main cabin.

The metal deck was buckled, bent into thirds. The bolts that had held Howard's jump seat were gone, popped free. Farther into the cabin, Jack could see torn metal, a flash of daylight through a ragged hole. Hoses swayed over the opening, leaking fluid.

Oily smoke gathered and gushed along the helicopter's upturned starboard bulkhead. It escaped through the shattered window off Jack's right shoulder.

"Howard!" Jack cried, coughing.

Whatever had been holding the *Belle* in place on the ground suddenly snapped. Jack heard metal tearing, grinding, and groaning. The *Belle* was sliding backward.

"Legs trapped," called Stephenson. He'd stopped hacking on the smoke just long enough to regain his voice. "She's sliding downhill, backward. We gotta get out. We gotta—"

Loud snaps from popping rivets cut him off. There was another grinding tear. The sliding helicopter came to a stop with a jarring thump.

"Think she's steadied up," said Jack. "Must have run into a tree or something. Let's get you out of here."

"I can't move," moaned Stephenson.

"What?"

"Legs trapped. Won't budge."

Jack released the three-point fitting at his belt and threw off his shoulder straps. He tumbled into the pilot, falling to the helicopter's port side. He could see instantly that Stephenson's thighs were pinned under the bent instrument panel. The helicopter's control surface had folded in on the pilot, pinching his knees against his seat like a vise.

"Can you move at all?"

Stephenson cast off his seat straps and yanked on his thighs. Jack pulled alongside him. Blood darkened the pilot's pants, saturating the fabric.

"Stuck," said Stephenson, coughing. "What about Howard? He get out?"

"I don't know. His jump seat's gone—like it was thrown free."

Stephenson winced. "Possible. I've seen it before."

Jack dug his fingers under the ruined dash panel and pulled with all his might.

He stopped when the cockpit rose, then slammed down like the butt end of a seesaw. Stephenson screamed in pain as the instrument panel bit deeper into his legs.

"Jack!"

Jack turned at the sound of his name. It was Howard's voice, calling to him from outside the wreck.

The banker scrambled up the hulk's side, reaching Jack's topside cockpit door. "Get out!" he was shouting, looking down at Jack and Stephenson. "If it slides back any farther it'll go over a cliff."

"Can't move," answered Stephenson. "Get Jack out."

Howard reached for Jack, trying to grab his shirt to pull him out.

Metal scraped and tore as the *Belle* slid backward another twenty feet. The cockpit rose a few degrees as the tail sunk down. Sunlight streamed through the broken forward window. Through the cracked chin bubble, Jack saw broken trees uphill and the wide furrow dug by the sliding *Belle*.

As the cockpit rose higher, Howard was thrown off. Jack could still hear him calling from outside—until the banker's voice was drowned out by tearing metal.

Jack knew they didn't have long.

"Come on," he said, turning to Stephenson, seizing the pilot with both hands. "The helo's shifted. Let's try again. Hang on to me." Jack braced his boot against the center console and yanked hard at Stephenson's arms. The pilot didn't budge.

The *Belle*'s ruined cockpit rose another few degrees. Jack recalled the view when they were airborne—the high plateaus, low valleys, and sheer limestone cliffs. He stole a glance to the rear. Through the open hole behind him, he saw a river valley a thousand feet straight down. The *Belle* had slid backward to the edge of the plateau.

Over Howard's insistent yells, Jack heard noisy *clunk*s. His hands stayed locked on Stephenson's elbows. The CEO relaxed his arms.

Jack looked at him. "What the hell are you doing?"

The pilot's hair was askew, but his expression was placid. "She's going to fall," he said over the popping metal. "You have to get out of here."

"Not without you," said Jack. His eyes stung. He coughed uncontrollably. The smoke that had been pouring from the ruined engine turned into fire. A yellow glow flickered in the cockpit. Jack felt heat building above his shoulders and reached for the CEO again.

Stephenson shook his arms loose from Jack's grip. "Let go of me, Jack. Get out of here. Right now. Go."

The cockpit stopped rising. It teetered down, then up a few degrees, precariously balanced.

"No way," said Jack, seizing Bruce again. "I'm pulling your crazy old ass out of here. Come on, now."

Stephenson didn't yell or carry on. He let his arms go limp. His voice was steady, his face resigned. "Take it from an old medevac man . . . You can't save everyone. Now go. Scramble out that window over your head while you still can."

"The moment I go," said Jack, his sleeve over his nose to guard against the smoke, "she's going to get out of balance. The tail will sink without my two hundred pounds. We have to leave together."

Stephenson wiped soot from his brow, his eyes suddenly distant. "Leave me. It's okay. You can't save me."

Jack ignored him. He propped his boot against the center console, fighting for more leverage to pry the dash up. "Give me your hands, Bruce. Now!"

Stephenson withdrew his arms, keeping them from Jack.

Realizing the fruitlessness of the attempt, Jack took a deep breath and looked the CEO in the eye. "Please, Bruce."

"I hope I made a difference here, Jack, in this country. I think I did. I think I built something important."

Jack tried once more to grab Bruce's hands. The CEO still wouldn't let him.

"Bruce," he said. "You're getting out of here with me."

Stephenson shook his head. "Do this for me, Jack. Make sure my kids know the significance of what I did here. I hope I turned America's long involvement in this country into something good, something lasting. I certainly tried to. Okay?"

The metal behind them screeched. Jack could see dirt moving again. The burned-out hulk was twisting. Stephenson still stared calmly into Jack's eyes. "Now go. God bless you, son. Go."

The cockpit rose a few degrees higher. The smoke thickened. Jack couldn't breathe. He had no choice now.

He used his foothold on the console to thrust himself up through the broken window of the starboard cockpit door above him, gasping for air. He got an elbow over the side, then pulled his body out, while the flames licked around him. He, rolled, fell, and thudded onto the dirt as the wreck slid away. Howard was on him instantly, tackling him to make sure Jack stayed put.

Without Jack's body weight in the cockpit, the *Belle*'s tail sunk.

Tilted vertically, on fire and smoking, the helicopter shot off the cliff face like a flaming arrow.

18

**PALMDALE, CALIFORNIA
SATURDAY, OCTOBER 5**

JACK RYAN, SR., WATCHED ARNIE VAN DAMM SHIFTING UNCOMFORTABLY IN THE first row. Flanked by Air Force generals in dress blue uniforms, Gerry Hendley, and executives in dark suits, the chief of staff was playing up his annoyed routine, tapping his wrist with two fingers.

Van Damm had granted the President his wish. Along with Hendley, the soon-to-be owner of GeoTech, Jack had demanded to get out to Quantum's Skunk Works airfield in Palmdale to meet the brilliant engineers who'd created UMBRA.

Now, though, van Damm seemed to have had enough. The taps at his wrist were getting faster.

Jack ignored his chief of staff.

Rather, he gazed out across the assembly of five hundred civilian workers, the employees of Quantum Atomics. They were sitting primly in folding chairs, listening politely and attentively, despite having given up a Saturday to be here for the President of the United States. Beyond them, on a shining hangar floor, sat a preproduction B-21 Raider. This was the latest stealth bomber, developed here at the Skunk Works facility, at a staggering cost of two billion apiece.

"And so . . ." continued Jack, his voice echoing off the hangar walls. He'd been reading from the glass teleprompter bolted to his podium. The blinking cursor was urging him to the next line. He put both hands on the edges of the podium and looked at the last row of the assembly, where the youngest and most junior Quantum employees listened politely.

He knew the whole next paragraph would be a recitation of platitudes about bringing America's defense into the next century, about the triumph of industry, the herculean effort of the American workforce, and the unrelenting drive of the Machinists Union. Arnie had stressed the importance of working in the pro-union message.

Ryan could tell they'd be bored by it.

So would he.

"You know," he said, interrupting himself. "This hangar here, on this base, Skunk Works, is one of the very few places I can give a speech where reporters can't pull me out of context—since they're not allowed to be here. So I don't feel like reading you the rest of this speech. Would, uh, that be okay with you all?"

Crowd murmurs. A few coughs.

The President looked through the teleprompter window at van Damm. The chief of staff's face was flushed, staring hard at Jack.

"Yeah," continued the President. "I don't feel like reading the rest of this speech. Instead, I'd rather just talk to you. Which means . . . that this damn thing is in my way."

He reached over the podium and swung the teleprompter to the side. There was a smattering of laughter as an Air Force technical sergeant ran in to wheel it away, stage left.

"Is this thing on?" joked the President as he came from around the podium and walked to the front of the stage, blowing on the handheld mic. "You guys don't mind, do you? I've got a ton of stuff to get done today. And there's something I really want to say to you before I go."

He meant it.

Soon enough van Damm would force him back onto Marine One, bound for the Port of Long Beach, where he'd have to stand around with Cobb and the union presidents to play nice in front of the cameras. Management, the union, and van Damm all wanted to showcase the PR win of the deal to head off a rail strike.

But that was work for later.

In the here and now, Jack stopped at the stage's front edge, held the microphone close to his lips, and looked across the sea of faces. Down there in the fourth row, he spotted the test pilot he'd met earlier—Lieutenant Colonel "Magic" Mike Holbrook, the one who'd flown the specialized F-15 Strike Eagle right over Mischief Reef, undetected, risking his life to test UMBRA. Magic Mike was one of about twenty-seven people in this crowd who knew about the project.

Feeling better now, Jack eased into a relaxed grin as he neared the audience. His voice echoed through the hangar. "I didn't come all the way out here to see that magnificent stealth bomber back there. She's a hell of a machine, but she's not why I came."

He looked again at workers in the rear. They looked back, a few of them leaning forward.

"No. And I *certainly* didn't come to see the brass up here in the front row—though I guarantee you, they all came to see me."

A roiling chuckle. A few hoots.

He lowered his voice, turning serious. "No. I came here to talk to you, to say something specific."

He cleared his throat and put one hand in his trouser pocket. "You know, folks, most of your fellow citizens don't know what you do way the hell out here in the middle of this godforsaken desert. In fact, I bet if you asked them, they'd say you're up here maintaining secret UFOs with dead aliens we've got frozen in cryo storage over in building fourteen."

Another chuckle.

"No. They don't know what you do. Well—maybe, just maybe, your families have an inkling. But your grocer or car mechanic or kids' teachers . . . *they*, your plain old fellow citizens . . . they have no clue. And why would they? They're too busy going about their lives to give you a second's worth of thought."

He raised his voice. "Life, liberty, and the pursuit of happiness. Thomas Jefferson wrote that phrase into the Declaration of Independence two and a half centuries ago. And what do you know? It's still in play. And that's precisely why your fellow citizens don't really know—or care, for that matter—what you do up here all day.

"See, they're too busy living out the promise of this country. They're too busy with life, liberty, and the pursuit of happiness in all its wild, modern, bewildering forms—especially the ones that aren't good for them."

Another polite chuckle.

"But have you ever wondered *why* your friends and neighbors never really ask you in-depth questions about your work? Sure, they might know it's defense-related and classified and all that.

But do they ever ask whether you like it or whether you'll keep doing it or believe in it? No one ever asks *me* those questions. But I have a theory as to why.

"As I see it, they don't ask us because they want to believe that we've got this." He waved his hand around to indicate the vast hangar, the plane, the flag. "All of this."

"See, about ninety-nine percent of your fellow citizens take their opportunities for granted. They think everything this country represents is solid, immutable, everlasting. Liberty and freedom in perpetuity. Theirs by the grace of God, just like Tom Jefferson said, endowed by our Creator with inalienable rights.

"And those ninety-nine percent almost *never* think about who's carrying the load. Who's standing on the wall, guarding their rights to *freedom, life, liberty,* and the *pursuit of happiness*. They just know it's someone else. And maybe, a few of them—like myself—know that someone else includes *you*."

Ryan raised his chin. He looked at the big vertical American flag that hung over the bomber, then down at the hulking aircraft itself, then at the junior people in the last row. There were no coughs now, no shuffling.

He went on.

"That's right. *You*."

"*You* are the people carrying that burden for them. And unlike the front row here, most of you folks don't wear colorful ribbons on your chest, stripes on your arms, or pins on your collars. So the worst part of the sacrifices you make for your fellow citizens, to give them that freedom, to allow them that pursuit of happiness . . . is that they never know to say thank you."

The President waited five seconds.

"Well, I, John Patrick Ryan, happen to hold the only elected office for which every citizen in this country has the right to vote. So, you see, in that respect, you can look on me as the representative of all those people, those ninety-nine percent.

"And *that's* why I came here today—as a representative of those American people whose freedoms you so vigilantly guard. On behalf of them, I came here to say thank you. To do it personally, to thank each and every one of you."

He looked left to the Air Force honor guard, standing at stiff attention. "Sergeant Kuhn. What do you think? Can we start with the back row?"

The President switched off the microphone and placed it on the red-carpeted platform floor. Then—much to the horror of his Secret Service guardians on either side of the stage—trotted down the center steps of the dais. Within seconds, he was immersed in the crowd, shaking hands, grinning, enjoying what was, for him, the very best part of the job.

It couldn't last, of course.

Though Jack was immersed in the crowd and loving it, van Damm eventually got to him. He took a firm grip on the President's triceps and urgently whispered in his ear.

Jack had been expecting his chief of staff to tell him to wrap this up, that they had to hurry down to Long Beach for the union meeting.

Instead, Arnie whispered that he had very critical news. Something that demanded his immediate attention.

It was about his son, Jack Junior.

UNDER PRESIDENT JACK RYAN, THE DIRECTOR OF NATIONAL INTELLIGENCE HAD been elevated to a cabinet-level position. Unlike many of his predecessors, Ryan was a leader who wanted regular interaction with his intelligence chief. He'd ordered Mary Pat Foley, his DNI, to relocate her office from her cubby at Liberty Crossing to the Eisenhower Executive Office Building, right next door to the White House.

Before then, Mary Pat had spent most of her time out at Langley, working closely with each of the leaders of her five so-called mission centers, which encompassed every counterthreat to just about anything a foreign actor could develop. But the President gets what the President wants, so she'd set up shop with her closest advisors on the third floor of the one-hundred-forty-year-old French Empire–style building on the White House grounds.

On this particular Saturday afternoon, the President was off in Los Angeles, which let her work in rare solace, undisturbed. She sat alone at her desk on the fourth floor beneath the broad attic windows that streamed in the autumn sun with her cardigan draped over her chairback. The radiator in this ancient marble edifice—once called the ugliest building in America by Mark Twain—never stopped ticking, even though the sun had raised the interior temperature to the high seventies.

In the Navy secretary's suite of offices down the hall, she could hear them listening to the Navy–Notre Dame football contest, groaning as the Midshipmen fell further behind. She pressed her hands hard over her ears as she concentrated on the satellite photo on her computer screen.

A sharp knock at the door interrupted her. She'd been expecting it.

John Clark shrugged out of his windbreaker as he strolled over the Persian carpet. "It's baking in here."

"I know. Too bad we sealed the windows shut and coated them with wave-deadening metallics to keep the snoops from the Russian embassy away."

The Campus director of operations rolled up his shirtsleeves and settled into the chair before her desk. He gestured at her computer monitor with the phone in his hand. "That the search area?"

"Yeah. The jungle around Lay Táo, where you said Jack was going—it's up near the Laotian border. Smack in the middle of the Golden Triangle."

"Right," said Clark. "How's our imagery quality out there? Any good?"

"No. NIIRS level three, at best. Not much better than Google Earth." She tilted the monitor so Clark could see the color photos.

Clark studied the screen, staring at the wide swath of green trees and brown rivers. The National Imagery Interpretability Rating Scale, used by all the intelligence agencies under Mary Pat's purview, went from zero to nine. A nine was good enough to read individual characters on license plates. Level three was only good enough to distinguish individual trees.

"I take it you've had no further reports on a crashed helicopter," said Clark.

"No." She removed her reading glasses and rubbed her eyes. "I've had some help from DEA. They say flights aren't monitored out in that area of Vietnam. There are no navaids, nothing. Out in that remote spot, if it crashed, it could go completely undetected."

"Right," said Clark. "And Howard Brennan reported in through Gerry that Stephenson liked to cowboy-it-up out there, flying around wherever he wanted. I doubt it was a direct flight from Hué to Lay Táo. What about SIGINT?"

"Still looking," she said. "But nothing so far. I've got—" She was interrupted when the Navy people down the hall briefly cheered at a rare Midshipmen touchdown against the Fighting Irish. "I've got NSA's ECHELON desk up, looking at intercepted phone calls. Nothing there. And since no one was operating a radar or communicating with the ground, there's just nothing to track when it comes to Stephenson's helo. Why was Jack flying out to the middle of nowhere, anyway?"

"According to Gerry and Howard, Jack saw some irregularities in GeoTech's mining operations. You know how he is. Once he sees a thread, he pulls it. He asked to get out to those mining sites to investigate directly."

"You think his helo going missing is an accident?"

"You don't?"

Mary Pat closed the satellite photos, finding them virtually useless. "I don't know, John. Seems like a mighty big coincidence that the principal executives involved in a deal for rare earth magnets with national security implications should just happen to disappear. Maybe this is MSS blowback for the Philippine op. That got messy, a lot of unwanted press. By now, MSS knows full well we were behind it."

Clark winced. "Yeah, I know. That's on me. But I'm not willing to conclude this crash is anything more than it appears. It was a private aircraft. Jack said Stephenson flew daringly. The man's seventy-three years old, piloting an old helo that he maintains himself. For all we know, it set down for maintenance. Old Army helos do that kind of stuff all the time."

She stared at him, unconvinced. "I think you know, John, that the rare earth magnets that come out of GeoTech are used by Quantum Atomics. They're used on some pretty sensitive, mission-critical projects—a sole supplier for us. The Chinese have every reason to want to screw this deal up."

"You mentioned NSA voice intercepts, ECHELON. I assume you're monitoring chatter with Beijing's Industrial Intelligence Directorate?"

She glanced up at the bright window over her head. "Yeah. I've looked."

"And?"

"Nothing there. But just like in the Philippines—this could be TALON. MSS has gotten much better at operating through surrogates. And if this is some kind of MSS op to take Jack alive through TALON, we're going to have a very nasty situation on our hands."

"If he's alive, we'll get him."

"How? It's not like I can send a CIA Special Activities team roaring around the jungles in Black Hawks. We can't refight the Vietnam War."

Clark, who'd cut his SEAL teeth in the old MACV SOG—the American special ops group from the Vietnam war—shoved at his drooping shirtsleeves. He found the heat in the office unbearable. "I've already got the Campus group from the Philippines heading over to Vietnam. They'll go in on business cover with legitimate visas obtained through Hendley Associates. They'll get up into those hills and conduct the search. They'll find him."

"The same Campus team that made us famous on YouTube? You sure that's a good idea?"

"It's the best idea we have. They'll be zero footprint, fully deniable. And if you're right . . . if this is TALON . . . then we'll want some tier-one operators on the ground. Even if it's . . . a recovery operation rather than an extract."

She held his gaze for a long while. The radiator ticked and the Navy people barked at their TV down the hall. She glanced at her desk clock. "Damnit," she said. "The President's speech just wrapped. Van Damm will have told him something by now."

"He should be on Marine One at this point. You ready for the call?"

A mother of two, the DNI sighed sadly. "No," she said. "I could never be ready for a call like this."

JACK RYAN, SR., FINISHED WAVING TO THE WELL-WISHERS THROUGH THE WINDOW as Marine One, the presidential helicopter, gained altitude.

Over the high desert plateau, he looked down at the small crowd, growing smaller. His eyes peered farther down the long runway, bleached nearly white. The second helicopter—a duplicate that acted as both spare and decoy—was just lifting off. Beyond it, two Black Hawks tilted forward, gaining speed in a swirl of dust. They carried his security people and the rest of his staff—including Arnie van Damm.

Gerry Hendley was leaning forward, elbows on knees. The helicopter had enough soundproofing that they had no need for headsets and intercoms. The President's old friend was the only one in the padded beige cabin with him.

Clark and Mary Pat Foley had been patched in via satellite. They'd just finished briefing Ryan on his son's missing helicopter.

Absorbing the bad news, the President watched jagged brown mountain peaks rise in the distance. Digital readouts on the forward bulkhead told him they were at three thousand feet, one hundred twenty knots. The clocks next to the gauges were listed in local time and Zulu, 1327 and 2127, respectively.

"What time is it in Vietnam?" he asked.

Mary Pat was quick to reply. "Half past one a.m., Sunday morning. They were expected up at the samarium mining sites about fourteen hours ago."

Ryan stared out the window, watching the helicopter's tiny shadow race over the sagebrush. He pressed his thumb and finger to his temple, the memory of his own Marine Corps helo crash ever fresh. That old Huey had left him with a broken back. One never forgets such things, he thought.

"Do we have actual evidence of a crash?" he asked. "Is it possible it could have landed for a maintenance issue?"

"Very possible," said Clark. "Especially in those remote hills. Tricky flying out there in that weather."

"But why can't we find the helo?"

"Mr. President," said Mary Pat over the speakerphone. "We've been scouring that area of the country, looking for any signs of a crash. The good news is that there are no prominent fires or smoke plumes or anything like that. That said, the canopy is thick out there and we don't have substantial surveillance coverage of that area. We're doing everything we can with what we can muster, quietly."

"Okay."

She went on. "That includes reaching out to trusted Vietnamese assets through Hanoi Station. Here's what I've got so far. The helo wasn't squawking on IFF, wasn't radioing with anyone. It wasn't on radar contact because it was flying low in the middle of nowhere, nap of the earth. Using the GeoTech sites as their intended landing point, we've boxed in a search area that extends southeast from the Laotian border, focused on the Ca river valley."

"What's it like?" he asked. "Are there villages? Some way to get to civilization?"

"The search grid maps to the Golden Triangle, according to DEA. Towns are scattered far apart with local gangs and cartels controlling the waterways."

"Drug trafficking?"

"Yes. Heroin. And human trafficking—a new growth area for them, according to DEA. Assuming Jack's helicopter landed safely, we'll want to get them into friendly hands quickly."

"Golden Triangle," Jack mumbled, thinking aloud. "Near Laos. We know Laos has gotten tight with China. Right?"

"Yes, sir," agreed his director of national intelligence. "Several Chinese party leaders have family ties to Laos. Beijing has gone big on Belt and Road there, building railways and a big hydroelectric dam on the Mekong. They see Laos as a bulwark against our strengthening ties with Vietnam."

"Right. With the Chinese influence in that region, could we get a CIA Ground Branch team in there for a search and extract? Quick? We can't let Jack fall into the wrong hands."

"We've got a level two presence in Vietnam, no permanent Special Activities people. We could get a team in undercover, maybe, but that takes a few days of planning to get right. There's also . . ."

"What?"

"Well, Mr. President, there's also the political aspect to consider. You're building a trusted relationship with the Vietnamese right now, a vital one. If we send Ground Branch door-kickers upriver into a denied-area op, it's going to dredge up a *lot* of unpleasant memories."

Staring at the blur of desert scrub below, the President knew she was right.

A CIA-backed team charging around the jungles of Vietnam could set back their relations fifty years, right when the United States needed Vietnam as a strategic ally—if for no other reason than to get their hands on enough samarium to power the next revolution in energy . . . and UMBRA.

"Okay, M.P.," he agreed. "What if I reached out to the Vietnamese government directly? I could speak with President Quang directly, couldn't I?"

"He'd inevitably confer with his own cabinet. DEA reporting tells us the Vietnamese government turns a blind eye to the Golden Triangle gangs. We assess that some of the old-guard Vietnamese ministers are on gang payrolls. If we go direct with our problem, it may well spark a race by the gangs to find Jack—and put scrutiny on the GeoTech deal that we don't want."

Ryan noted the time on the bulkhead clock again, trying to recall his schedule. After the rail union, he was to get back to the White House for a state dinner with the Indian prime minister. He couldn't cancel that. When it came to countering China, India was even more important than Vietnam—and twice as slippery.

"I'm working on another angle," said Clark. "I've got a Campus team headed there now."

"John and I have discussed all of it, Mr. President. We think that's our best option here," added Mary Pat.

The President turned to Gerry Hendley, who responded with a reassuring nod. He then looked out the windows, across the broad desert toward the picket line of brown mountains that marked the northern end of the San Fernando Valley. In just a few minutes they'd be at Long Beach, where he'd have to look happy in front of the cameras.

"I'm going to have to sign off here," he finally said.

"Yes, sir," Clark and Mary Pat answered in unison.

"Keep me updated."

"Jack," said Clark finally. "We'll bring him home. I promise you that."

The President continued staring out the window. "Thank you, John. I'm going to hold you to it."

19

**CA RIVER, VIETNAM
SUNDAY, OCTOBER 6**

"PUT YOUR ARM ON ME," SAID JACK RYAN, JR., AS HE DUG A FOOT INTO A LIMEstone divot. He could feel Howard's hand on his collarbone, hanging on for dear life. From the plateau where the *Belle* had crashed, they'd spent a dozen hours hiking to this bluff, judging it an easier descent to the river than the high cliff that had claimed Stephenson.

Now, trying to descend in the dark, ravaged by bugs and hunger, Jack wasn't sure it'd been worth it.

"My shoes aren't too good for this," mumbled the banker, painfully gouging his fingers deeper into Jack's shoulder.

Jack grunted under the strain of Howard's weight. "I got you. Just hang on to me. Only a few feet down until it levels a bit."

Getting through the jungle had been tougher than Jack had expected. The swollen trees grew tight as grass blades. They were strung with enormous creeping vines that grew in the canopy and hung to the jungle floor, tangling their feet. There were also liana wood vines that grew from the dirt, climbing up the trunks and spreading from tree to tree. Through it all, Jack and Howard had walked carefully, eyes darting to avoid poisonous snakes, venomous centipedes, and fire ants.

Worse, however, were the swarming mosquitoes.

"It's okay, Howard," Jack said, grunting to stay in position. "Use me like a railing, grab the vines around my chest . . . I have a good handhold here. I won't fall. Good, there you go. Get your right foot down another eighteen inches or so and press it into that divot. You'll feel a spot there. I swear it. Trust me."

If there was one paradoxical advantage to the jungle, Jack had thought on this trek, it had been those long vines. Using his necklace knife, he'd cut several lengths from tree branches. He'd peeled the leaves free, getting down to the strong fibrous stock. During their longest break, while Howard napped, Jack had woven together three strands of the denuded vines, forming a crude rope of sixty or seventy feet.

"I think I feel it," said Howard, hanging on the vines that wrapped Jack's chest.

"Good. I think you're there. If you let go, the most you'll fall is two or three feet."

"Right," answered the banker. He released his grip, fell to the loose slurry beneath him, and slid a few feet downhill with his hands in front of him.

"Nice!" Jack called from above. It was his turn now. He swatted a mosquito on his sweating neck and tried to see the terrain where Howard had come to a stop. It had rained twice that day, intense showers. The night sky was still overcast, silver in the moonlight.

"Look out," called Jack. "I'm going to have to jump."

Before Howard could protest, Jack jumped off the vertical boulder that had become such an obstacle. He flew two yards before landing in loose shale. His feet facing downhill, he fell to his back and dug his heels in. He skidded to a stop near Howard.

The banker had his hand extended, helping Jack up.

"Where do we go now?" panted Howard, looking down the next section of loose rocks.

Jack put his hands on his knees and caught his breath. The tree line that marked the end of the slope was still another two hundred yards down.

"That looks like a path there," Jack said, pointing. "See the shadows?"

"Pretty steep," muttered Howard.

Jack looked at the banker. He was leaning forward, his hands on his knees, rubbing them. His once-blue shirt looked like a mechanic's oily rag. His face was covered in bug bites. His Italian loafers were caked in mud.

"River's just on the other side of the trees," Jack reminded him.

"Yeah. Pretty thirsty. You?"

"I'm trying not to think about it."

"Same." Howard scratched a boil on his neck. "Sorry I mentioned it."

"There will be plenty of water as soon as we get through that last bit of jungle," added Jack. "You good?"

"All good," said the banker. "What's the plan to get down the rest of the way?"

From the beginning, Jack's thought had been to descend to a river and flag down a boat. Since Stephenson had been flying on a random course all his own, Jack didn't believe there'd be a significant search party looking for them in this area. The river, he thought, would be their only way out.

But they had to get to it first.

Jack looked at the rest of the slope. The dark trees were down there, a few hundred yards away. Somewhere beyond them lay the brown river. This last stretch of broken limestone marked the beginning of the end of their descent. The trouble, Jack realized, was that this final stretch of the bluff was steeper than it'd looked from above.

With his hands on his hips and the coil of vines around his neck, Jack leaned as far forward as he dared, looking for a suitable path. There was one, he saw in the moonlight, but it began below them, thirty feet away, nearly straight down.

Howard inched to the side of the ledge next to him. "Do we have to jump?"

Jack could imagine the damage that would do to the banker's wounded leg. Though he hadn't complained, Jack had seen Howard limping, rubbing his right knee whenever possible. Even now, the Hendley man was massaging it.

"If we jump," continued Howard gamely, "I'm thinking we'll land in some of that loose rock. The angle of the slope gets less severe. We'll slide to a stop before the trees."

There wasn't a chance in hell Jack was going to let Howard do that.

He looked back up the slope. Five feet over his head was a gnarled stump protruding from rocks. Whatever tree it had once been appeared to have died a century ago.

"Let me see something," said Jack. He pulled his coil of crudely woven vines from his neck and straightened it, letting its full length dangle over the edge to the looser rock below.

"You serious?" Howard asked, guessing what Jack had in mind.

"You're the one who proposed jumping, Howard. I'm suggesting we use the rope."

The banker picked up a section of vine. "You call it a rope. I call it a long weed."

"It's what we have."

Howard swatted hard at a mosquito on his neck. "I guess. Worst case, it's another form of falling. How's this going to work?"

Jack pointed to the stump over his head. "I'm going to loop it around that. Use it like a pulley."

Assured that it was long enough, Jack pulled his improvised rope back into a pile at his feet. At the rope's bitter end, he looped it around Howard's waist and tied a bowline knot, something he'd learned from his father when sailing on the Chesapeake.

"You hold on to this, okay?" He offered Howard a section of vine. "I'm climbing back up to put the rest of it around the stump."

"So I'm just going to jump?"

"No, Howard. You're going to walk backward with it. I'm going to feed it out to keep you from falling. You'll be fine."

"Okay. I get it."

Jack gave him a final clap on the arm and scrambled back up the slope with most of the coil around his shoulders. His feet slid often in the loose shale as he made his way up on hands and knees.

When he was parallel to the stump, he steadied himself and carved away a section of rough bark with his knife. It took him five minutes to expose a relatively smooth portion of wood. He looped his vine around it, then called down to Howard.

"Okay. You ready?"

"No."

"It won't be bad. Just walk backward. Look, the rope's taut. You'll be okay."

With the vine tied around his waist, Howard took a few steps in reverse while facing the bluff. Jack heard his feet slip, sending a shower of gravel down the slope. The banker cursed a few times as Jack paid out the vine. His head got lower and lower, finally disappearing over the far side of the ledge.

The vine continued sliding around the smooth portion of the stump. Jack looked at the remaining coil at his feet, suddenly worried there wouldn't be enough. If not, poor Howard would end up dangling like a marionette.

Then, mercifully, Jack saw the vine go slack.

"Woo-hoo!" Howard hollered up from below. The banker emerged from the shadows, sliding a few feet farther down. "Did it!" He pumped a fist in the air.

"You okay?" called Jack.

Howard gave him a thumbs-up. Though smeared with dirt and lumpy with bites, his face was exuberant in the moonlight. "Banged my knee up pretty good. But yeah." He bent to rub his leg, then looked up at Jack again. "Now how the hell are we supposed to get *you* down?"

"Let me bring up the rope."

After Howard took it off his waist, Jack pulled on his braided vine, hand over hand, until it was coiled near the stump. He tied a bowline around the stump's notch. He then detached his knife and shoved it in his pocket. He removed the carabiner that had held the knife to his neck chain.

He wrapped the end of the braided vine around his thighs in a figure-eight pattern, then clipped the carabiner to his belt buckle to form a makeshift rappeler's Swiss seat. He threaded the vine through the carabiner and threw the remainder over the edge, letting it hang down.

"You sure you're okay up there?" shouted Howard.

Jack ignored him. Facing the cliff, he fed the vine through the metal loop on his belt. When he leaned back, the friction on the carabiner acted like a break. When he leaned forward, the vine fed through the metal buckle with less resistance.

Backing over the loose shale, Jack kicked several shards loose, causing a mini avalanche.

"Hey!" called Howard from below. "Tell me what's going on!"

Jack leaned back, slowing his descent. He came to a stop, suspended by the vine. "I'm fine!" he yelled down.

"I just saw a bunch of rocks slide by. You sure?"

"Yeah. Sit tight. I'll be with you in a minute."

Leaning forward, he eased the vine out. His feet found the ledge where he and Howard had rested. Now for the hard part.

He stepped over the ledge, planting his feet, leaning at an angle that was nearly perpendicular to the bluff.

"How the hell are you doing that?" he heard Howard shout from below him.

Jack was too focused to answer. He was a few feet below the ledge, creeping down. His braided vine was taut and holding.

This is working, thought Jack with a glance over his shoulder. He glimpsed Howard below him, looking up while he scratched the bites on his face.

"You only have about ten feet left," Howard said. "Nice work, Jack. Amazing."

Indeed, thought Jack. He looked forward to telling Ding about his MacGyvered rappelling setup.

And then the stump gave way.

The vine above Jack broke free, going slack. He fell backward. Shoulders first, he landed on the loose shale slope just beyond Howard. He did three reverse somersaults, tumbling down the hill, smacking his head, before finally thumping into the base of a tree. As a final insult, the gnarled stump he'd so carefully prepared bounced down and hit him in the chest.

Howard was next to him a few seconds later. The banker had slid down the loose shale, coming to Jack's aid. He was on his knees. "Oh shit, Jack. Please tell me you're okay."

Jack ran his hands over his head and looked down his legs in a quick blood-sweep. "Yeah. I'm okay." His back against the tree trunk, he pushed himself to his feet, took the folding knife out of his pocket, and cut the vine from his waist. "Just a little embarrassed," he added. "Don't tell the boys around the office about that triple gainer I just did." He checked his old Rolex and removed the dust from its crystal. It was coming up on five a.m.

"Are you kidding me?" shot Howard. "That was spectacular! And look, we're at the tree line."

"Yeah," said Jack as he recoiled the vines around his chest and shoulders. "Let's go."

When Howard stepped forward, he winced and stopped.

"What?" Jack asked.

The banker pointed at his right knee. His pants had torn in the fall through the loose shale. "Banged this thing up pretty bad. Hurts like hell to bend it. Sorry, Jack."

"Don't be sorry. That was a bad fall. Stay here."

Jack wandered into the dark jungle. He found two fallen branches and cut them both to a length of about thirty inches. When he returned to Howard, the banker was sitting on the dirt, hugging his shoulders. "Getting cold," said the Hendley man.

"Hold these." Kneeling, Jack straightened Howard's right leg and put the two branches on either side of his damaged knee. Howard held them in place. Jack cut away a section of vine and wrapped the leg, forming a splint. "This ought to do you," he said. "Not much farther to go."

Jack felt the older man shudder. Glancing at the banker, he

saw that Howard was hugging himself tightly, shivering. Jack put the back of his hand to Howard's forehead. It was hot.

"Let's go," Jack said, pulling him up. "Lean on me. River's just on the other side of this thicket. Getting through it ought to be easy."

Getting through it was not easy.

With Howard clinging to Jack's shoulder, moving through the dense trees was slow. When they made it to level ground, the trees had broader leaves and were spaced farther apart. But the dirt got looser, grabbing at their feet. Every painful step through the muddy ground hurt Howard's wounded knee. The banker never complained.

When the sun was just coming up, they heard rushing water. The last obstacle in front of them was a thick tangle of thorny brush, growing at the river's edge, clutching at their every move. It took them an hour to cover the final twenty feet.

At seven a.m., the two men found a sandy bar along a wide river. Since they'd wound around the mountain all night looking for the easiest path down, Jack had lost his bearings. He didn't know if this was the Ca, where GeoTech sent its barges—or some other tributary.

For the moment, he didn't care.

He helped Howard to the river's edge. They cupped water in their hands, threw it on their scarred faces, and drank like animals. Then they lay on the sand, faces to the sky, and swatted at mosquitoes while the sun warmed them. Howard, Jack saw, was still hugging himself, shivering. Both men soon fell asleep.

Thunder woke Jack.

Sitting up, he saw Howard sleeping next to him, rolled to his side in a fetal position, his back covered in sand. Jack touched the banker's forehead and found it hot and sweaty. He hoped that meant the fever had broken.

Overhead, a dark overcast had crept in, streaked with purple. He heard another thunderclap and felt the first few pinpricks of rain.

He went back to the leafy bank and bent three saplings toward each other. He cut a section of his vine and tied the leaning trees together while the rain picked up. He tore several elephant ear–sized leaves from the ground shrubs, then layered them over the trees he'd tied together. He piled more leaves on the floor beneath the makeshift shelter.

"Have to get you out of the rain," he said to Howard, waking him.

The banker's eyes were wide and searching. "Oh, man," he said, rising. "I was having the weirdest dream."

"You've got a fever."

"I know. I'm not too worried about it. Think I just overdid it coming down the mountain." He went to stand, then nearly fell when he put weight on his injured knee. Jack lowered his shoulder and carried him to the bank, where he'd created the makeshift shelter. He gently lowered Howard to the leaves.

"You think we'll get out of here, Jack?" Howard asked, staring up at him, shivering.

Jack's mind wandered back to Stephenson, trapped in his pilot seat, crushed. He thought of his failure to pry that decent, honorable man loose. The crash had only happened because Jack had insisted on coming out to the mining sites personally. He bit his lip, anguished by guilt.

He squatted next to Howard and touched his face, turning it so they were eye to eye. "Listen, Mr. Brennan," said Jack. "If it's the last thing I ever do on this earth, I'm getting you back to Minnie. You hear me?"

Shaking with fever, Howard's lips quivered. "I appreciate that."

Jack helped him lie back, then covered him with a broad leaf.

The rain surged. Jack pushed his way back to the sandbar. He folded one of the broad leaves into a crude hat and strapped it to his chin with a vine. Water smashed into the river all around him, sizzling and popping. The thunder was louder, rolling through the hills.

Rolling thunder, he thought as he listened to it, recalling the massive American bombing operation in these hills, meant to break the back of the North Vietnamese Army. Bruce Stephenson, he thought, smiling faintly, would have appreciated the reference.

The sound of a slap on the water closer in forced Jack to turn his head upriver. He heard it twice more. Then, much to his relief, he realized the slaps were a hull banging against the current. Dark and low, a long sampan crested the bend.

Jack leaped to his feet and waved his leaf hat, flagging it down.

20

VIENTIANE, LAOS
SUNDAY, OCTOBER 6

A HUNDRED MILES WEST OF JACK, COLONEL CAI QI LISTENED TO THE THUNDER, too—though the rumbles hadn't woken him. Rather, he'd sprung awake when the girl sleeping next to him had stirred, jostling his sinewy arm and dragging the sheet from his chest.

To get free of her, Cai moved his elbow back, supporting himself at an angle in his bed. His heterochromatic eyes opened fully, taking in the morning. Gray light seeped through his window shades. His Mitsubishi wall-mounted air-conditioning unit hummed. The girl beside him lay still and naked. The sheet had slid from her brown waist.

Cai leaned his head back and yawned. Then he looked at the girl, studying her with a professional eye, pulling the sheet all the way off her. He knew she wouldn't wake up. The drugs they'd given her would make her sleep until eleven, at least.

She was small and slight with mocha skin and shining black hair. The mascara tattoo they'd applied to her lower lids accentuated her eyelashes. He could see her ribs. There wasn't an ounce of fat on this girl, Cai noticed. She was a good one.

He wondered where, exactly, they'd found her.

Based on her complexion, he guessed she'd come from somewhere up in the northwest—Chiang Mai, maybe Yangon. His men were getting a lot of them up in Yangon these days. They fetched a pretty penny on the markets in Ho Chi Minh and Bangkok.

Small wonder the men liked to forage up there. The farther one got out into the provinces, they'd told Cai, the easier the girls were to manage—since they knew so very little of the world. And look at the quality of them, he thought, noting the delicate curve of her calves, the slim ankles.

Cai yawned again. He heard the distant beat of thunder. A breeze thumped his shutters on the outside wall. His bedside clock told him it was nearing nine o'clock—later than usual for him.

Then again, as a Taoist, he saw nothing wrong with sleeping late. The natural rhythms of life were intricately interconnected, he believed—strung together by the mysterious Tao, the way of all things. Should the mighty, mysterious spirit decide that Cai should sleep a little longer today, then so be it.

Taoism, however, was not an excuse for sloth. He still had a schedule to keep, a routine to maintain. The girl's boat would leave at noon, running south along the Mekong, across Cambodia, and eventually on to Ho Chi Minh City. She might end up in Beijing, Pyongyang, Hanoi, or even Riyadh. None of that was of any real concern to Cai. The only thing that mattered was getting her to the dock on time.

Listening to the distant thunder, he found it hard to look away from her. He admired the swell of her slight breasts, the narrow cast of her thighs. With a solid decade of service ahead of her, she'd fetch a good price, he was sure.

Whoever had brought her in had a good eye. He almost wished he could keep her.

Ridiculous, he chided himself.

With the care of a merchant protecting his goods, he flopped the sheet back over her, then rotated his feet to the marble floor. Sitting on the side of the bed, he planted his hands at the base of his jaw and slowly twisted his neck. He felt for the usual pop at the bottom of his skull, then rotated his head several times, loosening up, preparing for the day.

He walked to his dresser and donned his black gym shorts, remaining shirtless. He picked up his phone and angled between the vertical blinds, stepping onto his wide veranda.

Though the thunder rumbled in the far foothills, the rain had yet to fall on the Mekong. He breathed deeply, taking in the smell of the river.

It was already hot outside, muggy, as it nearly always was in Vientiane, the Laotian capital. The monsoon breeze fluttered his short hair. Below, on the Mekong banks, he could hear the distant voice of a returning fisherman calling out instructions to his crew as they docked.

Cai leaned against his balcony rail and watched the river, sad to see its brown water running so low. He checked his text messages. Somewhat worryingly, Ling had yet to report in from his position on the Vietnamese border.

So be it. Cai placed the phone on the railing edge and looked out at the horizon. Up in the mountains where Ling was operating, the clouds were bunched, purple, and threatening. On the flatlands below them, a wispy curtain of rain dissipated before hitting the ground.

Cai hoped the monsoon was headed his way with a downpour for Vientiane. A week into October, the rainy season was approaching its end, the opportunity to swell the lakes nearly gone. It had been a relatively strong wet season—but looking at the high riverbanks, he thought, maybe not strong enough.

From the veranda where he stood, the river's near edge was obscured by wide palm trees. The far bank that Cai could see was cluttered with docks, boats, and houses with stilts planted in the mud.

Here, in Vientiane, the Mekong separated Laos from Thailand. Like the Amazon or Nile, it touched other national borders, flowing south through Cambodia and Vietnam before fanning into the South China Sea.

A shame to see it so low, Cai thought, sucking on his cheek, watching the fishermen drag their boats over the mud. Though he hoped this latest monsoon would help, he knew the real reason the Mekong was running low. It was because of the new Chinese hydroelectric dam twenty kilometers upstream.

Part of China's great Belt and Road Initiative, Cai had mixed feelings about that Chinese dam. On the one hand, he believed Laos needed the power to expand. On the other, if the river's flow sunk any lower, it would ruin the local economy. And, given how tightly the dam managers were constricting the flow, Cai guessed that most of the hydroelectric power must be feeding the Chinese grid up north.

That hardly seemed fair to him. As a man with some standing in Beijing, Cai's intent was to put in a word with the committee. But to do that properly, he needed to bring the GeoTech op to a successful conclusion.

He sighed and turned away from the river, walking the length of the veranda.

Cai's was a fine French house, built in the late forties, the honeymoon period after the Japanese occupation. French aristocrats had returned in force then. Profiting from exported rubber, jute, and sugar, they'd built houses with towering ceilings, charming balustrades, and wide, elevated porches to capture the river breeze—like Cai's.

The Laotian stopped walking in front of the hanging bag and leaned over to stretch his hamstrings. His glutes seemed a little tight from all the effort of the prior evening with the girl.

He whirled on the bag, leading with his elbow. After a step back, he slammed it with his bare foot. He repeated ten more warm-up kicks, steadily increasing his power.

After thirty minutes of the Muay Thai workout, Cai was glazed with sweat. Breathing hard, he stopped to check his phone again. There was a message there, finally—but not the one he'd been hoping for.

Panting and wet, he took a chair and read his phone carefully. The message consisted of a long string of numbers followed by a code that told him it was urgent, critical, priority one.

He dialed the number and held the phone to his damp ear. There was an answer on the other end, but no voice, just a series of clicks. Cai suspected those clicks were MSS's encryption regime, though he was no technician.

When the clicks finally stopped, he heard the quiet hiss of a live connection. Into it, he said, *"Zài ma?"* Who's there?

"Zǎoshang hǎo." Good morning.

Cai echoed the greeting. Control, his Beijing handler, started every conversation this way. Then, as always, without preamble, the first question came through. "Are you concerned about the acquisition, Cai Qi?"

Cai had never met the man he knew only as Control. "No," he answered. "The acquisition is proceeding."

After a delay of a few seconds, Control replied, "We do not think so here. We have concerns."

Cai thought about how to respond to that, wondering how hard he could push back. By statutory rank, he was an MSS colonel. More consequentially, however, his father had been a childhood friend of the chairman before coming back to Laos as a Beijing-friendly foreign minister. The old connection, Cai believed, afforded him a certain amount of leeway. He was never sure how much.

"You do not need to be concerned," he responded. "*Yángròu* is in place, as planned." *Yángròu*, Mandarin for "Lamb," was Control's code name for Cai's asset—David Highsmith.

There were a few clicks in the interval before Control came back. "Can you confirm that *Yángròu* has the authority to proceed? To finish the acquisition?"

"Yes. I can confirm that. *Yángròu* is the acting CEO now, as spelled out in company succession documents. I will make sure he stays there. I see no risk to the acquisition."

There was a hiss while Cai waited. The line clicked twice.

"And *Niu*?" asked Control. *Niu*, Bull, was their code name for Bruce Stephenson.

"As reported and approved, we took *Niu* out. He is confirmed dead."

There were several clicks on the line while Control remained silent. Cai was never sure if that meant someone was listening—or if it was just encryption. Probably both.

He watched the Mekong, waiting for Control's comment. In the clicking void, he thought of his parents, who'd also stood on this veranda with Cai when he was a boy. As the family of a senior government minister, they'd all lived well back then—until

Cai's parents had been murdered by Hmong rebels at a café, just two blocks into town.

Back then, the now-Chairman had sent condolences to the orphaned Cai, inviting him to Beijing, securing him a spot in the MSS's clandestine foreign directorate. After five years of training, they'd sent him back to Vientiane to build his network.

Control's delayed response had become worrying.

"Are you there?" Cai asked.

"Yes. I am here. You must know, Colonel, that we need to find the auditors."

And there's the problem, thought Cai.

One of Ling's boats had found the hulk of the dead helicopter along the Ca River. *Niu*, Stephenson, was found strapped to the smashed pilot's seat with much of his body burned. The two American auditors who'd been with him had yet to be located.

Still. Based on scorch marks in the jungle, Ling had reported that the helicopter had tumbled down a long slope before ending up overturned in the river. The auditors had surely been flung out somewhere along the way. The likelihood of survival was nil.

"I do not yet have confirmation on the auditors," confessed Cai. "But we suspect they were also killed in the crash."

A click-laden pause. Cai waited. Control's eventual response irritated him. "You must shut down trafficking operations until the auditors are recovered."

Cai squeezed the phone tightly. *Shut down trafficking operations?* Those operations were how he financed the Snakehead gang's operations in the Golden Triangle—at Control's direction, no less. It was how he'd managed to sink his hooks into *Yángròu*, David Highsmith, in the first place. He'd been told his work was highly strategic—now Control wanted him to shut it down?

"I cannot shut that down," he said firmly. He didn't bother to elaborate.

"Yes. You will shut down the operation, Cai Qi, until you either recover the bodies of the auditors or bring them in alive. We must be sure."

"I will find the auditors. But I will not shut down the operation. No."

A very long sequence of clicks while Cai waited. He wondered again about his real power, hoping he hadn't gone too far.

Finally, Control returned. "Explain yourself."

He took a deep breath before proceeding. "If I shut down the operation, I will lose the support of the Snakeheads. They are the ones who control the rivers and villages out there. They're the ones who can find the auditors, dead or alive. If I shut down the trafficking—drugs, women . . . all of it—then the men won't comply. You must understand that, Control."

Another blank interval, more clicks. Cai heard a second fisherman on the Thai side of the river barking at dockworkers.

"You have explained yourself, Colonel. Now let me do the same."

This is new, thought Cai. Then again, he'd never pushed back on a direct order. He waited.

"We have reasons to believe we may be compromised."

"Why?"

"You yourself reported a man missing in Hong Kong, where the auditors had been before coming to Vietnam. So had the Vietnamese woman your man had been following."

"You mean Twei. Yes, losing him was unfortunate. But *Yángròu* reports no trouble. And you told me the auditors were kept under strict surveillance in Hong Kong, that they only tended to HSBC business. We have no reason to believe the Vietnamese woman did anything in Hong Kong except shop."

"And yet. You lost Twei. In Kowloon. Our branch there disposed of his body."

Cai breathed deeply. That much was true—Twei, one of the two men he'd taken to Beijing for formal MSS training years ago, had been found dead in a Kowloon wet market.

Cai didn't know what, exactly, had happened to his man. He had a theory.

Men like Twei might accept formal MSS training, but they never really stopped being who they were. Cai had assumed Twei had been running drugs or women on the side and had run afoul of a rival in Hong Kong. He'd been garroted with a clothesline, according to the Hong Kong police reports obtained by MSS. Foreign intelligence services didn't operate that way.

"Moreover," continued Control. "We don't know how much the Hendley auditors know. If they're alive, we want you to bring them here, to Beijing. If not, you must make their bodies disappear. Either way, they must never be found. That is of grave importance to us. Your work is very strategic. Do you understand, Colonel?"

Cai looked back to the north at the rising thunderheads. A pre-storm breeze rippled the river water and cooled his sweaty forehead. He closed his eyes for a moment, listening to the faint cries of the fishermen as the first raindrops fell. The rain, he thought, was a good sign, a direct message from the Tao.

The Tao's message reminded him of the hydroelectric dam and his plan to put in a word with Beijing to increase the flow. He could only do that, he knew, if he remained in Control's good graces. Apparently, he realized now, that would mean finding these missing Hendley men in the northwestern Vietnamese jungle, dead or alive.

"I will have the men put a hold on the operation," he said.

"And I will find these auditors, quickly. I will direct the search myself, Control."

"We are very pleased to hear that. We expect better news tomorrow, Colonel."

When the connection closed, Cai stared at the distant storm clouds, rubbing his chin. His men would certainly rebel over ceasing the trafficking operations until they recovered the auditors' bodies. But in the end, if Cai satisfied Control, he could press his points to Beijing about the hydroelectric dam. Cai's own father would be proud of him for that.

As Cai saw it now, his search for the auditors was just another thread woven into the broad tapestry of the Tao, the way of all things. The storm, the river, his father's death, and even Control's call all fit together. Perfectly.

21

CA RIVER, VIETNAM
SUNDAY, OCTOBER 6

"**BẠN LÀ AI? BẠN LÀ AI?**" **SAID A MAN WITH THICK BLACK HAIR, PROTRUDING RIBS,** and crooked teeth. With his pockmarked face, lean arms, and muscled back, Jack thought he could be anywhere from twenty-five to sixty.

The ageless river pilot was clinging to a tiller, just forward of a large, exposed Ford truck engine. Behind the V8, a long drive-shaft angled back to the water where it cranked a submerged propeller.

Jack spoke slowly to him, trying to tell the man they needed to get to civilization. A hunched woman in black came to the stern from beneath the sampan's thatched roof. She tied a conical hat around her head and tried to understand Jack. Her face was lined and sympathetic.

After sorrowfully wagging her head, the woman went below the thatched roof. She returned with pieces of dried fish and cut melon. Abandoning all efforts to communicate, Jack brought the food under the shelter and shared it with Howard. The banker was leaning against the bulkhead, shivering.

The fish tasted like bland jerky, thought Jack, grateful nonetheless. When she returned with more melon, Jack pointed to Howard's pocked neck, where the mosquitoes had savaged him the worst. She went below and came back a few seconds later carrying a jar of light blue fluid.

"*Thuốc*," she said, pouring the oozy liquid into her fingers and smearing it on Howard's skin.

"Please say thank you to her," mumbled Howard. He was clutching his arms, shaking. The woman brought a blanket and put it over him. "*Thuốc*," she said again.

Jack stood up, looking over the thatched canopy, letting the rain pelt his face. The sampan was headed downstream. The Vietnamese pilot and his wife had pointed its bow that way, hopefully understanding Jack's hand gestures well enough to ferry them to the closest village. Jack assumed that would be with the eastward current, away from the mountains and Laos.

Confident that he would soon get Howard to safety, Jack thought of Stephenson again. He would want to find Stephenson's body, to bring him back to the U.S. for his family. It was the least Jack could do. He tapped the Vietnamese river pilot on the shoulder and mimed a helicopter crash with his hands, trying to ask if they'd seen a wreck.

The man's face twisted into a grin, as though he understood. Jack doubted it, but appreciated the effort.

He gave up and resumed his position next to Howard. The woman offered Jack some of the blue fluid. He smeared it on his own bug bites, covering his neck. Howard's eyes were closed. Jack could feel him shivering under the blanket.

The roar of the motor behind them fell to a clanking idle.

Drifting with the current, the man at the tiller steered them for a bank.

"*Ho ó dây,*" he shouted, pointing.

Unsteady in the boat's following wake, Jack got to his feet. He held on to the post of the canopy and followed the man's gesture. A large speedboat approached them, he saw, closing quickly. One man stood on the bow, another two at the stern.

Jack ducked down immediately.

Two of them were carrying AK-47s.

22

HO CHI MINH CITY, VIETNAM
SUNDAY, OCTOBER 6

"GOOD NEWS," SAID JOHN CLARK OVER THE VIDEO CONFERENCING CONNECTION ON Lisanne's Toughbook. "Your mission is a rescue, not a recovery."

Sandwiched between Cary and Jad in their Saigon hotel suite, Lisanne unconsciously touched her bandaged shoulder. It was the best news she'd heard in the last miserable twenty-four hours.

She was in the chair at the suite's small desk. Cary had slid an ottoman over to one side of her. Jad had perched himself on the arm of a stuffed chair. Master Chief Kendrick Moore stood behind them. It was late morning. Rain slapped hard against the hotel windows.

"Jack's alive?" she asked.

"Probably," hedged Clark. "We can't be sure. But the new intel puts the odds in his favor."

She frowned at Clark's equivocation. It was one thing to use the usual ambiguous words of the intelligence trade in a report on terrorist hits. It was quite another to use them when it came to Jack Ryan, Jr.

The previous day she'd left the Subic hospital with her new stitches and her deep chest bruise. Along with Moore, Mustafa, and Marks, she'd boarded a charter jet at Cubi Point, just down the hill. It was only then that she'd learned Jack was missing—and that the team's new mission was to find him, dead or alive.

"What's the intel?" she asked her boss curtly. Between the pain of her injury and the despair over Jack's crash, she hadn't slept since Subic.

"NSA's had ECHELON tuned in to that area," answered Gavin. The Campus infotech specialist was sitting across from Clark. They were in the underground Campus conference room that was buried below Hendley's Arlington office, abutting a pistol range. The cipher lock on the ground-floor stairwell door ensured that Hendley's white-side employees never entered it. "We got a hit that speaks of survivors. It even mentioned the word 'Americans.'"

Lisanne blinked at the mention of NSA's highly secretive voice intercept program. "ECHELON? Really? You have direct access into the feed?"

"Correct," Gavin confirmed. "And I can tell you this much, the NSA operators are all over the search area. I gather from cross talk that this is the highest priority for them. Sounds like the orders came direct from the White—"

Clark held a hand up, cutting Gavin off.

"Our high-level intel contact set us up with the feed," said the Campus director of operations. "The search area is within the Golden Triangle. DEA has used ECHELON in the past to go after narco-traffickers. We're just tapping into what already existed."

Lisanne studied the two men on her Toughbook screen. She thought they couldn't have looked much different from one another. Clark was rangy and hard with surprisingly bright blue eyes. Gavin was thirty pounds overweight, much of his face covered by a reddish beard.

Cary leaned sideways into her. He was in the new civvies they'd picked up in a Saigon market—blue jeans and a plaid short-sleeve shirt. "So—what did this ECHELON intercept say? It was definitive about Jack, Mr. C.?"

"No, not definitive. ECHELON intercepted a brief cell call conducted in Laotian," said Clark. "DEA reporting suggests the dialect and phone prefixes are consistent with the gang members they've seen operating up in the Golden Triangle."

Clark pulled Gavin's laptop in front of him. "Here, I'll read you the raw translation." He donned his reading glasses and mumbled for a moment. "Okay. According to the NSA translation, a remote caller in that region says he picked up two men that he called, and I quote, Americans."

"Two men."

"Yes." Clark nodded, removing his glasses.

"Then that could be Stephenson and Howard."

"It could be. Or Stephenson and Jack. Or Jack and Howard. Either way, we have two men to rescue. At least one of them is one of our own. And Stephenson's a good man—won the Silver Star for his medevac exploits at the tail end of the war."

"Maybe the caller's a friendly," suggested Jad. "Maybe they're on their way to a village or something."

"I doubt it," said Clark.

"Why?"

"Because I haven't read the rest of it, Sergeant Mustafa." Clark replaced his reading glasses and studied the screen. "The response from the other side of the call said—quote—bring them in immediately—alive."

Lisanne's spirits sank. "Bring them in *alive*? Like it's a choice? Really?"

"Yes. Really."

"And it's a Laotian dialect?" she followed up. "Can we triangulate the call?"

"It's Laotian. We don't have full triangulation because there aren't enough cell sites out there. One of the towers is near the border with Laos, close to a highway. The other one was an internet call through WhatsApp. Because of that, we have no location."

"That's bad," said Lisanne. "If they're near a highway, then they could already be moving farther inland, way out of reach."

"Agreed," said Clark. "Which is why you all need to move fast. Our high-level intel contact is concerned about the cozy relationship between Laos and China. And, without saying too much, you need to know that the white-side deal Jack and Howard were closing gives the U.S. critical access to non-China rare earth minerals. Without a doubt, we need to get our people back because they're our people—but also because they can't fall into Chinese hands. Clear?"

"Clear, sir," barked Moore. The master chief wore a blue T-shirt. In front of him, Lisanne leaned her chin on her hand, slowly shaking her head.

"Again," added Clark, reading her body language. "The good news is that this is an extraction op. Let's take some comfort in that."

"It's still a recovery op for one body," said Lisanne. "Goddamnit."

"True," said Clark. "But you can imagine which of those two missions takes priority for us. For now, anyway."

"Copy, sir," said the master chief. "We're on it."

"The cell communication is all we have?" asked Cary. "No other amplifying intel like imagery, thermals, any of that stuff?"

"Negative," Clark responded dryly. "So far, this is all we've got."

They were all silent for a moment. Gavin slid his laptop across the table, recovering it from Clark. He typed a few lines. "Hey, Lis, I'll work on getting as many other feeds going as I can. As soon as I have more intel, you'll be the first to get it."

She lifted her head from her hand. "All right. Thanks, Gav."

"Hey," added Clark. "Just like Mindanao, this needs to be a zero-footprint, deniable op. Whether the extract is Jack and Howard or some other combination doesn't matter. Get them back. ASAP. Quietly. Understood?"

"We won't let you down, sir," said Moore.

"Hell no," echoed Jad.

"We'll get 'em," finished Cary. "The Green Berets were born in this country. These mofos are about to find out we're back."

"Same with the SEALS," added Moore, looking at Clark. "But, of course you know that, sir." Clark's exploits with MACV had reached legend status.

Only Lisanne delayed her answer. "Listen. Before we all cry gung ho and dive out of C-130s, I have to ask, Mr. C.—why don't we have the Vietnamese government conduct a search? They could be out there with air assets right now."

Clark eyed her carefully. "Unfortunately . . . a Vietnamese government op is off the table. DEA tells us that several of the older government ministers are on the payroll of Golden Triangle traffickers. Our high-level intel contact thinks that involving the Hanoi government will all but ensure the kidnappers will kill the hostages, hiding the evidence of those relationships."

"I see," she said, swallowing. "And CIA? Couldn't we get help from Ground Branch?"

"Negative," Clark replied. "Ground Branch isn't in country. Sure, we could get them on a plane, but there are a lot of bad memories about the CIA operating in the Vietnamese countryside. Especially up there. Ever heard of Operation Phoenix? Lot of bad juju. The long and the short of it is that we've concluded Campus is our best option. Besides, we need to look after our own people."

"Understood," she said. She felt Moore's hand on her good shoulder, warm and comforting.

"Sir," said the master chief, leaning down to be seen in the camera. "While this intel is good . . . it's not actionable. We're going to need a lot more, quickly."

"Understood. You have ECHELON, which could spit out a new intercept any second. And it's probably safe to assume that if we're looking at a ransom demand, we'll be able to zero in on a location. When that happens, I need you to be ready. Consider yourselves on priority alert."

"Strong copy," said Moore, rising out of the frame.

"We'll be ready," echoed Cary. "Count on it, Mr. C. We'll get them."

23

GIANG RIVER, LAOS
SUNDAY, OCTOBER 6

JACK SAT ROCKING BACK AND FORTH ON THE METAL BENCH SEAT NEXT TO HOWARD. His wrists were zip-tied behind him, his ankles strapped to deck bolts. Howard had been given the same treatment.

They were just aft of the boat's center, covered by a fabric canopy that deflected some—not all—of the late-afternoon rain. The water fell in sheets from a low gray sky, roiling the brown current. Whenever the helmsman spun his wheel to keep the boat on its upstream course, rain stung their faces.

Sitting on the starboard bench opposite Jack and Howard was a man with a Fu Manchu goatee, an inked neck, and an AK-47. He was oblivious to the rain, his eyes never straying from the two hostages. The boat's third crewman was on the bow, sitting exposed to the elements on the grated metal platform over the anchor tackle. Most of the time, the bowman faced into the wind with his AK resting across his knees.

Behind the forecastle where the bowman sat was another metal bench that ran side to side. Jack had noticed the bench was hinged, doubling, he reckoned, as a storage locker. Somewhere below the forward bench, buried in the hull, was a piston engine, screaming like a hot rod.

As the speedboat raced on, Jack saw the bowman turn his head and call something back to Fu Man.

Fu Man swiveled his head with a shouted response. Over the clattering engine, the three-man crew had frequently barked at each other in their monosyllabic dialect. Having heard plenty of Vietnamese and Chinese at this point on his Asian trip, Jack heard the difference in this language. He believed it was Laotian.

Wet and shivering, noting their guards' distraction, Howard leaned into Jack. "What do they want from us? They're heroin guys, right?"

Jack waited for Fu Man to answer the bowman. He lowered his mouth to Howard's ear. "Remember my report on the political risks to the GeoTech acquisition?"

"*Khongyu!*" shrieked Fu Man. He raised his rifle stock and mock-jabbed it at Jack, staring threateningly.

Jack held the guard's stare. After a few seconds, Fu Man broke away, looking up the river. Three minutes passed before he was chattering with the bowman again.

Jack leaned close to Howard's ear. "We're in the Golden Triangle. I think these guys are druggies or traffickers of some kind. They're going to hold us for ransom."

Howard struggled through a shivering nod.

"Huddle next to me," said Jack. "Use my body warmth."

The banker scooted as close as he could to the Campus operative. The flat-bottomed boat bumped over a wake, slamming them down on their metal seats, jarring their spines. Howard winced.

"Hey," Jack whispered. "We're only good to them alive. We'll get out of this."

His eyes shut, the banker shook.

"*Bo!*" Fu Man hopped to his feet with his AK braced.

He viciously kicked Howard in the shin, then thrust his rifle stock to an inch in front of the banker's face.

Fu Man laughed when Howard flinched. He said something to the helmsman behind them, who snorted before pulling hard on the wheel, leaning the craft into another speeding turn. Fu Man sat down again, glowering at Howard.

One thing was for sure, thought Jack as the boat soared over a white boil of rapids. This was nothing like the old couple's sampan that had initially rescued them. This speedboat had a big gas engine under the metal deck and water jets at the stern that kept it on a plane, letting it ride easily over the rapids and shallows.

Though its metal decks were checkered with rust, the craft was solid. In addition to the center storage seat, its fore-and-aft benches were welded to the port and starboard bulkheads under the canopy. At the boat's stern, a three-foot-wide steering console was welded to the deck like an immovable lectern.

Jack felt a fresh dash of cold rain on his face and shook his head. He pushed himself closer to Howard, whose shivering had only gotten worse. Looking over Howard's head, Jack surveyed the narrowing river, trying to figure out where, exactly, they were.

Miles earlier, the craft had shot through a three-headed river fork, veering up the smallest of the three tributaries. Since then, the surrounding hills had gotten taller, crowding in on the river.

The sky had turned leaden, hiding the sun. Jack only knew the time of day through an occasional glimpse of his old Rolex, which now dangled on the helmsman's skinny wrist. The pirates had stolen it from Jack just as soon as they'd taken him and Howard off the old couple's sampan at gunpoint.

Though Jack didn't know anything about this tributary or how far they'd traveled up it, he was sure of one thing—his odds of escape were dropping the farther upriver they went.

With Howard shivering next to him and Fu Man calling to the foredeck once more, Jack resumed his attempt to sever the thick zip ties around his wrists. They were attached to a padlock that had been secured to a ringbolt welded to the port bench. By moving his hands back and forth over the padlock's hasp, Jack thought he might weaken the zip tie. After three hours of the motion, it hadn't worked. The restraints remained tight and strong.

When they'd first been taken aboard the speedboat, the crew of river pirates had wasted no time robbing Howard and Jack, relieving them of their wallets and watches. They'd even stripped Howard's wedding band from his finger.

The one thing they hadn't found, however, was the necklace knife below Jack's shirt. Now, straining against his zip ties, Jack fantasized about the knife. Its folding blade would make quick work of the plastic.

He looked aft to get another glimpse of the helmsman, who wore Jack's stolen watch. He appeared to be the oldest of the three crewmen. And since he steered the boat, barked out orders, and had taken possession of the stolen trinkets, Jack figured him as the leader. A few miles upriver of their capture, Jack had seen the helmsman use a flip phone. Among the foreign chatter, he thought he'd heard the man say a word that sounded like *Americans.*

The sky was getting darker. Whether that was due to a worsening storm or approaching dusk, Jack didn't know. He tried once again to snatch a glimpse at his watch on the leader's wrist—but the helmsman had turned away.

He was facing rearward, cupping his hands to his mouth, lighting a cigarette with a silver Zippo. Jack could see a stubby pistol tucked in the leader's leather belt. From here it looked like an old Russian Makarov.

When the leader turned around, Jack saw him flip the lid of the Zippo closed. He caught Jack looking at him. He glared at the American and called to Fu Man, who stood up and poked the sharp barrel of his AK into Jack's chest.

Yes, Jack thought. The helmsman was definitely the man in charge of this crew. When Fu Man sat down again, Jack resumed his covert hand motion against the padlock.

"*Heu ma! Heu ma!*" shouted the bowman a half hour later.

"*Heu ma!*" echoed Fu Man, his head snapping back at the helmsman.

The crew's leader yanked the engine throttles to idle. The boat slowed abruptly, throwing Jack and Howard forward against their restraints. Looking at the nearby banks, Jack saw that the boat was drifting backward with the current, turning slowly sideways.

Fu Man stood up, steadied himself against the roll, and pointed his AK at Jack's face. Out of reflex, Jack looked away. Fu Man backhanded him.

After tossing his cigarette overboard, the helmsman came forward. He barked a few instructions at Fu Man, then repeated them in a louder voice to the man up front.

Jack watched the lead pirate kneel on the metal deck. He was at the boat's center, under the canopy, slightly forward of Jack and Howard, but behind the sideways bench.

The leader's hands worked on flat buckles embedded in the

steel boat deck. As they drifted sideways in the current, Jack caught a brief, upriver view. He suddenly understood why the crew had sprung into action. Ahead, there were two sampans traveling together, rounding a distant bend, headed downriver—toward them.

Howard leaned into Jack. He'd seen them, too. "What do you think they're gonna do?"

"Not sure yet."

Fu Man saw Jack whispering. With his AK slung at his shoulder, he rose from the starboard bench and slapped Howard. The banker took it stoically, refusing even to wince, saying nothing.

Jack watched the crew's leader lift a long rectangular hatch from the deck, tilting it up. Craning farther, Jack could see into the storage compartment the hatch had covered.

His view was suddenly blocked by the bowman, who'd run down the port gunwale and stood in front of them. Now he leaned into Howard, cut the zip ties at his ankles, and opened the padlock that held the banker's wrists. Fu Man jerked Howard to his feet.

"*In!*" the helmsman shouted at the banker, gesturing with his left arm, the one with Jack's Rolex.

Howard stole a questioning glance at Jack. Fu Man saw it and slammed his AK stock into the back of Howard's knees. The banker fell.

With his zip ties pinning his wrists behind him, the bowman and Fu Man hoisted Howard into the belowdecks storage locker. Jack could only see his colleague's shoulder blades.

"*In!*" the helmsman shouted at Jack.

It was Jack's turn.

The bowman cut his ankles free, then opened Jack's lock and pulled him to his feet. Fu Man kept his AK aimed squarely at

Jack's forehead. The leader stood beside the hatch, pointing at the space in the belowdecks storage locker next to Howard.

On his feet, finally freed from the metal bench, Jack thought of his options. Going through his OODA loop, he considered jumping backward over the boat's side. The bank was close, the other sampans approaching. Even with his wrists pinned behind him and men shooting at him, he thought he could dive and escape.

Another glance at Howard's shaking shoulders redirected the thought. He wouldn't leave the banker alone, no matter what.

Fu Man swung his rifle butt into Jack's knees. Expecting it, Jack had already bent them, which helped cushion the blow.

He was thrown into the locker a moment later, banging his jaw against the flat-bottomed boat's metal hull. His immediate sensation was that of a bath. Warm liquid sloshed around him, bilgewater. He had to tilt his face to breathe. The metal hatch slammed down, banging his head. He heard them snapping the buckles on the deck above. Darkness closed in.

"You okay?" Howard mumbled a second later. The storage compartment was about eight feet long and two feet deep, spanning the boat's beam. The sloshing bilgewater smelled of oil. The boat's engine was a yard in front of them on the other side of a thin bulkhead, rumbling at idle.

"Yeah. I'm fine. You?" Jack replied. With arms behind him and only a few inches of free space over his back, he moved awkwardly toward the center.

"I get a little claustrophobic."

Jack rolled as far as he could onto his right side. He backed his hands until they touched Howard's arm.

"The compartment's wide. We can still move. And at least it's warm."

SHADOW STATE

"Right." Jack could feel Howard's arm trembling.

"Hey—we're only going to be down here for a minute or two. They're hiding us from approaching boat traffic. They need us alive for a ransom deal. Just remember that."

The engine suddenly roared to life. What before had been uncomfortable in the bilge, now became unbearable. Fuel fumes spewed from up forward. With the bow rising in acceleration, oily water from the boat's forward bilges streamed over them.

The engine was screaming like a dragster, maxed on RPMs. The hull bucked hard against a wave, slamming Jack's cheek off the metal. With the speedboat leveling on a plane, the bilgewater came sloshing back from behind. Jack heard Howard cough.

This, Jack thought, was a whole new level of suck.

He'd been through something like it once before. It had been his SERE training—survival, evasion, resistance, escape. Clark had brought a Special Forces SERE instructor out to his Virginia farm for the training. The man had done terrible things to Jack during that exercise. It'd been nearly as nightmarish as this.

Nearly.

The worst part, Jack recalled, was when the instructor stripped him naked, shoved him into a pickle barrel, covered it with a grate, and filled it with water. Jack's only way to breathe had been to press his lips against the grate for hours on end, fighting panic.

Your worst enemy is your imagination, the instructor had repeated over and over from outside the barrel. *It's the fear factory. You aren't drowning—you just fear you will. Master that fear, Jack, master it . . .*

Dizzy with fumes, Jack conjured the entire lecture—the man's navy-blue shirt, the greasy old workshop table in Clark's barn, the cast of the summer sunlight through the wooden planks.

The boat thudded over a swell, slamming him back to the present. He swallowed some of the disgusting bilgewater and spit it out, trying not to gag. To explore the cargo hold, he wiggled away from Howard, trying to get to the port side, banging his head off the closed hatch above.

When he got to the port bulkhead, a searing heat burned his left elbow. He jerked away from it. Oily water went up his nose when the boat went into a left turn. Jack was flung against the heat source again. He writhed furiously, trying to get away from it. Bilgewater went down his throat when he coughed.

Master that fear, Jack.

The boat leveled out. With the cough under control, Jack forced himself to lie still. The engine made it too loud to check on Howard.

What had scalded him? he wondered.

Give your head something to do, the SERE instructor had said to him back at Clark's farm.

There's an engine in front of me, he thought. He pictured the way a marine motor should work. Where a car's engine had a closed-loop system for liquid cooling, a boat used the water in which it traveled.

That meant, thought Jack, that there would be an impeller somewhere to let cool river water circulate around the engine. Similarly, once heated, that water would need to be ejected over the side.

He sloshed to the port bulkhead again. This time, he maneuvered his hands carefully near the heat source and felt three rubber hoses. One was warm, one cold, one neutral. He assumed the warm one was the water flowing back from the engine, headed over the side. But it wasn't hot enough to scald him.

Lying on his stomach, he twisted to his left and groped again.

Now he touched red hot metal and jerked away from it. He assumed it was the engine's exhaust pipe, running to the stern. Earlier, when the boat had idled, he'd noticed the smoke rising behind the helmsman.

The boat bucked again. Jostled, he accidentally bumped his knuckles against the hot exhaust pipe, burning them. Howard coughed furiously, knocking Jack in the leg.

Enough of this.

Jack scrunched himself up against the tubes. He shoved his bound hands against the hot exhaust pipe. The pain at his wrists was excruciating. He grit his teeth, enduring the searing hell, wondering if this would even work. Was it hot enough to melt plastic?

Clenching his jaw so tightly that it seemed his teeth might break, he jerked and pulled at the zip ties. He felt a slight give.

They snapped.

Yes, yes, yes!

He pulled his hands back along his sides, grateful for the bilgewater now, which cooled the burn.

With his hands freed, he pushed himself over to Howard and squeezed his shoulder. The engine was still maxed out, screaming just in front of them. Jack turned his head sideways and used his free right hand to cup Howard's ear. "Hey," he said into it. "My hands are free. I'm getting us out of here. Be ready to follow my lead."

Howard signaled his understanding by moving his head.

Sliding his burned wrists up his body to his neck, Jack found the knife on its chain and carabiner. He freed it, unfolded the blade, and cut Howard's wrists loose.

Still on his stomach, clutching the knife, Jack slid back to the port side of the boat. He avoided the hot exhaust pipe this time and concentrated on the three hoses. The warm and cold ones were both flexible, big enough for a golf ball to pass through them. The third hose was the diameter of a dime, stiffer. This close to the engine, it had to be the fuel line.

He jabbed the fuel line with the point of the knife. The rubber was tough. He had to shove hard, wiggling the blade.

It broke through. Gasoline spewed out with surprising force.

Now in addition to the sloshing bilgewater, gasoline was filling the compartment. The smell was overpowering, nauseating.

The engine sputtered once, twice, three times. It fell silent. Pushing against the current, the boat slowed instantly. Howard and Jack were nearly drowned in fuel and bilgewater as liquid sloshed forward. The compartment continued filling with gas.

Oh come on, thought Jack, struggling to keep his mouth free of the liquid. *What will it be? Five seconds? Ten?*

He could hear them shouting above, running down the steel deck. Still on his stomach, unable to roll all the way over, Jack pulled his hands under his chest. He gripped the knife in a fist, its two-inch blade jutting from the space between Jack's middle and ring fingers. He slid back to the port bulkhead.

In the relative quiet, now that the engine had died, he said to Howard, "Get ready. Move as far to the right as you can. When they—"

He stopped talking when he heard the metal over his head clanking, the heave of a rusted hinge. He saw daylight.

Jack flipped onto his back.

Fu Man was peering down, looking at the center of the bilge where he'd expected to see them. He held his AK in his left hand and the edge of the hatch in his right.

Jack swung his fist, embedding the blade just below the man's ear. He shoved it in hard, twisting it.

The boatman's eyes flickered. Jack snatched his rifle as he fell forward.

Scrambling over dead Fu Man, he rose to a knee. The helmsman was rushing from behind the steering console, his Makarov aimed forward. Jack fired a wild AK burst, sending hot brass jackets skittering over the steel deck. The shots went low, pockmarking the console. The helmsman dove behind it, taking cover.

Jack cursed himself.

He combat-crawled out of the cargo hold to the starboard bench seat. He sprung to his feet and fired again at the top of the helmsman's head, shattering the console's glass. There was no return fire. Jack crept aft, stealing a glance.

The crew's leader lay crumpled, the top half of his skull gone.

With no engine or steerage, the boat rocked and spun in the current. Howard was getting up, coming out of the hold. His face was shining with oil, his mouth open and gasping.

Jack spun on him. "Howard, *down!*" Beyond the banker, the bowman was aiming his AK.

Jack fired as Howard flopped back into the cargo hold. The bowman crouched behind the forward bench. He peered over it and fired. Jack fired back. The bullets bounced off the bench. Missed.

The bowman rose again, firing low from the starboard side of the bench, surprising Jack. He was forced to take cover behind the console, crouching next to the headless helmsman.

Poised and ready, Jack watched the bowman spring up to take another shot. With his iron sight firmly on the foredeck crewman's chest, Jack pulled the AK's trigger.

Nothing happened.

He was Winchester. Out of ammo.

Even worse, the man on the bow knew it. He crawled over the

bench, taking cover behind the raised hatch door that had trapped Jack and Howard moments before.

Jack dropped the useless rifle and dove for the dead helmsman's Makarov.

Leaning far to starboard, he could see part of the bowman's leg. He took two quick pistol shots at it. Whether it was the boat rocking in the current, the Makarov's pitifully short barrel, or Jack's agitation, he didn't know. But he'd missed again.

The foredeck hand appeared over the hatch with his AK. Jack ducked behind the console as the bullets thudded and sparked in front of him. The boat rotated in the current like a derelict wreck.

Taking a wave broadside, the craft listed abruptly to port. The boat's lean sent the bowman into one of the canopy posts, exposing him. Jack had him now. He aimed the Makarov and pulled the trigger. Missed again.

Son of a bitch!

He ducked behind the console. He ejected the Makarov's clip to see how many shots he had left. The clip was empty. The only bullet left was already chambered. So be it. Jack slammed the mag back into the grip.

The bowman stepped aft, cautiously aiming his AK at Jack, skulking down the boat's port side, still using the open hatch as cover. Jack thought he might have a shot—but with one bullet left, he had to be sure. He held fire.

The bowman crept around the port side of the hatch. He was low, abeam the open storage bay. His face was tilted over his AK, keeping the steering console in his sights.

Howard sprung from the bilge.

The banker tackled the bowman, slamming him into the port bulkhead. He clawed at the pirate's AK, forcing its barrel down.

The boatman hit Howard with an elbow, then jabbed the rifle stock into his chest. Howard clutched at the sling around the man's neck and pulled him close, trapping the gun between them.

Jack raised the pistol. He sighted the pirate's head as he grappled with Howard, their faces locked together.

He couldn't pull the trigger.

Having missed three times, he couldn't take the risk. With the gun still raised, he dashed forward. He slammed the butt of the Makarov into the pirate's face, knocking him backward, the AK still slung in front of him. Jack lowered the pistol to finish off the pirate—but Howard had fallen in the way. Jack knocked the banker to the side.

The pirate rolled behind the forward bench.

Outgunned, Jack hurriedly yanked Howard backward, pulling him behind the cover of the steering console. "Stay down!" he shouted. Howard fell to his knees on the dead helmsman's chest. Jack huddled next to him.

The banker was breathing hard, coughing. Having emerged from the bilge, he reeked of gas.

His chest heaving, Jack took stock of their situation. He had Howard to protect. He had one bullet—chambered in a pistol he couldn't shoot straight.

The bowman, on the other hand, had a machine gun, good concealment behind the steel bench, and two juicy targets. Unless Jack fired a magic bullet, the odds were that he and Howard would be gunned down. Even if they jumped and swam for it, the pirate would strafe them from the boat, almost certainly killing Howard.

Shaking with fever, his knees digging into the dead helmsman, the banker looked up, meeting Jack's eyes. His lower jaw jutted. "You're going to shoot that bastard, I hope."

"No. I have a better idea."

Jack riffled through the dead helmsman's pants pockets, splaying his legs. He found the Zippo lighter along with Howard's wedding band. He handed the ring over.

While Howard put it back on his finger, Jack returned his necklace knife to its rightful place on his chest. He then snatched his old Rolex off the dead man's arm.

"Okay," he said to Howard, buckling his watch in place. "Here's the deal. That guy's got a better weapon than this worthless piece of crap." He motioned his chin at the pistol lying on the dead helmsman's chest. "And I only have one round left. If we get into a gunfight, we're going to lose."

"Got it. So what, then?"

"You're going to jump over the side."

Howard sucked a quick breath. "I'm not a good swimmer. At all. And that river is—"

"It won't matter. I'll jump right after you. The bank's close. I'll have you."

"He'll shoot us when we're in the water."

"No," said Jack.

"Why not?"

The console in front of them rattled and sparked. They crouched low as more rounds bounced off the transom behind them.

"Just go, Howard—now, over the side before he fires again. When he hears a splash, he'll think we've both gone for it. He'll come back here to shoot. I'll have him then. Now go! Now!"

The banker signaled his doleful understanding, then scrambled over the transom. Jack heard a splash.

Alone behind the console, his knee resting on the dead helmsman, Jack ignored the Makarov. Instead, he flipped open the lid of the silver Zippo. He thumbed the wheel, generated a spark, and watched the steady flame. He put his hand over it, shielding it from the slowing rain.

In a single motion, he rose high from behind the console, lobbed the lighter into the fuel-filled bilge, and leaped.

He nearly landed on Howard at the waterline, who was still at the boat's side, clinging to the hull. Jack knocked him loose and forced him below the surface, dragging him down. He kicked furiously for more depth.

The boat blew four feet over their heads.

24

DA NANG, VIETNAM
MONDAY, OCTOBER 7

"GAVIN—YOU'RE NOT GIVING ME ENOUGH," SAID LISANNE AS SHE BLEW A STRAND of hair away from her face.

She was leaning forward over her desk in her Marine Corps tank top, the bandage at her shoulder plainly visible, her prosthetic arm lying on the bed.

With Kendrick Moore's embarrassed help, they'd changed the bandage at her collarbone a few hours before the chief, Cary, and Jad had gone shopping for equipment.

The stitches were holding up, though a little blood and pus tended to seep through from the contusion. Of concern to her vanity, the swollen bruise that crept from her breast to her shoulder was the most hideous thing she'd ever seen.

Gavin's mouth opened in a wide yawn, compressing the folds of his double chin. "I've been at this for twenty hours here, Lis . . . Can we wrap this? I'm dying to get some sleep."

Lisanne was on the verge of getting in his face, flat-out ripping it off. Three good Americans were missing, two confirmed alive.

She didn't know Howard Brennan well—though she'd seen him in the Hendley office a dozen times. She'd learned that Bruce Stephenson had won a Silver Star for his daring work evacuating Americans during the fall of Saigon. And then, of course, there was Jack.

She couldn't have cared less that Gavin Biery was drowsy. Leaning forward, she glared at him with fiery eyes.

Two seconds later, better judgment intervened. As a former state trooper and Marine, she knew it was possible to push people too far, which would be disastrous. Her forward-deployed Campus detachment would be utterly screwed without Gavin's help.

Empty water bottles, used coffee mugs, and energy bar wrappers cluttered the suite's kitchenette counter. Lisanne had thrown open the curtains to let the bright light of Da Nang stream in. They'd only arrived in the beach city that morning, riding the private charter jet north from Ho Chi Minh, retracing Jack and Howard's steps. It was two p.m. her time, fourteen hundred—exactly twelve hours ahead of the Arlington office.

"Sorry, Gavin," she said, softening. "I know it's late for you—we've all been going round the clock. If we could just get a better hit on where the hell these kidnappers are operating. The first forty-eight hours of a case are everything."

"Right," he said. "You were a cop, weren't you? Virginia statie?"

"Yes. And I'm telling you—the risk of the trail growing cold mounts by the second."

The Hendley infotech director looked back at her through his laptop camera, his whiskered chin drooping. "Yeah. Okay. I know."

"Can we just run over it again? There's got to be a way to get a better position fix. ECHELON must have some amplifying information."

"Here. I'll show you what I see."

She heard him typing. The screen swapped Gavin's face for a cascade of data, the back door into the NSA ECHELON program servers at Fort Meade, Maryland. "I'll take you back into the puzzle palace," he said, blowing a lung full of air through pursed lips. "What the hell."

"Thank you."

His keys clicked for a minute. Lisanne watched him maneuver through a directory tree, opening one file after another. "Okay," he finally said. "We're back in the ECHELON raw feed for that service area. Now. What search terms do you want me to use this time?"

Good question, she thought. The problem with the ECHELON intercepts was that without targeting a specific person, it was a true needle-haystack situation. "Try Americans, Hendley, GeoTech, Ryan, Stephenson, accountants, auditors."

"We did those already. There were three thousand conversations. Almost all business."

"I know. But let's refresh it. It's been an hour."

Gavin had already given her the download of Jack's computer and a full dossier workup on everything he could find about Bruce Stephenson, David Highsmith, and the rest of the GeoTech executive team. They'd come at the search with varying angles of GeoTech's business.

As far as she'd been able to tell, Jack's due diligence work had been straightforward. She'd seen his spreadsheets and followed his notes on the HSBC financing package from Hong Kong. After that, there'd been no new files. Gavin had told her that Jack had complained to him that many of GeoTech's records were paper-based. Maybe that was the reason Jack's digital path stopped so abruptly.

Or was it?

Outside of Jack's computer, she'd also retraced his movements in Ho Chi Minh City. He and Howard had only been there for one night, she'd learned, which they'd spent with the GeoTech executives at a fancy club atop Landmark 81, a glitzy new highrise. Stephenson had flown in from Singapore to meet them. Highsmith had traveled from Da Nang, where he lived. With Stephenson missing now, Highsmith had since flown back to Singapore to assume the acting CEO position.

Jack and Howard had taken a charter flight here to Da Nang on their second day in Vietnam. That's where his computer had become a blank. He hadn't even accessed it.

The only thing Lisanne knew for sure was that Gerry Hendley had had a call with Bruce Stephenson while the GeoTech CEO had been in Da Nang. Gerry had told her that Howard and Jack had been in the office there, with Stephenson, while Highsmith was in Hanoi lobbying the government. That was the last anyone had heard from the missing trio.

While Gavin manipulated search terms of the world's largest intelligence apparatus, Lisanne went back to her own laptop, scanning through Jack's due diligence files from his three days in Hong Kong.

A thought suddenly occurred to her. "Hey, Gav—Clark said Jack had gone to a suspected contact bump up in the hills of Kowloon the night before he came to Ho Chi Minh, right?"

"Mr. C. said there's no confirmation that it was a real bump. It ended up in a knife fight at the Temple Street Night Market."

"What do the surveillance cams show from that night?"

She heard him sigh. "I couldn't get into any surveillance cams there. Hong Kong's basically been folded back into the PRC now, Lisanne."

"*You* couldn't get in—but what about the CIA? It's a former Brit colony—maybe MI6? Our quote, unquote high-level intel contact has supposedly given us access to anything we need, right? Maybe there's a source somewhere within the Five Eyes intelligence agencies."

She watched the cursor on his screen blink as he thought about her point.

"What's that got to do with a helicopter crash and gangs in the Golden Triangle?"

"We don't know. Perhaps we should."

The cursor blinked for five more seconds. "Look," he said. "I'm one guy here. Which would you prefer? A tour through NSA's ECHELON? Or a mole hunt into the Chinese Communist Party's surveillance systems? As I see it, our team has gone down near the Laotian border. We have voice intercepts to indicate they've been kidnapped. Our job right now is to get them out, pronto, alpha priority the first forty-eight hours and all that. Right, Officer Robertson?"

He's right, she thought. *And he's getting pissy again.*

"I'll circle back to it later," she offered.

"Yeah. Later." He went back to his typing.

While waiting, she walked to the map she'd taped to the wall. With her hand on her hip, she looked at the terrain lines, river veins, and provincial borders. *Why'd you want to go out there, Jack? What the hell were you looking for?*

"Okay," said Gavin now. "I'm pulling up the latest comms hits with our search terms in that geographic area."

"Thank you."

"Nothing new," he reported a moment later.

"Then let's go back to what we have."

Gavin read off the fragment of the same voice conversation they'd analyzed earlier. "Speaker one says . . . we have two Americans . . . heading back. Then there's a gap where speaker two must have replied, which ECHELON didn't get because it terminated to an encrypted transceiver. Then there's speaker one saying they've taken, quote, precautions. At least that's NSA's translation from the original Laotian."

Lisanne had returned to her Toughbook to follow along with Gavin's reading. Around the dialogue were lines of metadata—geocoordinates, time stamps, and other character strings. She suddenly saw something in them she hadn't noticed before.

"Hang on, Gav." She stood up and went back to the wall maps. She'd already plotted the cell site in question. It was in far northwestern Vietnam, on a hill near a highway that ran north-south, parallel to the Laotian border.

She remembered the way the Virginia State Police would occasionally subpoena cell phone companies. "Hey, Gav—is there a way to ignore the voice traffic and simply concentrate on the signal strength of that cell call? I know we can't triangulate because we only have one tower, but maybe NSA captures more information about the signal itself."

She heard him typing. "Yeah. I think that's line five-oh-nine there. Let me try pasting that string into a separate query box."

She waited while he hammered on the keyboard.

"Whoa," he blurted. "Here we go. A whole new list file. You can see this, right?"

She leaned in close to examine the numbers that popped onto the screen. "Yeah. I see it." The numbers were all negative, ranging from 120 to 100. "That's what I was looking for. Those are decibel readings. Cellular signal strength."

"Concur. The identifier matches them to speaker one in the intercepted conversation."

"And the closer the negative number gets to zero, the weaker the signal, right? Isn't that how decibels work?"

"Yes. I think that's right. At least that's how they work on my home theater."

"Then, am I right about this? This seems to be saying that the signal strength is shifting in the middle of that short conversation, every second, somewhere within the radius of the tower. You see how the signal strength is changing?"

Gavin said little—he'd stopped typing. Lisanne had learned that was a good sign.

"Yeah," he announced. "I see what you mean. The time stamps indicate shifting signal values, which would in turn indicate movement of the remote radio within the cell radius. It was a mobile call, of course, so that adds up."

"It also means we could track the movement, right? As the decibel value weakens, the speaker should be moving away from the wave energy source, the cell tower."

Gavin took a few seconds before answering. "Correct. Whoever this guy is, he's probably driving. We know the cell towers out there are optimized for the highway near the border. Probably why that particular tower is even there."

"Yeah. Concur."

"That's Highway Eight," continued Gavin. "According to Google Maps anyway. Hey, according to the description on Google, that's the old Ho Chi Minh Trail, the way the Viet Cong got resupplied through Laos."

Lisanne went to the map and looked at the cell tower again. She saw Highway 8, just as Gavin had. She ran her finger outward from the plot, over the terrain marks, thinking about the fading signal and increasing time stamps.

A theory occurred to her. She scrawled out some quick algebra on a Post-it note, running through the time-honored formula of *rate times time equals distance.*

"Gav, based on those signal strength indicators, it means the guy is moving at a steady rate of about ten miles per hour. The interval between decibel changes is steady."

"Yeah. I see that, too."

"What goes at a steady rate of ten miles per hour?"

"Beltway traffic. On a good night."

"You know what else?"

"No," he said. "Enlighten me."

"A boat."

She heard a knock at the door, its rhythm following the code she'd established with the master chief.

"Gav, I have to run," she said. "Please keep me updated on anything new from ECHELON." She stuck the Post-it note next to the most prominent river within the radius of the cell site. Then she hurried to the door and unchained it.

Moore's big face stood blinking at her, a huge black bag slung over his shoulder. Jad and Cary were to either side of him, also carrying black duffels the size of golf bags. She stood aside to let them enter.

"The downside to being the one with the suite," said the master chief, grunting with his load, "is that you get to store all the kit. Sorry, Lisanne."

He shouldered past her, nearly knocking her over the sitting room's small coffee table.

The three of them put their burdens on the floor, then

maneuvered chairs close to the cases, unzipping them and inspecting their new gear. They were in civilian clothes. Moore had sweated through his short-sleeve Madras shirt.

"Jesus," said Lisanne. "You guys get enough stuff? Clark said you could spend liberally . . . But I'm the one who always ends up defending the budget."

Cary unzipped one of the long canvas bags. "You, of all people, should be able to appreciate quality in this type of gear." He pulled a Kevlar plate carrier free and held it up before him by the shoulders, as though inspecting a new sweater.

Master Chief Moore held a disassembled rifle stock in one hand, a long barrel in the other. "Look familiar?"

"Yup."

"We picked up an M249 SAW and an H&K 416 for each of us. Gas recoil on the HKs, none of that M4 piston crap like the Filipino SEALs had. Also grabbed a couple hundred rounds of five-six-two, frag grenades, some nine-bangers, and home-wrecker breaching charges. A few pistols, too. We'll want to swing by an electronics place for some radio equipment."

Lisanne gaped at the enormous arsenal now on the floor of her suite's kitchenette. "How is this even possible?"

"Clark knew a guy," replied Moore, wiping the sweat from his bald head with the inside of his elbow. "Took most of the day to establish safe contact with him. We finally met up with him down at the marina."

"Any surveillance?"

"Negative. We took precautions."

"Where at the marina was this arms dealer?"

"Pier Seventy, over by the fishing boats."

"Dude had *so* much shit stacked up in a container," chirped Jad. "It was like mercenary Costco."

"Who is this guy?"

Moore shrugged. "Clark said he runs an ex-im company for electronics. Based on some of the crate markings I saw, I'd say this stuff was stolen at sea. Probably on its way to Bangkok, Thai Special Forces. Does it matter?"

"It does if it means we're growing a tail," she said.

"I told you. We're black. We did an SDR in the rental van before getting there and used Stephenson's marina credentials to get on the docks. Nobody gave us a second look. Stephenson keeps a restored Navy riverboat over there, war vintage. We acted like we were a maintenance crew."

"Yeah? Was the boat in good shape?"

"Yes," said Cary. "Pretty awesome, actually. He restored an old Navy patrol boat the same way he restored that old Huey. Named it the *Longhorn*. Even has a pair of real horns mounted to the bow. The dude's a badass."

"*Hell* yeah," shot Jad, a shining black SIG Sauer raised to his eye, working the slide. "I haven't seen one of these in a while. This more than makes up for all the kit we left in the Philippines."

"Wait, Chief," interrupted Lisanne. "Stephenson keeps a restored riverboat at the Da Nang marina? You sure it's in working order?"

Moore glanced up at her. "Absolutely sure. We checked it out when we were playing maintenance men. It has a big diesel, new electronics, and water-jet propulsion. Looks like it's right out of *Apocalypse Now*. Painted up camo green, even a turret up front, though the fifty-cal machine gun is long gone. Why?"

"'Cause we're going to need it," she said.

25

VIENTIANE, LAOS
MONDAY, OCTOBER 7

CAI SAT ON HIS WIDE VERANDA, LEGS CROSSED, EYES SHUT, HANDS ON HIS KNEES, face at peace. He wore only his loose workout shorts.

His toned torso was wet, splashed occasionally by the rain that blew in under the roof. It had been raining all afternoon. Between his shoulder blades was a single tattoo, the bronze-age Chinese script that represented the Tao, his spiritual master, the quiet, steady force that wove all the threads of the universe together.

There were days—like this one—when Cai sought harmony with that force. He'd been in this position for nearly four hours, searching for understanding. Now the day was nearly done.

Ling had called him the prior evening. Cai's MSS protégé was up at the lake on the plateau, near the Vietnamese border, directing the search. He'd reported that the auditors from the private equity firm, Hendley Associates, had been picked up by one of the boat crews on the Giang River, north of the fork, and that they were on their way into Laos.

SHADOW STATE

Cai had instructed Ling to transport the auditors directly to him here, in Vientiane, which would take some time. He'd been waiting all day to question them. His intent was to keep them at the Vientiane safe house and use the intelligence he gained as leverage with Control to force action on the hydroelectric dam.

But earlier that afternoon, when Cai had been over at the safe house preparing his tools for an intense interrogation, Ling had called again.

The boat with the auditors hadn't reported in since the prior day. Now it had been found, torched, beached on a sandbar, its three dead crewmen charred and smoking. There was no sign of the auditors.

Cai couldn't understand what the Tao was trying to tell him.

A splash of early evening rain hit his forehead. His eyes remained closed, his body oblivious to hunger. *A little longer*, he thought to himself. His spirit, he believed, was balanced on that invisible line between order and chaos, walking the path, the way, searching out the Tao, searching for the meaning of this strange setback.

He heard his phone ring. It was Control's tone.

He let it trill on, four, five, six times. Finally, knowing that even *this* was part of the Tao's path, he stood and whisked water off his chest with his palms.

The harsh realities of the physical world intruded. He suddenly felt cold and hungry. He picked up the phone and went inside while it kept ringing. He found a robe and sat on his bed, looking at the insistent Android.

With one hand pressed beneath his chin and the other pulling from above an ear, he twisted his head until his neck popped.

He was ready for the world now, ready to play the Tao's

selected part, whether he wanted to or not. He answered the phone.

It took several clicks before Control's voice drifted over the line. "Have you found the auditors?"

"Yes. My people found them. On the river."

There was no delay this time. "Found them alive?"

"Yes. Alive. They survived the helicopter crash."

"And you have them, then? In custody?"

Sometimes, Cai thought, it was better to handle things on his own. Control didn't always need the exact details. "Correct," he lied. "We have them. They are in transit, upriver. I'm bringing them here to Vientiane. Because the rivers are low, that can take some time."

"That is excellent, Colonel. We want you to bring them in. Beijing. MSS headquarters at Tiananmen. Immediately."

The wind gusted. Cai realized he'd left the sliding glass door cracked. He rose to shut it, noting the frothing whitecaps on the river. "It would be easier," he responded, "to let them disappear. The weather is poor here. The logistics are always challenging with human cargo. They will never be found."

Clicks, static, a buzz. "No," said Control. "You will bring them in. Immediately. Here."

Cai waited, watching the river. Even if they'd survived the burning boat, Cai genuinely believed there was no way two American accountants could survive on their own in those mountains. He saw no point in worrying Control.

"We should minimize witnesses. I would suggest, Control, that we make these men disappear."

"No. We are still concerned about the acquisition."

"The acquisition is completed," said Cai. "*Yángròu* is in Singapore, now the acting CEO. I spoke with him yesterday. He,

Hendley, and the HSBC bankers have worked out a new arrangement. There will be no loose ends if the auditors stay missing. That will be a good thing. Better for them to be dead."

Clicks. "No, Colonel. We . . . want them here. It's imperative we understand their motives for going to the samarium mines. What if they know we've penetrated their UMBRA program and that our radars can see their new stealth capability? Can you imagine the repercussions, the vast failure that would represent? All your strategic efforts, Colonel Qi, would be for naught. The Chairman himself would know."

Cai closed his eyes and inhaled. "It will be done."

"As with your direct action on Mischief Reef, we do not trust the transport of the auditors to your lower-level people. You will report here with them personally. Do you understand?"

Perhaps, thought Cai, that wasn't such a bad thing. If he came in personally, he could use the trip to press on the committee that ran the hydroelectric dam. Now that the GeoTech acquisition was completed, now that Highsmith had become CEO, he'd carried off the master infiltration strategy into Quantum Atomics and UMBRA. He'd be lauded at headquarters, maybe even promoted to general. Surely the committee would have to listen to him.

The Tao, he thought further, had come through again.

There was only one problem. He still had to find the missing Americans.

"I understand," he said, his voice even. "I will see to the transport of the auditors personally. I will bring them to you, Control."

26

**LAOTIAN HIGHLANDS
MONDAY, OCTOBER 7**

THOUGH THE SUN HAD SET, JACK COULD STILL MAKE OUT THE RIVER DOWN IN THE valley. From his perch on the bluff, he noted the thin seam running between the black hills. The rushing water was deceptively still at this distance.

The rain had stopped. Under the racing cloud fragments of a broken overcast, he'd watched strobes of moonlight hit the highlands. He studied the shadows now, trying to discern a path through the craggy mountaintops that pushed eastward.

His eyes shifted back to the river. The distant warble of an engine had broken his concentration. *No,* he thought. *Another one?*

The speck on the river appeared around a bend. It was just a dot, but was quickly growing into a slanted line. Jack watched and listened. He knew it wasn't a peasant boat. It moved too fast, throwing a long wake behind it. It was another gang speedboat.

The distant craft curved around the shallows and angled toward a bank. Jack lost sight of it beneath the tall tree canopy. He heard the engine cut. He suspected it would be putting men ashore.

Looking for them.

Staying low, he scooted backward on the exposed limestone bluff. He scraped in reverse until he was deep inside the stony hollow, next to Howard.

"Another one," he whispered to the banker. "Men probably coming ashore."

Howard continued lying sideways, his hands clasping his knees. He raised his head. "A second boat?"

"Yeah. I think so."

"Where?"

"About the same spot we came ashore."

Howard rose to an elbow. He swallowed and winced. "Do we need to keep climbing?"

Jack touched a hand to the banker's forehead. It was sizzling. "You need some rest."

"No. I'm okay. Did you find a good path up the mountain?"

"Sort of. I may have spotted a saddle through the peaks just north of here," said Jack. "I figure that if we can get through it before sunrise, we lose the river guys. How's your knee?"

Howard shifted and extended his leg, gritting his teeth. "Damn thing. Hurts. Mostly though, I'm just cold." He shuddered. "I'd give anything to get dry."

"We can't make a fire. Not with those men down there."

"I know." The banker shivered briefly. "If my head's so hot, why am I so goddamned cold?"

"You're sick. Get some sleep. I'll take watch." Jack briefly left the hollow to gather some long, dry grass. He piled it over the banker, trying to warm him.

Howard closed his eyes and cleared his throat. "Thanks, Jack."

Jack moved back to the edge of the bluff. He scanned the river and checked his Rolex. It was nearing ten p.m. He decided he could give Howard thirty minutes. Waiting out the interval, he picked up a stick, detached his necklace knife, and whittled away branches to make a fresh leg splint.

Thirty minutes on, Jack found Howard shivering beneath his grass blanket. Without waking him, Jack tied the new splint to the banker's leg. Finally, he felt he had no choice but to shake the sick man.

His eyes were distant and yellow as Jack hoisted him to his feet, telling him it wouldn't be far until they made it to the pass through the mountains, where he was sure they'd be safe. Leaving the hollow behind with Howard draped over his shoulder, Jack could see the clouds thickening and feel the wind picking up.

Damn, worried Jack. This country had a lot of ways to kill them.

With Howard's arm slung over his neck, Jack guided them along on a diagonal course. Sliding often in loose shale, Jack carried a long stick in his left hand, using it like a ski pole. With his right, he leaned into Howard to keep him upslope. By one-thirty a.m. they made it to another tree line. Though the going would be slower in the thick foliage, Jack was grateful for the concealment.

For the next two hours, they limped over downed logs, through thick swaths of vine, and between tightly packed trees, zigzagging their way uphill.

Finally, they stepped into a clearing with long silvery grass waving in the breeze. The rain had resumed—but Jack had heard no signs of the men following them. With his hand sheltering his eyes from the rain and wind, Jack studied the peaks that loomed ahead. He spotted the saddle. He believed that if they could make it over it before first light, they'd be free of their pursuers.

As Jack studied the ridge, Howard slid off his arm. The banker collapsed in the long grass, shivering uncontrollably.

Jack squatted to his knees, put his arms under Howard, and hoisted him up. He could feel the heat coming off the banker's body.

"You doing all right, Howard?" he asked as he carried him.

"Yes. I just slipped. Turns out I wore the wrong shoes."

Jack found a thick tree trunk and deposited Howard on the comparatively dry dirt. He listened to the squall hammer the forest canopy over their heads.

On either side of Howard, he saw dark lumps of what appeared to be rotting fruit. He picked one up. It was the size of a coconut, but with a studded, rubbery skin. He searched around the tree roots and found a fresh one before sitting next to Howard.

Howard saw Jack inspecting it. "That's a jackfruit," he said. He laughed. "How fitting."

"What is it?"

The banker shivered. "They served it at the hotel in Da Nang. Remember?"

"Any good?"

"Our bar is pretty low right now."

Pulling his necklace knife free, Jack cut into the strange fruit and sampled a bite. It had the consistency of pulled pork and was otherwise bland. He cut several hunks for Howard, who forced them down with chattering teeth.

A few feet away, Jack saw another ground plant with large leaves, shaking under the onslaught. After propping Howard against the jackfruit trunk, he left the shelter of the canopy and gathered one of the leaves. He bent it like a taco, collecting rainwater.

He drank greedily. When he'd had his fill, he used the knife to cut another leaf and folded it into a makeshift cup. Five times he shuttled the leaky vessel to Howard's mouth, who sucked it down while leaning against the tree trunk. On the sixth trip, Jack brought four whole leaves, intending to make hats for the next phase of the journey.

Howard picked up one of the leaves and laid it across his lap. "That's a butterbur," he mumbled.

"A what?"

"Minnie and I . . . we do a lot of gardening. Planted some butterburs along our back fence at our lake house. Oh damn, that rain's really picking up."

The rain spattered the ground, even overwhelming the thick canopy. Jack pushed his back hard against the tree trunk, balancing on the roots. He did the same with Howard, trying to keep him out of the runoff that was pooling around him. The tree roots were an island in a rising tide.

To stay dry, Jack folded the butterbur leaves into hats and blankets. He huddled next to Howard, who radiated heat like a woodstove.

A single clap of thunder echoed from the far side of the valley. The rain fell harder, dripping down their leaves.

Howard slumped over, leaning into Jack's shoulder, mumbling through another fever dream. Jack put his arm around the banker, hugging him, stealing some of the warmth that poured out of his body.

The rain sizzled. The leaves whispered. After eating more fruit, Jack's eyelids drooped.

He let his head fall back against the tree trunk.

SHADOW STATE

He was soon asleep.

A poke in the chest woke him twenty minutes later.

STILL IN THE CLUTCHES OF A DREAM, JACK IMAGINED HIS OWN WALKING STICK HIT-ting his chest. He shifted against the tree root, trying to get more comfortable. He felt Howard's familiar form shivering under the butterbur leaf next to him.

The poke happened again, more insistently. Jack's eyes slowly opened.

A man was standing over him with an AK-47 in his hands. After jamming the barrel into Jack's chest for the second time, he'd taken a step back. His finger was in the trigger guard, his eyes were steady and black.

With cold alarm, Jack thought of the OODA loop, the knife around his neck—and the unconscious banker beside him.

Beyond the gunman, Jack saw another man with an AK, aiming it at Howard.

Without moving, Jack took them in. Like the men on the river, they had dark faces and narrow eyes. But unlike the river pirates, these men wore black hats with turned-up earflaps, faded camouflage fatigues, and reddish fabric wrapped around their shoulders. They were impervious to the pounding rain.

"*Ma!*" called the man aiming at Howard. He put a hand to his mouth and whistled, a shrill sound that pierced the squall.

A third man arrived behind them. He was dressed the same way, scowling under a hat with similarly upturned earflaps. He had a long machete hanging from the rope belt around his waist. His face was lined. He looked much older than the other two men.

With Howard shivering next to him, Jack slowly raised his

hands from beneath the massive butterbur leaf, wondering if he could make a move. As though sensing the thought, one of the men kicked the stick away from Jack's side, then swatted away the leaves. The gunman shoved Howard's chest with his boot.

The banker opened his eyes in shock. He said nothing.

"It's okay," Jack mumbled. "They want us alive. We know that. Go ahead and put your hands up like mine. Keep them pinned to the tree trunk."

Howard raised his shaking arms.

The AK-wielding man closest to them jerked his barrel upward.

Recognizing the gesture, Jack got to his feet, then pulled Howard up. They stood with their backs against the jackfruit tree trunk.

The older man, the one with the machete, came forward out of the rain, shaking his head briskly. Since he was short, he looked up at Jack, studying the Campus operative's face from below. As the two Americans kept their arms raised, the newcomer surveyed Howard with the same dubious expression.

The older man turned his head and said something to the other gunmen over his shoulder. All three men were short, no more than five five or five six. Jack could have easily overpowered any of them—had they not been armed with Kalashnikovs.

A strong gust shook water from the overhead canopy, dousing all of them. Unfazed, the older man continued studying Jack's face.

"What do you want?" Jack finally asked, weary of the staredown. He could see that the man's curious hat was covered in decorative embroidery. He noticed the boar's tooth necklace that hung around his neck on a strip of rawhide.

"*Qui es-tu?*" the old man growled in reply.

SHADOW STATE

French.

Jack thought of Henri Claré and the French colonial rubber-field lands that had given GeoTech its start.

"He wants to know who we are," Howard said hoarsely, raising his voice over the drumming precipitation.

"You speak French?"

Howard shivered under his raised hands. "Yeah. Sort of. I did six months in the Paris office for Goldman Sachs in the late nineties. Met Minnie there. She made me learn some."

"Tell him we're Americans. Businessmen. They probably hate French people. Don't tell him about Paris—or that your wife is French."

Howard thought for a moment, formulating the words. *"Ah . . . Nous sommes Américains,"* he said. *"Nous sommes . . . des hommes d'affaires . . . ah . . . ah . . . perdu."*

The old man's strange hat tilted back at that. His eyes shifted back and forth between Jack and Howard.

"Hurry up. Tell him about the helicopter," added Jack. "Quick."

Howard cleared his throat. *"Ah . . . Notre hèlicoptère . . . Est . . . ah . . . Caput."*

The old man's squint tightened. He extended his hands, palm down, lowering them. The men behind him pointed their AK barrels at the dirt.

"Vou êtes Americains? Vraiment?" snarled the leader. The look on his face was pure disbelief.

"He doubts we're Americans," Howard said.

"Yeah. I got that. Convince him."

Howard slurred out more French, shivering through the entire exchange.

Jack lowered his hands, cautiously. The old man didn't seem

to object. Instead, he squinted up at Jack with interest. The rifle barrels stayed down. "Howard . . . come on. Make sure he knows we're not a threat. Quick."

Howard and the old man went back and forth in halting French. Occasionally, the man with the machete relayed the conversation to the two gunmen. He spoke in a dialect Jack didn't recognize; different, even, from the men on the boats.

Howard threw out another French phrase. It made the leader shoot another doubting glance at Jack.

"What did you say?" asked Jack.

"Told him I'm sick, that we both need food and water, that some bad guys held us hostage on the river, that we're on the run from them. I told him we killed some."

Jack watched the man carefully, worried now. Howard had informed this crew that he and Howard were wanted men, valuable to the thugs who ruled the rivers.

The leader seemed to be making the same calculation, thought Jack. His narrowed eyes darted. His hand went to his hip, touching the top of his machete handle.

He stepped forward.

He bowed at a slight angle, a rapid jerk. The abrupt maneuver made the boar's tooth around his neck slap against his chest. After a second quick bow, he removed his cap and extended his small, leathery hand, grinning with a closed mouth.

"*Bienvenue, Americains. Cela fait longtemps.*"

"What did he say?" Jack asked, taking the hand and bowing in response.

"He said, 'Welcome Americans. It's been a long time.'"

27

WOODSMOKE MADE JACK RISE. SPURRED BY THE COMFORTING, FAMILIAR SMELL, his semiconscious mind lazed in a distant sense of well-being, reluctant to stir.

The woodsy aroma evoked cozy Maryland winters at Peregrine Cliff, beachside campfires along the Chesapeake, and hiking trips in the Adirondacks. He drifted back to sleep.

Until rough fingers touched his forehead, tapping him, shaking his face. Jack's eyes sprang open. Reality flooded in.

Alang, the old man who'd found them in the jungle, was leaning over Jack. They were in a shelter made from plastic tarps and stretched animal skins bent over a rigid frame of green wood. A low fire smoldered near Jack's feet. Its smoke channeled up through a rusted pipe that angled out a flap.

Jack glanced at his Rolex. He could hardly believe it was already two p.m. Had he really slept that long? The last thing he remembered was the licorice-flavored medicine the old man's wife had given him to drink while smiling kindly.

What the hell was in that?

"*Ton ami*," Alang said, tapping Jack's chest with one hand and gesturing at Howard.

Still groggy, his French nonexistent, Jack shook his head.

"*Ton ami*," Alang said again, pointing at Howard, who was still asleep.

Jack cast off the bristly boar skin that covered his legs. Stripped to his underwear—another thing he didn't quite remember—he sat up. Next to him, Howard's face was blue in the dim firelight.

Memories of the previous night flooded in. After a long climb in the rain on a narrow, rocky path, Howard had finally collapsed. The two riflemen had taken turns carrying the banker, staying silent. It took them another three hours to complete the climb to this small cluster of roughly hewn tents.

Once they'd arrived, a stooped old woman had insisted he and Howard strip off their wet clothes and climb under the furs next to the fire. She'd wasted no time smearing blue paste over Howard's bug bites while he shook with fever. Then she'd given them biscuits and that sour, syrupy drink. Whatever the hell it was, it had knocked both men out cold. Jack had slept for nine hours.

"*Ton ami*," the old man repeated.

Jack grasped Howard's shoulder, shaking him gently. Smeared in blue, the banker slowly opened his eyes. Then, as reality dawned, they flipped wide open.

"Are we okay?" he croaked, eyes red and glassy.

Jack squeezed his colleague's naked shoulder, finding a spot without the pale blue salve. "Yeah. We're okay."

"How'd we get here?"

"We climbed. Alang's men carried you up the final ascent. You don't remember?"

Howard shut his eyes and rubbed his temples. "Oh yeah. Sort of. Alang . . . the machete guy. Man . . . I've been having the weirdest dreams."

Alang leaned forward and offered Howard water in a carved wooden mug. The banker drank greedily, holding Alang's arm in place so he wouldn't spill. Finally, he pushed it away with a *merci*. "What is this place? How long have we been here?"

"It's a little after two p.m, so about nine hours. Our host has been speaking to me in French, but I only know a few words. I get the feeling this is their family hunting camp. Based on these sleep skins, I think they're after wild boar."

Howard looked up at the ceiling, then at the hide over his chest. Wind rustled the plastic tent flaps as rain drummed against them. "Right. He said the two guys with the rifles were his sons. Can they get us out of here?"

Jack looked at Alang. "Can you ask him to get us to a town or something, Howard? Before those guys from the river track us down?"

Howard raised his arms over his eyes, noticing the blue paint that went all the way down to his hands. "Boy, they really love this blue crap, don't they?"

"For the mosquito bites. I think. How are you feeling, anyway?"

"Lightheaded." He clutched his arms to his chest and shivered. "I just can't get warm. But . . . it's nice to be dry."

"I think you have malaria, maybe dengue fever. Some kind of jungle parasite."

"Yeah. I know. It's not like we had time to get our shots before we were dropped in the jungle. I don't suppose they have any real medicine? Have you asked him?"

"You're the one who speaks French."

Howard rolled to face his host. "*Ah . . . Bonjour, Monsier Alang. Avez vous de . . .* ah *. . . quinine? Médicaments?*"

The old man nodded sagely, then pointed to the blue salve on Howard's arms.

"I think that's a no," said Howard, lying back again.

Alang continued with a combination of halting French and his native language while backing against the tent flap. When he was done speaking, he tossed the flap open and shuffled outside, into the blowing rain.

"What did he say?" asked Jack.

"He says his wife is the doctor. And a bunch of other stuff I couldn't follow." Howard closed his eyes. "Jesus, I'm dizzy."

Jack put a hand to the banker's forehead. "You're red-hot again."

"I'm sorry about this, Jack. Really, I am. I'm not cut out for this."

"Don't be ridiculous. You escaped a gang of kidnappers, slashed your way through a jungle, and damn near climbed a mountain. You're a tough old bastard, Howard."

The banker's lips curved slightly upward. "Something to tell the grandkids. You saved our lives on that boat . . . the way you got us out of there. Were you in the Army or something? Did I miss that about you?"

"I almost drowned you in that river."

"Not what I remember, but . . . Yeah, my head is all over the place . . ." He swallowed heavily, his eyelids lowering. A moment later, they opened wide again. "Hey, is there any way we can get word back to Gerry—let him know we're okay?"

"I'd imagine the crashed Huey's been found by now. They'll see that Stephenson didn't make it out. They'll know we survived. I'm sure word's gotten back to them."

Howard shut his eyes again.

The mention of Stephenson made Jack think of the deal. He wasn't sure how much longer his colleague would stay lucid. "Hey, Howard, I know this isn't the time or place to talk about business . . . But with Stephenson gone, do you think HSBC will back out of the financing for GeoTech? You think the deal will go south?"

Howard pressed his hands to his temples, his eyes still closed. "Well, the loss of Stephenson wouldn't necessarily stop the deal. GeoTech's corporate bylaws would have made Highsmith acting CEO, per their business continuity policy. He wants that deal. He'll sign off on it, no problem. This is his ticket to retirement back in England."

"Won't my missing due diligence report stall the funding?"

"No . . . not necessarily. Gerry could have stepped in and covered their risk with richer terms. Last I spoke to him, he said he was prepared to take it that far to close this."

"Wait." Jack abruptly sat up. "Are you serious? He could do that?"

"Uh-huh. Kind of like buying a house without an inspection—if you want it bad enough, you'll take the risk."

"So . . . what I've been doing here in Vietnam . . . chasing these anomalies in GeoTech's refined samarium flows . . . You're saying it didn't even matter. The deal was going to happen anyway."

Howard squeezed his head tighter. "If you'd found a problem, that could have stopped it. I thought you were onto something about the samarium. I told Gerry I agreed with you, that we should get out in the mountains and check out the operation. But, you know, it's his company. If he wants to pay a higher premium for GeoTech, that's his call."

"So it doesn't matter that you, me, and Stephenson all disappeared."

Over the prior two hellish days, Jack had pondered that helicopter crash, wondering if it could have involved foul play because someone didn't want the deal to go through. But the dots didn't connect. The deal would have happened anyway.

The tent flap opened, sending in a fresh gust of wet wind. Alang entered, tied the flap shut, and settled into a cross-legged pose next to Howard. On his lap, he placed a folded piece of brown boar skin. He still wore his brimless hat.

"*La fièvre?*" he asked, touching Howard's head.

"*Oui,*" said Jack. He then grabbed Howard's shoulder, gently shaking it. "Hey, Howard. Don't go down on me yet. Alang's back. Can you stay with me? Need you to translate."

Howard dipped his chin in agreement, but kept his eyes closed. "Yeah. I'm here. Just . . . keep it simple. *Parlez vous* . . . Simple."

The old man unwrapped the boar skin, and pulled a folded yellowed envelope free. With the envelope on his lap, he pointed to his strange hat. "*Béret vert,*" he said, looking Jack in the eye, tapping one of the raised earflaps.

"What?"

"Green beret," mumbled Howard. "That's what he said."

Jack thought of Cary and Jad, the two Campus Green Berets. "Okay. Got it. Tell him I'm friends with some Green Berets. Quick, Howard."

The banker relayed the message, slurring the French pronunciation as his voice slackened.

The old man's lips puckered as he sifted through Howard's mumbled words. He then extended the yellow envelope, reaching over Howard's body. He held it before Jack with both hands.

Jack accepted the envelope and scooted under the chimney flap for more light. He carefully pulled a single sheet of typed paper free, then read the faded type aloud to Howard.

SHADOW STATE

FROM: Commander, U.S. Forces, Vietnam
TO: Caporal Alang Nik Trong
SUBJ: Expedited Visa

To whom it may concern,

Caporal Alang Nik Trong, Indochina Free French Montagnards, served with distinction as an advisor and mountain guide for the 315th Special Forces Group, Military Assistance Command Vietnam (MACV) in the operational period 12MAY69 to 23FEB71.

In appreciation of Caporal Nik Trong's valor, he is to be afforded entry to the American embassy, Saigon, RSVN, and given priority Delta 02 with respect to emigration and citizenship, should Caporal Nik Trong desire it.

Caporal Nik Trong's service reflects the highest traditions of the United States Armed Forces.

In gratitude,
LCOL Stanley Wilcox
By direction of
Creighton Abrams
General, United States Army

"Ah. He's a Montagnard," Howard mumbled faintly, eyes still closed. "Good for him."

"A what?"

"I remember a John Wayne movie . . . Think it was called *Green Berets* . . . Something like that. It had Montagnards in it . . . I think they're Hmong. There was a Clint Eastwood movie about Hmong people living in the U.S. . . . *Gran Torino* . . ." His voice drifted away.

Alang watched Jack. Not sure how best to respond, he smiled politely, replaced the paper in the envelope, and handed it back with a *merci*. The old Montagnard tucked it in the folds of his boar skin, then gave Jack a second paper.

As before, Jack carefully unfolded it and looked it over in the stream of daylight—a bizarre foreign script, handwritten, almost like calligraphy, but with a much different alphabet. Based on the repeating lines, Jack assumed it was a paragraph, then a list with twelve entries. It meant nothing to him.

"Howard, can you ask him what this is?"

"*Nos filles*," answered Alang after Howard had relayed the question without opening his eyes. The old Montagnard continued on in a halting mixture of French and his native language.

"He says it's a list of girls . . . Something about them being taken by the men on the river. Wants American help getting them back. Says the Green Berets will help them. They owe him. Getting sort of wishy-washy here, Jack . . ."

Jack thought back to the boat that had held them captive, remembering the long metal benches with the welded bolts at regular intervals. Their cargo, he realized now, wasn't drugs. It was girls. With revulsion, he recalled Highsmith's club, the impossibly young women with painted eyes and lips, and how he used their charms to gain influence with the government.

Alang went on, speaking with his hand over his heart, his dark eyes shining.

Believing the speech significant, Jack shook Howard's shoulder. "Hey, stay awake. Stay with me. I think this might be important. Did you get that? What did he just say?"

"He said they took his daughters-in-law . . . Maybe

granddaughters . . . Lots of girls this past year that . . . I couldn't follow him . . . Hey . . . Jack, I'm not sure I . . ." Howard's eyes closed and twitched.

"One more minute," said Jack.

"Okay. I'll try."

"Tell him if he guides us out of here safely I'll have some Green Berets return to help find his girls. Tell him, Howard. Hey . . . Tell him."

Howard labored through half of a French sentence, slurring badly. The old man nodded once, then asked a clarifying question. This time, Howard didn't respond.

Jack shook him harder. "Hey. What'd he say? Did he agree? Will he guide us out?"

The banker didn't answer. His breath was husky and uneven. His eyes darted behind smeared blue lids.

The Montagnard motioned for Jack to keep the foreign letter. Jack tucked it in his shirt pocket. Then, clutching the folded boar skin with the precious U.S. Army memo, the Montagnard shuffled backward to the tent flap, untied it, and exited into the rain.

He returned a half minute later with his wife. Wearing a strange, peaked hat and a drapey smock that looked to Jack like a toga, she cupped the back of Howard's neck, holding him up. She forced his mouth open and poured a trickle of water from the wooden cup. Howard shook so intensely with fever that much of the water spilled down his stubbled, blue chin.

The old woman carefully laid Howard's head on the boar skin. She looked sadly at Jack, scaring him.

"I'm sorry, Minnie," Howard said with shocking clarity. The Montagnard's wife caressed the banker's cheek with her thumb. She shook her head.

"Alang," snapped Jack, getting the Montagnard's attention. He tapped his breast pocket, rattling the handwritten list he'd been given.

Racking his brain for the few French words he knew, Jack began, "*Les filles. Je . . . je . . .*"

The old Montagnard angled his eyebrows inward, confused.

Jack didn't know how to tell him that he'd get the Hmong girls back. To improvise, he pointed to his head. "*Béret vert*. The *béret vert* will come for your *filles*. Okay?"

The mountain man grunted at that.

"You have to get me and my . . . ah . . . *ami* out of here. To a . . . *ville*. To Hué. Or Da Nang. A *ville*. *Un hōpitale*. Right away." Jack pointed to Howard, then himself. Then he gestured with his hands to indicate they must all walk out. Finally, he tapped his old Rolex. "Immediate. *Oui?*"

Looking past his hunched wife, the old Montagnard squinted at Jack's face. Finally, he shuffled forward, disturbing the carpet of animal skins. "*Bon Américain*," he said, extending his hand. "*Pour ton ami, nous irons en bateau. Ce soir, ce soir.*"

Jack shook the outstretched hand.

He was unaware that the Montagnard had just told him that, come sunset, they would be headed straight back to the river they'd just escaped.

28

**CA RIVER, VIETNAM
TUESDAY, OCTOBER 8**

AS A COLLECTOR OF WAR MEMORABILIA, BRUCE STEPHENSON HAD DONE AN ADMIrable job on the old U.S. Navy PBR—Patrol Boat, River—that he kept at the Da Nang marina. The thirty-one-foot craft, propelled by hydrojets manufactured by the Jacuzzi company of Irvine, California, had been sunk by a Viet Cong rocket-propelled grenade in a marshy, wooded section of the Mekong Delta once called the Forest of Assassins.

In the heat of that battle on June 14, 1969, a trailing boat pulled the survivors out of the water. But the stricken PBR, USN Bureau Number 98053, dropped to the bottom of the Mekong that day. There she'd remain, entombed in silt until a 2018 dredging project spat her onto the shores of the very forest that had once concealed her killers.

On learning of her discovery, Bruce Stephenson wired the Vietnamese government a hundred thousand dollars for the wreck's rights. He doubled that sum in payment to a Malaysian marine salvage outfit to crane her onto a floating dry dock. He tripled it for a Massachusetts company to come restore the PBR to her former glory.

By 2020, the only thing missing was the PBR's bow-mounted .50-caliber machine gun, which the Vietnamese government had on display in Ho Chi Minh City's War Remnants Museum, built in the old American embassy. In its place, Stephenson had bolted a three-foot-wide set of Texas cattle horns and stenciled a new name on the PBR's stern. From that day hence, she was the *Longhorn*.

All this was detailed in Stephenson's spiral-bound documentation—complete with before and after photos—that Special Operations Master Chief Kendrick Moore had found in the *Longhorn*'s cabin belowdecks, shortly after Jad had broken into the harbormaster's shack and stolen the keys.

"Eyes!" Moore whispered huskily from the PBR's helm. He flipped down the NOD tubes mounted to his helmet and looked out over the dark water. His hands gripped the *Longhorn*'s wheel, steadying the bow into the current. "Jad, I got a possible target boat ahead. You tally?"

In the eerie green light of the NODs, the chief watched Jad Mustafa at the bow turret. The Green Beret rested his M249 Squad Automatic Weapon on the big horns and flipped down his NOD tubes. "Yeah. I got it, Chief," he said after a moment's inspection. "Contact. Two o'clock. On the waterline."

Lisanne rose from the elevated starboard seat she'd taken next to Moore. She wasn't wearing NODs, since her job was to keep her eyes steady on the dash-mounted Garmin marine radar and navigation system Stephenson had installed. "On radar now," she declared. "Opposite heading, five knots, coming closer to us. Small craft."

With his eyes still on the water, the chief pulled back on the throttles, slowing the PBR. "A small craft with no running lights. That's suspect."

Lisanne studied the Garmin screen. Though the restored Navy boat was sturdy and fast, it had taken them a full day to load their weapons, gas up, and run north along the coast to the Ca river delta, where they'd turned inland.

Gavin's NSA ECHELON tap had intercepted another one-sided voice call near the original cell site referencing captured American hostages. Via Lisanne's analytical algebra, she'd fingered this second call as coming from one of three Laotian tributaries to the Ca. She'd since plotted a course to the fork where the smaller rivers converged.

"Thermo scope 'em," said the chief over his shoulder to Cary. "Let's see if we can get a positive ID." He backed the throttles to idle and killed the diesel. The *Longhorn* drifted silently beneath racing clouds, gray in the half-moon.

Two hours earlier, just before sunset, the chief had run the PBR up a side stream and anchored under a swampy jungle overhang. Invisible from the heavy traffic of the main river, he'd waded ashore with Cary and Jad to cut brush, which they'd then zip-tied to the boat's struts to disguise the old war boat.

Cary stood at Lisanne's rear, leaning on the back of her seat as he raised his Heckler & Koch rifle to his eyes. The Da Nang weapons dealer had sold him a three-eyed scope that could go laser, red-dot optical, or infrared in a single package. Cary adjusted to the thermal view, twisting a knob to tighten the focus.

"Thermal has five people on the boat," he whispered, just loud enough to be heard over the water splashing against the hull. "Contact has a rear-mounted engine. Long canopy . . . I can see one tango at the back. Two tangos forward on the bow. Looks like two others standing near the cabin. Engine is exposed, big block from the size of her, glowing white-hot. You guys hear it?"

With the clarity of sound moving over flat water, they could now make out the low rumble of the boat's distant V8.

Lisanne maneuvered closer to Master Chief Moore, leaning into him, whispering. "Moving at night. No lights, powerful engine. Could be them, right?"

Moore studied the unknown boat through his NODs.

"Fits DEA's intel profile for drug traffickers on these rivers," added Lisanne. "They said kidnappers would most likely travel at night."

The master chief's jaw tensed. He cupped his mouth with his hands, projecting his voice forward in a hoarse whisper. "Sergeant. Stay frosty up there. That two o'clock might be our target."

Jad didn't answer. Instead, he pulled the arming lever on the heavy M249 and tucked the rifle between his right arm and waist, resting the barrel on the bull horns. With his left hand, he pulled some slack into the long brass belt of bullets that slinked down into the cabin below, pooling at his feet. He shot Moore a thumbs-up.

The unknown boat came closer. Its rumbling V8 got louder.

Moore squinted through the green light of the NODs. He could start to make out the tiny figures across the water. He needed to get closer for PID, positive identification.

He started the engines and edged the *Longhorn*'s throttles forward. The diesel shook the deck plates, squirting water from the jets at the stern. The chief steered her at a shallow angle, crabbing across the current, noting the moon's reflection on the rippling water.

"Stand down!" Cary suddenly erupted from behind. "Not a target. Repeat, not a target. Stand down."

Lisanne looked back at the Green Beret standing with one foot on the deck, one on a bench seat. He was still studying the boat through his thermal scope, his finger outside the trigger guard of his green and tan HK416 assault rifle.

"I got two adults, three children," Cary continued without breaking his aim. "Zero weapons visible. I see kids."

Lisanne wasn't so sure. "DEA intel said they might easily employ women. They're small. Those kids might be adults."

"Jack Junior is six three. Howard's pushing two-thirty and is nearly six feet tall himself. All these people are small."

"Maybe Jack and Howard are lying flat," she countered. "You can't see through the bulkhead."

"True. But I got a little boy taking a leak off the stern now, Lis," said Cary. "He's about three feet tall. I can even see his pecker. His mom's holding him up on the side. This ain't our boat. Sorry."

Lisanne cursed and settled back behind the Garmin.

The master chief flipped his NODs up and cupped his hands to his mouth. "Jad, weapons lock. Stand down. This ain't our boat." While Jad stowed the heavy SAW below, Moore shoved the throttles forward, swooping past the oncoming sampan.

For the next two hours, the *Longhorn* sped through the night, zigzagging up the river with her running lights off. The chief kept the PBR at a steady fifteen knots, making good progress toward the fork where the Ca's tributaries converged.

Three times they slowed to inspect a possible target boat. Each turned out to be a dry hole. Finally, Lisanne looked up from the Garmin and tugged at Moore's plaid short sleeve. In the glow of the navigation screen, she held up three fingers, the symbol for the three-pronged fork.

The master chief slowed the *Longhorn* to a few knots, flipped his NODs up, and removed his helmet. He shuffled closer to her. "Is this it? We there?"

"Yeah. The fork's just around this next bend. We're only about a hundred yards south of it on the map. About a half klick by river transit."

"Right." Moore pulled the throttles to idle. He rubbed his bare scalp with his fingers as he looked up at the fat moon glowing between the clouds.

"Clear night. I wouldn't be surprised if we have a little fog rising from the river in a few hours."

"That won't help us."

"No." The master chief cracked his knuckles and then looked at her shoulder. "How's your wound doing? You all right?"

She glanced at the bandage. "It hasn't bled in a while. It's really just a bad bruise."

"Swelling looks better."

He scanned the dark banks to either side of the river. Then he inspected the Garmin. "Okay. So we're here, near the village of Nâm Căn, which must be those scattered lights off that way. Another quarter mile upriver on one of those tribs and we're going to be in Laos."

"Right."

He tapped the Garmin screen. "We need to decide which of the tribs to take."

"I know. I was hoping we'd get a fresh feed from ECHELON. It's about all we have to go on."

Cary came forward. He, too, had removed his helmet. He slung his rifle over his T-shirt. "What gives? We stopping for the night?"

"Yeah," answered Moore. "We're just about to the fork below Nâm Căn. We still don't know which river to take into Laos."

The master chief tilted the Garmin, taking full control of it. Standing next to Lisanne, he zoomed in on the shoreline, panning northward, verifying the bend in the river and the shape of the fork. A peninsula separated the convergence from where they idled now. He glanced at the Garmin's time display. It was ten p.m.

The *Longhorn* had begun to drift backward in the current. A light breeze rattled the palm fronds strapped to the canopy.

Moore zoomed in on a section of the riverbank close to the digital display of their boat. "This little finger inlet looks like a place we could hole up while we wait for better intel. I say we use it."

"Agreed." Lisanne reached for her Toughbook. "I'll check in with Gavin over the sat link to see if he's got any new leads."

"Okay. But after that I want you to get some sleep. We'll set up a rotating watch to get us to daylight. Cary, you're up first. Relieve Jad up front. Tell him to get below, eat an MRE, and rack out. He'll relieve you in two hours."

"Roger, Master Chief."

Moore turned to Lisanne. "Let's hope the druggies have gotten chatty."

"Or that Jack's found a way to signal us."

The chief chose his words carefully before answering. "From what I've heard of him, I wouldn't be surprised."

29

GIANG RIVER, LAOS
TUESDAY, OCTOBER 8

TWENTY MILES TO THE NORTHWEST, CAI WALKED ALONG THE DOCK WITH HIS HANDS folded behind his back. The last of the rain drummed on his shoulders. A gust coming down out of the mountains shoved the floating docks against each other.

He didn't mind that he'd been soaked through during his walk. To him, the passing squall was a welcome reminder that the rainy season still had legs.

Surely, he thought as his feet thumped along the floating deck planks, the Chinese reservoir downriver would be at full capacity by now. The deluge of the past week should present an ironclad case to the committee for the release of more water into Laotian waterways.

The wind eased. The river was slow here, close to the lake. He watched the moonlight rippling on the water. Raising his bicolored eyes, he saw a widening hole of clear sky, a smattering of stars. He thought of his father, the Mekong, and the case he would make to the committee in Beijing.

SHADOW STATE

So much had gone right in the past few weeks, Cai mulled. Highsmith, his star recruit, was in place and functioning. Stephenson was out of the way. The acquisition was closed. The Americans had no idea that the breakthrough stealth technology GeoTech's magnets enabled for Quantum Atomics was visible on Chinese radars. His direct action at Mischief Reef had proven that.

Given all he'd done, could the committee really deny his simple request to raise the Mekong's flow?

Yes, he thought grimly—if he failed to find the missing American auditors.

He heard a fast boat approaching, quivering the moonlit waters. As it neared, Cai studied the man at the helm. He recognized Ling, precisely who he'd been waiting for.

Ling slowed the jet boat and guided it in. A man on the bow tossed Cai a line, then jumped to the dock. Cai tied the rope to a cleat while the other four crew members jumped off with their AKs slung at their backs. Ling stayed behind the wheel, lighting a cigarette.

"Nothing?" Cai asked in Laotian, climbing aboard.

Ling inhaled smoke. "Nothing."

Of all the men who worked for Cai, only Ling and Twei had ever understood the full scope of the GeoTech operation. Years earlier, Cai had plucked them from the Golden Triangle trafficking gang known as the Snakeheads. He'd initially chosen them because, like him, they had family who'd been killed by Hmong rebels in Vientiane.

He'd offered Ling and Twei an opportunity. If they worked for him as an agent within the Snakeheads, they'd have permanent legal immunity for their crimes. They'd also be paid extra money in Chinese yuan and perform the occasional direct action under Cai's leadership.

They'd jumped at the chance and gone to Beijing for formalized training. With that under their belts, Control had authorized them for direct-action missions where ethnic Chinese intelligence officers couldn't be involved—like the one on Mischief Reef.

"You searched civilian boats?" asked Cai.

"We did. Ten of them. At least. And that was just my crew. The others have all been doing the same."

"How many boats are still out?"

Ling cast his eyes down the length of the empty dock. "Every boat we have. Six stretching all the way to the Ca. One or two might even have gone south of the fork by now, across the border."

"And the search on land, near the burned boat?"

"Six men on foot in those hills. The rain hasn't helped."

Colonel Cai Qi inhaled deeply, then let it out slowly. "What do you think, Ling? Could those Americans really still be alive?"

"I hope so."

"Why?"

"Because I'd like the pleasure of killing them myself."

Ling was convinced the Americans had killed his closest friend, Twei, in Hong Kong.

Cai knew better. Control had told him that the Hendley men had never strayed from MSS surveillance while conducting their business with HSBC. But he didn't want to disabuse Ling of the notion. It was good to have him angry.

"Our orders are to bring the auditors in alive," he reminded Ling. "Control wants us to fly with them to Beijing. He thinks it's important to learn what they know."

A woman screamed from one of the low buildings on the shore. Ling looked up the bank at the group of Quonset huts. This facility had once been a secret American air base, a forward combat outpost where they flew bombing raids targeting the Ho Chi Minh Trail.

"The men are getting hard to control," said Ling, noting a second scream. "Product's still coming in. None's going out. It's not good for anyone. Even the girls."

Cai listened to the young woman wailing. "We have no choice."

"We'll only be able to stop them for so long." Ling flicked his dying cigarette into the water. "Come on. I need something to eat."

Together, the two Laotian MSS men made their way up the bank to the buildings. As they got closer to the longest Quonset hut, the screaming got louder.

"The Rangoon girl?" asked Cai.

Ling stopped to listen more carefully. The screams had faded to whimpers. "Yes," he confirmed. A man laughed inside the hut. "I told you. The men are getting harder to control."

Cai listened too, wondering if he should push back on Control's order to stop sex-trafficking operations. Then again, that kind of push at this point might destroy the broader balance. It could threaten his arguments about the hydroelectric dam.

"You must find the auditors," he said to Ling after another three seconds of reflection. "If you want to kill them, go ahead. We'll tell Control they died in action. Just bring me the proof."

Ling was about to respond when his MSS-issued encrypted satellite phone buzzed on his hip. He stepped behind a wall to listen, taking shelter from the breeze, and placed a hand over the phone to silence the mic.

"Did you mean it?" Ling asked Cai.

"Mean what?"

"That it's okay to kill the auditors?"

"Yes. I meant it. As long as you bring back the bodies. Why?"

"Because the men on the banks just saw them floating by in a canoe. They're on the Giang River, near the fork where it enters the Ca."

Cai squinted. "How long until one of your boats can pick them up?"

"Fifteen minutes. They're already on the way."

30

GIANG RIVER TRIBUTARY
TUESDAY, OCTOBER 8

"*VOUS TROUVEZ NOS FILLES*" WERE THE LAST WORDS THE MONTAGNARD SAID TO Jack before pushing him off in the dugout canoe. Jack didn't know the exact translation of that, but he got the message when the old man poked at Jack's shirt pocket, his finger stabbing the letter. So that it wouldn't get wet, the Montagnard's wife had sealed it in a ziplock bag.

"*Béret vert*," Jack had answered, tapping his fingers over the pocket. "We'll be back for them. I promise."

That had been a few hours ago. Jack and Howard were well downriver now, the water flowing faster as it came out of the mountains.

Using it like a rudder, Jack dipped his oar in the water and angled it, straightening the bow, trying to see in the dark. When he thought he was back near the river's center, he dipped his hand and sprinkled cool water on Howard's forehead. The banker was sitting between Jack's legs, his head lying on Jack's chest.

When the water ran over his cheeks, Howard shifted beneath the boar skin but didn't wake.

Nor had he woken during the descent from the hunting camp to the river. The hike had been steep, but much shorter than Jack had expected, which made it easier on Howard. Their expert Hmong guides had made all the difference.

The elder Montagnard had led the way down the slope, walking point with an ancient M1 carbine in his arms—as though a Viet Cong patrol might leap from the jungle at any moment. Alang's younger son pulled rear security, sweeping the brush with his AK-47.

Between them, Jack and Alang's older son carried Howard on a stretcher. It was made of two long branches and the stretched boar skin under which Howard now lay. Doped up with another cup of the old woman's sour medicine, the banker remained unconscious.

The dugout's bow rose, then came down with a splash. Jack heard a rush of upcoming water somewhere ahead in the dark. With the overhanging trees blocking most of the moonlight, he couldn't see much. The scratch of a leafy branch poked his forehead, running quickly past him.

Shit.

He'd drifted into the fast water along the banks. At the risk of upsetting the unstable dugout, he grunted through five oar strokes and got them to safer water.

Once they'd finished the mountain descent and arrived at the riverbank, Alang Nik Trong had uncovered the overturned dugout. Motioning Jack forward, the Montagnard had flipped it over and shoved its bow into the water. The family hunting canoe was adorned with a carved prow and an oar the size of a tennis racket made of wood and boar skin. The three men took great care in loading Jack at the stern, and then laying Howard in front of him.

Before sending Jack and Howard into the river flow, Alang had placed his M1 carbine in the boat and tucked the boar skin over the banker. With a final shove in the dark, Jack had no time to look back before they were shooting along in the swift current.

Up ahead, Jack sensed rather than saw that the river was getting bigger, perhaps nearing the fork he'd seen on Alang's map. Overhead, he saw stars filtered by a thin fog. He kept his eyes forward, anxiously looking for rocks and shadows.

Without landmarks, he couldn't know how much farther they had to go. His hope was that this steady, rapid current would get Howard to a hospital by first light. Alang's war-era map had shown a village about ten miles to the south, near a river fork, just over the Vietnamese border.

With their prospects brightening, Jack reached forward and rearranged Howard's boar skin to keep him warm. He'd noticed the banker shifting restlessly again, almost tipping the boat. Now that it'd settled, Jack found the hunk of dried pork Alang's wife had given him. He chewed it vigorously, occasionally dipping his hand into the water for a drink.

It was much better than the awful jackfruit, he thought.

For the first time since his departure from the Hmong, he heard a motor on the river. Turning his head, he established that it was behind him, upstream.

He dropped the pork next to the carbine and angled the paddle to direct them closer to the leafy bank, risking the faster water to stay out of sight. The motor behind him rose and fell in pitch upstream as it rounded one bend after another. He heard its hull slapping against the water as it raced forward.

The last time he'd heard a hull doing that had been when the kidnappers had snatched them.

Moments later, the engine was shrieking just behind Jack. There was no doubting it. The approaching craft was a speedboat.

He paddled furiously, alternating sides, trying to keep the ungainly dugout upright. With horror, he saw his own shadow stretching long on the water as a searchlight swept over him.

He concentrated on gaining the bank, digging deep with the oars, trying to cut across the strong current.

Yet the closer he got to the bank, the faster the river's flow. When he was within a few yards of the overhanging foliage, a wave flopped over the upstream side of the canoe, dousing Howard. A second wave hit them, followed by a third. Jack nearly capsized before he could straighten the bow, aiming it downstream.

Sloshing with water, the boat rode lower on the river. The bright searchlight flashed again. Jack collapsed onto his back, holding the oar at his side, just above the carbine. When the light passed over them it lit the leafy overhang. It kept sweeping.

At least it hasn't spotted us yet, thought Jack.

The river got much louder.

The bow in front of him dipped. A flood of water rushed over it. He felt the dugout's bottom scrape over a rock. The roaring rapids wiped out the engine noise of the searching boat. White water boiled around them.

Howard was suddenly awake. He tried to sit up, rocking the boat.

"Hang on!" shouted Jack over the roar of the water. "We're in the rapids. Stay low!" Jack seized the oar and tried to guide them farther to the river center now that the search boat had seemed to move on.

Still mostly out of it and racked with fever, the banker threw off the soaking boar skin and moaned, just as the bow slammed into a frothing white wall. His eyes went wide.

The rushing water tore the paddle from Jack's hands as the canoe careened down a three-foot drop and swept them into a fast right turn.

A thousand points of Campus training flashed into Jack's head. He'd learned how to shoot, fight with knives, disarm bombs. None of that—none of the OODA loops or SERE torture or marksmanship—had prepared him for *this*.

His fingers dug into the wood gunwales. The dugout dipped left and right, tossing more water into the boat. Howard tried to sit up, right when the searchlight swerved over them. Jack pulled him down forcefully.

"Stay down!" he shouted.

The rapids wouldn't last much longer. Under the previous sweep of the searchlight, he'd seen where the white water would flatten. After that, the current would shoot them right back to the middle, making them sitting ducks for the speedboat.

There was one bend left before that happened. He scanned the banks. Amid the scraggly brush, he saw a stark, leafless limb from a tree that leaned far over the river, partially uprooted. It hung low enough to the water that Jack thought he could reach it if he could only—

"Howard!" he screamed.

In a full-blown fevered panic, the banker was trying to stand up, nearly knocking the boat over.

"Get back down! Now!"

Thankfully Howard was used to following Jack's direction. He collapsed between Jack's legs. The leaning tree was fast approaching. As Jack got closer, he identified an almost horizontal limb.

He wrapped his legs around Howard's torso, locking his ankles, clamping the banker's waist like a vise.

"Get ready!" he yelled, unsure if his words penetrated Howard's delirium.

Bouncing on the white water, Jack heaved up and caught a low-hanging limb on the leaning tree. With Howard still clamped between his thighs, the canoe shot out from beneath them, continuing on its way, riding higher on the rapids.

The tree limb was a foot thick, its bark long since stripped, making it slippery. Jack tried to improve his grip on the branch while squeezing Howard with his legs. He hooked his right elbow around it, giving him better leverage. The speeding white water gushed around both of them.

Dangling in the rushing water, Howard was yelling insensibly, his voice gurgling. He would drown in another few seconds if Jack couldn't get him higher.

Jack pulled as hard as he could toward the slimy, dead limb, trying to edge Howard's mouth up, out of the immediate danger.

It was no use. A pull-up onto an overhanging tree branch was one thing if he'd been alone. A pull-up while hanging on to a two-hundred-plus-pound man being torn away by white water was quite another. Jack's stomach twisted in terror. If he let go, Howard was a goner.

Uncorking all the pent-up anger at his luck, the water, and the relentless sons of bitches chasing them down, Jack contracted his whole body and managed to get his second elbow over the limb. Howard was eight inches higher in the water now. The pull of the rapids lessened slightly.

Looking to his right beyond the dead tree's trunk, he could make out the bank, less than four feet away. Rocking on his elbows, Jack swung his legs. If he could get enough momentum, he thought he might be able to throw Howard close enough to shore for the banker to gain a handhold.

Jack rocked back and forth. "Howard!" he roared. The rapids were as loud as a jet engine. "I'm hoisting you to the bank. Grab whatever you can!"

He wasn't sure whether the banker had heard him and was somewhat amazed when Howard nodded briskly. Swinging faster, Jack saw Howard's hands waving, readying for the release. Just one more swing . . .

The limb snapped.

They plunged back into the white water. Feet first, Jack held on to the thick limb while continuing to squeeze Howard between his legs. The bottom of the river fell away. Its roar abated when it dumped Jack and Howard into a swirling eddy, then a narrow sluicing stream, before finally ejecting them back into the river's main current.

Jack clutched at Howard's shoulders and forced the banker's elbows over the log. Side by side, they clung to it, their drift slowing from seven knots to two.

"Still with me?" asked Jack, turning his head.

His face squashed against the log, his teeth clamped to keep from chattering, Howard jerked his head. "Till the bitter end, Jack."

The din of the rapids was falling away behind them. Jack's feet found no bottom. They were back in deep water.

"Keep your head low," said Jack. "We'll use this thing for cover from that speedboat. I'll try to kick us to the bank. I think the rapids are gone."

"I know I'm a terrible swimmer," said Howard. "But I can kick."

"Damn straight. Let's do it. Follow my angle. No splashing."

Jack and Howard kicked hard, making slow progress for the bank, while the searchlight shined in the distance, scanning for them.

Stealing a glance downstream, Jack saw the beam sweep over the empty canoe and alter course. He watched in horror as a big, bow-mounted machine gun followed the search beam and spat yellow fire, shredding the Montagnard family's dugout canoe.

With the machine-gun fire echoing off the banks, Jack suddenly realized that this was no longer a kidnap-for-ransom operation.

These men were out to kill them.

31

**CA RIVER FORK
TUESDAY, OCTOBER 8**

"YOU HEAR THAT?" ASKED MOORE. THE MASTER CHIEF WAS BEHIND THE WHEEL, his helmet on his lap. He quickly put it on and lowered the NOD tubes over his eyes, scanning upriver.

"Yeah," said Cary, next to him. "That's a big-ass gun. Maybe a fifty cal?"

There was another ripple of heavy machine-gun fire echoing over the water. It seemed to come from the far tributary, across the land bridge that separated them from the fork.

Moore started the engines. "Get Lisanne and Jad up!" he barked. "Let's roll!"

"Should I hop out and untie the line from the tree?"

"I got it!" cried Moore, already reaching for his knife to cut it. "Weapons up! Right now!"

Lisanne had been below, dozing next to Jad. By the time she scrambled to her seat behind the Garmin, Master Chief Moore had the *Longhorn* spinning into a quick one-eighty, exiting the small inlet where they'd hidden for the past few hours.

Lisanne kept her voice steady, studying the Garmin. "Guess we got our intel. Where'd that gunfire come from?"

"The trib to the far left," the chief returned. "Sounded like dishka rounds to me."

"Dishka?"

"Heavy Soviet machine gun. Numbskulls all over the third world mount them to pickups and boats." He cupped a hand to his mouth. "Jad!" he called. "I want you on the SAW at the turret. We're headed into a gunfight. Lock and load."

Just as Jad's head emerged in the front turret with his big machine gun resting on the horns, Moore sped up, watching the river through his NODs.

"Sandbar!" bellowed the master chief. "Brace!"

Lisanne was horrified to see that they were about to run aground on a fifty-foot-wide strip of sandy earth. "Turn!"

"Too late!" growled Moore, jamming the throttles all the way to the stops. "Let's hope it's narrow enough."

With her powerful diesel engine and quad-water-jets, the *Longhorn* leaped forward, running high on the water. Seconds later, she was amphibious, her metal hull scraping over sand and rock.

"We're aground!" shrieked Lisanne. She was sick that all they'd done had suddenly come to naught. That heavy machine gun had sounded so close. They'd been ready and waiting—and now the *Longhorn* was useless, a fish out of water.

"Stay with me!" hollered the master chief, gripping the wheel tightly as it shook in his hands.

Jad was thrown back against the hatch. His heavy SAW slid from the cattle horns and dropped into the cabin below.

Behind the chief in the cockpit, Cary hugged the metal canopy post, burying his face in palm fronds so he wouldn't get thrown out of the bucking boat. The *Longhorn* rumbled over sand, its water jets exposed to air, screaming, wheezing, threatening to melt if they weren't submerged in the next few seconds.

She tumbled over a last row of smooth river rocks before splashing into the shallows, still maintaining two knots of headway. As soon as her stern met water, the *Longhorn* shot a thirty-foot rooster tail out her backside. In seconds she accelerated to fifteen, twenty, twenty-five knots.

Lisanne could see on the Garmin that they were careening into a sharp S-turn at the mouth of the tributary. "Left, Chief, left!"

Moore was already spinning the wheel, studying the black banks through his NODs. He aimed the *Longhorn*'s bow up the river mouth, the diesel roaring below the deck plates.

The stout tributary was narrow, fast, and deep. Crowded by thick shrubs and overhanging trees on either side, it curved into one blind turn after another. The *Longhorn* was up to thirty knots in the dark. Lisanne was sure the master chief would slam into a bank.

"I got thermals!" shouted Cary from the cockpit.

Lisanne turned to look at the Green Beret behind her. He had his H&K rifle pointed forward, scanning with his infrared scope. He had one eye closed under his helmet. His T-shirt flapped in the breeze, strapped down by the same type of Kevlar plate carrier vest she was wearing.

Cary bellowed, "I see two men floating on a log, three hundred yards, heads just above water. PID! PID! That's Jack and Howard. *Shit!* A big boat just shot around the bank, gun on the bow, sweeping searchlight—just steadied on the log! It's firing! Chief, should—"

Ignoring him, seeing the boat with the bow-mounted DShK

and two warm arms on the floating log in his NODs, Moore whipped the *Longhorn*'s wheel left and jammed the throttles forward. At nearly forty knots, he steered an intercept path.

Jad had recovered his position at the turret with the SAW and swung the weapon at the boat.

"Jad! Take out the dishka!" roared the master chief over the rushing wind. "Hammer it hard!"

From the forward turret, Jad unleashed a fully automatic barrage. A stream of pink tracers poured from the *Longhorn*'s bow, clanging and sparking off the target's hull.

32

"UNDER!" SHOUTED JACK AS BULLETS THUDDED INTO THE LOG IN FRONT OF THEM.

After inspecting the canoe and finding it empty, the kidnappers had reversed course and turned upriver, slowly approaching Jack and Howard's hiding spot behind the log. Now, after two passes with the searchlight, they were firing at it.

Jack and Howard dipped below the surface, holding tight to the limb from below, stretching out their arms to get as deep as they could.

Yellow in the searchlight's beam, the water over their heads churned and boiled. The wood rattled and twisted as round after round from the murderous boat's DShK thudded into it. Growing desperate for a fresh breath, Jack prayed the bullets would stop and that the light would swing away.

Three beats later, his prayer was answered. The log stopped shaking, the water settled, the light was gone. Jack kicked to the surface and dragged Howard up with him.

"What's that?" cried the banker, pointing past the log, downstream, spitting.

Jack snapped his head to the right, shocked by what he saw.

A bright magenta line of tracer fire was pouring out of a second boat.

SCATTERED PINK ROUNDS RICOCHETED AND SOARED INTO THE NIGHT SKY. JAD walked the tracer stream into the bow-mounted DShK as the *Longhorn* closed in at high speed. Scalding brass jackets from the SAW's spent rounds skittered on the deck, flying rearward, bouncing up and stinging Lisanne and Moore.

Behind them in the cockpit, Cary opened up with his H&K, using his thermal scope to sight individual tangos on the enemy boat.

The DShK swung at them and belched fire. Jad walked the pink tracers directly into the muzzle flash, killing the big gun's operator. Unmanned, the black DShK barrel swiveled to the sky.

"Got him!" shouted Jad. "Chief! I need to get below for a fresh belt!"

Moore looked at the target boat through his NODs. There was still a man behind its steering console, whipping the wheel, arcing into a retreating turn that would take the speedboat directly over Jack and Howard's log. "Cary! You need to hit that tango at the wheel. I'll swing us right to get you a better angle."

As the *Longhorn* leaned into a fast starboard turn, Cary's rifle banged twice behind the chief. "Last tango down!" he called.

Lisanne kept her eyes fixed on the target. The man who'd been at the wheel was gone. But the boat hadn't slowed.

"It's going to run them over!" she screamed.

"SWIM!" JACK YELLED, YANKING HOWARD FROM THE SCARRED TREE LIMB. THE speedboat was angling for them, its engines screaming. The tracer fire from the second boat had stopped.

Jack hooked one arm around the banker while paddling frantically with the other as he abandoned the log to escape the oncoming boat.

The speedboat rammed the log and knocked it aside, missing Howard's head by two feet. At thirty knots, the force of its bow wave plucked the banker from Jack's grip, sweeping him away.

"Howard!" Jack screamed as he rose on the swell, the water breaking over his head.

Searching wildly for the banker, treading water, Jack watched from behind as the roaring speedboat neared the bank, its engine maxed. He heard it crash into a boulder and saw its bow pitch up and catch air. The flat-bottomed jet boat took flight and flipped end over end, snapping trees as it cartwheeled into the dense jungle.

Before Jack could process what had happened, the water around him rose in a fury of competing waves, sucking him swiftly downriver, swirling over his face. "Howard!" he cried again, spitting. He stroked against the current, trying to swim back to the bobbing log, hoping the banker had regained it.

Seemingly out of nowhere, he felt a thump against his leg. A hand gripped his shoulder.

For a moment he was relieved, thinking Howard had found him. But the force of the grip on his shoulder was strong, propelling Jack backward.

"I got you!" growled whoever was holding him.

Jack tried to shake free. "Howard!" he screamed.

"Jack Ryan! We're here for you! Lay back! Stop fighting me!"

Bewildered, Jack turned his eyes toward the swimmer who held him, and stared into the face of a big bald man. He was pulling Jack across the current in a sidestroke.

"Howard can't swim!" Jack protested, trying again to shake free. "Go for *him*, you idiot!"

"Don't have to," returned the bald man. "We have him."

A flashlight beam strobed the water. Jack could see that it was coming from the boat that had rushed upstream with the pink tracer fire. The craft was idling, drifting five yards away from him. The beam lit two other swimmers. Jack recognized Cary Marks, face up, frog-kicking in a backstroke. The Green Beret's arms were hugging Howard tightly.

The banker raised a shaking arm.

He gave Jack a thumbs-up.

33

A LIGHT IN JACK'S EYES. A FAMILIAR BRAID OF HAIR HANGING DOWN, TICKLING HIS chin.

"You okay?" asked Lisanne.

Jack felt the rattle of his rescuers' engine below the deck plates vibrating against his head. He pushed himself up, chilled by the rush of wind. Lisanne threw her arm around him, saying nothing, holding his face next to hers. He returned the hug as the *Longhorn* sped downstream, racing with the current.

"How?" he asked.

She squeezed him tight. "Doesn't matter. Are you hurt?"

He gently pulled her arm free as the boat flew over white water, jostling them. "I'm fine. How's Howard?" He rolled to his knees, then got to his feet. She stood next to him, her arm around his waist.

She shined her flashlight sideways. "Jad's got him."

Jack saw the medically trained Green Beret perched over the banker. He'd removed his helmet, but still wore his plate carrier vest over a short-sleeve plaid shirt. Jack squatted next to the banker, taking his hand.

Howard raised his head from the deck plate, eyes wide and

staring. "Jack, did I imagine Lisanne here?" he croaked. "Did I . . . dream that?"

Jack grinned. "Lie back, Howard. We're going home."

Howard lowered his head to the deck and closed his eyes. He gave Jack's hand a squeeze. "We beat those fuckers didn't we?"

"Yeah. We got 'em. Like I said, you're one tough old bastard, Mr. Brennan."

Shaking with fever, his face deathly pale, Howard smiled weakly. His hand went limp.

"He's in rough shape," said Jad, butting in. "Let me take care of him."

Reluctant to let Howard's hand free, Jack leaned in and said to the banker, "Don't give up on me. Hang in there."

Howard bobbed his head once. His eyes stayed closed.

"What can I do?" Jack asked Jad.

"He's going into shock." Jad's hands swept down Howard's arms and legs in a blood sweep, looking for wounds. "Damn. I thought he'd have hypothermia with you guys in the water for so long—but he's burning up. Is he hit? Wounded? Internal bleeding?"

Jack caught Jad's eye and gave a shrug. "His leg's messed up, but not seriously wounded. He's sick as hell, shaking with fever for the last couple days, off and on."

"Got it," said Jad. "Lisanne, grab his legs. We need to elevate 'em." She slid an ammo box, cushioned it with a boat fender, and levered Howard's legs over it. She removed the banker's ruined leather loafers and dripping dress socks.

Howard shivered awake and tried to raise his head. "Careful with those. They're Guccis." His head went back down.

Lisanne handed the ruined shoes to Jack.

SHADOW STATE

"I'll buy him new ones," he said, tossing them over the side.

"Blanket, Lis," said Jad. "Get it. One for Jack, too. I need to get this shock under control. Then we'll deal with the fever."

Lisanne returned with a wool blanket and threw it over Jack's shoulders. She put another across Howard, tucking it around his legs.

"He's been like this for a few days?" Jad asked as he inspected Howard's yellowed eyes.

"Yeah. Really sick."

The light passed over the banker's lumpy forehead and neck. "Jesus. Mosquitoes ate him alive. Complexion's yellow. Classic malaria. Didn't you guys get vaxed for jungle travel before you left D.C.?"

Jack glanced up and frowned. "We were supposed to be in and out of Hong Kong in three days, tops."

"A wonder this old guy survived." Jad withdrew a clear IV bag from his medical pouch and tapped it.

"He's tougher than he looks."

"Must be. Malaria might have killed him by now."

"I should mention," said Jack, "that these great people helped us out . . . a Hmong family. They took us in for a night and gave us medicine. It knocked us out cold. They gave Howard a second dose of medicine earlier tonight."

"What do you mean, *medicine*? Like what?"

"It was a drink . . . Tasted like sour licorice . . . Some home-made remedy."

Jad was pumping up a blood pressure cuff on Howard's arm. "Sounds like you had laudanum. Hope Mr. C. doesn't drug test us when we get back."

"What's laudanum?"

"Distilled opium, basically." He glanced at the pressure meter. "Shit. BP's low. Yeah, I think Howard maybe had a little too much opium."

"Did you say *opium?*" Lisanne's eyebrows shot up in surprise. "Interesting new friends."

Jack wrapped the blanket around his shoulders. He thought of the folded paper in his breast pocket, hoping the ziplock bag had held up. "Yes. Long story. I'll get to it. I assume you know we were in a helo crash with the GeoTech CEO? Bruce Stephenson? He didn't make it."

"At first, we only knew that two of you survived the crash and that river pirates were looking for you. We didn't know which two." She briefly touched Jack's arm before continuing. "You were a juicy kidnapping target for one of the gangs that runs the Golden Triangle. DEA said they're called the Snakeheads, operate out of Laos. Druggies."

Not druggies, thought Jack. *Sex traffickers*. He stood up with the blanket around him. He looked past the big man behind the wheel and over the bow. He saw the wide cattle horns mounted to the turret. "Lis, what the hell is this boat?"

"Stephenson's. Restored Navy river patrol boat. She's called *Longhorn*."

Jack thought of Bruce Stephenson's Huey, the *Austin Belle*. "Of course it is," he said, chuckling.

"Hey, Chief!" Jad hollered from the deck, still leaning over Howard. "Can we slow it down? Working an IV needle here."

The engines slowed to idle. The rushing wind fell away. Master Chief Moore faced Jack and Lisanne.

"River's wide enough to drift for a minute." He stuck out his hand. "I'm Kendrick Moore. Nice to meet you, sir."

"Sir?"

"Kendrick's a SEAL master chief. DEVGRU," said Lisanne. "Clark hired him."

"*Former* SEAL," corrected Moore. He pulled off his plate carrier vest and dropped it on the deck with a noisy clank.

"He's Campus," added Lisanne.

"More like a temp," explained Moore. "Mr. Clark thought I could help with some of this jungle stuff. Hey, Lisanne, probably be good for you to check Gavin's intel feed again. Let's make sure we don't have anybody chasing us down."

"Good idea," she said, sliding into her seat behind the Garmin. She opened her Toughbook.

"Gavin's intel feed?" asked Jack, standing next to her.

"Yeah," she said. "He hooked us up with live access to NSA's ECHELON."

Jack crowded closer, studying the screen as she logged in. "Show me?"

"Sure." She clicked open a file. "Right here. These top numbers were how we figured out you were on a boat. We could read the changes in signal strength as the caller moved. Plotting those waypoints matched a boat's profile. Down here . . . that's the raw voice conversation, translated into English from Laotian."

"Can I read it?"

"Yeah." She pushed the Toughbook in his direction, then reached for her sat phone. "I should call Clark to let him know we have you. A lot of people are going to be relieved. Especially your father."

Jack nodded absently, paging down through the transcript. After a few seconds, he grabbed the phone out of Lisanne's hand, mid-dial.

"Hey!" she shouted. "What the hell?"

Jack put the phone on the dash, then pointed to a line in the ECHELON transcript. "Look. Right there. See that?"

"Yeah, I see it. I told you. They were looking for you."

"Right. But whoever this guy is . . . he's calling me and Howard *the American auditors.* He's saying the *auditors* have to be found."

"I see that. So what? That's how we knew they were looking for you."

"Lis . . . these aren't just regular old gang members. If they're calling us *auditors*, then they must know something about the GeoTech deal. We were flying out to the remote mines where the company does its samarium refining, which eventually goes into rare earth magnets. I'd seen something funny about the books and wanted to investigate."

"So what?"

Jack glanced at the Garmin, then turned to the chief. "Kendrick, can we get this boat all the way back to Hué? Would we be able to make it to the Perfume River?"

The chief was behind the wheel, watching the banks through his NODs. "Possibly. We have a half tank of diesel left. Lisanne, you have the track. Could we make it?"

She manipulated the Garmin. It showed the boat's range and the distance back to the river mouth near Hué where they'd come in from the sea. "We can make it." She looked at Jack, her face glowing in the Garmin's light. "Jack, I have *got* to get word to Clark that you're okay. Everyone's terrified you guys have been kidnapped or killed."

"Who's everyone?"

"Clark, Gavin, Gerry . . . Your father."

"That it? Anyone else?"

"Not that I know of. Clark was adamant that this stay covert on orders from your dad and Gerry."

"Do we know why?"

"Clark said it had to do with sensitivities to Americans operating here in Vietnam. There's also some fear of Chinese blowback after our Philippine op—which didn't go as smoothly as planned."

She filled him in on the op in Mindanao, the hurry-up offense due to Adnan Al Sheikh's plot to kill the Philippine president, and the YouTube videos blaming the U.S.

"But why would Clark be worried about Chinese blowback for a hit on Sayyaf?" asked Jack. "They're an Islamic fundamentalist sect."

"We were told Adnan Al Sheikh was a Chinese asset. Mary Pat Foley's been working on a theory that China's built a shadow state using gangs as deniable operatives. She calls it TALON. Ding's deeply embedded on a non-official cover assignment, chasing another TALON lead down in Venezuela right now."

Jack listened with his hand rubbing his jaw, watching the dark coastline as the new man, Moore, maneuvered the boat downriver.

"There were also concerns," she added, "that you'd get burned, outed as a Campus operative, black side. Clark made it clear that couldn't happen."

Jack grunted his understanding. "So no one else knows about this?"

"Not yet, no. Clark wanted to give us a crack at getting you out first, quietly."

"And what about the GeoTech deal? What's the status?"

"Gerry pushed it through. That's the good news, I guess. If this *was* a TALON industrial espionage op, then it obviously didn't succeed. And we don't have any evidence that the Chinese were involved."

Jack watched the bow as the boat turned. His eyes rested on the wide cattle horns mounted up front. He thought of his MSS minders in Hong Kong, Brown and Blue. He thought of the woman who'd tried to contact him, the fight in the alley at the wet market. He remembered the helicopter going down.

Lisanne nudged his arm. "I've seen that look before. What's on your mind?"

"Just thinking," he said. "Howard told me the deal would happen, even with Stephenson gone and my unfinished due diligence."

"Exactly." She reached for the phone. "Which is why I'm going to call it in now. Whatever crap someone tried to pull out here, it's over. Gerry got his high-growth source for rare earth magnets to power the clean energy revolution." She started to dial again.

Once more, Jack pushed her hand down. "Don't. Those magnets aren't just about green energy. GeoTech's biggest customer is Quantum Atomics, the defense contractor. The deal may be done . . . But something's not right here."

"Jesus, Jack. Of course something's not right. You were damn near killed in the Golden Triangle when your helo crashed."

"I'm not so sure it was an accident."

She lowered the phone to her lap. "What—you think you were *shot down*?"

"I'm starting to wonder if that crash wasn't from an IED."

Her mouth had partly opened. "A bomb? Why would you think that?"

"Because, when we were going down in a spin, I could see behind me that a hole had blown open. And it smelled a certain way, sweet, almost like . . ."

Moore leaned in. "Almonds?"

"Exactly. There was this French guy. He packed the lunch cooler. Along with it, he'd tucked away some almond croissants. So I'd thought it was just that."

Lisanne looked back and forth between them. "Jack . . . how much opium did you have?"

"He's talking about Semtex," the chief explained. "Manufacturers put a distinct smell in it for safety, like they do with natural gas. Once you smell it, you don't forget it. We use C4 for breaching charges. It smells the same way."

"Correct," said Jack.

Moore rubbed his head. "So . . . You're thinking this French guy used the croissants to disguise the odor. Wouldn't surprise me. I saw the same thing in Aleppo. ISIS terrorists kept their IED factories in the backs of bakeries."

Jack nodded quickly. "There we go. So Howard and I survive a deliberate bombing—and since then, a well-organized gang is looking for the *auditors*. Maybe Mary Pat's right about TALON. Maybe the Chinese wanted to mess with our strategic stockpile of samarium magnets."

"Well, if so . . ." Lisanne shook her head. "It didn't work. They may have tried to derail it, but the deal's done."

"That's just it," said Jack. "I don't think they were trying to derail it—I think they wanted to make sure it happened."

Her dark brows slanting inward, she looked him in the eye. "If this was a TALON op, then why would they want it to go through?"

Jack tapped the Garmin. "Get me back to Hué and we'll figure that out."

34

SINGAPORE
WEDNESDAY, OCTOBER 9

DAVID HIGHSMITH CROSSED HIS LEGS, SIPPED HIS LEMON WATER, AND SMOOTHED his receding hair. He'd been gazing between the tall buildings of downtown Singapore, snatching glimpses of the South China Sea, noting the towering cumulus and the hundreds of anchored ships in the channel below them. He remembered how Bruce Stephenson had long said how much he admired the view from this high floor. Now Highsmith could understand why—though he cared little for it himself.

The desk phone buzzed next to a framed photo of Stephenson's adult children standing on a sailboat bunched around their father, grinning at the camera. Before answering, Highsmith tossed the frame in a drawer.

"Is he here?" he asked into the speakerphone.

"Yes. Shall I show him in?"

The acting CEO took a deep breath. It would all be over soon. "Yes. I'm ready."

The Singapore bureau chief of the *Financial Times* walked into the vast office, shook hands with Highsmith, and installed himself at the mirror-shined conference table. He was young, wearing an untucked chambray shirt, blue jeans, and Adidas sneakers. Highsmith frowned. He'd expected more from a prestigious British broadsheet like the *FT*.

The correspondent pulled a small device from his canvas bag and placed it at the table's center. "You don't mind if I record this, do you?"

"Of course not." Highsmith took the chair opposite, disdaining the reporter's long hair and four-day beard.

He had no fear of his words being recorded. Alice, his new PR manager, said this would be a puff piece, an opportunity to introduce David Highsmith to global industry. And given the kid's age, Highsmith was confident he'd run rings around him.

He also wasn't concerned about fielding questions regarding the Hendley acquisition or the circumstances of Stephenson's missing helicopter. While there was a fear that a shuffle at the top might worry customers, Highsmith felt he had matters well in hand. And besides, GeoTech and Hendley were both private companies. If the questions got too sensitive, he didn't have to say a thing.

"There we are," began the reporter, positioning his pen over a yellow pad. "I suppose I should begin with my condolences for the loss of Bruce Stephenson. I'm . . . sorry to be here under these circumstances."

"Well," countered Highsmith. "Condolences would be premature."

The reporter studied the man in front of him. "Quite right. I suppose there's still the chance he'll be found."

It had been three days since Bruce had gone missing, presumed crashed in the remote Vietnamese highlands. The presence of the two American auditors hadn't been reported—more insistence from Hendley.

Highsmith tapped a knuckle on the conference table. "All of us here at GeoTech are optimistic that Bruce *will* be found."

Legs crossed, the reporter bobbed his sneaker, irritating Highsmith. "While the search goes on, you've assumed the highest post in the company. How does it feel to be the new CEO?"

"*Acting*," corrected the Englishman.

"But even in an acting role . . . GeoTech's operations go on. A complex enterprise, balancing foreign governments, high-tech customers, a vast supply chain . . . I should think it quite the challenge to assume the top job."

Oh, thought Highsmith, *you don't know the half of it, sonny boy.*

What a strange seventy-two hours it had been since Stephenson had gone missing. After grieving video conferences with far-flung regional offices, he'd spent a full day hugging the staff here at the Singapore headquarters. All the while, he'd been closing out the legal documents that transferred the company to Gerry Hendley—and put twenty-seven million dollars into his own bank account.

"You must remember," said Highsmith. "I, too, am a founding member of this firm. We've had no interruption in the work."

"That's right. You are a founding member. I understand many of GeoTech's landholdings were once rubber plantations owned by your wife's family. She's French, right? Claudette Claré? Quite the advantage."

Highsmith forced a polite smile.

What could a boy like this understand about the risks he'd endured? For fifteen years he and Claudette had burned through their holdings, mortgaging his family estate to stay afloat, taking a job with HSBC's private equity division, where he'd studied the burgeoning market for rare earth minerals.

On reading that Vietnam was rich in them, he'd had his wife's family's lands tested. The geologist reported rich concentrations of samarium, though its mining was restricted by the Vietnamese government. Claudette's brother, Henri, had used his wife Marie's connections to curry favor with Hanoi. With the path clearing, Highsmith recruited Bruce Stephenson as CEO, whom he'd met at HSBC when Bruce worked for a Texas oil company. Dear old Bruce.

The journalist referenced his notes. "I understand your wife still has family in Hué, but she stays in Paris. Is that right?"

Time to get rid of this kid, thought the Englishman.

Ignoring the question, he segued into his prepared remarks. "Let me just say this, for the record. We sincerely hope Bruce Stephenson will be found alive and well. Until he is, our operations continue apace. GeoTech has an unequaled supply chain, robust refining works, and enough scale to power the green energy future. Under my *temporary* leadership, we will . . ."

He didn't stop for questions. The *Financial Times* or not, Highsmith wasn't about to let this little snot call him a product of nepotism.

And, as he rode the elevator down the tall, glassy building, he thought through his performance, declaring it a good one, making himself proud. Even Bruce, he thought, would have approved of it.

Then again, he reconsidered, as the floor numbers counted down, what did it matter? Why did he even care?

After all, he finally had enough money to spring his Gloucestershire estate from hock. Soon he'd be free to stride across its rolling green hills, rehire the long-furloughed house staff, and reopen the stables. After appropriately hiding the money in offshore accounts, he'd finally be able to afford a divorce and free himself from Claudette and the rest of the bloodsucking Clarés.

It was over. He was free—from all of them.

Before the elevator reached the lobby floor, he scrolled through his phone, noting the long list of emails. Most were from customers—high-tech components manufacturers, electric vehicle makers, and the big American defense contractor Quantum Atomics.

He ignored them. With his personal payout gaining interest in his Caymans account, he considered this all Hendley's problem now. He tucked the phone back into his breast pocket and walked out the revolving door. Let Gerry worry about all this.

The Singapore humidity covered him like a wet wool blanket. He wouldn't miss that. Was there anything he'd miss?

Ah, he thought as he sweated near the curb. *There was one thing.*

The girls.

One was supposed to be waiting for him right now at his Raffles suite. Taking her for a spin would be a good way to quell the irritation he still felt at the reporter's inference that his route to success had only come because of his wife.

The thought quickened his step.

A blacked-out Mercedes S 500 pulled to the curb in front of him, right on time. He opened the door and felt a cool blast of air. Relief, at last.

Thinking of the girl at Raffles, he collapsed into the luxurious cabin feeling lighter, eager to celebrate what would prove to be, he rejoiced, the last workday he would ever endure.

Work.

Ghastly.

It wasn't until he'd slid fully into the right rear passenger seat and reached for the water in the armrest that he realized there was a man sitting on the opposite side.

Cai.

"Go," the Laotian snapped at the driver.

Highsmith's heart sank as the car accelerated. Leaning back into the plush leather, he could see the driver's long hair pulled into a bun. Below it, the familiar garish red and green Snakehead gang tattoo.

Cai, he saw, was dressed in a short-sleeve white shirt, his hair closely cropped, his bicolored eyes calm. The gang leader pressed a button to raise the privacy screen.

The locks clicked. "You can't be serious," groaned the Englishman.

The Laotian shot Highsmith a dyspectic look. "There are things we need to discuss, *Sir* David."

Highsmith looked out the window, his hopes about this being his final workday dimming. "The Hendley deal is done, Cai. So are we." They were on Orchard Road in the business district. It was crowded with rich Chinese shoppers carrying big white bags with ropy handles.

"Look at me," demanded Cai.

Highsmith glanced at him. He'd never been comfortable with the Laotian's strange blue and brown eyes. "I've done everything asked of me," he said.

"Not yet, Sir David. There are still some loose ends."

Staring out the window, Highsmith sighed. "Such as?"

"Such as the Hendley auditors."

"They're not my problem. I told you about the flight. Henri gave you access to the helicopter. And look . . . Stephenson and the auditors will never be heard from again. Congratulations, Cai. What more could you possibly want from me?"

Cai snorted. "Stephenson's dead, yes. But the auditors aren't. They've made it to safety. And it's just a matter of time before they turn up again."

"So?"

"*So?*" Cai mocked, imitating Highsmith's pursed lips. "*So?*" he said again, exaggerating Highsmith's pinched, indignant frown.

Insulted, the Englishman watched the shoppers recede as they reached the outskirts of the city. They'd passed the roundabout that would have taken him to Raffles—and the girl. "I don't understand the purpose of this meeting," he mumbled.

"It's to give you a ride to the airport," answered Cai. "You're going back to Da Nang."

"Da Nang? Surely not. Thanks to you, Cai, I'm the acting CEO of GeoTech. My desk is here in Singapore."

"No. You're going to Da Nang."

"Why?"

"Because as soon as those auditors make it to safety, they'll call you."

"Oh, will they?"

"Yes. And once they do, you'll welcome them with open arms."

"Will I?"

"Yes. And when that happens, you'll call me."

35

HUÉ, VIETNAM
THURSDAY, OCTOBER 10

"*MON DIEU!*" CHORTLED HENRI CLARÉ. "YOU ARE ALIVE, JACQUES! IT IS A MIRACLE! *Dieu merci!*"

Jack stood at the threshold, accepting Henri's hand. The Frenchman was wearing silk pajama bottoms and a T-shirt. Jack was in the jeans and button-down he'd borrowed from Cary. It was nearing midnight, and the rest of the expansive colonial home was dark.

"Come in, come in, Jacques. You must be exhausted. You must tell me, please, what happened?"

Jack followed Henri inside, accepting the offer of a leather club chair before settling into it. The Frenchman busied himself with turning on lamps. "You must let me cook you something. Are you hungry? Thirsty?"

"I'm fine," said Jack, crossing his legs. The Campus was holed up in the guest villa across the ravine from the Clarés' majestic home. Cary had picked the lock of the cottage where Jack and Howard had been staying before the ill-fated helicopter flight.

Jad had stopped by a Hué hospital for chloroquine tablets and other medical sundries. Howard was in the villa bed with another IV drip, coming in and out of fever. They'd agreed it best to keep him sedated.

"You look incredibly well, Jacques, considering . . ."

Considering what? Jack asked inwardly, waiting for the Frenchman to finish.

". . . the crash. We have all been sick about it. Bruce is okay? Your friend, 'Oward, is okay? You are all fine? It has been nearly six days, such a long time to be in the wild mountains."

Jack eyed this potential TALON operative who'd tried to kill him with a bomb in a cooler. Bluntly he said, "Bruce is dead. Howard is sick with malaria."

Henri swallowed. "Oh my. *C'est terrible*. Tell me what happened. *S'il vous plaît*, you must tell me everything."

"Oh, I will," assured Jack. "But maybe we should get your wife in here as well?"

"Ah. Marie is upstairs, asleep. I see no reason to wake her with this sad news—it will shock her deeply. Tell me now, Jacques, what happened to you?"

Jack gave the answer he'd concocted with the team a few hours earlier.

"Bruce took the scenic route when he flew us up to the samarium mines near Lay Táo. Something failed in the helicopter—a hydraulic line, probably. We went into a spin. I think you know Bruce liked to fly fast and low."

The Frenchman shook his head sadly. "Ah, *oui*. We have warned Bruce of his antics. It finally caught up with him. That must have been terrifying."

"Yes. We crashed into a plateau. Howard and I were thrown

free. Bruce, unfortunately, was killed when the helo went over the side, falling to the river."

"*Mon Dieu*. And then? How, may I ask, did you make it out?"

Jack watched the Frenchman wring his hands. Had he been informed of the capture on the river? The escape? "We hitchhiked," said Jack. "It took us a few days to get through the jungle, but we finally made it south to Highway Eight."

"Highway Eight," echoed Henri. "The old Ho Chi Minh Trail."

"Yes," Jack replied coolly. "The old Ho Chi Minh Trail. I suppose Bruce would have appreciated the irony."

The Frenchman stood. The table lamp cast a shadow across his face. The rest of the house was still dark—but Jack thought he'd heard a footstep upstairs. The lovely Madame Anh was awake.

"Please, let me get you some bread, at least. I baked it today. Some curry soup? Wine? You look well, considering, but I see the scrapes on your neck, the mosquito bites. You have been to hell and back."

Jack was sitting up straight in the chair, staring intently at the Frenchman's shifting eyes. "Sit down, Henri. You've had several questions for me. Now I have some for you."

"I should get you something first." The Frenchman remained standing.

"I've lost the taste for your cooking."

Henri blanched and turned through the arch. "I will at least get us some water."

Jack let him leave. He listened to the Frenchman as he made his way down the hall to the kitchen. Then he heard a pained cry.

When Henri returned, Kendrick Moore held him by a bent wrist behind his back. The master chief roughly propelled the Frenchman into a chair.

"Seems like he wanted to go somewhere," said Moore.

"What a shock," returned Jack. "Honestly, Henri. That was your best move? Going out the back door?"

Henri said nothing as he massaged his pained wrist. Moore stood over him, rolling his sleeves over his thick forearms.

"Cat got your tongue?" asked Jack, scooting his chair closer to the Frenchman.

A Gallic shrug.

"Maybe we can free that tongue up."

Jack jerked his head at the chief.

Moore grabbed the Frenchman by the head and thrust his thumbs down the man's throat, choking him.

While he was gagging, Jack said, "That was a hell of a special lunch you packed for us, Henri. I've never had banh mi sandwiches with a side of Semtex. The almond croissants were a nice touch."

Moore removed his hands.

"I did no such thing," blubbered the Frenchman, coughing, his nose running. He wiped it with a shaking hand. "I packed a cooler for you. I didn't put it on the helicopter."

"Then who did?"

His lips quivered. "I don't know. The maintenance people. The workers . . ."

"But you *knew*," said Jack. "You knew something was going to happen to that helicopter."

A light from the hall reflected off the window. Jack turned to see Madame Anh under the arch. She was dressed in a black silk robe over matching pajamas, her hair down, barefoot. She was wagging her head at Henri, her lips drawn tight. She made no effort to stop Moore from slapping the Frenchman.

"Jack, we meet again." She glanced at Moore. "I do not know your friend."

Moore took a step back from Henri in response, as though embarrassed to have been hitting her husband.

"It's all right," she said. "He deserves it."

She stood with hands by her sides, stroking her silk pajama pants, and addressed Jack. "Thank you for returning. I didn't think you would."

"I guess there's no need to slip me a note for a meeting like you did on the *Star Ferry* in Hong Kong. You already have my full attention."

Her head drooped in a resigned nod. "So you *did* recognize me in Kowloon."

"It took me a while. Perhaps too long. Maybe now I can figure out why you lured me to an attack in an alley behind a wet market. I got to know the Snakeheads quite well on the river. I realize now that's who you sent after me in Hong Kong."

"No. It isn't at all as it appears," she said.

"It *appears* . . . that you and your husband have both tried to kill me. You're quite the pair."

Eyes blazing, Madame Anh recoiled. "Jack, no. I planned the shopping trip to Hong Kong specifically to speak to you. I had no idea you'd be attacked. I didn't know I was followed by a Snakehead. I suppose I can thank Henri for that."

The Frenchman winced. "Marie . . ." He shut up when Moore glowered at him.

Jack continued. "Let's say for a minute that you're not lying. Let's say you didn't know anything about the Hong Kong attack. Even so, you still sat by while your husband planted a bomb in Bruce's helicopter. You knew Howard and I would be killed, too."

She gasped and put a hand over her heart. "I had no idea about the helicopter. I swear it. I was shocked to hear that it crashed."

"Really? Why should I believe you, Madame Anh?"

While Jack's question was genuine, there was a part of his gut that already believed her. She wasn't acting like someone caught in the act. She'd also looked genuinely scared in that wet market in Hong Kong. Either she was very good . . . or she was telling the truth.

"They are detestable men," she said acidly. "I didn't think they would be desperate enough to try to kill Bruce along with you and Howard. I was wrong."

Jack and Moore traded a look.

"What makes them detestable?" asked Jack.

"Marie!" barked her husband. "You say nothing!"

Moore slammed his elbow into the side of the Frenchman's head, then shoved his finger in Henri's ear.

"Shut up, Henri," said Jack. "You had your chance." Moore retracted his hand. Jack turned back to Madame Anh. "Answer me. What makes them detestable men? Who exactly are they? Why did you go to Hong Kong for my help?"

She took the club chair next to Jack and crossed her legs, artfully arranging her satin robe across them. She stared at her hands, which she'd folded over her knee. Though married, Jack saw her fingers were ringless.

"I wanted you to see what they've been doing here," she began. "I was relieved to hear you were flying up to the remote mining regions. You must believe me when I say I was horrified when you didn't return."

"What was it you wanted me to see up there? What did you think I would find?"

She looked at him, her eyes glazed. "The trafficking of young women, girls really. The Snakeheads steal them from their families, ship them south to Saigon. They sell them. They end up in Beijing or Pyongyang. They're a . . . commodity. I could not stand by, I—" Her voice caught. She took a rapid breath.

"I figured out that the Snakeheads are active in sex trafficking up there," said Jack. "I saw it firsthand, even met a victimized family. But I don't see what that has to do with GeoTech."

"GeoTech is part of it."

Jack squinted. "Why would anyone in this company allow that? GeoTech's making a fortune. It has a bright future, the next big thing in green energy. Why get tangled up in all this?"

"GeoTech is successful now," she replied, "partly because of the Snakeheads."

Jack waited a few seconds before responding, wondering if he could trust this woman. His gut told him he should at least hear her out.

"Okay. Tell me how it started, then."

She sat up a littler straighter, stiffening her spine, her eyes fixed on the far wall. After a deep breath, she began, "Years ago, when we first learned of the samarium deposits, a Snakehead leader approached the Claré family, beginning with Henri."

"Marie, don't—" Moore pressed his finger and thumb over a pressure point on the Frenchman's shoulder. He whimpered and fell silent.

"Why?" Jack asked Madame Anh. "What did they want from the Clarés?"

She shot him a pleading glance. "You must understand, Jack. The Snakeheads run the lands where the mines are, the old rubber fields. That area out there has become lawless. When it started, it was a pay-for-protection scheme, like mobsters everywhere."

"Okay. How did that affect the mining operations?"

"The Snakeheads wouldn't bother the GeoTech mine workers or rob cargo on the rivers—as long they got regular payments. And"—she swallowed—"as long as David looked the other way when it came to moving girls through the same territory into Laos."

"Stop!" shouted Henri. "You'll get us killed, Marie!"

Moore clamped a hand over the Frenchman's mouth. "Enough," he growled. "You heard Jack. You had your turn."

"Wait," said Jack. "You're saying *Highsmith* is in on all this? David Highsmith? The acting CEO?"

"Yes. Soon after it began, it became impossible to stop. The Snakeheads kept increasing their demands. Eventually, they wanted more than money. They wanted equipment, boats, unfettered access to all the territory. David found ways to give them everything they wanted, skimming from the company."

"But why would he do that? GeoTech is big enough to hire its own security. Why didn't he go to the government? Why not tell the truth?"

"Because he was guilty by then. All the Clarés were guilty . . . including myself. We would all become the face of the traffickers, lose everything, and spend the rest of our lives in a Hanoi jail. David has wanted out for years. Except . . ."

"What?"

"He likes the girls. Not only does he frequent the exclusive brothels in Saigon and Hanoi, he takes some of the corrupt old government ministers there, too. He finds it a pleasurable way to advance his business, to get more mining certificates." Her eyes shifted to her husband. "Isn't that right, Henri? You've made several of those trips with him."

The Frenchman looked away, staring out the dark window.

"And when Hendley came along," said Jack, "Highsmith finally found a path to get out unscathed. He'd be rich, to boot."

She dipped her head again. "Yes."

"But once Hendley took over, we'd have figured all this out."

"Perhaps," she said. "The Snakeheads might have receded if they couldn't find a way to manipulate you. But ask yourself—were you planning on moving here? My understanding is that you would own the company, but that operations would continue as before. Bruce was to stay on for two more years as operating CEO in Singapore. He would have hired whomever David recommended."

True, thought Jack. No one from Hendley would have actually set foot in Vietnam.

"I'd hoped this was a chance to put a stop to them completely. And I wanted you to know about David. And *him*." Her eyes flashed at her husband.

"Oh, go on, Marie. You allowed it, too," sneered the Frenchman. "Stop playing like you're a victimized Vietnamese girl."

She looked down at her hands, speaking softly. "I tried to rescue as many girls as I could." She glanced at Jack. "You even met one here, Danielle, at dinner. I saved her from being shipped to Saigon." Her eyes lowered again. "But it is true. Saving a girl here and there doesn't make a real difference. I thought meeting you in Hong Kong would."

Jack unfolded the paper in his pocket the Montagnard had given him. "A man in the mountains on the Laotian border gave me this. I could be wrong, but I believe it's a list of missing girls taken from their village by this Snakehead gang."

She took it from him and inspected it. "Yes. I think you are right. I don't read Hmong . . . but Danielle does. She can translate it for us. The Snakeheads have taken many girls from the Hmong in those mountains." She handed the letter back.

"There's one thing I can't wrap my head around," Jack said, scratching one of the mosquito bites on the back of his neck. "I can't imagine Bruce Stephenson would have allowed this to happen in his company. He was an honorable man. He cared deeply about his legacy. In his way, he loved Vietnam."

"You are right. Bruce was a very decent, honorable man. And he did love this country. He had no idea what was happening, of course. He trusted David to run the business here."

"Then why didn't you go to Bruce with all this? He would have shut it down."

"The Snakeheads would have killed him. He was but a single man, easily stopped. If you disbelieve that," she said, looking at her hands again, "consider that is just what they've done."

Jack tipped back in his chair, thinking. Perhaps this wasn't TALON. Maybe it was just as it appeared—a sad, sordid business within a legitimate one, a chain of secret blackmail by immoral people begun years ago.

Even if China had been involved in the gang, would it have mattered?

Then he thought of the big order from Quantum Atomics and GeoTech's emerging significance to national security.

Something was still off.

Jack thudded his chair back to the floor.

He looked over at Henri, who slumped against an armrest while Master Chief Moore hovered over him. "Did you have help when you packed the Semtex in the cooler?"

"Ach. No, Jacques. You must believe me. I am not a bomber. I am not a killer."

"But you made a call. I remember you saying you would make sure the helicopter was loaded."

The Frenchman sunk lower in his chair. "Yes."

"Henri, I'm sure I could find your phone and check out the call records from that night. Or, I could have Chief Moore here beat it out of you. But there happens to be a third option that's both faster and easier—why don't you just tell me?"

The Frenchman gave a resigned shrug. "I called David Highsmith, of course."

36

**DA NANG, VIETNAM
FRIDAY, OCTOBER 11**

DAVID HIGHSMITH, ACTING CEO, HAD BEEN GRATIFIED BY THE RESPONSE FROM HIS Da Nang staff. Though they all maintained the "acting CEO" title as a manner of propriety, he rather liked the extra attention. He'd become the big boss, afforded the respectful glances and deferential gestures. He could see himself enjoying it—for a while, anyway.

While the requests for customer calls had been piling up, Highsmith didn't do much work that morning. He was tired. Cai had forced him onto a red-eye—coach, of all things—and escorted him back to his Da Nang apartment. The movers had already half-emptied it, shipping his goods back to the UK. Cai and his henchman Ling had flown with him from Singapore. They'd followed him on his walk to the office that morning.

At least here on the fifth floor, Highsmith was treated with respect. Presently, he was lunching in Bruce Stephenson's office under the picture of the war vet getting his Silver Star for evacuating Americans during the fall of Saigon. Fearing the staff would notice, Highsmith hadn't taken that photo down.

Lunch was good. Vietnamese food, he reflected, just might be something else he would miss. He was holding a sauced prawn to his mouth when the desk phone rang.

"Yes?" he asked.

"A call for you, sir. Shall I put it through?"

He put the chopsticks down and wiped his mouth with a cloth napkin. He had a rule against using paper napkins. "I told you, Corrine. I don't want to be disturbed. Especially over lunch."

"It's a personal call, sir. Sounds important."

Oh Christ, thought Highsmith. *Goddamned Cai.*

He shoved his plate aside, picked up the handset, and stabbed the blinking light.

"This is David."

"Hello," said Madame Anh.

"Marie," he answered abruptly, relieved it wasn't Cai. "I'm pleased to hear from you. Is everything all right?"

"I read your interview in the *Financial Times*."

Highsmith smirked. He'd read it on his phone an hour ago. It'd come off better than he'd expected, suggesting the firm was in steady hands with Stephenson missing. Just as he'd predicted, he'd run rings around that kid.

"You are very kind, Marie. Thank you."

"When did you get into Da Nang? I called the Singapore office and they said you were here."

He twisted in his chair to take in the ocean view. Stephenson's office in Da Nang was nicer than his office here. That had always irritated him, not that it mattered anymore.

"I came in on a late flight," he said. "Much to do, as you might imagine. Frantically busy."

"Yes, of course. The circumstances are tragic. But at least the company remains in your firm hands."

He puzzled at that choice of words. *Firm hands.*

Mouthing his thanks, he wondered about this woman. He knew the flame of her marriage to Henri had blown out long ago. They slept at opposite ends of the hall at their Hué home, he'd learned from the servants.

What's her agenda?

After all these years, she'd maintained her exotic looks, he thought, along with a certain glamour he'd long found attractive. Two years back, he'd dropped a few hints that he wouldn't mind diving into bed with her, some stronger than others. None had done the trick. If anything, she'd treated him coldly, as though too good for him.

A Vietnamese . . . too good for him.

Well. Perhaps she'd realized he was a man with options now. She knew he'd be leaving soon. Was this her desperate plea to join him, to finally get out?

If so, it was too little, too late. That didn't mean, though, he wouldn't try one more time . . .

"Marie," he ventured, "I was thinking—perhaps you could come down here and help me. I'm suddenly aswim in government contracts. You're as good as *anyone* at deciphering those ridiculous things. By the time they pass through all the translators I can't make heads or tails of them. Would it be nice to come down? To help this old fellow out and take a break from Hué?"

And from Henri.

"Actually, I was going to ask you to come here," she said.

He held his breath for a moment. "You want me to come up to Hué?"

"Yes. Henri has gone off to shop in Hanoi."

His heart thudded. Cai would let him go up to Hué, wouldn't he?

"I was thinking of heading up to my Hué house for the weekend," he answered. "Since Bruce, well . . . you know, won't be there. Poor Bruce. Dear man. I . . . suppose I could be talked into coming sooner. If you want me to, that is. You must be a little lonely rattling around that house."

"I think you should come now."

He swiveled back and forth in the chair, smiling. "Well . . . All right, Marie. I need to wrap up a few things here . . . But I can be up in Hué tonight. We can have dinner, just the two of us."

"I'm relieved to hear it," she said.

Relieved? Highsmith's face fell. "What do you mean *relieved*? Why?"

"Because we have a situation here. With Henri gone, I need your help to manage it."

"What situation?"

"The Hendley man—Jack Ryan. He's here. He showed up an hour ago. I'm not sure what I'm supposed to do with him."

"Are you serious?" shot Highsmith, sitting bolt upright. He could see his narrow little secretary, Corrine, through the glass outside his office. He lowered his voice and swiveled away from her, facing the wall with Bruce's war memorabilia. "You're saying Ryan is in *Hué*?"

"I'm saying he's right here. At the plantation."

"What? How is that possible?"

"Jack said he and Howard made it to a highway and caught a ride. He told me Bruce was killed in the helicopter crash. Now he's here, staying in the guest villa, bruised but uninjured. Howard is at the hospital in Hué—he has severe malaria. Jack said he wanted to talk to you immediately. No one but you."

Highsmith clamped a hand to his forehead. "Well, if nothing else, I suppose this confirms Bruce's death. Terrible. Tell Jack I'm on my way, will you? Tell him not to go anywhere."

"Yes, I will. He is insistent that you come as soon as you can. You can leave soon? When will you get here?"

"Six o'clock. See you then."

He put the handset in its cradle and sat staring through the office glass, past Corrine, out toward the rest of the floor. In the far corner, across three rows of cubicles, was the conference room where Jack Ryan had gathered the bankers boxes with the carbon receipts. With the deal done, Highsmith had since ordered an underling to destroy those files. Apparently, he thought, that might not be enough.

He sighed, then dug out his cell phone.

He called Cai.

37

HUÉ, VIETNAM
FRIDAY, OCTOBER 11

THE LARGE KITCHEN WHERE HENRI LIKED TO EXPERIMENT WITH ASIAN-FRENCH FU-sion dishes was at the back of the Clarés' plantation house. Cleaned daily by Danielle, the Hmong girl Madame Anh had rescued, its marble countertops, chrome fixtures, and black-and-white-checkered floor gleamed like a French café.

Abeam the double-wide refrigerator, directly facing the home's rear entry, was a frosted-glass door that led to the pantry. Inside that windowless room were the usual dry staples—flour, oats, nuts, and cans—and a small desk with three flat-screen monitors, a landline phone, and French-language cookbooks.

At the moment, Lisanne Robertson was sitting uncomfortably at the pantry desk in a straight-backed wooden kitchen chair. She watched the split screens on each monitor, adjusting the angles of the cameras with a mouse to test the fields of view.

Just as she was maneuvering the camera to sight the guest villa on the other side of the ravine, where they'd installed

Madame Anh and Danielle for safekeeping, Jack Ryan, Jr., came through the door and set his radio on the desk.

"What are they doing?" he asked, leaning on his knuckles, studying the view of the guest villa. The lights were on, but the curtains drawn.

"I can't see Madame Anh or Danielle," answered Lisanne.

"And her phone? Anything new?"

Lisanne picked up Madame Anh's iPhone. Eager to help in any way, the Vietnamese woman had surrendered it willingly along with her security code. "Nothing new," said Lisanne.

"Okay." Jack bent slightly to peer at the monitor. "What's that view you've got there?"

"I was just checking Cary's overwatch position on the roof." She resumed pointing the camera at the villa. At maximum zoom, they could both see Cary Marks lying prone, his Heckler and Koch 416 rifle set up on a tripod, his head close to its scope.

"Radio check," said Jack into his walkie-talkie, holding it close to his mouth.

They watched as Cary picked up his own device. *"I have you Lima Charlie, Jack,"* he responded. *"How about me?"*

"Five by five."

"Any change in plans from our HVT?" asked Cary. He was referring to their high-value target, David Highsmith.

Jack checked his old Rolex. It was five forty-five. Highsmith had texted Madame Anh's phone twenty minutes earlier, confirming he'd arrive at the plantation at six.

"Negative," answered Jack. "We assess the HVT's still on schedule." He looked at the split screen that showed the plantation's front gate and asked Lisanne to zoom in on it.

"Master Chief Moore," Jack said into the radio. "You have eyes on the road? Any traffic?"

SHADOW STATE

"*I've got eyes,*" confirmed the chief. "*All quiet out here. Two cars passed by earlier. One was a working van, the other an old SUV. Locals.*"

Though Jack was watching the chief's position intently on the split screen, he couldn't see any movement. Somewhere out there by the gate, buried in the undergrowth along the hilly road, he knew Moore was waiting with the heavy, belt-fed M249 SAW.

"How about you, Jad?" Jack asked into the radio. "How are comms?"

"*I got you Lima Charlie, boss,*" answered the Green Beret. Jack could see Jad out at the edge of the property, standing near a beachside cliff with his rifle slung on his back. He was twenty yards from a small masonry structure with a shed-style roof, the plantation's old freshwater springhouse, where they'd locked Henri Claré, much to the Frenchman's frustration. Locked inside with him was the *Lone Star*, Stephenson's restored Vietnam War–era jeep.

Jack clipped the radio to his belt and touched Lisanne's shoulder. "Looks like we're all set. Should we go check on Howard?"

She scraped her chair back. "Sure. As long as we keep it quick."

They climbed the polished mahogany stairs to the second floor. The front room on that floor, just off the landing, belonged to Madame Anh.

Her husband's room was at the rear end of the hall, the back of the house. Judging by the arrangement of clothes, furniture, and toiletries in Marie Anh's room, it seemed clear to both Jack and Lisanne that the couple rarely comingled—if ever.

Lisanne quietly opened the door to the bedroom. Howard was lying flat on his back in Madame Anh's huge bed, shrouded in a veil that draped from the canopy. Lisanne parted the sheer fabric and found him asleep. The IV drip was taped to the headboard, keeping him sedated.

"His IV bag's getting a little low," she said. "Think it will be okay?"

"Jad said he'd stay sedated for the next few hours. Should be fine."

Lisanne stroked Howard's warm forehead. The bug bites had gotten smaller—but still marked his skin like a kid getting over chicken pox. "Fever's gone down a little," she said.

Jack lifted Howard's wrist and felt for a pulse. Relieved, he found it stronger than it had been earlier that day.

Lisanne let the veil close around the banker. "We'd better get back," she said.

At the bottom of the stairs, Jack took a right, into the front parlor. The exterior casement window on the room's far side had been left open, its large plantation shutters flattened against the outside walls. Jack positioned himself on the chair opposite the open window, while Lisanne stood under the arch that went to the foyer. It was quiet. He could hear the birds cawing in the ravine.

Jack turned on a table lamp, then settled into the chair and put the radio to his lips. "Cary, I'm in the HVT's seat. How's the view from your pos?"

A red laser dot suddenly appeared on Jack's chest. He looked down at it and moved from side to side, intentionally shifting his body. The dot followed him, trained on his rib cage—it gave him the creeps.

"That oughtta do it," he said into the radio, standing up, eager to get clear of the laser.

The red dot stayed fixed to the back of the club chair Jack had vacated. *"It's a clean shot,"* said Cary over the radio. *"Three hun-*

dred yards. No breeze, wide-open window. Let's hope I don't have to take it."

"Roger that," answered Jack. "You won't. The dot should do it."

Lisanne stuck her head out the open window and noted the setting sun at the treetops. "We should get in position," she said. "He could be here any minute."

Jack gave her the radio. "Right. Here. Take this."

She was wearing her prosthetic arm and had buttoned the long sleeve of her blouse tightly at the wrist. She kept her good arm at her side, staring at the radio in Jack's hand. "I don't like that you won't have a radio on you."

"We only have the four to work with. We all agreed—it's better for you to keep an eye on the monitors and stay connected to the trigger pullers." She reluctantly took the radio.

"What if he tries something in here?" she asked. "I won't have eyes or ears on this room."

He took a deep breath. "I know. But Cary's on overwatch. Jad and the chief are within shouting distance. And don't forget . . . I've met Highsmith. He's going to fold like a tent when that dot shows up on his chest. Trust me. There's also this." Jack lifted his shirt to show the SIG Sauer in his belt.

"Don't underestimate him, Jack. Highsmith killed Stephenson. He damn near killed you and Howard, too."

"He *ordered* us killed. Big difference."

She shot him a dismissive glance. "Fine." With the radio at her side, she walked briskly to the pantry and sat behind the desk. She looked over the camera views again, and keyed the radio, leaving the mic open, since she needed her single hand to adjust the camera views. "Final radio check," she called.

One by one, Cary, Jad, and the chief told her they could hear her Lima Charlie, loud and clear. Just as they finished reporting in, Jack appeared in the doorway, slouching against the threshold, his hands in his pockets.

"Hey, Lis," he said. "I didn't mean to blow off your concerns."

"Yeah you did," she said.

"I didn't. But if I came across that way, I'm sorry. You make a good point. If we had a fifth radio, I'd take it. But we don't. I'm just saying—we all agreed on this plan."

"I know. We did."

Jack scratched his freshly shaved chin, then put his hand back in his pocket. "Hey—I'm sorry about the way I left things back in Arlington. I'm glad you're here."

She glanced at him briefly, then went back to looking at the monitors. She switched off the radio microphone for privacy. "We're in the middle of an op, Jack. This isn't the time."

"I'm just saying. Clark was right to promote you. I should never have doubted it. It's important to me that you believe that."

She chose to stay silent and kept her eyes focused on the monitors.

"You know," continued Jack. "Mostly I was pissed off at Clark for putting me on this white-side gig, boxing me out of the Philippines. And . . . I know I'm not supposed to say this . . . I was worried about you over there in Mindanao. I was worried about what would become of Emily. You can't fault me for that—you took a round to your breastplate."

She still hadn't turned away from the monitors. "Yeah. Well, Emily's fine. So am I."

Moore's voice came through the radio. *"All call signs, I have headlights at the road junction that match our description. Vehicle approaching. Repeat, vehicle approaching. Confirming with optics, stand by."*

Lisanne used the mouse to shift the view at the gate, while Jack hunched over her. Neither of them could see the chief.

"I've got a silver Range Rover, full-size," Moore reported on the net.

Lisanne spoke into the radio. "Roger, Chief. Copy. That's the car Madame Anh told us to expect. We're a go."

"Roger that. Waiting for him to pass through . . . Wait. Hang on. Vehicle must have pulled over. I lost sight of it where the road dips in the ravine. Now it's not coming up. You have eyes on your cameras?"

"Negative," said Lisanne, studying the split view that showed the gate. She turned to Jack. "What do you make of that?"

"I don't know."

Madame Anh's smartphone buzzed on the desk. Jack looked at it. He let out a long breath of relief. "It's Highsmith texting. Says he'll be here in a minute."

She nodded. "Good. Why do you think he pulled over?"

"Highsmith doesn't live here anymore, since he rented his house to Stephenson. We already know that he and Madame Anh aren't exactly on 'pop-in' terms."

He typed an answer into Madame Anh's phone. *We're waiting for you at my house. See you soon.*

"Got eyes on suspect vehicle," said Moore a half minute later. *"Silver Range Rover headed into the gates."*

Through the split-screen monitor on the right, Lisanne and Jack watched the twin iron gates parting. They knew Highsmith had a remote control for them. As expected, a moment later, Highsmith's Range Rover sped through.

"Chief, can you confirm he's alone?" Lisanne asked.

"Single driver," whispered Moore. *"That's all I saw. Headlights in my face."*

Jack looked at Lisanne. "You set?"

"Yeah."

"I'll head to the front door as soon as Highsmith gets out of the car."

Through the video feed, Jack and Lisanne could see the edge of the vehicle's roof. The Range Rover idled for a moment as though Highsmith was unsure where to park. Then it angled down a graveled driveway extension designed for a three-point turn. Because the SUV had come so close to the house, they could only see its hood.

"Looks like he's setting up to get out of here in a hurry," said Jack.

Madame Anh's phone buzzed next to Lisanne. She picked it up and read the message aloud. "Highsmith says he's at the side door. Says it's locked."

Jack hesitated. The plan had been for Highsmith to come through the front door, where Cary had an unobstructed view on overwatch. "Tell him to come around front."

There was a knock at the side door. Another.

"It's a huge house," she said. "That's going to sound like a weird request, considering his familiarity with the place. He can probably see the light in the kitchen."

Jack rubbed his chin for a second. The knocking got louder. "Yeah. Good point. Tell him you're on your way. I can meet him at the side."

"Cary won't have eyes on you."

"Not for long," he said. "I need him comfortable, ready to talk." He pulled the SIG Sauer from his waistband. "You cover me, okay?"

Jack jerked the slide and chambered a round for her. He put the gun on the desk.

She picked it up and stood, preparing to follow him. "I can't operate a weapon and a radio at the same time."

He motioned her into the hall. "Won't matter. It'll just be a second. Stay in the kitchen, out of sight."

The knocking at the side door grew insistent.

Jack gave her a final thumbs-up, then walked to the side entry. After pausing to gather his thoughts before confronting the man who'd tried to kill him, he reached for the deadbolt.

That's when he heard Lisanne's stifled scream behind him.

38

THE SIDE DOOR BURST OPEN, KNOCKING JACK BACKWARD. HE FELT A KICK AT HIS ankle and went down hard, slamming his hip on the cold marble floor.

Lisanne had screamed once, then gone silent.

Jack rolled, trying to scramble into the kitchen. He saw her backlit, trapped in the grip of a man who'd stripped her of the SIG. His hand muffled her mouth. The assaulter had long hair and a familiar tattoo on his neck.

Jack felt a hard kick to his temple.

A knee fell on his back, knocking the air from his lungs. He twisted sideways, trying to throw his assailant off. He felt a pistol barrel at the back of his neck. "Stop, or she dies."

Jack froze.

He could see the Snakehead in the kitchen pulling Lisanne's prosthetic arm free with a laugh. The Snakehead then wrapped duct tape around her other arm, pinning it to her torso. He dragged Lisanne next to Jack and slammed the SIG down onto the base of his head, grip-first. The shock of the pistol whip allowed the assailant on Jack's back to gain control of his arms.

Jack's shoulders ached as his elbows were yanked behind him.

He felt duct tape around his forearms. The binding moved to his head and over his mouth. He heard Lisanne grunt. One of the assailants howled in pain.

Go, Marine.

From his position on the floor, Jack could see her running for it, trying to get to the back door of the kitchen. When she got to the door, she turned, trying to twist the knob with the hand taped to her side—but the deadbolt had been thrown. She couldn't reach it. Abandoning the effort, she ran for the front parlor, headed for the open casement window.

Too late.

The assaulter who'd pistol-whipped Jack tackled her in the kitchen. He gripped her braid and yanked it back. "Cary!" she screamed.

The Snakehead wrapped a ring of tape over her mouth and towed her to a chair. He secured her to it with more tape before returning to Jack.

Two sets of hands dragged Jack to the front foyer.

They heaved him into a wooden chair they'd taken from the dining room. Then they wound tape around his chest, pinning him to it. After securing Jack, they dragged him to the post that held up one end of the arch that separated the front foyer and the parlor.

They returned for Lisanne's chair. As they did so, Jack got a look at them.

One man had close-cropped hair, tawny skin, a pressed white shirt. The other was younger. His long hair was in a ponytail. The cobra tattoo on his neck resembled the one on the man Jack had killed in the Kowloon wet market.

"Ling!" barked the man in the white shirt. "Bring her over here."

The invaders pulled Lisanne's chair to the arch post opposite Jack, facing him. They placed her against it the same way they'd done to Jack. Their eyes met.

By holding her gaze, Jack tried to reassure her. With the tape over his mouth, he did his best to regulate his breathing.

The man with short hair and a pressed white shirt leaned over to inspect Jack, nearly bowing. He was broad-shouldered with muscled forearms. His most distinguishing feature, Jack saw now, was that he had one brown and one blue eye. There was a pistol in a compact plastic holster clipped to his belt. Jack recognized it as a Chinese Type 92.

Highsmith's handler, thought Jack.

TALON has a face.

The man patted Jack down. He found the folded paper in his breast pocket and withdrew it.

Standing in front of Jack, the handler read it and snorted.

"So the Hmong have given you a letter," he said in accented English. "Now I know how you got out of the jungle with a native canoe." He shook the paper. "Very helpful that they wrote down the location of their village."

The man tapped the paper with his fingers. His dual-colored eyes focused on Jack while his Snakehead partner stood near Lisanne.

"Hmong rebels killed my parents when I was fifteen," he said. "They stabbed Ling's brother three years ago." He glanced at the Snakehead, then back at Jack. "Ling doesn't speak English. Let me tell him."

The TALON operative rattled off a few words of Laotian. Jack watched the Snakehead's expression change. After the younger man responded in his native language, he stared at Jack, his mouth in a tight line, shaking his head.

"Do you want to know what Ling said?" the man with bicolored eyes asked Jack. "He said he'd been looking forward to putting a bullet in your head because you murdered his best friend, Twei, in Kowloon. Now he says a bullet's too good for you."

While Jack shook his head slowly, they heard a thump upstairs.

Highsmith's TALON handler looked up at the ceiling. Jack saw no tattoo on his neck, though he detected a pale patch of skin where one might have been removed.

"That must be Madame Marie Anh Claré," the Laotian said, still looking at the ceiling. "You didn't realize she would set you up, did you? Of course she would hide upstairs."

Lisanne's eyes were glassy, looking down. Jack knew she was thinking the same thing he was—that Howard's sedatives were fading. The banker was probably trying to get out of bed—if for no other reason than to figure out where the hell he was.

The Snakehead next to Lisanne spat angry, guttural Laotian. He pulled a knife from behind his back and flicked out the blade with his wrist. It was the same curved karambit Jack had seen in Kowloon. The Snakehead twirled the weapon around his finger, just as his friend had done in the wet market. He pulled back Lisanne's long braid and held the curved knife to her throat.

Keeping her eyes steady, Lisanne's breath quickened.

Jack heard a second, softer thump from the floor above. He didn't react. The knife-wielding Snakehead spoke again while pushing the blade harder on Lisanne's neck.

"Ling says he will cut her head off right in front of you. He said you deserve it for killing Twei—and for being a friend of the Hmong."

Jack stayed still, saying nothing, determined not to show a reaction. Bravely, Lisanne did the same.

"I have a better idea," continued the MSS agent. He exchanged a few words of Laotian with his Snakehead partner.

The gang member crouched in front of Lisanne. With the karambit still wrapped around his finger, he seized her hand. Since Lisanne's arm was taped to her torso, all she could do in resistance was make a fist. The Snakehead wrenched Lisanne's index finger free and straightened it. He pressed the blade against her knuckle.

"He's going to cut off her finger now," explained the TALON man as he stood directly in front of Jack. "I told him to wait until I could see how cooperative you might be."

He put his face very close to Jack, cutting off his view of Lisanne. Jack studied the strange brown and blue eyes.

"You had this one-armed woman pulling security for you, did you?" He glanced condescendingly at her, scoffing. "A curious choice. I wouldn't think an American agent could have one arm."

Jack kept his eyes steady, determined not to react.

The TALON man went on, his face close to Jack's "You know, I thought you and that bumbling old man were just bothersome accountants. Why is it now that I think you're something very different?"

Jack could smell his breath. He flinched, turning away.

"We know all the DEA people in Vietnam," the TALON operative said. "We know them in Laos, too. And you just don't *look* like DEA."

He suddenly jammed his thumb in Jack's eye, pressing it hard, scraping it with his nail. Jack tried to move his head back. The man held him in a firm grip, then lowered his hand.

"The FBI has accountants," he said. "Are you FBI? Building a cover as a Hendley financial analyst must have been a lot of trouble." He stopped moving in a moment of reflection. "Is your partner at the hospital in Hué FBI, too? A little old for an agent. I guess we'll find out when we visit him next."

Jack kept his bleeding, throbbing eye screwed shut. He could feel blood trickling down his cheek.

"So. Are you ready to talk? Ready to tell me who you really are?" The man whipped the tape off Jack's mouth. Jack stayed silent.

"Yes. I thought you'd do that."

The TALON handler turned to face the Snakehead, then stood aside. Jack could see the gang member press the karambit blade hard against Lisanne's finger, drawing blood.

"Can you imagine?" continued the man in the white shirt, his mouth close to Jack's ear. "Imagine if you had only one hand—and then you lost your fingers, too. That's about to be her unless you tell me who you really are—and what you think you know about GeoTech."

Lisanne's eyes widened. Her breath quickened.

There was another bump from the ceiling, then footsteps on the stairs.

Oh dear God, thought Jack.

Howard was about to walk into a melee. Jack saw the TALON operative in front of him draw the Chinese pistol from his belt, raising it toward the stairs.

The lights went out.

A noisy explosion sucked the air out of Jack's lungs. And then another and another, each accompanied by a blinding flash of light, as though looking point-blank into a camera flash. Sulfur gas invaded Jack's nose, making him cough. He held his breath, waiting for the ninth explosion, recognizing the familiar pattern of a flash-bang grenade.

Jad Mustafa was suddenly in front of him, the red light from his helmet shining in Jack's good eye. He was slicing the tape from Jack's chest and wrists. Jack leaped to his feet. The room was still dark and smoky, lit only by the red light on Jad's helmet.

He ran to Lisanne's side. The Snakehead who'd been in front of her was on the ground, a puddle of blood spreading under his long hair. Jack ripped the gag off her mouth. "You okay?"

"Yes. Howard!"

Jack used his necklace knife to cut Lisanne free.

"Clear!" shouted Cary Marks behind him. The second Green Beret was standing under the arch at the foyer, his H&K 416 sweeping the room.

Jack leaped for the stair landing behind Cary. Howard was there, lying on his side with both hands pressed to his ears. As Jack searched the banker for a wound, he shouted at Cary. "Are there two tangos down? I only saw one."

Jad was already running through the parlor. He bounded out the open window with his rifle in front of him.

"The other guy got out," explained Cary, lowering his gun.

Lisanne was at Jack's side, leaning over Howard. The banker was out of it, speaking nonsense, racked by fever, sedatives, and—of all things—a flash-bang grenade.

"I got Howard!" she cried.

Jack hoisted himself to his feet and went out the front door. Cary followed him.

The Range Rover was skidding down the crushed granite parking area. It ran over a hedge before careening wildly onto the main driveway. Engine roaring, the SUV sped for the gate with its lights off.

Jad was standing with his H&K 416 to his eye, shooting at the driver. Cary raised his rifle beside him. A round sparked off the SUV's rear liftgate. Another shattered the window. But a dip in the long driveway and a thick copse of trees gave the retreating Rover cover. It accelerated through the gate.

Over the revving engine, Jack heard a distant, ripping tear like a chain saw coming up to speed. Hot-pink tracer fire flew from the jungle, glowing like molten steel. The rounds slammed into the Rover's hood. Fire licked from the engine bay. The SUV charged straight into the tracers, closing the distance with the gun and slamming into it

The tracer fire stopped.

Jack heard the dying hiss of the Rover's engine—but nothing else.

"On me!" he cried to Cary and Jad, already racing for the gate.

39

DA NANG, VIETNAM
MONDAY, OCTOBER 14

WEARING A BLACK PATCH OVER HIS RIGHT EYE, JACK RYAN, JR., EMERGED FROM the fifth-floor elevator and stood aside. He let Kendrick Moore and Lisanne Robertson pass by him. They returned the favor a few yards later when they reached the glass double doors with the GeoTech logo.

"Oh," said the startled receptionist at the desk. "I didn't realize there'd be three of you."

The Campus operatives were dressed in business attire—Jack in the suit he'd worn in Hong Kong, Moore in a long-sleeve button-down and gabardine trousers picked up at a local shop, and Lisanne in a black pantsuit she'd acquired when they'd first landed at Ho Chi Minh City.

She was wearing her prosthetic arm under her jacket. After its abuse at the hands of the Snakehead, the arm was none the worse for wear.

The receptionist inspected their fully legitimate Hendley Associates ID cards. Gavin had sent the digital images to a FedEx branch in Da Nang. Jack spent twelve bucks getting them printed and laminated.

"Welcome," greeted the receptionist, satisfied. "Not every day we get to meet new owners. I'm sorry I didn't set up desk space for you. Can I get you a conference room?"

"That's all right," said Jack, winking at her with his exposed eye. "Just give us a badge to get through the security doors and we'll make ourselves at home."

Badged in, the trio walked past rows of cubicles filled with workers typing on keyboards or talking into headsets. Beyond them, the midsize buildings of Da Nang stretched all the way to the sea.

They rounded a corner and approached a large, glass-partitioned office.

A young secretary stood up to intercept them. The name at the edge of her cubicle was Corrine Nguyen.

"Mr. Ryan. Hello. Do you have an appointment?" she asked, trying—and failing—to block them.

"No," he said. "But we own the company. We don't need an appointment." He pulled the door open and waved Moore and Lisanne through.

David Highsmith didn't see them coming. He'd been on the phone, his chair turned away, his feet up on the credenza behind the desk. Stephenson's old war plaques were still mounted over his head.

Highsmith sounded chipper—and for good reason, Jack knew, thanks to some handy hacks from Gavin Biery into the GeoTech systems.

With his oxford shoes waggling happily on the credenza, Highsmith was speaking to his private bank in the Caymans, giving instructions to get his beloved Gloucestershire back into his possession, out of the UK Exchequer's hands. NSA's ECHELON was monitoring the call, sending the real-time feed to Lisanne's phone. She'd let Jack read the contents in the elevator.

Jack didn't need the ECHELON feed now. He listened to Highsmith with his own ears from the threshold of Bruce Stephenson's old office.

"Yes," said Highsmith while inspecting the cuticles of his free hand. "You'll need to wire the funds to the His Majesty's Revenue and Customs Service, office of the Exchequer, tax receivables. Correct. Seven million. You'll . . ."

He finally turned. He glanced up to find Kendrick Moore staring down at him. Every ounce of blood drained from the Englishman's face as he lowered his feet to the floor.

"I'll call you back," he said, choking off the last word and hanging up the phone.

He surveyed his visitors and stood. "My God, Jack! Your eye. The crash must have been horrifying! Thank God you . . . Well, I'm so, so sorry about Bruce. How is Howard? Is he still in the hospital in Hué?"

"Howard's fine," returned Jack. "We've got him in the infirmary over at the U.S. consulate in Da Nang. He'll be headed back to the States in a couple of hours."

"Oh, thank God. I'm so glad you came directly here. You should have called me. I could have set you up with everything you need." Highsmith looked at Moore and held out his hand. "I'm afraid I haven't had the pleasure."

Moore glared at the extended hand. He didn't shake it. Highsmith let it fall to his side.

Behind Moore, Jack was lowering the blinds on the glass wall that separated Bruce Stephenson's old office from the rest of the floor. He smiled reassuringly at Corrine as the last one came down. Then he threw the door's lock.

"We missed you last night, Sir David," said Jack. He leaned over to unplug Highsmith's desk phone. "Funny thing. Madame Anh told me she called you."

"What?" shot the Englishman. "Oh . . . that. Yes, she called and said something. But I told her I couldn't make it out to Hué. Too much to do here as acting CEO . . . as you might imagine. Congratulations on the acquisition, by the way. Well done, old boy."

"You couldn't make it to Hué," echoed Jack.

"No. I'm afraid not. Rude of me, I know."

Moore cracked the knuckles on his right hand, one at a time.

"Yeah," said Jack. "So you sent someone else."

"I don't know what you're talking about."

Lisanne withdrew a big Chinese Huawei smartphone from her jacket pocket. She swiped it, revealing a bright-flash photo of Highsmith's battered, overturned Range Rover. It was lying in thick jungle foliage, black smoke pouring from its engine bay.

The former Virginia state trooper said, "This *is* your Rover, correct? The plates are registered to you."

Highsmith's eye rotated from the phone's display to Lisanne's face. "I'm sorry. Who are you?"

Jack replied. "This is Lisanne Robertson. She and Mr. Moore are with Hendley security. They help the firm clean up messes . . . One of the benefits you'll come to enjoy, now that the deal's closed."

"I see."

"Not yet, you don't," said Jack, the corners of his lips tilted in the hint of a grin. "But you will."

Kendrick Moore walked behind Highsmith. He perched

himself on the credenza, the same spot where the Englishman's feet had been resting a few moments earlier. "Mr. Ryan would like to ask you a few questions," said the master chief.

Highsmith's eyes darted between the phone, the window, and Kendrick Moore. "That's fine, of course. I have nothing to hide."

"Except for a sex-trafficking business," said Jack. "And payoffs to the Snakeheads. Just a few little things like that."

After a sharp breath, Highsmith blustered, "You have no idea how hard I tried to stop that. It was all Marie Anh Claré's doing. And Henri. That family has been a terrible leech on this business. All started with my wife, Claudette."

"Really? Madame Anh and Henri said *you* were the one who has the relationship with the Snakeheads."

"That's ridiculous. I may have been coerced into an illegal payment, but that's it. Ghastly people." He sniffed. "I'm the victim here. It's so good to have competent security here to help me."

"Is that so?" asked Jack.

"Absolutely. I've had nothing to do with those horrible people."

"Really? Because we found the Snakehead leader in *your* car. You know, the upside-down Range Rover Ms. Robertson just showed you."

"I don't know any Snakehead leaders. Obviously, they stole my car—they stop at nothing. It's so good you're finally going to get a handle on them."

"Oh, I think you probably do know this guy," said Lisanne, swiping forward on the Huawei screen. There was Cai Qi, his shoulders shredded and bloody from Kendrick Moore's onslaught. Before snapping the photo, the Campus operatives had laid Cai's body on the jungle grass.

Highsmith glanced at the grisly photo, then hurriedly looked away. "I don't know him."

"Sure you do." Jack took the phone and swiped to the messaging app. "In fact, you two guys have been doing a lot of communicating."

Highsmith looked at the phone screen, then glanced away. "I don't know what that is."

"Oh, this?" Jack's eyebrows arched as he thumbed the length of the text message inbox. "See, this is the Snakehead leader's phone. A lot of interesting stuff in here. You guys were chatty." Jack stopped scrolling, landing on the top message. "This last one—the one that says the problem's taken care of and that you can head back to the UK when you want . . . Well, that was me, actually. I sent you that this morning."

Silent, Highsmith kept his gaze out the window.

"Sooo much interesting stuff in here," Jack continued. He put the phone on the desk and pointed to it. "See, we have this hacker guy at Hendley. Friggin' genius. Anyway, since we got this phone last night, he was able to hack into it, so we can see *all* these messages. And here's the really cool part."

The acting CEO stared out the window.

Jack went on. "See, our hacker dug around the phone's IP addresses, VPNs, subnet masks, yada yada . . . All technical stuff none of us really understand. Anyway, he's able to make a direct match back to *your* GeoTech account that shares a bunch of data on one of the customers. Which customer was it, Lisanne?"

"Quantum Atomics."

Jack snapped his fingers. "That's right. They're the ones who signed the contract for all those special samarium rare earth magnets. It seems, *Sir* David, that your account also has a back door that lets your Snakehead friend into GeoTech's servers, exactly where the Quantum Atomics technical files are stored.

Now why is that? What does that have to do with your *other* criminal enterprise? You know, the sex-trafficking ring."

Moore put a heavy hand on Highsmith's shoulder. He squeezed tightly.

"Henri and Marie let the Snakeheads in the door. I told you that. Once they were in, I . . . I will admit that I was subjected to blackmail. *Terrifying* blackmail. That man regularly threatened my life. I was *forced* to do what he wanted."

"Wow," said Jack. "That sounds harrowing. Doesn't it, Lisanne?"

"Scary," she said.

Jack whistled softly. "Tough for you. Well. Did you ever ask yourself why this Snakehead guy would want a back door into the GeoTech technical records for an American defense contractor?"

"No."

"Great. I have the privilege of enlightening you, then. See, when we dug further into this guy's phone, we discovered he's been passing that data to another long, complicated string of IP addresses that we now know leads back to the Chinese. Specifically, the Ministry of State Security. And, well, see, that makes you a Chinese spy."

"I'm no such thing."

"Yes you are. And, while you might think you're an English guy operating out of Vietnam, muddying the jurisdiction—turns out you were spying on an American company while also working for one. That's industrial espionage—and the United States has jurisdiction over you."

Highsmith's panicked eyes shifted to his desk, then back to Jack. "You're not an FBI agent."

"No. But the FBI works for my father. Well, technically, they work for Dan Murray, the attorney general. *He* works for my father."

"I will only speak to a lawyer now," Highsmith said. "You can leave. Good day." He swept his eyes over his monitor and put his hands on the keyboard, as though getting back to work.

"Now, don't be like that," said Jack. "I haven't told you how I'm going to give you a way to keep your sorry ass out of prison."

The Englishman stopped typing and rotated his eyes to Jack. "All right. I'm listening. How?"

"You're going to spy for us."

"I told you. I'm not a spy."

Jack held up the phone. "Au contraire. You're absolutely a spy. All we want you to do is switch teams."

"I don't understand. What *exactly* are you asking me to do?"

"Nothing! That's the beautiful part. You're going to spend your days here, doing some make-work job as executive vice president of flower arranging or whatever. Pretty soon, a new Chinese handler is going to show up and ask you for information on Quantum Atomics that you're going to get out of the Geo-Tech servers. And we're going to give you the files to pass on to them. Got it?"

"You're mad. All of you. I want no part of this."

"You sure? Let me restate your options. One, life in prison, where you'll be free to endlessly ponder your crimes for the rest of your days. Two, Mr. Moore, here, fakes a suicide note for you and throws you off the roof—he's partial to that one, by the way. Or three, you keep working here, enjoying this beautiful view. You won't be corrupting young women anymore, you sick bastard—but you can keep your apartment here in Da Nang. Highly monitored, of course. Our hacker is a wiz with that surveillance stuff."

Highsmith's face fell. After a five-second silence, he shot an exasperated glance at Jack. "All right. You have a deal."

"Wonderful," said Jack. "Oh, one other thing I forgot. Our hacker also messed around with your account in the Caymans. Since you violated pretty much every fiduciary duty of a Geo-Tech company officer, Hendley has taken your money back. Sorry, Sir Dave. You're back to being broke."

Highsmith glared furiously at Jack, breathing slowly.

"Shall we shake on it?" asked Jack, extending his hand over the desk.

Highsmith stood. After a moment, he slowly raised his hand, his eyes cast down.

Jack removed his hand. "Don't you dare, Sir David. Now, get the hell out of Bruce Stephenson's office."

EPILOGUE

**THE WHITE HOUSE, WASHINGTON, D.C.
ONE WEEK LATER**

GARY MONTGOMERY, HEAD OF THE WEST WING DETAIL, WAS THE FIRST OF THE SE-cret Service people to see Jack, who he knew better by his call sign, SHORTSTOP.

The senior agent had been making his morning rounds, checking on his people. He was hardwired into every security post around the White House—the snipers on the roof, the uniforms at the bane-of-his-existence public entrances, and the fifteen suited agents spread across the three floors. He liked to check in with each of them in person, a few times a day.

His pace brisk, he'd just come in from the West Colonnade. As his route wound on, he said good morning to Kate, his agent stationed at the Cabinet Room doors, where the President was meeting with his labor secretary, going over the finer points of the deal that had held off the rail strike. Kate returned the greeting but stayed still as a red-coated Beefeater at the gates of Buckingham Palace.

Montgomery saw SHORTSTOP standing outside the Roosevelt

Room, slouching against the wall with his hands in his pockets. The Secret Service agent also saw SHORTSTOP's fiancée next to him, looking up and down the hall in the manner of the former cop that she was.

Between them was another man. Montgomery took a double take. The man was enormous, bald, wearing a suit that seemed a size too small. He was holding one of the White House bone china cups in his hand. In the clutches of this awkward giant, the cup looked no larger than a shot glass.

"Well," said Montgomery, sidling up next to the President's son. "I saw your name on the briefing sheet. I didn't know you were bringing guests." He offered his hand. Jack shook it, then introduced Lisanne and Kendrick Moore.

"Sorry about that, Gary. These two were a late addition," said Jack. "You know Lisanne, of course. I work with Mr. Moore, here, in risk analysis at Hendley."

Moore and Montgomery shook hands. "You going to tell me about that eye?" asked the lead Secret Service agent, squinting at the eye patch Jack wore. The eye was healing up nicely, but Jack's mother—an ophthalmologist of some renown—had said to wear the patch for a few more days. Besides—Jack rather liked it.

"Looking through too many keyholes," he joked to Montgomery. "Finally caught up with me."

A voice crackled in Montgomery's ear. It was Kate. The President was on his way, moving from the Cabinet Room to the Oval Office.

"I gotta go," said Montgomery. "It may be a while before the President's ready for you. Think he's having a busy morning. Excuse me."

Jack turned to Moore, noting the bulging vein at his neck.

"You can loosen that shirt collar, Mr. Moore. I told you the tie wasn't necessary."

The SEAL shook his head briskly and sipped from the tiny cup in his hands. "I'm fine."

Arnie van Damm came rushing toward the Oval Office, folder in hand. Seeing them standing there caused his pace to slow—barely.

"Nobody's come to get you guys yet?" he asked, stride steady.

"Negative," said Jack.

Arnie looked at his watch. "Goddamnit. Crazy day. Someone will be along. Sit tight."

"That's what he said twenty minutes ago," noted Lisanne. She watched the President's chief of staff disappear around a corner and shook her head.

This time, the promise held.

A Navy captain in dress blues approached them. Jack Junior noticed the aviator wings on the officer's chest and the five rows of colorful decorations by his lapel. Moore stood ramrod straight when the captain introduced himself, nearly spilling the coffee in his hand.

The Navy captain said his name was Gronemeyer. No first name. Just Gronemeyer. He told them he was the White House military liaison to the National Security Council.

"Come on," he said then. "I have orders to bring you all into the pit."

"Oh," said Jack, surprised. His father had only said this was going to be a quick meet-and-greet in the Oval Office. He hadn't expected an invitation into the White House basement, the underground home of the six-thousand-square-foot intelligence operations center known as the Situation Room—and the *pit*.

"Follow," said Captain Gronemeyer.

He led them through heavy doors, down back stairs that smelled like a freshly painted ship, and past a security check manned by an Army Ranger and a bomb-sniffing beagle. Finally, they entered a conference room with thick black leather chairs, red LED clocks, flat-screen monitors, and a polished table with a phone at each station.

The captain told the three Campus operatives to get comfortable. He left them alone.

One of the flat-screens lit up. At first, it was nothing but the National Security Council seal against a blue background. The monitor buzzed noisily. The logo went away. They were looking at John Clark's creased face, peering down on them from midway up the wall.

"Nobody else there, yet?" asked Clark.

"He can see us?" whispered Moore.

Jack nodded briskly to him. "Hi, Mr. C. No, nobody else is here."

Clark adjusted the reading glasses on his nose, apparently scanning a paper that was out of view. "POTUS should be along. How's the eye, Jack? Your mother fix you up?"

"Yeah. She said it's going to heal up fine."

Clark lowered his reading glasses and stared down at the President's son. "Huh," he announced. "Kind of a good look for you. Must have rubbed off from those river pirates you fought off."

"Good one, Mr. C."

"Looks like you got a new suit, too."

Jack grinned. "It was shipped to me from Hong Kong. I know a hell of a tailor there."

Clark grunted, then looked away, reading something else on his desk.

"What is this?" whispered Moore, trying not to move his lips.

Clark heard the question anyway. "Mr. Moore, sit tight. You'll see soon enough."

The heavy door cracked open. Captain Gronemeyer peeked inside for a moment, saw Clark on the screen, compressed his lips in a look of satisfaction, and closed it again with a thump.

"While we wait," said Clark, looking up, removing his glasses. "Cary and Jad checked in a few hours ago. From Bangkok."

Lisanne shot Jack a look. Then she turned to the monitor. "Bangkok? Was that part of the plan, Mr. C.?"

"Not originally, no. But your lady . . ."

"Madame Anh," Lisanne prompted.

"Yes. Madame Anh. She told us these Snakeheads generally stay out of Bangkok. Evidently, Thailand's controlled by a different gang. Their thing is drugs—not sex trafficking."

"That's comforting," said Jack. "Who's working on getting the girls back to their families?"

"We're working that problem with the UN High Commissioner for Refugees. As you might imagine, we don't want a lot of direct involvement, since that could raise questions about The Campus. We have someone from State in the UNHCR helping out."

"Got it," said Jack. "What did Cary and Jad have to say? They give you a debrief?"

Clark's eyes reflected a touch of wistful appreciation. "They said they had a hell of a time finding that Montagnard. Then they had an even harder time convincing him they were real Green Berets. Damn near got in a firefight with the man and his sons."

"Well . . . not surprised. How'd they find the Hmong?"

"The coordinates in his letter checked out, but led to an abandoned camp. They didn't say as much, but I get the feeling that

Montagnard may have gotten the drop on our Green Berets. They'd never admit that, of course."

"Where's the Montagnard now?"

"Bangkok. Cary and Jad are still with him. They're looking for the women on his list."

"Are we putting him up?"

"State is. As it turns out, his old Army letter was legitimate. We're honoring it, offering him citizenship. Not sure he'll take it. He didn't back in 'seventy."

"The guy saved my life. And Howard's. I wish we could do more for him."

Papers shuffled in Clark's hand. "Well. As you'll see in a minute, that's why we're here."

Gronemeyer, the Navy man, opened the door again, but this time held it ajar. President Jack Ryan, Sr., strode in. His tie was loosened, his suit jacket unbuttoned, his graying hair slightly mussed. Van Damm was marching behind him with a folder, as ever.

The three Campus operatives stood. The President went directly to his son, putting a hand on each shoulder, holding him at arm's length, grinning.

"I like the patch, boy."

"Yeah. Everyone seems to like it."

Jack Ryan, Sr., took his privilege not only as a President, but as a father. He peeled away the eye patch for a moment and looked at Jack's swollen bruise, his reddened iris. "Mom said it will heal. You're taking the antibiotics?"

"Yeah, Dad, of course I am." Jack put the patch back in place. "Think I'd go against Mom on this one?"

"And the malaria meds? Just in case?"

"Yes, Dad."

The President let his hands fall to his sides. "Gerry said your coworker, Howard Brennan, had it pretty bad."

"Very bad," confirmed Jack, no trace of humor left in his voice.

"Have you seen him since you've been back?"

"I caught up with him at Johns Hopkins a few days ago. They said he narrowly averted a coma. The parasites had really eaten into him."

The President looked up at Clark on the monitor. "Gerry said Howard is back at work. Have you seen him, John?"

"I just saw him an hour ago wearing the new Gucci shoes you gave him, Jack. The boss over here is giving him a big bonus for closing that GeoTech deal."

"Sorry to interrupt, sir." The Navy captain poked his head in again. "We have the live feed."

The President made his way to his place at the head of the table. He gave Lisanne a swift hug. He shook hands solemnly with Kendrick Moore, who mumbled a greeting that was indecipherable, other than starting and ending with the word *sir*.

Arnie van Damm cleared his throat. "I want to say for the record that I don't think you should be here, Mr. President. We do our damnedest to keep you out of these ops."

The President settled into his chair. He looked up at the three monitors. They were glowing black and white, an image of scrolling terrain marked with ticking telemetry numbers in the corners.

Van Damm went on. "There's still time to get out of here, sir. We keep you in the dark on things like this for a reason."

Ryan tilted his chair, studying the monitors. "Knock it off, Arnie. This is the good part of the job."

Mary Pat Foley came through the door. Before taking a seat, she took in Clark on one monitor, the gray scrolling terrain on the others, and the people around the table. She said her brief hellos, then sat down, spread her portfolio, and opened her laptop.

She donned her reading glasses and peered into the portfolio. "Okay," she began. "We're all set." She looked around the table one last time, ending her scan with the President. "You're sure about this, sir? We could still call it off. It's not without risk."

"M.P., you said there was zero Chinese naval activity. No change to their sensor profiles."

"Correct."

"And you said NSA ECHELON detects no special communications activity out of Beijing."

"Correct."

The President looked at his director of national intelligence. "And we know the Chinese air force is using the new software?"

"Yes. We have confirmation from our new asset, HAMLET."

HAMLET was the code name she'd assigned to David Highsmith, GeoTech's executive vice president of special projects based in Da Nang. The Campus's first double agent—though the President didn't need to know that.

The President tilted his head forward. "And, M.P.—DIA also confirmed the Chinese radar signatures from their side, right?"

"Yesterday. Yes, sir. Our recon birds picked up the new emissions profiles."

The President stared at his DNI. "Final question. You're sure this target is an operating base for TALON? And that there are no innocent civilians there?"

"Affirmative," answered Mary Pat. Clark had confirmed to her that the Montagnard, Alang Nik Trong, had led Cary and Jad to the Snakehead base, where they'd found only gang members.

"And," the DNI added, "this TALON target is as juicy as it's ever going to get. It's going to make a statement, sir, about Chinese meddling in American companies."

"Well," said the President, rubbing his hands together. "Then, yes, I'd like to go ahead with this. Captain Gronemeyer, shall you brief us up?"

The naval aviator stood before them, motioning at the three monitors. "Ladies and gentlemen," he began, "this feed is from sensors on a specially modified F-15 Strike Eagle on a code word–classified mission called UMBRA. The feed you're looking at is live, nearing the Laotian border."

Though Jack Junior was familiar with the program now, he kept his face neutral, saying nothing. Clark had told him not to speak with *anyone* about the specialized rare earth magnets produced by GeoTech for Quantum Atomics, which gave the F-15 and UMBRA new stealth capability.

The Campus director of ops had only briefed Jack Junior about UMBRA because the spy Jack had recruited, Highsmith, would be critical in keeping the Chinese off the scent of it.

"Target's coming into view now," said the aviator. "It's zero-two-hundred local time. Target's an old CIA base, once used to direct air interdiction missions out of Laos. Awaiting your order, sir."

Jack could see five Quonset huts coming into view. He could see the narrow black river, the tall mountains to either side, the docks where the Snakeheads kept the long speedboats Highsmith had bought for them, specially equipped to smuggle girls down the rivers like livestock.

"You sure, Mr. President?" Mary Pat asked the man at the head of the table.

"Very," he said, eyes locked on the monitor. "Send it."

Captain Gronemeyer touched a button on the speakerphone.

"Magic, this is Shotgun, you're weapons free," he said into it. "Cleared hot."

"Roger, Shotgun. Magic is hot," came the tinny reply.

Jack watched the Quonset huts grow larger. He could see the boats in crisper detail. They were identical to the one he and Howard had escaped—and the one that had nearly run them over.

The huts loomed very large in the monitor.

The screens suddenly flashed white as if they'd broken. Then the brightness faded and an image returned. Jack could see drifting black smoke. Through it, he watched flying chunks of debris. The smoke cleared, blown by the mountain wind.

The buildings and boats were gone. There was nothing but a smoking hole next to the river.

"I'd call that a direct hit," said the President.

"Affirmative, sir. Confirm hit. Target destroyed." Captain Gronemeyer touched the speakerphone again. "Magic, you are RTB. Shotgun out." He glanced at the civilians looking at him from the table. "That's return to base. The Strike Eagle's headed back to Kadena, Okinawa. Mission complete."

Mary Pat Foley was looking at her open laptop. "And, as of now, I can confirm that there is no response from China," she said. "Or Laos. Or Vietnam."

The President pressed his hands together. "Nice work, everyone."

Van Damm leaned far over the table and tapped his watch, deliberately entering the President's field of view. "Press briefing in an hour on the railroad strike deal. We need to prep you."

"I know. I'll be along." He looked at the end of the table. "Captain Gronemeyer, you're dismissed. Cut the feed."

"Aye, sir." The aviator hurried from the room.

"Arnie. Get back upstairs and keep the wolves at bay. I'd like a private word with my son."

On hearing that, Mary Pat shut her laptop. Moore and Lisanne pushed their chairs back. Clark started punching keys on his computer, preparing to sign off.

"Hang on," said the President. "I want Lisanne and Mr. Moore to stick around. You too, M.P."

When the Situation Room was reduced to Jack, Moore, Lisanne, Mary Pat Foley, and John Clark, the President appeared to relax. He leaned farther back in his chair.

"A good day," he said.

"Agreed," replied his son.

"Between this and the Abu Sayyaf op, we put a serious dent in TALON." The President looked up at his DNI. "M.P., is TALON hot anywhere else?"

The director of national intelligence reopened her laptop. "Yes, unfortunately. Venezuela. I'll save you the details for later—the ones I think you need to know about, anyway."

The President chuckled. "Perfect."

She clicked around her computer, then glanced around the table. "For now . . . suffice to say that we've put MSS on notice. But we don't know how widely TALON goes. Another lead has come in from down south."

"That thing south of the border?"

"Yes. An MS-13 offshoot operating all over Central America. We got a COMINT hit out of ECHELON. A call between a shipping company and a gang member. The shipping company's a front for the Cubans. It will be in tomorrow's PDB."

"Well," said the President, smiling. "I'm sure you'll find an asset down there to get to the bottom of it."

"I know a few people," said Clark. "M.P., call me after this. I may be able to help."

The President laughed. "Yeah. I bet you do." He turned suddenly serious. He looked directly at Kendrick Moore, as though noticing the big SEAL for the first time. "I understand you led the rescue op in Vietnam, Master Chief. Must have felt different working as a contractor outside of DEVGRU."

Tongue-tied, Moore mumbled, "It was my honor, sir. Very much. Thank you, sir."

"It's not lost on me, Mr. Moore," the President told him, "that you saved my son's life. And Howard Brennan's. And Cary's and Jad's."

"And mine," added Lisanne. She touched Moore's beefy hand.

Moore mumbled something else as he pulled his hand back and stared at his knuckles.

The President leaned forward to catch Moore's eye. "As a father and a President, I want to thank you, Mr. Moore."

The master chief nodded. He glanced quickly at the President, then swiveled his head back to the table, his carefully shaved scalp reddening.

The President stood up. The rest of the room came to their feet.

As Jack Ryan, Sr., headed for the door, ready to walk out, he paused and reached in his trouser pocket. He turned and took two steps back to the polished table.

"And, Mr. Moore," he said, looking at the master chief. "This belongs to you."

The President slid a shining SEAL trident across the table to Moore. The chief looked down at it. His hands twitched. He seemed scared to pick it up.

There it was—the golden eagle clutching a flintlock pistol and trident for which he'd sacrificed so much. There on the Situation Room table lay the gleaming pin he'd spent his life honoring, so much so that he'd left instructions in his will that it was to be pounded into the top of his coffin by his brothers. There lay the golden badge his commanders had pulled from his chest, sending him into the wilderness.

His knuckles whitening, the chief pressed his thick hands to the table to keep them from trembling. He looked hopefully into the President's face.

"For the record . . . As far as this commander in chief is concerned," said Jack Ryan, Sr., "you never lost that trident in the first place."